A Matter of Time

A Matter of
Time

by Jessamyn West

Harcourt, Brace & World, Inc., New York

The first quotation on page vii is from page 743 of *You Can't Go Home Again* by Thomas Wolfe. Copyright 1940 by Maxwell Perkins as Executor. Used by permission of Harper & Row, Publishers. The second quotation on the same page is from page 56 of *Joyce Cary: A Preface to His Novels* by Andrew Wright (Harper & Brothers, 1958). The quotations from Albert Camus are from *Notebooks 1942-1951*, translated by Justin O'Brien, and *Notebooks 1935-1942*, translated by Philip Thody (Alfred A. Knopf, Inc., 1965 and 1963). The quotation on page 94 is from "Oh see how thick the goldcup flowers" from "A Shropshire Lad"—Authorised Edition—from *The Collected Poems of A. E. Housman*. Copyright 1939, 1940, © 1959 by Holt, Rinehart and Winston, Inc. Reprinted by permission of Holt, Rinehart and Winston, Inc.

First edition
Library of Congress Catalog Card Number: 66-22289
Printed in the United States of America

For Henry Volkening
a matter of time

LINDA

"But before I go, I have just one more thing to tell you:

"Something has spoken to me in the night, burning the tapers of the waning year; something has spoken in the night, and told me I shall die, I know not where. Saying:

" 'To lose the earth you know, for greater knowing; to lose the life you have, for greater life; to leave the friends you loved, for greater loving; to find a land more kind than home, more large than earth—

" '—Whereon the pillars of this earth are founded, toward which the conscience of the world is tending—a wind is rising, and the rivers flow.' "   —*Thomas Wolfe*

BRENNER

The truth is "that life is hard and dangerous; that he who seeks his own happiness, does not find it; that he who is weak, must suffer; that he who demands love, will be disappointed . . . that joy is only to him who does not fear to be alone; that life is only for the one who is not afraid to die."   —*Joyce Cary*

BARANCA

"There is but one freedom, to put oneself right with death. . . . When you have accepted death, the problem of God will be solved, and not the reverse."   —*Albert Camus*

THE DESERT

"I shall tell of nothing but my love of life. But I shall tell of it in my own way . . ."   —*Albert Camus*

A Matter of Time

I

Blix's letter came addressed to my maiden name, Tasmania Murphy. This wasn't Blix's way of saying, "Whatever your name may be now." I've had only two husbands; and I've been Mrs. Pete Orcino for the last twenty years. No, that slip of the pen came out of Blix's remembrance as she wrote of the days when she had been able to depend upon me as big sister and sub-stitute mother. What that address said unconsciously, was: "Be to me what once you were."

The letter began, "Sister, dear sister, there are things I must know."

The things she must know were medical and not of a nature to be found in volumes of "What to Do Till the Doctor Comes." I might have laid my hands on other books, but I wanted the information to be explicit and from someone I knew and trusted. I went to my own doctor. I pretended a piece of writing for which I needed certain facts.

Dr. Benedict was delighted. He saw a new and unsuspected facet in his patient. "Why, Tassie, what have you been hiding from me? I didn't know you had ambitions along that line."

I didn't have ambitions along that line, but I let him think so. We all get so much less attention than we crave that any suggestion that something of ours can be used in a piece of writing inclines us to be co-operative.

I know. I was taken in at the age of seventeen by just such a ruse myself.

The would-be housemother at the college dormitory where I lived had her son pose as a writer of college stories. I didn't know he was her son, and I was greatly flattered to be chosen as the resident most likely to have the inside dope on forbidden goings-on. Because this impression was so wrong, I worked hard not to let him down. I didn't make up anything, but every report I had heard of study by candlelight after "lights-out" or forbidden chafing-dish parties I repeated to him. What he was interested in though was boys and sex; as well he should have been. In Pilgrim College, founded by the Church of the Pilgrims, boys, at least for the girls I knew, were the only sources of excitement available. Our classes were dull, our teachers unlearned; we were forbidden to play cards, to dance, to go to the theater. (Since the theater for us meant "White Cargo" in Los Angeles, twenty-five miles distant, our deprivation wasn't, however, as great as we imagined.) If we went anywhere by car on a date, a school chaperone accompanied us. Under such circumstances any overt necking was out. But in the dark of the back seat of a big Reo and with the chaperone on a jump seat, a system of pretty intimate fondling developed. And the dear ladies, spinsters usually, never seemed to suspect that our feverish conversation with them on high-minded subjects of their choosing was a cover-up for hand play that wasn't.

But the pseudo-writer son—I found out later that he owned a hardware store—wasn't interested in what happened in cars; what happened outside the dormitory was no responsibility of his mother's. "Were boys ever smuggled into the dormitory?" If so, I didn't know anything about it, and I left the interview feeling I had failed as a writer's assistant. I didn't know anything about sex! Even straightforward, hallowed-by-the-church, and practiced-

4

in-a-conjugal-bed sex! And what this pseudo-writer, son of a putative housemother, wanted to know about was forbidden sex: "Boys in girls' rooms? Girls in girls' beds?" Girls in girls' beds! What was he talking about? I knew we had single beds and weren't supposed to double up. For health reasons, I supposed. What else?

2

Once, my mother, when I was fifteen or sixteen, had come into my room, had awakened me at nine or ten in the morning out of a sound sleep. "Tassie, you know some girls fall into the bad habit of playing with themselves."

I didn't know it, and I was irked, as I often was, with my mother's suspicion and gullibility.

"Well, I don't know what they've got to play with," I told her. "Boys have got something to play with, and I can understand how they get into a bad habit." The whole business appeared to me to be on the level of nail biting and nose picking, only more vulgar, since it had to do with private, not public, parts. It disgusted me that my mother would speculate about such things; that she would be taken in by somebody's ignorant gossip.

Perhaps it was some glint of humor in my mother's face that melted my own exasperation. Suddenly it all seemed like a big joke to me. Perhaps I became jocular to protect myself from the embarrassment of hearing my mother display her ignorance—and on such a subject, too. "You tell me, Mama, what they've got to play with. Because maybe they've got something that was left off me."

It seems now that a fifteen-year-old with an iota of curiosity would have asked some questions then, or made some explorations later; I didn't. I had a kind of complacency about what I knew. I was impervious to the wisdom of others. I learned by doing—or failed to learn, by not doing. This retards learning, but it also prolongs it, so that at an age when all is known to more

5

gifted assimilators, the plodding experiencers are still making exciting discoveries.

My mother said, "I reckon you've got all the parts the Lord intended you to have, Tassie," and left the room.

I reckoned I had, too. No one was ever more content with her physical equipment than I. I could run fast, kick high, sing loud; I breathed with excitement, ate with gusto, could smell fog, feel the movement of air when it was scarcely moving, and see in our sunsets, red and black like burning sump holes, some grandeur way beyond the fact of color and the earth's turning. The physical equipment that I had, and knew I had, kept me so occupied I had no time to speculate about what I might be missing.

I had read late the night before, as I always did unless I ran out of books, so, after my mother left the room, I flopped over on my face, twitched the bungalow apron I was wearing as a nightgown out of its binding twist and prepared to sleep some more. The apron belonged to my mother. The only difference between it and a nightgown was the material it was made of, and the fullness of the cut. I don't know why I found the idea of sleeping in my clothes thrilling. I believe I thought it bohemian.

So I jerked the bungalow apron out from around my arms—I was larger than my mother, and it tended to bind—plumped up my pillow, put my cheek back on the cool unbleached muslin pillowcase, and slid off to sleep filled with scorn for my mother's silliness. Then a sound from Blix's bed made me turn to face her. She was the real sleeper in our family. She didn't need the excuse of staying up late to sleep late. And since she was never routed out early, as I was, to work, either at home or in a packing house, or helping some recent mother with diaper washing, she had the habit of sleep. And it, like everything else she did, became her. Whatever Blix did or refused to do delighted us all. She had that knack. She was at that time (if I was fifteen) eleven. And she was, at that age, lazy, dirty, a successful operator. And doted upon. She was twenty years old before it occurred to me that she also had the strength to hold up a broom. Either water or the effort washing took did not appeal to her. We kept track,

6

hoping for a record, of the weeks that passed without her taking a bath. She was beautiful, girl and woman, and gave much attention, girl and woman, to her appearance. So from the neck up, if you didn't scan ears and hairline too closely, she was, even at eleven, as white as her olive skin permitted her to be. Beneath that, who knows? Because, though *what* we wore was not a matter of concern in our home, nakedness was; there was no sashaying around in our birthday suits. But she smelled good. "And why not?" I used to ask. "She never moves fast enough to get up a sweat." I did. I moved fast, sweated, and bathed. Not, I admit, because I cared about being clean or smelling sweet, but because I loved movement, the feel of water on my body. Because I liked the feel of bathing so much, I would have hopped into tubs even if I had come out dirtier than when I got in. I can't remember how Blix looked the morning Mother talked to me of the bad habits girls could get into, except that when I lifted myself on my elbow to see if she was awake, she appeared not to be. But I wasn't sure. Her eyelids didn't twitch, and her mouth was relaxed; but beneath her smooth olive-and-apricot skin, some tide of more than sleeping consciousness appeared to move. Perhaps I imagined it, for, though younger than I, Blix always convinced me that she had been born with knowledge I would never acquire.

"Tassie believes everything anybody tells her. Don't you, Tassie?" Blix often teased me.

I don't know about "everything." Perhaps I do incline to take what people say at face value.

3

I certainly believed that letter of hers. "Sister, dear sister": the very salutation twisted my heart. I never for a minute doubted that Blix's cry came from desperate need.

Pete tried to ease my anxiety. He said, "Tass, you know how it is with letters. The writer gets his worst fears out of his system by telling someone else about them. By the time his letter arrives, he's already feeling better."

"Maybe," I said, but I didn't believe it. Blix was different.

Blix's letter came in August. A month before, in July, she had been visiting us. In July, we were all still being brave. But the threat was there, and I had wanted to let Blix know how much I had always loved and admired her. Since such openness wasn't characteristic of our family in normal times, such a declaration would have been an admission of the threat we were determined to ignore. I got around that by showing her an old letter written by me to her when she was twenty, and never mailed. Never mailed, probably, because I had thought it "too emotional."

I was twenty-four when I wrote that letter and had been married for four years to my first husband. Marriage, added to the four years' difference in our ages, made me feel more than ever Blix's mother.

I had felt that from the beginning. They had awakened me the morning she was born, the dawn of a hot August day and led me into the big, still dusky, and somehow frightening bedroom where my mother lay in bed. They had seated me in a rocking chair and placed my little sister into, I am sure, my willing and eager arms. She was a big baby, eleven pounds, though the runt of my mother's five, and must have extended a four-year-old's reach and endurance. I was told, "This is your baby sister. You must always take care of her, put her first, and be an example to her." This is too much to ask of any four-year-old, let alone one already determined to please. The four-year-old is doomed, with those words, to fail. And doomed too, if that is her nature, never to forgive herself for her failure.

The letter I gave Blix last July was written on the stationery of "Benbow's Feed and Fuel Store," where I at twenty-four had been the incompetent bookkeeper, secretary, and office saleslady. They didn't pay me much, but they did supply me with a lot of free paper.

8

Blix took the letter without enthusiasm. "What's this?"

"A letter I wrote you when you were twenty and never mailed."

"You hang onto everything, don't you?" Blix asked. "Why're you giving it to me now?"

"Oh, just to remember the days of our youth and beauty," I said.

Blix unfolded the letter gingerly. "There are days of *my* youth and beauty I'd just as lief forget," she said.

But she began to read.

"What were you trying to do? Flatter me?"

"I didn't send it to you," I reminded her.

Blix had too much tact to observe that I was showing it to her then.

I read the letter over her shoulder.

"Dear Blix," I had written, "The last time I sat at this table you were sitting across from me, copying poems. I remember exactly how you looked—like a young Gloria Swanson, but honey blonde instead of a brunette. You had on that green wool crepe with the cinnamon-colored scarf. You were prying coconut out of the shell we had cracked.

"Now you are at home and I wish you were back across the table from me.

"I had counted the days until you came up—and then, when you arrived, I didn't tell you I had counted them. The last thing you said to me was, 'I wanted to stay longer, but you didn't give me much encouragement.'

"Oh, Blixy, how can two people be so mixed up about what each other wants?

"You wanted to stay. I wanted you to stay. But Mama told me, aside, that she wanted you home and for me not to urge you. Honestly, you're the only person in the world I can really talk to. Do you know what? I can't bear to throw away that coconut you were eating from. It's half-eaten and turning yellow. But it's a symbol to me of our visit. But not, I hope, of our lives—where nothing must be halfway.

9

"Be good to yourself. Eat more.

"Love and kisses, always, Tassie."

Blix handed the letter back to me. "Do you still have that coconut?" she asked dryly.

I laughed a little, shamefaced.

"You did a lot of suffering, didn't you? In those early days?"

"I don't remember it that way," I answered, truthfully.

"It was the same old story, wasn't it? Right from the very beginning?"

"Which old story are you talking about?"

"You and Mama. Your trying to please her."

"You tried to please her sometimes. Didn't you?"

"I hope so. But I wasn't ever willing to sacrifice you, just to please her."

I might have defended myself; but last July Blix had too many burdens for me to add any old ones to her supply.

4

When our mother died five years ago, Blix told me, "I've always resented you."

At the time—it was the afternoon following the funeral (a February afternoon of tender sunshine, washed free of smog by morning rain)—I took her words to be an accusation. I think now that they were a confession. But then I thought they were an accusation, and that I had done nothing to deserve them. I was the oldest in a family of five, with one sister and three brothers. Perhaps the oldest always runs the danger of feeling overresponsible for everything.

In any case I got mad when Blix told me she had always resented me. What had I ever done to be resented? I had borne myself humbly and lovingly before her all the days of my life. I cried. I argued with her. How incredibly stupid I was! She was, I can see now, confessing a fault she thought her own, not accusing me of having one. I wonder that she didn't wash her hands of me then and there. *She* knew she was taking blame, not passing it on.

But what she said was news to me, absolute and bitter. I refused to be resented. This shows my stupidity.

Not every member of my family seemed as fascinating to me as Blix, or as my mother. But they all fascinated me pretty much. My father, in his early days at least, was too reasonable to be fascinating; and Marmion, the brother just younger than I, decided, I don't know why, to make "doing without" his life's glory. This trait, while not very charming, did, and still does, interest me; and when it came to talking about my family, and this I loved to do, even Marmion's determination to abstain provided many good anecdotes. Le Cid (called Cid outside the family), the brother just younger than Blix, was fascinating all right; but his gifts were too great to be wasted on the family circle. He moved on early, and thereafter the public knew just as much about him as we did. Basil (called Blackie), seven years younger than Blix, the baby of the family, after the first quick bunching, didn't so much fascinate as enchant me; but I told my friends about him, too.

Tasmania, Marmion, Blix, Le Cid, Basil. Once, Blix, speaking of a story she was reading, said, "I like everything about it, except the outlandish names of the characters."

"Well, look at *our* names," I told her. "I just can't believe in people called Mary, Jane, and John. They have about as much personality for me as one, two, three, four."

Blix said, "Nine tenths of the world *is* John, Mary, and Jane. I bet these outlandish names put most readers off."

She was probably right. But it's a relief, in writing of my own family, not to have any choice. My mother named these people, not I—and names may have more to do with people's characters than we think. If Blix had been Jane or Sarah instead of being named for the heroine of Frank Norris's novel would she have been a different woman? Or if I had been Hannah? Or Ethel? Not Tasmania.

The names of my sister and brothers were a part, at least, of

11

my attention-getting equipment when I told my friends about my family. "My brother Marmion," "my sister Blix" made a better anecdotal beginning than "Brother John, Sister Jane."

When Blix told me she had always resented me, I remembered what Jim Wylie, a librarian friend of mine, had said after listening to me talk about her. "I've got a kid sister like a princess," I had told him (and anybody else at the party who would listen). "She can feel a pea under twenty mattresses. Once when she was sick I boiled an egg too hard to suit her and she threw it at me. Talk about sex appeal. Boys were bringing their ponies over for her to ride at ten. At fifteen she was having two dates a night. 'Thanks for a good time' at the side door at ten o'clock and 'Hello, I thought you'd never get here' at the front door at ten-fifteen. She can take two yards of material, a scarf, and a string of pearls and concoct an outfit better-looking than anyone else can buy at I. Magnin's. Once she told me to take the dress off my back and lend it to her for a date. Imagine having the nerve to do that? And I was dressed for a date myself. It was like living with an F. Scott Fitzgerald character. Beautiful and damned. Only Blix wasn't damned, just a little in advance of Southern California."

"How did you feel about such a paragon?" Jim asked. "All beauty, grace, infallible clothes sense, et cetera. Didn't you ever resent her?"

What he was saying, of course, was, "Don't you, a woman without these attributes, envy the sister who has them?"

This didn't faze me. It never had. We were sisters, and what I didn't have, she had. And vice versa. So it evened out.

"And you don't resent her?" Jim persisted.

"No."

He said something else, but the idea he had planted in my head kept me so busy thinking that I only half heard him.

"You're lucky to feel that way."

"She feels the same," I assured him.

5

But she didn't. It was a part of my blindness; what I felt, everyone felt. I didn't resent Blix, hence Blix didn't resent me. She, as Cornelia said of her children, was one of *my* jewels. But who knows what the children thought of Cornelia? Who wants to be someone's jewel, anyway? An ornament for another person.

The first thing I had done after my mother's funeral was to get out of my dress-up clothes, put on a pair of Capris and a blouse. I was like Mama in that. Not that she ever wore pants; but she, like me, had two ways of dressing: dressed up or not dressed up. Blix was always dressed up; her clothes for staying home were as attractive as her clothes for going out. When she came upstairs after the funeral and into the room that was always mine when I was home, she, too, had changed her clothes and she, too, wore pants. But no makeshift combination of whatever blouse was clean and whatever pants were available. She had on light blue ski pants, darker blue Navajo boots, a soft white sweater with a sleeveless jerkin of quilted flowered material over it. She could have posed just as she was for any Bullocks-Wilshire or J. W. Robinson ad.

I told her so.

"Do you think that's good?"

"Of course. Not like me. I could stop sales."

"It's your choice."

"It's not. Nothing I could do would make anyone want to buy a dress I was wearing."

"Tassie, you'll never know; because you're so darned sure of yourself, you don't care how you look."

This was not true. "I'm not sure, and I do care. Whenever I have to be seen in public, I try hard."

"You try hard for about ten minutes."

I couldn't help laughing. "Well, it's only good sense to recognize when you've reached the point of diminishing returns."

I went over to the opened casement windows. The house,

which had been built by mother's father, was a gray Swiss chalet, a second-generation Southern California building. Second-generation Southern California American building, that is. The Spaniards had built their tile-roofed adobes in the open barley fields a hundred years before the first orange ranchers knocked together their bungalows of pine planks and stained them green or brown. When the oranges came into bearing, these bungalows were converted into foremen's houses, or carted away. They were then replaced by imitation Spanish, stucco with wrought-iron grilling about the windows to keep the hidalgos away; or by imitation Swiss chalets, with shingled exteriors and a second story set like a small cube on the larger cube below. My grandfather, a consecrated Pilgrim, believed in keeping the boys away from the girls. But, brought up in the clapboard country of Southern Kentucky, he couldn't go for all that stucco and tile. Besides, the chalets were cheaper to build.

On the day my mother was buried, my grandfather's Swiss chalet was fifty years old; it had been my mother's and father's home for twenty years. I had stood, as a child visiting Grandpa and Grandma, at the very window out of which I was now gazing. All, except the Coyote Hills across the valley, and the oil tanks that topped them, had changed. The orange orchards and walnut groves had been leveled by bulldozers, and what I looked out on now were the glittering varicolored rooftops of the endless subdivisions. My grandfather's ranch had contributed its share of fifty rooftops to the flood. But when my father subdivided, he had kept an acre of orange trees about the Swiss chalet. So, if I looked downward, instead of outward, I was, for all my eyes could tell me, still in a place I had always known.

"Long old January," I said to Blix, turning away from the window. "Remember how often Mama used to say that? And how she longed for January to be over? It's ironic for her to have made it through January, suffered through all the rain and fog, only to be buried in the sunshine of February. It's like a soldier's being killed after the peace treaty's signed."

"The idea would make her laugh."

"It's not a very funny idea."

"You could always make her laugh. Anything you said."

"She liked to laugh. She often had the blues. It was a treat to her to laugh. She was looking for laughs."

"But it was always you who could make her. I've always resented you, Tassie."

"Because I could make Mama laugh?" I spoke automatically, knowing this wasn't the real answer, or at least the whole answer, but too astounded to make a better reply.

"That was part of it, perhaps. But I've always resented you. I can't remember when I didn't. Mother cast you up at me from the beginning. 'Tassie did the entire washing for me.' 'Tassie is never out after midnight.' "

"I never had much chance to be out after midnight."

"You've been married twice."

"I took the only two who asked me."

Blix ignored this. "It was the same at school. 'Your sister was president of the Girls' League.' 'Your sister was the best hockey player we ever had.' Even my own husband says, 'If you had a job like your sister's, I'd give up work and spend my time playing games like Pete.' "

"Pete's a professional. Golf's no game for him. It's the way he earns money. He works as hard as anyone else."

"I didn't mean to fire you up about Pete. Pete's a sweet fellow. Some men couldn't lead the life he leads. But he can, and I admire him for it."

I was astounded all over again, but I didn't say another word to her about Pete. If Pete resented me, Pete would have to tell me himself.

"Blix," I said, "how could you resent me? And I not know it."

"Oh, it was easy as hell," Blix said cheerfully, as if it were a pleasure to get it out at last. "Except for you, I would've had a pretty happy life as a girl."

"I thought you did."

"*I* was satisfied with it. Except people kept telling me I oughtn't to be. 'Your sister did this.' 'Tasmania did that.' "

"But *what* did I *do?*"

"Just a lot of hard-working, unselfish things I wasn't up to. And that everyone expected of me, because of you."

I wanted to fall on my knees, to clasp Blix's hands. I had lost my mother. I didn't want to lose my sister.

"Blix, you were all I ever wanted to be. I've always been so proud of you. I supposed it was the same with you."

Blix snuffed out her cigarette in one of Mama's old pin trays, and got up from the edge of the bed where she'd been sitting.

"I suppose that's what makes you such a spellbinder with audiences."

"I'm not a spellbinder."

Blix ignored this. "What *you* feel, you're convinced everyone else will feel. They can't resist your confidence."

"Blix, I thought we were close."

"I'm trying to stay that way."

"Saying you've always resented me?"

Blix pulled the crease straight in her taut-legged stretch pants, looked at me speculatively, and without saying another word left the room. She walked slowly, closed the door quietly, the way a nurse might who has an overwrought patient.

6

And I was overwrought. The tears I had been able to control at my mother's funeral now ran down my face. I had lost the only one who would ever really understand me. Mother would have known how unfair Blix was. Accusing me of being a person who could be resented. I pitied myself. I pitied my mother, a dreaming girl, whose dreams were all extinguished now. I pitied the bedroom I was in, fresh and pretty fifty years ago, now going downhill with faded ingrain carpet, loose wallpaper, spots like the age marks of the elderly marring the mirror of the bird's-eye maple dressing table. I pitied the doves, once my mother's tame pampered beauties, who had lived in a room-sized cage at one

16

end of the lath house. When she had her first stroke, they were set free; but freedom came too late for them. They had settled as near their old home as they could, in the big palm at the end of the driveway. Here they were preyed on by cats and attacked by boys with BB guns. When, toward the end of the afternoons, they began to call in their soft plaintive voices, they sounded like children who couldn't understand why the gates of home have been locked against them.

I walked up and down the room. Oh doves! Oh decay! Oh the passage of time! Oh carpet faded, and wallpaper sagging, and hand-painted hair receivers outdated, and powder box whose German silver top had tarnished. An enlarged photograph, framed and under glass, of two people, a man and a woman, standing in the snow in front of a back-East farmhouse, the picture labeled, in the jaunty nervous hand of my grandmother, "Christmas, 1900: Waiting for the children to come home."

One of the children she had waited for, my mother, would never again be waited for; and the doves my mother had fed were crying. I stopped my walking to peer up into the crown of the palm tree where they roosted, disconsolate, iridescent, and calling softly to be let in, to come home.

I began to walk again. The doves continued to call. Someone, Blix or I, was in trouble. Where, once before, a long time ago, had someone else walked? Doves cried? Blix been excluded? Only that night, the wind was blowing; and mother, the dreaming girl, was a young woman, imagining the sin she'd been taught to fear as the worst of all, in the backwoods of Kentucky.

Linda, Linda. It was in Linda, the Murphys' first home in California. There the doves were wild. They lived among the cottonwood and wild tobacco trees at the edge of the reservoir. At nightfall, when other birds were quiet, they began to call, and if the wind was right we heard them—even inside our bungalow. I had heard them before I began to play so sweetly, so dutifully, while Blix, aged eight, walked up and down, up and down the gusty, dusty driveway. If I took my eyes from my music, which

17

was dangerous, for I was no musician, I could see her in the half-light, her butternut hair spread out by the wind, her blue-and-white gingham dress, first wrapped around her, then torn away from her by the gritty Santa Ana wind. And she, who even at eight was so careful of her appearance, never put out a hand to pull it down or straighten it. Little and stoical, light as a dried mullein stalk, she looked ahead; and if she saw how snug we were inside, or smelled supper cooking, or heard my sugar-sweet playing of the "Barcarolle" from the *Tales of Hoffmann,* she gave no sign.

Was that why the doves in the palm tree seemed to be saying to me now "Let me in. Let me in"? Was it Blix, speaking from more than thirty years ago and using their voices? Blix outside, tramping the driveway, punished? Tasmania inside, straight as a soldier, playing the "Barcarolle" like "Onward, Christian Soldiers"? And Mama smiling approvingly? Was this what Blix meant when she said I could always make Mama laugh? Or at least smile?

Mother would never believe that Blix wasn't boy crazy. The shoe was on the other foot, insofar as I could see. The boys were crazy about Blix. *I* was the one who was boy crazy; but I was so completely crazy, I had to be crazy like a fox. I was so crazy I knew enough to keep it hidden. I don't know to this day why the boys fell so hard for Blix. She *was* pretty. But plenty of pretty girls get the go-by from boys. I think it was because she didn't make boys feel that she was going to throw her arms around them and squeeze them to death. She wasn't afraid to say good-by.

But Mother saw the boys hanging around, and I would hear her talking to Blix about girls "who got in trouble" and how she'd rather have a girl of hers "in her grave." Since we never doubted, or I didn't, at least, that Mother loved us, this prefer-ence for us in our graves rather than "in trouble" told us some-thing about the terribleness of this kind of trouble; but not about its nature. I was in on these talks, too. I was actually of a more suitable age for them than Blix, and my face burned and my scalp tingled just to hear Mother; though Blix was the one who got the full benefit of Mother's big blue-green blazing eyes, and of her lips taut with hate and oratory.

It wasn't Blix she hated. I knew that, even then. It wasn't even girls who "got in trouble." It was whatever "caused" the trouble. But to see her bending over Blix, shaking her finger, her lips, which were shaped like Blix's, hard as boards, the long ugly lines extending from nostrils to mouth, and her eyebrows lifted so that the bony ridges below them were exposed—it must have been easy for Blix to think *she* was hated. Toward whom else were those gestures and grimaces directed?

I read the other day that every child considers his own mother beautiful. Kate O'Brien said this in *Presentation Parlour*, and the person to whom she was talking replied, "Oh, but my mother *was* beautiful." This passage astounded me. I disliked my mother's looks. I remember the exact times and places when I watched her and thought, "So ugly, so terribly ugly." I think now that what I thought ugly were some expressions my mother had. She had ten thousand, for she was an ardent woman if ever there was one; and the ardent, kindling, loving expressions I took for granted. Like moon and stars. It is the eclipses I remember; the times when fear and anger and disgust shaped her mouth and blazed in her eyes. Blix never had anything to say during these tirades. Or after. She was always pretty self-contained. Except for occasional wild bitter flares of anger. She'd saunter off by herself, down by the reservoir where the wild doves nested. There she'd skip stones across the water; or try to, for she wasn't put together for throwing or jumping; and when she disappeared, Mother would believe she was off playing with the boys again. And she'd send me to look for her and bring her back. So long as I was with her, Mother didn't worry about the boys. Actually, that wasn't very flattering; but at that time—and perhaps always, as Blix said—I took what people said pretty much at face value. So I thought Mother trusted me because of my sterling character. That's what she said.

The Linda reservoir was about a mile from where we lived.

It was a great wonder in a dry foothill country. Toward sundown, with the slanting light on its pewter-colored water, and the carp rising, leaving circles of water which, as they died, grew larger, it was a magical place as well. When I was sent after Blix, I'd see her before I got to the reservoir, standing on the shore line, and I'd hear the doves calling; so the two are associated in my mind. Of course I didn't see her then as I do now. I think I felt *some* pity for her then, but what I felt mostly was a mixture of complacency and irritation. The darned little towhead in the wind-whipped dress was causing trouble. Mother was grieving; that was the trouble. Once, feeling sorry for myself, I told Blix the story I half believed, and which we both always remembered. I'd like to think I told it with some idea of making her feel better, of showing her that while life wasn't easy for her, it was even worse for me. But self-pity and self-dramatization were probably my real incentives.

"Come on back to the house, Blix," I said. "Mama wants you."

"I don't want to go back."

"Well, you have to, whether you want to or not."

"I could walk out into the reservoir and never come back to anyone."

Her words weren't boastful or threatening. Just thoughtful. Something to do if the worst came to the worst. They frightened me.

"Blix," I shouted, "what would you do, if you were me? If you didn't really belong to the family?" Blix merely looked at me. "I'm not really your sister. I'm a stranger. I work for my room and board."

"Who are you?" she asked. "If you're not my sister."

"I don't know who I am. How long can you remember me?"

"When I was six, you took me to school. I remember that."

"I can remember when you were born. They had got me to work for them then. I am no relation to any of you. I'm an orphan picked up to be a scullery maid."

"What's a scullery maid?"

"A servant. But I don't get paid. I work from dawn to dark just to pay for my board and keep."

"You go to school."

"It's against the law to keep kids out of school."

"You call them mama and papa."

"They told me to. But they're total strangers to me."

"Why don't you run away?"

"Where would I run? Besides, I love them even though they work me to the bone and make me take care of all their real children. You don't ever have to do any work, do you?"

"No."

"Didn't you ever think that was funny?"

"No."

"If I was your real sister you would."

"You are my real sister."

"No, I'm not. I'm homeless. Nobody really loves me. I'm just kept here for the work I do. When I see the woman I call mama loving you, and you don't do a lick of work, sometimes I cry."

"I never see you cry."

"I hide it. I go out in the barn. I don't want people to feel sorry for me. I go out with the horses and I talk to them and I say, 'We are alone in the world. No one likes us for ourselves. It's the work we do.'"

Blix was crying now, as I had intended.

"It's sad to be an orphan and not loved for your own sake."

"I love you, Tassie."

"I work for you, too, Blix," I told her. "I make your bed and iron your clothes."

She didn't say, as I reminded her afterward, "I'll help you," or "You don't need to, any more." What she said was, "I'd love you, anyway, Tassie," as if she wouldn't let the work I did stand between us.

And maybe if I hadn't been, as it appears now, so determined to be an orphan, no matter what, she would have offered to help.

Once, Mother said to me, "Tassie, I want you to tiptoe out to the arbor and see what's going on there. Blix is out there with that big Sam Foss, and I haven't heard a sound out of either of them for an hour or more."

The "arbor" was a kind of little bower covered with honeysuckle. Strands of honeysuckle hung down over the door. Blix and I played house there sometimes. I didn't like the idea of spying on Blix. If Mother wanted to know what they were doing, why didn't she tiptoe out? But orphans want to please—that's about their only stock in trade—so I crept out, holding my breath till I had a pain in my chest. I didn't know it then, but you can't do a thing without becoming that thing. When I started to look for Blix, I was, at the very least, her loving foster sister; creeping, holding my breath, spying, I became a spy. My hands got heavy and hot; my mouth, dry. I wanted to see Blix doing whatever it was Mother thought she might be doing that was so terribly wrong.

When I got to the arbor and peeped in, I saw Le Cid was there with Blix and Sam Foss; and that all three of them were practicing deaf-and-dumb language. That was the rage with all of us kids that summer. There was that big Sam Foss, old as I was, sitting there cross-legged, practicing sign language so hard he was sweating. Natural spoken language was hard enough for Sam Foss, let alone a made-up sign language. They had oranges, rolled soft, and straws stuck in them so they could suck out the juice. Real straws, I mean, not the manufactured pasteboard tubes that are called straws. Sam Foss sucked so hard I thought he would turn his orange, and maybe himself, wrong side out.

That's all they were doing. Practicing sign language and sucking oranges. Blix saw me, and it never crossed her mind that I was spying. She spelled out, "Hello, come in." And gave Le Cid a shove so there'd be room for me. My hands were so thick and hot I couldn't spell anything back; and I couldn't move either, until I heard Mother calling.

She was on the back porch. The bones, which her eyebrows should have covered, were showing; her mouth had gone hard as a bucket rim.

"What are they doing?" she asked, in a half-whisper.

"Playing sign language with Le Cid," I said scornfully.

"Is Le Cid with them? I didn't know that."

She looked shamefaced, and I felt sorry for her. But things like that were always happening. Sometimes I hated Mother for her suspiciousness, for the black thoughts, whose true nature, except for their blackness, I didn't know. But I wanted people to love me. And especially you want your mother to love you; and the way to be loved, I thought, was to please people. I wasn't free, the way Blix was, able to say "Good-by for now," and let people go to hell if they didn't like it. I was afraid they'd never come back. Something had orphaned me.

7

Linda, Linda and the wild doves. I remember that.

One evening in September I was coming home from the Linda library, coasting across lots that weren't built on yet, with a hot dry Santa Ana blowing at my back. There was dust everywhere when a Santa Ana was blowing. The first thing we did in the morning when we got to school was to write our names in the dust on the desks. Tumbleweeds blew past me; and the wind, in the clump of eucalyptus by the barn, had its usual Santa Ana sound of waves breaking against rocks, falling back, then coming on to break again.

When I saw Blix, the poor little tyke, walking up and down in the driveway, I wondered why, but was glad. I had one of the Andrew Lang fairy books for her, a new one she hadn't read. Blix depended on me to get books for her; and I loved to do it, to find the exact book I knew would please her. This one was Lang's *Yellow Fairy Book*. It was too far down in the stack I carried for me to get it out myself. I ran toward Blix so she could pull it out. But as I got near her she turned her back on me, and before I could call to her, Mother came to the door.

"You're not to talk to Blix," she said. "Come on in the house." Then she called to Blix. "Blix, you're to keep walking and not to stop. You understand? I want to hear footsteps and I want them to be brisk." Blix didn't pause, didn't look up, didn't hasten. She was a little girl, eight years old, and in the windy dusk her butternut hair looked white, and it lay horizontal on the air, as if floated by water, not wind. Mother closed the door behind us, though it took force to do so.

I didn't put down my books, but, still holding them, went to the dining-room windows where I could see Blix, never stopping, head bent, ignoring the wind. It made me sick to my stomach to see her walking up and down there in the wind like a homeless dog, while I was snug inside. But as I stood there, Mother came to me, took the curtain out of my hand, and put it back down over the glass. She took my books and put them on the dining-room table and gave my shoulder a little pat, which was unusual from Mother. She was never one to cuddle or fondle her children. I've forgotten many a box on the ear, but that caress I can still remember. I betrayed Blix because of it.

"I'm glad you're crazy about books, not boys," she said. I *was* crazy about boys, and my books got on Mother's nerves. She was forever hiding them, or snatching them away from me, so that I could get some work done.

"Tasmania, you've never given me a moment's cause for worry."

That wasn't strictly true either. I have a letter she wrote to her mother. "The babies are well." (I was two, Marmion one.) "Marmion is so good, and Tassie is good, I guess. But she is never still for a moment, body or tongue, and sometimes I think she'll drive me out of my mind."

So it was sweet now to be praised and patted, to be unorphaned, not expected to peel potatoes or start the fire, or stir the mush. Yes, I thought, I am Mother's comfort. I didn't know what Blix had done, but I was sure it was something underhanded, something I would never do. I had some consideration for my family. But that little snipe out there in the wind, she didn't care.

Father and Marmion came home, and Mother took Father out

to the kitchen and talked to him there in a voice that only now and then became high and shrill so that we could catch a word: "Dress," "Mrs. Hayden," "before," "Aunt Mamie," "too late."

"What's Blix doing out there?" Marmion asked me.

"Something bad again," I answered, smugness leaving no room for sorrow.

Marmion had to feed his rabbits. I was left alone in the house, which was almost dark, listening to the wind, to my mother's voice, to Blix's light footsteps and the papery sound of the pepper leaves and berries as she crushed them in her walk, up and down, up and down in the driveway. I lit the lamps—this was before we moved to Baranca, and our ranch house, out in the hills of Linda, was lit by acetylene. But the blue-white glare made me feel more alone than the dark, so I turned them out.

Pretty soon Father and Mother went outside; Blix's footsteps stopped, and Father's voice was the one I heard. Father was like me. He wanted to please Mother.

Marmion came back in from feeding, and I had what I thought at the time was a nice idea. Mother, who was musical herself and could play Sousa's marches with enough military fervor to make a bedfast man enlist, believed music to be genteel. So Marmion and I, both unmusical, were taking music lessons: Marmion on the violin and I on the piano; that was the standard arrangement for brother and sister then. And we, I judge, were equally bad. But the sounds we made were, I knew, music to Mother's ears.

"Let's play something for Mother," I told Marmion.

Marmion, though he considered our playing "practice," played with me. It was more than practice to me. In the contest that rages between children for parental favor, and a contest in which I thought I was at a disadvantage, it was the celebration of a victory. And it was making sure that Mother didn't miss the point. I had not only stayed out of trouble; I was capable of playing sweet music to comfort her when one of her less dependable kids did something wrong. And I knew this. Oh, I knew it. To this day I've not been able to hear the "Barcarolle" without pain. The knowledge of what I was doing made me sick to my stomach, but I kept right on. A Peter in pigtails, denying; a Judas at the Kurtzman upright, throwing kisses.

The three of them came in, finally. Blix, without supper, went right to bed. Father got as far behind a paper as he could. Mother made a skilletful of dried-beef gravy, but only the three boys were hungry. I went to bed, too. Blix and I still slept together, and I saw tear tracks in the dust on her face. I got into bed without touching her. Or saying a word. What could I say? Confess my nastiness and ask about hers? Mine was too complex for eight and twelve to discuss. And hers, I guessed, from all the hullabaloo about it, was of the kind we had been taught never to mention, or even to think of, if we could help it. Since we didn't know, or I didn't at least, what it was I wasn't to think about, I spent a good deal of time on the subject. What could be so awful that I was never even to think about it? I supposed Blix knew, and I wanted to wake and ask her. But she looked too tired and too sorrowful. And while I racked my brain about what it could be that I wasn't to think about, the Santa Ana, whistling mournfully around the corners of the bungalow, put me to sleep; and if I dreamed about what was forbidden, I have forgotten.

But I've always remembered that night and my guilt, not Blix's. In the days of her last sickness Mother said to me, "Once, I listened to a tale a neighbor carried to me about Blix. I hope God has forgiven me for listening to that woman and refusing to listen to my own daughter."

I didn't know then what she was talking about. I'm not yet positive, of course, that she was speaking of that September evening of wind and dust when Marmion and I played our duet, but I think she was.

II

In a later September, the September of last year, after I had rounded up by hook and by crook, by fiction pretended and falsehood direct, the medical information Blix needed, I went to stay with her. And there in her Arabic house of azure tiles, green plants, and falling water, the house she had longed for all of her life, we fell into our happy-tragic nighttime pattern.

The time was autumn. But an autumn day on the desert contains every season. Keeping my strange hours, I knew them all. Before dawn it was bitter winter, with the stars sparkling in the black desert sky. At six there was a short spring. The mountains were rosy and sudden thunderstorms moving down from Snow Peak dampened the sand and set loose the scents of all the countless flowers that had blossomed and perished there. By noon it was blazing summer. Outside, the thermometer would register 105°, 108°, 110°; but inside, the air conditioner maintained a steady 75°. Sundown would bring the day and the season into some congruity. Dusk brought not only nightfall, but the year's fall as well, a real autumn of an hour's duration. Something was visibly dying away then, something was visibly changing color, losing warmth, shortening. It was a time of peace; the clock had resolved the conflict between earth and the calendar. The day no longer contradicted the equinox.

Between ten and eleven o'clock, Blix usually prepared for sleep. The two of us would then be alone. Milt, Blix's husband, who was not well himself, went to bed soon after the dinner the three of us ate together in Blix's room. The minute he left, the ritual of bedtime began, the ritual of Sparine and Seconal, of Numorphan and Skin Dew. Of drugs and cosmetics. And of the past remembered. For the mind needs room to turn around in, and when the future doesn't provide this dimension, one chooses of necessity whatever spaciousness the past affords. These were not the best of the ten hours that were to follow. And under the circumstances it is difficult to understand how any of them could be good; but as proof that they were good, I have the memory of my own feelings and of what Blix said.

After Milt left us, Blix turned the TV on; and out came the ten o'clockers, Danny Kaye with his rueful smile; Jack Paar, who, whatever he protested, kidded us quite a lot; and Mitch, whose old men Blix derided but watched.

While Blix listened (and I did, too), I collected and stacked the day's accumulation of papers and magazines. I emptied ashtrays, threw away dead flowers and watered those that still lived; I put chairs back into the places in which they looked best to a bedfast viewer. Blix watched me with one eye, and Jack Paar with the other. We both loved this nightly transformation of her room: order out of confusion, tranquillity out of distraction. We told ourselves that we decked the room each night like two fairy godmothers preparing Cinderella for a ball.

"The room is Cinderella," Blix agreed, "and we deck it, or you do. But what's the ball?"

"Nighttime itself," I told her. "That's the ball." And in some ways, because night was so much easier for Blix than day, this was the truth.

"And when midnight strikes?" Blix asked. "Then what?"

"Then you sleep on," I told her. "The ball continues, the room is still beautiful. But you sleep."

There was more to it than this, but Blix was instinctively tactful. She had a sharp tongue at her disposal and could wound with it when she chose. But she wasn't one to maunder into the painful through lack of foresight.

Blix's room connected, by way of sliding glass doors, with a walled Japanese garden. Sometimes the evening cooled rapidly enough for these doors to be opened. This also was a part of the bedtime ritual. Day was done. It had been survived; and like all who live besieged, we relished the freedom of dark and fresh air, of gates opened to the world.

Night on the desert is quiet. Birds, which have celebrated sundown and coming coolness with a burst of song, are silent. The insect choir sings on, but in bleached moonlight tones. The stub-tailed cat, not Blix's, not Milt's, but inherited with the house, unloved, and unnamed—which proves it—comes to silent life at this hour. She is not allowed inside, and during the rest of the day lies deep in the leafy shade of a clump of oleanders. Her fur is hot and dry and charged with electricity. Now she, like Blix, enters the larger world of night. She crosses and recrosses the arch of the persimmon-colored bridge in the Japanese garden: a bridge whose whole utility is pleasure to the eye. It spans nothing but gravel bought at a nursery and goes nowhere; and the cat, who has no name, does not mind this. She has no destination in mind. At the top of the arch she often pauses and lifts her sad little monkey face to the moths which are attracted to the light overhead. She simply watches and never, like other cats I have known, tries, with a paw spread large and thin, to bat one down. She watches, meditates: on the succession of day and night? On the ways of moths and candles? Sometimes she looks into the bedroom. She is a gray cat, but around her eyes the fur is black, so that she looks a little like those fifteen-year-olds who believe that being Cleopatra is mostly a matter of mascara. I wait for Blix to say, "Kitty kitty." She never does. She is loosening ties, not making them. And besides, she is house-proud, and doesn't want perfection marred with tracks or scents of fur.

It is usually later that we hear coyotes. At this hour, though, we sometimes hear from down the street the good-bys of departing dinner guests. The sound of coyotes is easier to listen to. Blix, though she loves their cries, never was a coyote, and she *has* been a dinner guest and a party girl; she, too, has left the living rooms, with their concealed lighting and ankle-deep rugs, full of bourbon and memories of success. The voices take her back, and she can't go back. And they make decking her room for a night of pain and drugs, while pretending to be fairy godmothers, a thin pretense. Usually, however, the doors slide open to silence, to the smell of sage and greasewood, to a black wall of mountains, and, above the mountains, the glitter of stars; we may hear the thin dry rustle of olive leaves and of palm fronds scraping the night air. This comes to us like the breath of the desert itself and is reassuring because unchanging.

When Blix and I are washed and pajamaed, I pull my chair close to her night table, which is given over in about equal proportions to cosmetics and drugs. And I go part of the way with her in both lines.

We begin with Skin Dew; and stroking that fragrant grease into our faces, we are linked by its sweetness, by the hour, and by the motion of our hands to the past. Our mother and her mother before her had busied themselves at bedtime with skin care. At bedtime, Blix and I are bound to the past not by memories of prayers said or Bible stories read to us, but by memories of devotions of another kind. Face creams hold the generations together. Stroking, we remember, we wonder, we ask each other questions and hazard answers.

We must have been a family of thin-skinned women, whose faces, unless lubricated, burned and chapped. Neither Blix nor I had any idea that Skin Dew was going to restore us to our youth or make us, once again, daisy-fresh. We used it because it made our faces feel better. God knows what is in Skin Dew. It may be, for all I know, a frappé of Crisco, slightly scented.

Grandma *knew* what she put on her face. She made it herself of equal parts of honey, glycerin, and rosewater. Short and round, with the black hair and white skin of an Irishwoman, she stood in front of her mirror at night, and her hands, applying lotion, flew around her face and neck as fast as bees around a hive.

Mother, like us, bought her face creams ready-mixed. She said Grandmother's mixture would make a good cough syrup. She once pretended to drink some. Mother was a clown, a cutup, a card; and these characteristics contradicted a dozen others. She was shy, puritanical, an actress, a mystic, a verbal genius, possessive, ambitious, quick to take offense. Sexually responsive and attractive, but determined, in spite of this, to be a good woman and an ornament to the Church of the Pilgrims. And to have the neighbors recognize this fact. I think the neighbors did. But her daughters, for the first half of their lives, didn't know what to make of her. And now, five years after her death, we were still speculating about her. On one point we were agreed. She was a great woman for face creams. "Rejuvenate," "Restore," "Banish," "Texturize," "Replenish"? She believed all their claims.

"But what did she think after they *didn't?*" Blix asked. "Why did she keep on using them?"

"She blamed herself. She thought *she'd* failed in some way, skipped a night, not spent the required ten minutes rubbing it in, or given the necessary forty pats. She was brought up on Bible promises, and *they* never panned out either. But she never blamed her Maker. She was the one who had failed. It was the same way with face creams."

"She changed creams, though."

"That's not denying God, though. That's just saying a different prayer."

Elmo was the cream we remembered best.

"Semper Jovenay, Ingram's Milkweed Cream, Pond's Vanishing Cream: she tried them all. But Elmo! When she found Elmo, I think she stuck to it the rest of her life."

All the Elmo "preparations," with the exception of Cucumber

31

Cream, of course, were the color of crushed raspberries and clotted cream. And they smelled as rich and sweet as they looked. Mama's bedroom at night, after the creaming started, was a garden of lilies and honeysuckle.

"And in spite of all the failures," I told Blix, "Mama may have expected a miracle, someday. She believed in miracles."

Blix looked at me, and I stopped short. There were words we didn't say, and "miracle" was one of them. A miracle was desperately needed, and neither of us had the faith for it. Mother might have; we both believed that. There were things in our lives that Mother had said she wouldn't tolerate—and they had never happened. But Blix was only my sister, and I had tolerated much. I tolerated disease and I had tolerated the death of my mother. I tried to erase the word, not "death," but "miracle," by bringing back that other word we had been using, "Elmo." "Do you remember the smell of Elmo?" I asked.

Blix had finished with the Skin Dew, and her face was pink from the massage. She didn't answer my question, but asked instead, "Do you remember the night Mama walked me up and down the driveway?"

"The night I played the piano?"

"I don't remember anything about a piano. But I'll always remember Mama's smell as she leaned over me. I kept thinking, How can she smell so sweet and talk so mean? Then I thought, That's not her own smell. It's Elmo."

When the cosmetics were finished, we started on drugs. There was an array of them, most to be swallowed, one to be inserted, one injected.

As I filled the hypodermic needle, Blix said, "You don't give it a second thought any more, do you?"

"A second, maybe. Not a fifteenth, or a twentieth."

2

The first night I gave Blix a shot, Milt was away.

Milt had a Southern Counties' automobile agency, and every time a new man took over the agency in a nearby town, or a new model came out, or a new record was set, the new man, and the company itself, liked the "big boss," for that area, to be present.

Blix always urged Milt to go. Milt had been wounded on Luzon; a bullet still roamed around in his body, and when he wasn't fully occupied, he could feel it nearing a vital organ. His heart began to flutter. His liver didn't function at all. His stomach rejected all but liquid food. Busy breaking sales records, organizing sales campaigns, and setting up additional automobile-financing operations, Milt was the healthiest man south of Bakersfield.

"That bullet plus what's happened to me would finish Milt," Blix told me.

"How can you change what's happened to you?" I asked. "Or Milt's knowing about it?"

Blix was impatient with me. "Oh Milt knows about it, of course. Who do you think took me to hospitals and doctors' offices? But if I don't talk about it to him, and if I don't look like the wrath of God, he doesn't have to feel it. Not twenty-four hours a day, anyway."

I accepted, with no further expression of surprise, Milt's absences. Blix wanted him to go.

So Blix and I were alone on the night when an infection, which had nothing to do with her real trouble, began to give her intense pain. Milt was a hundred and fifty miles away and staying on for a "kickoff" breakfast next morning.

Blix's doctor's name was John Reyes. I located him finally at the hospital in Oasis. It was ten-thirty before he reached the house.

The minute I saw him, I was reminded of someone—who, I couldn't for the life of me remember. He was a tall young man, not very good-looking, very dark, but with the beetling brow, button nose, and long upper lip of a stage Irishman. His eyes were his own, though: thoroughly Johnny Reyes, gray, intelligent, and, on that first night, very tired. He had been up working since seven that morning; he suspected that he was dealing with an alarmist and he hoped to settle my fears quickly and get home and into bed.

He gave up that idea at once. Blix had an infected bladder and a temperature of 103°. I was able to help him, though awkwardly, with the catheter. The hypodermic was another story.

"Mrs. Orcino," he said, then paused. "Orcino? Where does that come from?"

"Portugal," I told him. "A long time ago."

If the origin of the name meant anything to him, he didn't show it.

"Please watch me closely, Mrs. Orcino. The pills your sister has been taking aren't giving her enough relief. I am going to give her a shot. She'll probably need another before I can get back in the morning. You'll have to give it to her. Please watch me carefully."

I watched him carefully. But a hummingbird might as well have said to me, "Please watch me carefully, Mrs. Orcino. Before morning you are going to have to fly."

No more than a hummingbird could fly in slow motion for purposes of pedagogy, could Dr. Reyes give a shot slowly for purposes of instructing me. His hands flew: syringe assembled, syringe filled, needle in flesh, plunger pushed, needle out, cotton to puncture, needle bent and thrown in the wastepaper basket.

"It's eleven now," Dr. Reyes said. "This should take care of the pain for four hours at least."

It did better than that. Blix's room was pink with dawn before she asked for another. She watched me, her eyes large with pain, as I tried to duplicate Dr. Reyes's hummingbird motions. Everything went wrong. I could not assemble the syringe. I could not fill it. But, finally, the part that I had expected to be most difficult was easiest. The flesh ate up the needle. It took it as if starving. It drank Numorphan as a famished calf drinks milk after a day's separation from its mother. Everything human is easy, I told myself. Everything mechanical is difficult. There is no truth in this. The human can accommodate itself more easily to the inept than the mechanical, that is all. And neither was easy for Blix that night: the inhuman needle, the clumsy human sister, the lacerating human pain. Only the Numorphan blessed and eased.

After a while, lying back against the pillows, Blix said, "I didn't think you were going to be able to do it." Then, a little later, she added, "Anything we have to do, we can do, I guess." And finally, "Anyway, I believe *you* could do anything you really wanted to do."

3

With that, the forbidden word was once more with us: "miracle." The trouble was we both half believed in the possibility of the miraculous. Half of what had happened in our lives was miraculous. Miraculous, but unbidden. Was that the nature of the miraculous? That it had to come unbidden? Had we been on the wrong track with our belief in the miracle induced by prayer and sacrifice?

When I was fifteen I attempted a miracle by sacrifice—the supreme sacrifice, as they say. A young cousin was dying of tuberculosis, and I offered the Lord, with every bit of willingness I had, my life in exchange for Harvey's. I knelt on the floor of the bathroom, my head against the rim of the tub, and paid no attention to those who, desiring the bathroom for purposes more practical than prayer, were pounding on the door. I offered my life to the Lord in exchange for Harvey's. The Lord preferred Harvey.

I no longer believe in the efficacy—or even the decency—of such proposals for swapping. God may, and probably should, look on them as attempts at bribery. The willingness to assume the affliction of a sufferer may be good for the would-be miracle-maker. Or maybe not. Christ's miracles didn't involve martyrdom —unless you believe that the efficacy of all of them, early and late, hinged upon that final martyrdom on the cross. But walking on water? Providing a plethora of food at a picnic? Prestidigitating water into wine at a wedding? Raising the dead? Especially yourself? Fun, sheer fun, all of it. No sacrifice involved. Nothing whatsoever required—except what is perhaps far more difficult than laying down your life: a desire for joy.

Blix and I were brought up in the shadow of the cross. *Was* sacrifice the price demanded by God as payment for gifts of joy? I, Sunday school grounded, was still haunted by the old mercantile theory of an eye for an eye. If you asked for a life, shouldn't you be ready to pay the price, by giving one? Of course I had tried that with Harvey and failed. Did I now refuse to try it with Blix because I believed that there might be elements of Russian roulette in such sacrificial miracle-making? And that this time my luck might have run out?

I didn't know. I don't know. But I do know that there lay between Blix and me an awareness of the possibility of a miracle: an awareness stronger with me than with Blix, because I knew something she didn't.

Blix, even when a girl, didn't like pain. (Who does, at any age?) She hadn't had many pains, but she had found a way to deal with those she had. Her best friend was Aggie Kilgrew. Aggie's mother was a Christian Science practitioner, and Mrs. Kilgrew, whenever Blix felt a pang, gave her a treatment. Absent or present, distance made no difference; Mrs. Kilgrew could cure her of anything—or of anything Blix had in those days. Blix's only, but usual, disease then was an afternoon once a month of cramps. The Kilgrews lived a mile and a half away from us across the Linda Hills. If Blix was smitten when I was at home, she would have me scoot over the hills to Mrs. Kilgrew. Mrs. Kilgrew would institute treatment the minute she got the word, and by the time I returned home, Blix would be cured.

One afternoon in early fall (the first rain of the season was drizzling down, sweeter than honey after the dry, hot days), Blix asked me to get word to Mrs. Kilgrew as fast as I could. She was really suffering. I left her curled around a hot-water bottle and sped toward the Kilgrews', licking the sweet rain off my dry, chapped face.

The Kilgrews were not at home.

On the way back, sorry for Blix, I began to do what I knew Mrs. Kilgrew did: I declared Blix's wholeness. I declared that God was love and that Blix was a child of God, and that she was filled with God. And this being so, where in Blix was there room for pain? Logic left no room for pain. I jogged, licked rain, and made my declarations. When I reached home I found that my treatment had worked as well as Mrs. Kilgrew's. Blix was fully recovered, uncurled, un-hot-water-bottled, and dressing to go to a roller-skating party. I was afraid to tell her the declaring had been done by me, not Mrs. Kilgrew, for fear of causing a set-back.

Actually, though God's name had been used, I don't remember giving *Him* the credit for Blix's recovery. The recovery came about, I thought, because Blix could not exist outside my mind other than as I was imagining her. All life then still seemed miraculous to me; and there was nothing extraordinary to me in the idea that two miraculous persons like Blix and me should be capable of influencing each other. Particularly in such a minor matter as the cramps.

Miraculous or not, and minor or not, changing other people's sensations by what you think is very demanding. It requires the ability to concentrate; it requires self-forgetfulness and time. None of which I've ever possessed in abundance.

Fortunately for me, and probably for Blix, I was soon away in college. After college I married; and never again until last year, the autumn of her sickness, were Blix and I together again as we had been when we were girls.

4

But in this latter autumn, last year's autumn, the boundaries between our minds got thin again. Last fall what was in her mind often entered mine. Asleep, I would awaken suddenly, plunge from my bed, and start down the hall toward Blix. Before I reached her room, her light would go on. She had awakened in pain and was about to ring for me. I could receive these messages of her need far better asleep than awake. Asleep, I awaited her call; awake, my mind was filled with all kinds of odds and ends of distractions which made it more difficult for her to get through to me. I alternated, for various reasons, between sleeping in a room of my own, connected with Blix's by a bell, and sleeping in one of the twin beds in her room. She used the second bed during the day as book table, magazine rack, telephone stand, and horizontal clothes closet. I cleared it off, of course, when I slept there. When I first came to stay with Blix, both of us took for granted that sharing the same room would be intolerable. When that week of infection required that I be very close at all times, I did sleep there. And, to our amazement, we discovered that sharing the same room wasn't at all intolerable. The drugs had something to do with it, of course. Each time I wakened to give Blix her medication—I did this three or four times a night—I took a sleeping pill myself. If I hadn't done this, I would never have closed an eye the night long. In the twenty minutes or so it took for her Numorphan and my Seconal to uncoil their tentacles, we talked. We said what we had never said before. The truths we spoke amazed us as much as the truths we heard from each other.

During the time we waited, Blix smoked; or perhaps she would eat a small dish of custard or drink a glass of warm milk. "Some married couples wake up in the night," she told me, "and smoke and talk. I couldn't ever do that with Milt, because if he talked in the night, he couldn't go back to sleep again."

Without the pill, I would have been like Milt. Trusting it, I, too, talked. Blix's night lamp had a bronze shade, and the light it shed was more like that of a study than a sickroom. In the silence of the desert, separated from our daytime selves (and lifetime selves) by drugs, there was a snowbound contentment about our conversations. We might have sat the clean-winged hearth about.

On the night of the Elmo talk, I gave Blix her first shot about eleven o'clock. She had been watching Mitch and his singers as I tidied the room. She despised them all, she said: fat old fellows, trying to be agile and flirtatious; all except one, a dark, stocky fellow under forty, an Italian by his looks.

She snapped off the TV. "He's the only one there with an iota of sex appeal." Hearing Blix say that made me so cheerful. That was my old highhanded Blix: flat on her back, dependent on shots, and talking as if out of forty men (hers for the asking) she would choose only one.

Mitch faded to a point of light. We settled into our beds. Covered with Skin Dew, tranquilized and sedated, we drifted toward sleep, and as we drifted we talked. Drugs affected us as drink affects strangers. In fact, made us strangers, which is the first requirement for confessions. Night, darkness, the desert, illness, the drugs: under circumstances that were strange, we became strangers. We were unsistered. And if at any time we were appalled by what we heard ourselves saying, we had the drugs to blame it on. "We must have been out of our minds." We hadn't been; but in our minds so much deeper than usual, we didn't recognize the landscape.

I was still smiling because of Blix's turndown of the thirty-nine singers when she asked in her nighttime voice, soft but drug-roughened, "Do you remember Harvey?"

"Cousin Harvey? He died," I told Blix, absorbed in *my* relationship with Harvey.

"Before he died," said Blix, "Harvey and I looked at each other."

"Looked at each other?" Sometimes my Seconal, having less to overcome than Blix's Numorphan, took hold faster. I was already drowsy and had forgotten our talk, earlier, about the evening she walked up and down the driveway while Marmion and I played sweet music. Besides, I didn't know that Harvey had anything to do with that walk.

"That's all we did. Harvey said, 'If you'll show me what you've got, I'll show you what I've got.' "

I woke up. I understood her. "Is that why Mama marched you up and down?"

"Yes."

"But you already knew what Harvey had. The same as Marmion and Le Cid and Blackie. What was the temptation?"

"He was so sickly I felt sorry for him. There wasn't much he *could* do, except look. Besides, I thought *he* might not have anything to look *at*. I thought sickness might have eaten it away, the way I thought sore throats destroyed tonsils."

"Not Harvey, I bet."

"No, not Harvey. He was all he promised and more. He scared me."

"How old was Harvey then?"

"Twelve or thirteen."

"My age," I said. Neither of us said what was obvious: Why didn't he ask me, someone nearer his own age?

"This is the first time I've ever mentioned that evening to anyone. I never felt the same about Mama again. She wouldn't listen to a word I said. She believed I did more than look. She didn't care that I felt sorry."

There was something characteristic of Blix and of me in the kind of gifts we had offered Harvey; and Mama's reaction to both (had she known of my offer) would have been characteristic of her, too. I was willing to die for Harvey (I thought), and this was Christian, and she would have approved. Blix, more practical, was willing to enhance the life he had with a smaller donation; and this was un-Christian and evil. Better a dead Christian than a live sensualist.

"She said she'd rather see me in my grave than 'bad.' "

"All mothers said that then."

"She meant it."

"Do you really think that if she'd had her choice, you in bed with a boy or run over by an auto, she would have said, 'Run over her'?"

"That's what she said."

"She was fooling herself. She would have clawed you out of any grave with her bare fingers."

"I wish she'd said that to me, then."

"Sex was so much more important to them."

"Why?"

Before I could answer that and I couldn't, Blix said, "Was Mother a lot sexier than we are?"

Drugs had taken us a long way, but not far enough to allow us this kind of talk about our own mother. There had been too many walks, too early, up and down too many dark and windy driveways.

"What would you have done if *you'd* thought you were going to have a baby before you were married?" Blix asked.

"Jumped in the reservoir."

"Then you believed it, too?"

"Believed what?"

"That she would rather have you in your grave."

"I believed *I* would rather have me in my grave."

"She never told you about me and Harvey?"

"No."

"She thought you were too pure to know."

III

The time came after my marriage to Everett when my mother didn't think me too pure to know. On the fourth Christmas of my married life, which Everett and I spent with my family in Baranca, she told me something about Blix.

Because of the concentration of misfortunes, mine and Blix's, I remember that Christmas very clearly. And I remember it, bad as it was, with pleasure.

Marmion was twenty-three that Christmas, a senior in the agricultural college at Davis, the handsomest of the three boys. He looked as if he were made of living marble: long smooth muscles, a chiseled nose, classic curls. When we were toddlers, Mama had enjoyed fooling the neighbors by switching our clothes. What I got in rompers was freedom. What Marmion got in skirts was embarrassment. A boy's virtues make a girl a jolly tomboy. A girl's virtues in a boy make him what even a girl doesn't want to be: a sissy.

He was engaged that Christmas to a black-eyed rake-handle girl. When pleased, she would lie on the floor and kick up her long shapely legs until you could see the tatting on her teddy-bears. More, if you didn't, out of embarrassment, look the other way. When displeased she pulled hair. Once she conked Marmion on the head with the telephone. When they weren't around, we speculated endlessly on what he saw in her. We supposed that out in the car she must be a whirlwind at necking.

We were too young then to understand that Marmion had already chosen resistance as his lot; not what he could accomplish, but what he could put up with. Set down second in a family like ours, his older sister wearing the pants at two, and his next younger brother a wild-eyed genius, what else could he do to make his mark?

Marmion didn't marry Olive, the impassioned rake-handle. But for his purposes he could scarcely have chosen better. She would have made him a winner in his chosen career.

Blix was having a go at my old alma mater. She wasn't, like Marmion, engaged, but she had, as always, a boy friend. A special one, that is, in addition to the regular band of admirers: Vurl Seaman. We were all agreed that Christmas that Blix had at last made up her mind. How could she find anyone better than Vurl? He was intelligent. He was an athlete. Vitality blazed from his blue eyes, curved about his full-lipped mouth, crested in the cockscomb of his blue-black hair. We weren't a colorless family ourselves, but we were blonds and redheads; and blonds and redheads have never been able to hold a candle to any authentic prince of darkness. And we were handicapped, except for Le Cid, by the humility and self-doubt instilled by the Church of the Pilgrims. Nothing had ever instilled any visible self-doubt in Vurl.

Le Cid and Blackie were still at home. Thus the five Murphy children ranged in age that Christmas from my twenty-four to Blackie's thirteen. We were a houseful of young people together.

Whenever I looked at Blix and my brothers I took pride in their youth. True, our parents were in their forties; but age in a parent didn't count. Young or old, they were already out of it. And Mother acted, actually, too young for a mother. I would have whitened her hair if I could, amplified her bosom, and thickened her waist. And certainly I would have given her some more motherly lines than those she usually spoke. But the five of us were exactly right. We inhabited among us, I thought, life's best years; and those who had more, or fewer, were to be pitied.

Except for being the right age, and for being with my family, all of whom I loved, I didn't really have much cause to rejoice that Christmas. I was ill and had been for a year. Everett and I, though I was too ignorant to know it then, were engaged not in matrimony but in an endurance contest.

Because Everett is a part of my youth, I now regard him with the tenderness we have for what we once were. And I pity him for those five years with me at least as much as I pity myself. And I thank him from the bottom of my heart for having had the strength to cast me off. For I, with my pride in endurance, would never have left him. The more I suffered the stronger the scar tissue would have grown, binding us finally like Siamese twins in the inescapable misery of two who were never intended to be one.

On the day before Christmas Everett and I left the ranch we were renting in Brenner. This ranch, which was seventy-five miles southeast of the town of Baranca, where my parents then lived, was failing. Apricots were no longer a money crop, and Everett, on any ranch and with any crop, would have failed as a rancher.

My father-in-law, before I was married, had taken me aside to warn me. I had expected him to tell me about some wild act out of Everett's past. I even hoped so. But it wasn't wild and it wasn't past.

"Tassie, I hope you know you are marrying the caboose," he said.

I marched right away from Mr. Henshaw. It was a part of my dream of myself as a wife that I would never listen to a word against my husband. Besides, I thought Mr. Henshaw was doing a terrible thing, running down his own son. Actually, he was trying to protect Everett, by preparing me for the facts. And the fact was, Everett couldn't qualify as a caboose, even. He

44

didn't just come in *last*. He never came in at all. Everett wasn't scheduled. He wasn't attached to any train.

My mother also took me aside before I was married (this was the whole of any heart-to-heart talk we had about marriage) and said, "Tassie, I hope you've faced up to the fact that you're in for a lot of waiting with Everett."

I hadn't. But I didn't want anyone telling me a thing about marriage. I did not want one word of advice about Everett, myself, or the married state. I awaited marriage as revelation. I no more wanted a premarriage résumé of what lay ahead than I wanted an inventory of Christmas presents before Christmas. I intended to launch into the state of holy matrimony unnourished by so much as a crumb of worldly knowledge; and I did so launch. The trouble was, Everett was launched in exactly the same manner. And what we were headed for was not so much a collision course as a complete miss. Everett was chiefly a romanticist, and I chiefly a sentimentalist. One looks to the future; the other to the past; and the present, on the unlikely chance that both ever happen to be in it at the same time, is, under such circumstances, foredoomed to be disappointing.

When my mother told me I had better be prepared to be patient, I told her I was.

"You don't show any sign of it around here."

I didn't deign to explain to my mother that marriage automatically changed many things.

It really did. But Everett's relationship with time wasn't one of them. Psychologists are busy trying to unhook modern man from the alarm clock and the conveyor belt. They would love Everett. *He* never got hooked. Time was as ample for him as for any caricatured peon, shaded under a sombrero, and dozing against an adobe wall. The difference between them was that Everett had this dream of himself as a rancher, a master among his herds and crops. And a master among animals, or even alfalfa, if the crops and animals are to survive, let alone pay a profit, must be, at the very least, a caboose. He can be the last to irrigate, cultivate, milk; but he must be last, regularly. Cows milked late, regularly, can adapt themselves to such a schedule. But cows milked now late, now later, dry up. And they don't even freshen if not taken to the bull in the proper season. Some of our cows got to bulls anyway; fences weren't Everett's long suit, either. I dreaded to hear the phone ring. It usually meant that livestock of ours was browsing on somebody's pole beans or rooting up their strawberries.

So we made no money; and it never occurred to Everett to say to himself, "The point of ranching is to make a living, and I'm not doing it." And, actually, for Everett that *wasn't* the point of ranching. The point of ranching was to be a rancher. And he was a rancher.

Long before that fourth Christmas, I saw the way we were heading financially. I got my Benbow job to help. But a better wife would have tried to help Everett by pointing out to him some of his mistakes. I have always found this difficult to do. I'm not sure whether I keep silent out of a reluctance to cause pain, or out of pleasure in a secret knowledge. Both, probably. Secret knowledge is power. You live like a spy among unsuspecting people. You listen, you watch. You collect the data: "Stupid. Unfeeling. Pretentious. Ignorant." I have never spoken these words to another human being. (Except to myself about myself, every day of my life.) But about others! Thousands of times and for minutes on end!

Finally, I became two persons with Everett. And he never knew the difference. Never knew that even in the closest relationships one remained aloof, commenting. Ironically amused, even, at the silent uninvolved discomfiture of the other young woman. What a hell of a life for a young man and woman.

This all seems to be the truth now. But that fourth Christmas of our married life, neither Everett nor I believed ourselves to be in hell. We thought of ourselves as any happy young couple heading home for Christmas. Our car was laden with produce from the ranch. Everett was, as they say, generous to a fault. He not only saw himself as a rancher, but as an openhanded one. His agricultural failures made openhandedness practicable. The

46

turkeys hadn't matured early enough for the Christmas market, so we brought two birds, a little on the scrawny side, with us. We brought three gallons of milk. Sometimes after a period of irregular delivery or early and unaccountable souring we had more milk than customers. Such was the case now. We had a two-gallon crock of home-cured olives. This year's "cure" had stayed a couple of days too long in the brine and had turned out both salty and flabby—unsalable but not inedible. There was a flour sack of dried apricots, undersulphured and destined to spoil before spring, but delicious at the moment. Two dozen brown eggs, and not a thing wrong with these.

In any case, my parents, with a large family to feed and not too much money, never thought of looking any of these gift horses in the mouth. They welcomed them—and they welcomed Everett in the role he wanted to play: openhanded rancher. And I liked being the daughter who had married the openhanded rancher who brought home the produce at Christmas time. But once again I was ambivalent. I had reservations and didn't express them. I knew that Everett's openhandedness was made possible by the jobs I was holding down. And I disliked myself for being capable of having such a thought. How mean-spirited can you get? Here was Everett, brimming with the spirit of Santa Claus himself, and my family, joyously reaching their hands into his pack of peculiar goodies, while I, sullen as Santa Claus's wife, sulking unthanked, thought, Little do you know to whom you owe it all.

Actually, such thoughts never lasted long. Even before we reached Baranca the change in climate began to excite me. Baranca is fifteen miles from the Pacific and has an elevation of only twenty feet. Brenner, where Everett and I lived, is eighty miles from the sea and fifteen hundred feet high. Also, the coastal range lies between it and the Pacific, so that, compared with Baranca, it is high and dry. In December, Brenner's orchards are leafless, its lawns frostbitten, its air clear and sharp as a knife. We felt, mile by mile as we ran downhill toward Baranca, that we were not only going home for Christmas but also leaving winter for spring. The grass on the foothills outside Baranca was already thick and green. The Valencia orchards were blooming, and the air was sweet as well as balmy. Baranca lawns didn't turn brown in winter; paper narcissus had bloomed and were past their prime; the whole town was decorated with the Christmas red of bougainvillaea and poinsettias.

My parents' house stood at the corner of Water and Palm Streets. These names alone would tell anyone who knows Southern California that Southern California was its location. Hibiscus hedges gave the house privacy. The back yard was a hodgepodge of flowers and vegetables, sweetpeas and pole beans, pansies and pieplants. In the midst of jungle was a big birdcage whose chief resident was a pouter pigeon named Bolivar.

Usually Mother, Blackie, Le Cid, and Blix, in that order, reached the car before Everett could bring it to a stop. Today, the day before Christmas, we drove in, stopped, and were as ungreeted as though it were any day in the year, and were parked in a stranger's driveway to boot. It was very strange. The excitement I was feeling needed to expend itself against an oncoming wave of equal excitement. Everett, possibly, was glad to have the clamor of a Murphy reunion postponed as long as possible. Everett was genial but didn't care for the Murphy rambunctiousness and exaggerations.

We parked alongside my father's tow car, which stood on the driveway in front of the garage. My father usually had some smalltime business or other to supplement his ranch income. The tow car was bright yellow with the advertisement for his garage painted in royal blue.

ACME GARAGE

ORLAND MURPHY, PROP.

TWENTY-FOUR HOUR TOWING SERVICE

As we sat in the car waiting to be discovered and welcomed, Everett said, "Orland! I bet your mother married your father for his name."

I pretended not to understand. "He didn't have to make an honest woman of her."

"Orland," Everett said, "not Murphy. Why's your mother always been so crazy about crazy names?"

"She likes crazy names."

Mother and Everett were beginning to tangle. In the days of our courtship, she had been, in spite of his slowness, his champion. She admired his good looks and his nice manners. She exchanged fuchsia and pelargonium cuttings with him. Whenever I had shown signs of discontent, she reminded me of the girls who searched the length of the woods, only to pick up, finally, a crooked stick. Lately she had changed her tune.

Looking at father's tow car in the driveway, Everett said, "If your father's name had been Henry, I bet your mother would never have married him."

"Yes, she would."

"If his name wasn't what won her, why did she give all her kids such outlandish names?"

"Because she hated her name so. Maude. Maude Hobhouse. She says Maude is a mule's name."

"Do you really think Tasmania is a better name than Maude?"

"Everybody calls me Tassie."

"Not your mother. Does she even know it's an island?"

"Of course she does. It's no different from being called Virginia or Georgia."

Before Everett could think up a reply to this, the screen door banged and out came the welcomers for whom we had been waiting.

Two didn't come at all, and I hadn't expected them: Father and Marmion.

Father was never a man to run. And Marmion, as I have said, had decided years ago against enthusiasm. But Blix, though no runner, would have been there if at home. Her absence made me sorrowful. "Hi," she would have said, in her soft warm voice. "Gee, I bet you're tired."

Mother came as fast as she could. Her brown bobbed hair was bouncing; the gold inlay in one front tooth flashed; her apron, made out of the back of one of Papa's shirts, was flying. She was never a person for hugging or kissing, but her welcome of

49

words and looks was so warm you felt kissed. She never participated partially, insofar as I know, in any act in her life. She was often sick, and when she was, her participation was feebler than when she was in health, but it was still complete.

She never cried. She was often "blue," "heartsick," "down in the mouth." But she didn't cry. Father did. Mellow, manly sobs, and tears that appeared to be tan-colored as they ran down his bronzed cheeks. Perhaps Mother, with some understanding of her own nature, knew that for her there could be no such thing as the "good cry" with which other women relieved their feelings. With her energy and enthusiasm, a "good cry" would become a full-blown case of hysteria.

She called out to Everett before she did to me, for she was capable of tact with her in-laws, particularly when they were men.

"Everett, I'd about give you up. Tasmania, how're you feeling, petty? Still got the side ache? Orland," she called back into the house, "the least you can do when your children provide the food is to help carry it in the house. Loaded with things as usual!" She excused Father. "He's listening to the radio. A terrible thing happened. A little girl's been kidnapped. The kidnapper's driving her around in a car, and the police can't get near for fear he'll kill her. He throws out notes for them. Being Christmas makes it worse. Look at those turkeys! It's Christmas every time you kids come home, no matter what the month."

Mother always greeted us with a long speech. It was her natural reaction to the hours of anticipation which had, I knew from her letters, been building up all week. But once that was out, long speeches were over.

Blackie was more like Mother than any of the rest of us, probably, though with masculinity blunting some of her feminine responsiveness. At thirteen he was a big boy, big shoulders, big thighs, built like a football lineman. His hair was the color of the red in the American flag, his eyes were the same blue, and his body as white as the white. Run him up a flagpole without his clothes on, and people would start saluting.

Blackie was Mother's love (though I had heard her say that Marmion was her favorite child) and her constant headache. She had staked him out like a dog in the back yard when he was two, to keep him from running away. She had threatened him at four, scissors in hand, with amputation, for his own good and to preserve his sanity. (I know. As Blix said, I believed everything I heard, and I, a big fourteen-year-old, heard the threat and took those scissors away from Mother. Blackie was my love, too.) Blackie came through it all, sane, unamputated, still a wanderer.

Behind Blackie came Le Cid. Nobody is ever satisfied with a sister's picture of a public figure. If she appreciates him, it's taken to be a filial build-up. If she doesn't, it's taken to be sibling envy. Look at the brothers and sisters of Hemingway and Faulkner! The public *knows* what those two men were like and doesn't want what they know contradicted by pictures from old family albums.

Though Le Cid was only seventeen that Christmas, no one doubted, inside our family or out, that he was a cut or two (more likely ten) above the ordinary; still no one was figuring him then as a combination of Howard Hawks, the Wright Brothers, and Richard Burton. Burton as actor, that is, not international lover, though Le Cid hasn't been celibate either. I think Le Cid combined the characteristics of his sisters and brothers. He had Marmion's brains, Blackie's openness, Blix's power of making people want to help her, and my energy—without my fatal reluctance to use it to change the *status quo*.

He didn't run out to the car as fast as Mother and Blackie, who were willing to break their necks in order to get any place they wanted to be in a hurry. But he came swiftly. He wasn't as handsome as Marmion, or as big as Blackie, but he was big enough and he was handsome enough. I was less at ease with Le Cid than with any of the others. He wasn't as classifiable. Blackie was my baby; Blix my ideal; Marmion my brother. But Le Cid's number I didn't have. And I thought he probably did have mine. I loved him, he loved me; but with Le Cid love

51

wasn't a finished thing, something that shaped up like Jell-O in a mold of recognizable form. It stayed fluid. It assumed hour by hour differing forms. It expressed itself now this way, now that way. You couldn't simply memorize the shape it had taken last time, and thus have love pegged.

Blackie, the minute he reached the car, had begun to rummage through the stuff we had brought with us.

"Tassie, did you forget it?"

"It's there," I told him. "Somewhere. Watch out, don't spill anything."

At Thanksgiving, in Brenner, I had promised Blackie a basketball. I finally had to fish the ball out myself; it was hard to locate among the presents, the produce, and the extra bedcovers we had brought. Blackie stroked the curve of its bright leather, the way he did Bolivar's breast.

"It's a real league ball," Blackie exulted. He dribbled it down the driveway and sank it in the basket above the garage door with a neat singlehanded jump shot. The net swished with the satisfying sound of a shot put in hard and at an angle.

"I can't miss," Blackie yelled, and he couldn't; but on the next rebound, Le Cid took the ball, threw it to me, and the game was on. I was very good for a matron of twenty-four; Le Cid was good; and poor old Blackie, except when our hearts softened, had to play middleman. We got carried away in the warm afternoon, jumping for rebounds, dribbling, centering the ball with the swish of the sword in a Chinese beheading, and tormenting Blackie, too. My side ached with the jumping and twisting, but even the ache was a part of my pleasure. My side had been troubling *me;* now I felt as if I were getting even, troubling it. Le Cid, with more brains than I, shifted to the inside spot so that Blackie, who was working up to one of his bellows, wouldn't be odd man out forever. It was winter, but in the warmth of play it was summer; it was pain, but it was pleasure; it was marriage and matronhood, but it was home and the old-time unforgotten scramble with my brothers; it was the earth and gravity, but it was flying and floating, too. Blackie and I were red as beets and sweating. Le Cid, who had Blix's coloring, had no more than the flush of a good ripe apricot, and his hair, which wasn't curly like Blackie's and Marmion's, was the color of fresh cedar shingles.

Le Cid, also for Blackie's sake (but I was glad), had slowed the game down. I could see Mother, never a sports fan, in the vacant lot next to ours, gathering an armful of mustard bloom. Except when it first comes out, mustard is a weed, and no one picks it, unless for greens. But that winter it was especially early, and a vase of mustard, though it shatters fast, will light up a wintry house like a shaft of sunshine, for a day or two.

I saw Everett, as well as Mother. He had the olives, the two turkeys, and a couple of comforters. He didn't look happy, and I didn't blame him. He had donated the produce of his ranch to his in-laws, and I didn't even have the decency to help him unload it. He was always telling me, "When you get mixed up with your family you forget that I exist." What I had gotten mixed up with wasn't actually so much my family as a game. But since my family was always getting mixed up in games, Everett probably didn't see the difference.

"I've got to go help Everett unpack," I told Le Cid.

Le Cid threw the ball to Blackie. "I'll help," he volunteered.

I held out my arms to Everett.

He looked at me with a hard face. "Aren't you afraid you'll hurt your side?"

This was sarcasm. Everett thought I noticed my side ache more at some times than at others. And the truth is, I did.

"Nothing to lose," I told him. "I already have."

Everett refused to relinquish his load, so I grabbed a load of my own from the car. Even Blackie parted with the ball long enough to help. Mother, with her arms filled with mustard, joined us as we headed under the leafless arbor for the back door. She, leading the way, church organist and harmonica player as she was, began to sing "Bringing in the sheaves." Everett had taken singing lessons but he wouldn't lift his voice to join a bunch of Murphys, strung along like bearers on a safari, singing, "We shall come rejoicing, bringing in the sheaves": this didn't strike him as a dignified performance in broad daylight on the afternoon of Christmas Eve.

Father, as we entered the kitchen, called out, "Be quiet, I want to hear this."

We all wanted to hear it. We put down our loads noiselessly and tiptoed into the living room. Father was seated in front of the Stewart-Warner, leaning forward so that he could quickly make adjustments if the sound faded or the tone blurred.

The radio announcer said, "The Police Department has made public the sixth note it has received from the abductor of little Marian Parsons. The note reads as follows: 'Trust me. This is Christmas time. So have a little trust. Not a hair of this child's head will be harmed if you trust me. I have bought her a Christmas doll and one pound of gumdrops. She is happy. Stop following me. You are being tested. God is using me to test you. I am His instrument. "Have those people any trust?" is the question He is asking. If Marian Parsons is harmed, her blood will be on your hands. Do not persecute an innocent child. We are praying together. "Let the people be filled with trust." We trust you. Are you worthy of *our* trust?'

"That is the end of the note.

"The police fear that little Marian Parsons may already be dead."

"Turn that thing off, Orland," my mother ordered.

My father turned it off. You would have thought a man named Orland Murphy would be a flashing Irishman, and a woman named Maude Hobhouse would be a sober Englishwoman. I don't know where Father's flash went, or even if he ever had any. Maybe a Murphy girl had an affair with an Indian sachem who wouldn't marry her, and Father inherited the Indian nature and the Irish name. He looked more Indian than Irish, that's for sure: a handsome, dark-skinned fellow with an Indian's characteristic meeting of lower and upper teeth, an Indian's outward calm, and his willingness to let the women wait on him. Only he'd got the

54

wrong woman in his wigwam for that role. Mother was, in fact, three quarters Irish, flashy as all get out, ready to die for Orland, but strictly on a volunteer basis. No Indian smoke signals saying, "Do this, do that."

2

The Murphys weren't the only ones celebrating Christmas that weekend in Baranca. We had, in addition to what the radio was telling us, reports from other sources.

Le Cid, who had a vacation job as delivery boy for the Bon Ton department store, had been given a gift-wrapped package to be delivered to Mrs. Dewey Hoben, who lived over on Zeyn Street. No one answered the front door when he rang. It was locked, and he thought he shouldn't leave the package out there on the front porch, visible to every passer-by. Mrs. Hoben's back yard was enclosed by a fence of redwood palings. Le Cid opened the gate and went in. Before he got in, he heard an awful squawking, and when he got in he saw why. Mrs. Hoben, flat on the ground, was at the fence opposite the gate he'd entered, trying to pull a chicken through a gap in the palings. She couldn't do it because Mr. Wetzel, her neighbor on the other side of the fence, had hold of the chicken's feet and was pulling in the opposite direction.

"Didn't it hurt the chicken?" Mother asked.

"It sure sounded like it."

"Whose chicken was it?"

"I never asked."

"Were they mad at each other? Fighting?"

"They didn't sound like it. They were laughing fit to kill."

"They must've been drunk," Father said.

"That's what I decided," said Le Cid. "Mrs. Hoben didn't have any clothes on."

No one said a word for a minute, busy doing, I suppose, what I was: seeing Mrs. Hoben's white bottom sticking up into the air and that chicken halfway through the palings, and hearing the mingled squawking and laughing.

Mother and Blackie asked simultaneous questions, each showing where his heart was.

"Why didn't you rescue the chicken?" asked softhearted Blackie. And sex-conscious Mother, "Was she stark naked?"

Le Cid answered Mother's question. "All I could see was her back."

"Did Mr. Wetzel have his clothes on?" Mother asked.

"I didn't pay much attention to Mr. Wetzel."

"Where was Mrs. Hoben's husband?" Father asked. "And Mrs. Wetzel?"

"Search me," said Le Cid. "All I wanted to do was to get out of there. So I gave the box a toss onto the back steps and started to beat it."

"Started to?" Marmion asked. "What stopped you?"

"When Mrs. Hoben heard the box hit, she let go the chicken and jumped up."

"Well, then, you know if she was stark naked or not," Mother accused him. "Don't you?"

"Yeh, I know," said Le Cid.

Even Blackie forgot the poor chicken now. "Was she?" he asked.

"Yeh," said Le Cid. "She was."

Father said, "How old a woman is Mrs. Hoben?" and Mother, turning on him with a glare, said, "Do you think Le Cid was examining her teeth?"

Le Cid said, "Without her clothes to judge by, it's hard to say."

We were all laughing, even Marmion, we couldn't help it, holding in a little, though, so that we could stop when Mother called a halt, as she was bound to sooner or later.

Everett, who despised anything off-color, and didn't have much stomach for people like Le Cid who, in his opinion, were show-offs, was making his face of disapproval. When the story reached nakedness, close up, he rose ostentatiously and said, "I think I'd better see to unpacking the rest of our things." I knew I ought to

When Everett's pinching and tickling recalled me from prayer, I felt as some people do when awakened from a sleep. Blackie was like that with sleep. If he dozed off on the sofa, and you poked him so that he could undress and go to bed properly, he woke up fighting mad, and struck out at you or anyone else within flailing distance.

It's one thing to come out of sleep fighting mad, and another to emerge from prayer mad. But that's what Everett's fingers nibbling along my thigh made me: mad, and wanting to hit. And that proved his point, I guess. He *was* stronger than God; and my praying, if that was the word for it, *was* pretty shallow. For quite a long time I continued to bow my head, to keep my eyes shut, and to give no sign that I wasn't in the timeless realm. But I wasn't. I was in the present, hearing a voice—my own—saying, "Stop that, Everett, stop it, or I'll hit you."

So I gave up returning thanks before meals. I couldn't endure sitting there, a whited sepulcher, posture saying one thing, thoughts another. I had spoken to Everett about it, I had asked him to stop, but he had laughed and said, "If a little tickling takes your mind off God, I guess you aren't very close to Him anyway."

Maybe I wasn't. Anyway, I gave up "returning thanks," though I missed it. For a long time, even though I picked up my knife and fork as briskly as Everett at the beginning of a meal, I had, for a second or two, a hollow unsatisfied feeling.

Everett, so far as I know, never realized that I *had* given up "returning thanks."

I told Blix about this in one of our nighttime exchanges in the long autumn of her sickness. Not about Le Cid and the pulled chicken, a story she would have enjoyed, but about Everett and silent prayer.

This was selfish of me. Everett and silent prayer were nothing to her, while Le Cid, away in London, remembering her with cables and French perfumes and hand-knit Irish sweaters far too hot for the desert, was often in her mind. Sometimes when the

say, "Let me help you," but I couldn't tear myself away f
the increasing laughter and the awfulness of it all. Drunk
naked! Anything might happen. Perhaps anything had. So Ev
stalked out; without anyone, so far as I could tell, noticin
had gone, or hearing him deliver further packages with reso
ing thumps on the breakfast-nook table. I felt miserable (th
I was laughing) and knew that later Everett would say to
"When you get with your family, you don't know that I exist.

3

It had been a shocking account for any season and downrig
religious for Christmas Eve. Every one of us, except Everett,
this and had laughed anyway. Everett hadn't left because h
religious. I don't know why he wasn't. His family were s
Pilgrims than mine; maybe their very strictness had turne
against religion.

We were all brought up in the practice of "returning th
before eating. Nothing was said. We bowed our heads and
was a minute or two of silence. Blix told me she always co
to ten, then looked up. I actually said thanks; it was a m
of floating, of nonbeing, or of being everything; I'm no
which, but I enjoyed it. I continued the practice of "ret
thanks" after Everett and I were married. Or tried to. I
bow my head, close my eyes, become everything or nothi
joicing in creamed carrots (and glad I was finished with so
and cooking the damned things), floating, beginning to fl
away from all earthly trivia; then, just as I made it, E
hand would come under the tablecloth, caressing and p
up and down the length of my thigh. I think he thought
contest between him and God for my attention; as he tho
home-coming to Baranca as a contest between himself
family. In Baranca he lost. But at the supper table he wo
proves nothing about God or Everett, but does, I thin
some comment about me.

sand blew against the windows and even the combination of Percodan and Numorphan was slow to act, she'd say, "I wonder what Le Cid is doing this very minute?" It would be getting on for morning in London, but Le Cid had always been a night owl, and we envisioned him eating and drinking with theatrical cronies in some fashionable café, the modern version of the Café Royale about which we had read.

Once Blix said, "Someday science will find a way for us to trade lives for a day or a week with someone else. It wouldn't be too bad for someone to lead my life, even for a week, if he knew he could stop at the end of the week. Le Cid would trade with me for a week, I know."

"I would trade with you for a week."

"And me take care of you? I think I'd better trade with Le Cid."

"Would Le Cid be *you* sick? Or himself?"

"Himself. I want to be *me*, well."

"In London? Leading Le Cid's life?"

"You know I couldn't do that." Then she added, "It doesn't take any talent to be sick, does it? Or to die?"

"It takes talent to do it with style."

"Do you think I'll have a stylish death?"

"Yes," I said, "I think you will."

"And Mama?"

"Style wasn't Mama's line. She was just . . . intrepid."

"I'd like to be . . . intrepid."

"You will be," I told her. "Both. Stylish and intrepid."

But Le Cid, though Blix liked to speculate about him and what our lives might have been had we had his ability to break away from the family and the limitations of the backwoods and the inhibitions of a run-down Pilgrimism, wasn't the subject I asked her to consider that night.

Everett was. Everett, I thought, had been trying to have his cake and eat it. A man who was too good for plain talk ought also to be too good to interrupt a woman returning thanks.

Blix didn't see it that way at all. "I don't blame Everett.

59

Having to sit there while the food got cold. Nothing to do but twiddle his thumbs while you held a long silent conversation with God."

"I told you Everett found something to do besides twiddle his thumbs."

"Well, good for John Everett."

I didn't answer her.

In the darkness, half whispering, Blix said, "Tassie? Are you still awake?"

"Yes."

"You've never forgiven him, have you?"

"I don't know about forgive. There are things I haven't forgotten."

"Why didn't you do your praying in some private place? Where Everett didn't have to watch?"

"I tried that later," I told her. "The trouble was that with Everett there was no private place."

I would have told her about that, too, but I heard a change in her breathing. As the drugs took effect an automatic pilot took over her respiration. Blix, undrugged, breathed soundlessly, light as thistledown. The automatic pilot was heavy-handed. He dragged her breath in and shoved it out.

I thought about Blix's question. They say to understand is to forgive. If so, I *have* forgiven Everett (and myself) for many of the acts—and failures to act—of our youth. And I understand now that religion, or the lack of it, had nothing to do with Everett's responses.

It wasn't religion that had taken him out of the room during Le Cid's account of nakedness and chicken stretching. It was a kind of inborn squeamishness. Everett couldn't stand any joke, no matter how sidesplitting, if it was the least off-color.

None of us Murphys were like that. We were a million miles away from today's four-letter words, but we didn't boggle at facing a few earthy facts, and even at joking about them.

Lacking Everett's little grain of sensitivity, neither Father nor

Mother had asked Le Cid to spare us any of the details of the Bon Ton delivery to Mrs. Hoben. We had all managed to stop laughing long enough to get our breath back, and we supposed (I, anyway) that we had heard the last of Le Cid's story. But Mother, with that strain of sorrow in her that made her hate to let the laughing stop, hoped for more.

"Le Cid," she said, "you haven't said a word about what Mr. Wetzel was wearing."

We knew (I knew) from the way Le Cid began his answer that Mother was going to get her wish. Whether or not Le Cid was telling the truth, I don't know to this day. He knew that Mother wanted to laugh—and probably understood the causes better than I.

"Mr. Wetzel," Le Cid began, wrinkling his olive-colored brow in the effort, it appeared, to recall the whole elaborate outfit, "had on, to begin at the top, a vest, unbuttoned. To begin at the bottom, and work up, he had on a pair of black socks, held up tight by a pair of bright red Paris garters."

"No shoes?" Blackie asked.

"No shoes."

Le Cid appeared once again to make an inventory of his memories.

"What else?" Mother asked.

"Between the socks and the vest?"

Mother had to admit this was the region she was inquiring about.

"Nothing," said Le Cid.

"Nothing! My gosh," said Mother, and she had the laugh she had reached for. "Nothing but a pair of socks, and a vest above them?"

"You're forgetting the Paris garters," said Le Cid.

"And a lot of hard liquor," said Father, trying, in spite of his laughing, to get the affair into some kind of proper moral focus. "Between them they had consumed quite a lot of hard liquor."

"And on Christmas Eve, too," Mother said, wiping her eyes and recognizing her duty.

4

Christmas, to Mother, apart from the home-coming of her children, didn't mean a twit. We had never had a tree; often, no presents. And when there were presents, Mother usually couldn't wait until Christmas to give them to us. She had not been brought up to celebrate Christmas, as, indeed, none of the Pilgrims had been. The historical birth of Jesus on a possible December 25 meant nothing to them. What counted was the birth in the heart of the spirit of Jesus. *Then* He was born, and only then. The folderol of a tree, of a play crib, of a toy Babe surrounded by a toy Mother and Father and assorted sheep and shepherds struck many Pilgrims as idolatrous; and Mother, as so much child's play. She didn't condemn them or the people who found pleasure in them. But she couldn't pretend, herself, to find their use other than childish, like a grownup still cherishing a doll received at the age of six.

If Pilgrim religious spontaneity hadn't existed, Mother would probably have invented it; it so suited her nature. So Christmas was a celebration of the children's home-coming; and it was, since her children now observed the growing commercialization of Christmas, an exchange of presents. It was also, since feeding her children was one of her delights, popcorn balls and Blix's specialty, pans of walnut fudge; it was fondant made with English walnuts in a back-East washbowl and called "heavenly hash"; it was an enormous amount of talk, of hilarity, for the real goal of any Murphy statement was to make a listening Murphy laugh; it was joy in each other's presence, which is love's face when it does not pretend. It was not prayer or Scripture reading or going to church, or thinking of the poor, or singing carols, or any other activity that can be labeled religious.

But Christmas Eve or no Christmas Eve, Le Cid's story had to do with sex—and with liquor—and Mother never wanted her children to take either lightly. Or to think that she did.

None of us, insofar as I know, had had any inclination to take either liquor or sex lightly, no matter how hard we laughed at Le Cid's Bon Ton delivery story; and Mrs. Hoben and Mr. Wetzel drunk in their birthday suits made us thank God for water, God's good ale, and the fires of sex banked down within the bounds of holy matrimony. And actually, Christmas Eve in Baranca was being celebrated, for the most part, more traditionally than with either the Murphys or the Hobens and Wetzels.

5

There were Christmas Eve services at the churches. Organs played "O Little Town of Bethlehem"; sopranos sang "Adeste, Fideles." There were Sunday-school programs at which six-year-olds recited "Away in a Manger," and where Sunday-school superintendents handed out red mosquito-net stockings filled with hard candy. Trees, decorated with ornaments saved for over fifty years, were lit, and Christmas gifts wrapped in Christmas paper were under the trees. Traditional meals were already in ovens, or cooling on pantry shelves. Prayers were being said at hearthsides, and drinks, which neither impoverished nor impassioned their imbibers, were passed.

At the Murphys', Christmas Eve fell somewhere between chicken pulling and the traditional. There was no silver punch bowl foaming with a traditional drink, no lighted candles flashing messages either religious or sociable, not even a tree, a bell, a wreath. But, on the other hand, no orgies either.

So there we were, at the corner of Water and Palm (both religiously symbolic), with no symbols, religious or otherwise, to sustain us, and no ribaldry to free us. But this is today's conclusion. The Murphys on that Christmas Eve felt no lack.

There was tension and excitement in our coming together. We were forgathered because of a religious holiday. But we were nearer, in some respects, performers than religious celebrants. We were about to run through a dialogue as yet unknown

63

to us, but of which we expected much. Hilarious gags, mordant lines, scathing witticisms. Since the script for our performance would shape up as we went along, each performer was nervously alert, determined not to miss cues or to fail in delivery or tone.

We had talked, or listened, the sun down; but it wasn't dark yet. On either side of the fireplace, above the bookcases that flanked it, were casement windows. These were open, and through them the hibiscus foliage was now bronze-black in the December twilight.

The Murphys did not, on that brief December day, like the Whittiers of John Greenleaf's poem, "sit the clean-winged hearth about." We sat a hearth about, but it was neither clean nor winged. In the center, lemonwood logs, wrist-sized, sent wisps of mustard-colored flame through an encrustation of peanut hulls, orange peel, walnut shells, unpoppable popcorn, apple cores, gum wrappers, and an old bone discarded by Blackie's dog, Beanie. I, a Martha in season and out (and this should have been Mary's hour), worked at keeping unburnables out of the fireplace; and, this being impossible, of keeping what fire there was going, in spite of them. It was a losing job amid such a gathering of carefree Marys.

With no one to remind me, I stopped my cleaning and reminded myself that it was Mary who had chosen the better part. I sat down in a chair away from the unclean, unwinged hearth and those who were crowded about it. Withdrawn, I indulged in another activity resulting in a state not unlike that which I achieved by grace-saying. I looked at my family as though absent from them in time and space. Or as though this absence would soon be a fact. And saw them as vividly as though imagined—or remembered.

Look, oh look, I told myself. Hear, oh hear. For the forty-eighth Christmas save this, the twenty-fourth. Record the voices. Memorize the attitudes. Store up the sayings. Recall the laughter. Soon they will be gone. As smoke riseth upward. As the grass withereth. I dispossessed myself of my family in time in order to possess them in eternity. The smell of lemonwood and the smoke of unburnables was my incense. I was trying to take in simultaneously the presence of life and the fact of death. In youth we have the energy to sustain such emotions, and the freshness of heart to be stirred by the facts that call them forth. The talkers did not miss me. Mother threw back her head and brought her hands together in a spontaneous clap of pleasure. Blackie rolled on the floor, snorting. Le Cid showed his white teeth and pink tongue in pure merriment. Even Marmion smiled, if a little shamefacedly. Father, tinkering with radio knobs and tubes, looked sly. The sound of the present laughter took my family out of the eternity where I had banished them in order to enhance them.

I saw how selfish I was. Imaginatively separated from my family, though physically present; and absent from my poor husband, not even to be *with* my family, but only to exercise my imagination about them. I went immediately to search for Everett. I found him, stretched on the bed in Le Cid's gloomy little back bedroom, reading a Scattergood Baines story. I sat on the edge of the bed, but Everett gave no sign that he had noticed my arrival.

"You are right," I said. "There is nothing funny about nakedness and chicken pulling."

Everett put down the magazine which had hidden his face from me and let me see his expression. It was disgust, enduring interruption. "I'd rather not talk about it," he said, and put his magazine up again.

"I'm sorry," I told him. "I just wanted you to know I understood, and that I missed you."

He put his magazine down again. "Understood what?"

"How you felt."

"But you sided with your family. You laughed with them." He couldn't go on. He didn't want to get into those subjects *again*.

"I don't side with them. I side with you."

"You sure laughed."

"You can laugh at things that you know aren't right . . . the same way you can do things that aren't right."

He didn't put his magazine up again, but he didn't look at me either. Instead, he gazed out of the window which opened onto the back yard and Bolivar's cage. But it was a sign of relenting.

"Come on," I urged. "It's Christmas Eve. Blix'll be here soon. The first thing she'll say is, 'Where's John Everett?' "

I began to stroke Everett's pompadour and to straighten his eyebrows and to kiss his small ears, which were frosted with white hairs and rather bristly. Everett put down his magazine, grasped my wrist, and began to pull me toward him.

"Lock the door," he told me.

"Oh, no, Blix will be here any minute. It's almost suppertime. Le Cid will be trying to get in."

Everett shrugged, reached once more for his magazine.

"Always thinking of your family."

I was thinking of myself, to tell the truth. There was not time . . . this was not the time . . . my side did ache. . . . Everett's face was hard again, a fine little gimlet. I had the choice, I knew, of an evening, perhaps a whole day, of Everett's polite removal, in all but his physical presence, from the holiday festivities, and the five minutes he was now proposing.

I thought I made a spiritual choice. I said to myself, The body doesn't count; the spirit does. You have the choice, body or spirit. Five minutes of body against a friendly evening and a Christmas of good will. I locked the door.

When I left Blackie's room, Everett was finishing Scattergood Baines. But he would be out presently, smiling. He didn't think it would look just right for the two of us, after such an absence, to return together. If anyone asked about him, I would be able to say, quite truthfully, "Everett's in Le Cid's room, reading."

No one asked.

6

I hadn't been away from the living room more than ten minutes, even counting the stopover in the bathroom.

When I got back someone had placed our "Christmas tree" (Mother's big straw laundry basket, decorated by Blackie with two red bows of crepe paper, and filled with our Christmas presents) at the corner of the hearth. This year almost all of the presents had been taken out of their store wrappings and re-wrapped in gift paper, a great advance in formality for us. Blackie wasn't able to stay away from the basket for long. He counted, read tags, hefted, and shook.

"There's fourteen for me," he told us. "That's an average of two from everybody. Counting Tassie and Everett as one. Did you give together?" he asked me.

"Wait and see," I told him.

"I only gave you one present," said Le Cid.

"Everybody else gave me more than you, then."

"I figured they would," said Le Cid, "so I could lay off."

Blackie took advantage of the silence provided by Father's radio repairing to play the phonograph. Blackie really "played" the phonograph; the music that came out was Blackie's, not any composer's or band leader's. He wasn't tied down by the tempo of the recording; with the use of a couple of fingers he hastened it up or slowed it down, he improvised on the theme provided by the record. The record was "Piccolo Pete." Blackie let us hear enough of it straight so that we could appreciate what he was accomplishing. When Piccolo Pete went "tweet, tweet, tweet," Blackie pulled Pete through a knothole. The piccolo whined like a mosquito imprisoned and dying of starvation. Hardly enough strength to lift his voice and no space to lift it in. Blackie got the sound down so thin that only Beanie, pricking his ears, truly heard it. Then he hustled the record until the notes came so fast they were as indistinguishable individually as cicada cries in a burst of 110° weather in September. Machine-gun rattle of insect artillery. Why were these sounds funny, rather than ugly or irritating or meaningless? Because, I think, Blackie made drama out of them. He would let us hear three or four bars of "Piccolo Pete," his own voice, then whammie, mos-quito or katydid would take over. He made it a struggle, Piccolo Pete the good guy, the blond boy in the high-school orchestra, trying to speak to us, but overwhelmed every time before he could get his message out, by insects, by his own breakdown, by

67

chance. It shouldn't have been funny, but it was: "Piccolo Pete," tormented by Blackie, while Blackie's family laughed.

Le Cid made it funnier and sadder. He began to dance, and he danced as if he'd spent a thousand years rehearsing those interludes of sanity and eras of incoherence. He danced the history of the race. He knew Blackie's intentions ahead of time. He became gnatlike, long, thin, and fragile, but at the beginning complete, equipped with wings and able to fly. He lost his wings. His eyelash-thin legs broke; he was reduced to a whine as thin as the thread for a #3 needle. He would momentarily become Piccolo Pete himself, face as fresh as a new-laid egg, a whole new world inside and revelation due any minute. But the bugs always took over, or madness or misfortune; and his dance showed it.

I wished Blix would come home. She would discuss Le Cid's dancing with me—and Blackie's manipulation of the Victrola. I would imitate Le Cid imitating a gnat. And Blix would laugh at my imitation.

What greater gift can anyone give a clown? Applause is nothing compared with laughter. Anyone can clap hands, and the mind be miles away. A laugh comes right from the center. No wonder comedians love their audiences. No wonder men hate women comediennes. It's a masculine prerogative, men think, this ability to cause a response like laughter: a paroxysm, the breath short, tears in the eyes, pleasure so near pain the victim pleads, "Stop, stop. You're killing me." But he is ready, the minute he has caught his breath, to be killed all over again.

I never ceased to be able to make Blix laugh. My God, what a blessing that was to me. Every time I did so I felt good and powerful.

In the July of her last visit here—was it only seven months ago?—Blix, though I didn't realize it then, was living through a time worse than the autumn that followed. I was protecting Blix, I thought, by my hopefulness, my optimism. Perhaps. But I was protecting myself even more so. The body accepts the

68

possibility of death more quietly than the mind. In July Blix was accustoming her mind to death. Death embraces the body. But the mind must reach out toward death and make a part of its thinking the very state that will annihilate all thinking.

In July I didn't understand this. I did see that Blix didn't want to speak of the future. So we talked of old times, looked through my bountiful supply of old letters, and examined my stacks of old photographs.

Blix came upon a picture of herself taken when she graduated at the age of fourteen from the eighth grade. Of all my pictures of Blix it is my favorite.

By some happy meeting of photographer's art and sitter's mood, there looks out from Blix's dark eyes and wide sweet mouth every bit of the longing and uncertainty that characterize a girl of that age. Plus Blix's real beauty. She was wearing a soft, ruffled white chiffon. You can see the slippery abundance of her butternut hair and the shadows under her high cheekbones. She looks like a Russian princess, elegant, pampered, but imprisoned. And outside on the snow the blood of serfs.

Blix gazed and gazed at that picture of herself. Then she said, "Oh, how terribly sad I look."

As if she saw somehow, in the face of the fourteen-year-old, some foreboding of the fate toward which every day of her life she was to take another step.

Luckily the next picture was of me: aged fifteen, a junior in high school, wearing a blue serge middy blouse and, for some reason impossible now to fathom, for this was not a snapshot but a studio photograph, a jaunty white sailor cap balanced above a strained-back straw-colored coiffure.

What I looked like was not a Russian princess but a Russian peasant, serving a term as a proud midshipman in the Russian navy.

Blix gave my picture the same long brooding examination she had given her own.

Then, shaking her head, she said, finally, "Oh, Tassie, you look so sad, too."

"And I," I promptly told Blix, saying exactly what occurred to me, "look as if I had plenty to be sad about."

Blix laughed. She took another look at the picture, and tried not to, for laughing admitted the unflattering truth of what I'd said, and laughed some more. For a minute, perhaps two, she was free of the future, and of the past, which seemed to her to look toward the future with haunted eyes. She was in the midst of now and laughing.

Those words may not be the funniest I'll ever say, or Blix's laughter the loudest. But I'll remember that sound and those words when funnier and louder are forgotten.

7

On that Christmas Eve, with Blix absent and Le Cid holding down the job of court jester, there was no one I could make laugh.

Mother, who had headed for the kitchen when Le Cid's dance was over, came back to the door to speak to Father. "Orland," she said, "I need a hand in here."

Father was busy again with pliers and screw driver. He didn't answer. It may be that he didn't hear. He always had an unusual ability to exclude what he didn't want to be bothered with.

In those days I felt sorry for Father. Nowadays I feel sorry for Mother. Give me another twenty years and I may feel sorry for myself, or Marmion.

Mother ate, read, talked, worked, and drove faster than Father—and was more generous. She had more initiative—and more tenacity. She ate with a larger spoon, wrote with a blunter pen, and sneezed with a louder sneeze. Yet she was not loud, large, or masculine.

Father was in many ways more "ladylike" than Mother, without being in any way feminine. He looked like a man and acted like one. The difference between them (apart from sex) was that her feminine engine had a higher compression ratio than his. She responded with more to more, and more quickly. (Though not always more wisely.)

At twenty-four, I thought Father was henpecked. I'm not sure he wasn't; but I'm not sure now, either, that he didn't need a little henpecking, or that he didn't relish and even ask for it. Mother pecked him out of his procrastination, defeatism, and the opinion that moving on would solve most problems.

Orland Murphy was about as handsome as a man can be, and Maude Hobhouse was about as plain as a woman can be. Orland was high-minded, and Maude was highhanded, which, given the circumstances of their respective physical endowments, was just as well. Orland believed philandering to be wrong and, whatever his beliefs, one wink from him in the wrong direction would have finished him with Maude. And he didn't want to be finished with Maude. He had had the rare good luck of falling in love completely and enduringly, thus knowing all the ardor and none of the inconvenience of a series of love affairs. He had begun his wooing in the backwoods of Kentucky when he was seventeen and Maude was fourteen. In that bend of the Rush Creek the Hobhouses were long-time landowners and the Murphys were unknown renters drifting through. Only Orland, after meeting Maude, stopped drifting, went to Normal, and started teaching.

Maude, for all that she was plain, had been a backwoods belle with suitors galore. She was witty, daring (as this was judged in a Pilgrim community), and exuded a kind of excitement which, if you were a young male, was thought to be sexual. And possibly was. She also valued herself highly. She wasn't giving anything away, which always convinces boys that there is something worth working for. And in that work, being of the kind all young men feel themselves designed for, Orland had much competition. This may have enhanced Maude in his eyes.

What Maude saw in Orland besides his looks was his good heart, his love of learning (that was what his going to Normal meant to her), his romanticism, his strong emotions—which he expressed in fist fights, twenty-page letters, and a physical responsiveness that made his heart beat so hard when he embraced her that he set, merely by contact, her hatpins, side combs, and brooches to jouncing.

The Hobhouses opposed the marriage, saying that Maude would have a dozen children in as many years, live in two dozen houses, none of them good, and be lucky to have clothes on her back and food in her stomach.

Maude married Orland anyway; but she never forgot her family's prophecies. And Orland's inclinations gave substance to them. But with Maude for a wife, he found himself, in spite of his hankerings to trade the garage for a bakery, the orange ranch for four hundred acres of rich bottom land (the advertisement said) in South Carolina, or to advertise towing only twelve instead of twenty-four hours a day, hanging onto the garage, keeping up payments on the ranch, and advertising towing for twenty-four hours a day. He was even postmaster of Baranca for a couple of years, with Mother doing the actual work. In the long run, he became wonderfully proud of his business acumen and his dogged application to duty. But I thought then, as Mother forced acumen and application upon him, that he was being henpecked.

When Mother called to him from the kitchen, I went to her at once—as much to protect Father as to help her.

"What is it you want?" I asked. "I'll do it."

"No, you won't, petty. What's he mean, sitting in there tinkering on that radio? Don't he know what day it is?"

"There's a lot of good programs to hear today."

"We were hearing them till he took it into his head to take the radio apart."

"He's about finished."

"What'd he think if I took it into my head to spend the day taking the stove apart?"

Mother had a tamale pie about as long and wide, though not as thick, as a bale of hay baking in the oven. I opened the door to look at it. The olive oil, stained red by the chili powder, bubbled up in miniature blowholes through the crust of the corn meal, and the crust itself was the color of foothills in October.

"What a smell!" I told Mother. "I could live on it."

"Are you hungry?" she asked. Before I could answer, she scooped out a saucerful with a long-handled wooden spoon. "How's it taste?" she asked.

Mother never in her life said, "Don't cut the cake," or "I'm saving that for supper," or "Watch out, you'll spoil its looks." She liked to eat when she was hungry and she wanted others to do the same.

"Did I get too much chili in it?"

"Just right," I said. Mother made her gravies rich and brown, her pie dough rich and short, her tamale pie rich and hot. "As the old lady said," she always told us, " 'When I make water, I make water. When I make tea, I make tea.' "

I was smacking my lips over the rich hot pie when Everett stuck his head in the kitchen door. My first impulse was to hide the saucer and stop in mid-chew. Everett didn't approve of Mother's harum-scarum come-and-get-it methods of serving meals. I didn't either, as a matter of fact, but constitutionally I was evidently like her. Without coaching from some power that I considered higher than my body's appetites, I, too, was a grabber and a gobbler.

But there wasn't time to hide the saucer or stop the chewing, and Everett was in a good mood. "I see you've worked up an appetite someplace," he said meaningfully.

I got the drift. "Starving to death," I agreed, "for some unknown reason."

"Save some for me," Everett said, and, as once again the radio went into operation, turned back to the living room. "News bulletin from KFI," Mother and I heard.

I shut the swinging door between the kitchen and dining room. "Papa had to see if what he did works," I explained to Mother.

I took over the job of cracking English walnuts for the Waldorf salad, and Mother climbed onto a chair so that she could reach the top shelves where the special china and glassware was

73

stored: the celery vases, spoon holders, gravy boats, casters, and toothpick holders of past generations. She told me about them (she had done so many times before) as she placed them on the table. They represented persons and occasions to her: mother, grandmothers, aunts; wedding anniversaries, birthdays, fairs, exhibitions, reunions.

Mother hadn't a touch of the antiquarian about her. These dishes, the hand-whittled potato mashers and butter paddles (now used for oleo), the ivory-handled case knives, and the lusterware pitchers were people, her people. She didn't live in the past, but she knew where she came from, and pretty much *how* she had come.

Mother, as I cracked nuts with a hammer that had been made for tacking down rag rugs in Kentucky, small-headed so that you could get in close to the walls, was setting out dishes and serving up family history.

"That fruit bowl belonged to your great-great-grandmother Pryce. She was eighty and Great-great-grandfather eighty-seven when they sold their farms, packed their belongings, and with children and grandchildren left the slave state of South Carolina for the free state of Indiana."

I finished the walnuts. As I cleared away the shells, Mother took down a big teacup, bespattered with faded violets.

"Grandpa Macmanaman's," she told me. "He was a tobacco chewer till the last year of his life. His sight had failed, and when he wanted to spit, he aimed at the fireplace by the feel of the heat on his face. One day a visiting Quaker lady—it never entered her head, I suppose, that anybody *she* knew could be a chewer—got between him and the fireplace just as he let fly. She got the whole stream, plus some of the chaw, full on her fichu. She may have been a Quaker, but she wasn't the silent kind. She told Grandpa exactly what she thought: That a man who couldn't see where he was spitting ought to stop chewing. Grandpa agreed. 'Ma'am,' he said, 'a man who can't tell a female from a fireplace had as well admit his knell has tolled.' Grandpa never chewed another chaw from that day on."

Mother, with her dishes set out for the meal, gave me a hand with peeling and chopping apples for the salad.

"These California Bellflowers," she said disdainfully, "can't hold a candle to the apples we grew back in Kentucky. The Early Harvest was likely nearest to it. The Yellow Transparent was earlier, and Mama liked it far better for pies and sauces. My favorite for eating was a Red Tallman's Sweet. It was no good for cooking, but I used to keep a supply of Tallmans on hand to eat with hickory nuts."

We peeled, cored, and chopped to a litany of named apples, apples Grandpa Hobhouse had grown (better than anyone else) back in Kentucky: Rambos, Rome Beauties, Grime's Golden (after the Tallman, Mother's favorite eating apple), Benoni, Ben Davis, Black Sweet, Sheep's Nose, Black Twig, Baldwin, Early Harvest, Smith's Cider.

I was transported to the hilly apple orchards of Kentucky, to orchards of trees long dead and to a land I had never seen. But I saw them, while Mother talked; I saw the orchards in blossom-time, pink and white, loud with bees; I saw the trees bright with Rome Beauties, aglow with Winesaps; I saw fruit rotting in the grass, the wasps at their harvest; and I saw the leaves turn yellow, then drop, leaving the summer orchard nothing but a tangle of gaunt gray limbs. I saw snow cover and soften the bare limbs, cover the fallen leaves, hide the summer residue of bees and apples.

So where did I live? In a kitchen or in an orchard? In the East or the West? In the twentieth century or the nineteenth? In summer or winter? As wife? Or as daughter, *and* granddaughter? And *great*-granddaughter? And what did I believe? What I saw practiced? Or what I was told had once been practiced?

Listening to Mother, I learned to live where I wasn't. Compelled by her art, I had my most vivid life in her memories. I imagined those hills and branches, those creeks and springs; the Aunt Libs and Uncle Steves, the Great-grandfather Amoses and Grandmother Elizas. And everything we imagine is, because it is a part of ourselves, more real than reality. It is the reality *we* have manufactured. We possess it, as God does the world *He* created. It is the dust into which we have blown the breath of life.

So fruits I had never eaten, Rambos and Black Twigs, were sweeter to me by far than fruits I ate every day: loquats and tangerines and guavas. Snow was a greater wonder than sunshine. A Santa Ana wind, strong, dusty blower off the desert, couldn't hold a candle to the blizzard I had never experienced. What was a seen rattlesnake to an unseen hoop snake putting its tail in its mouth and coming after you like a wheel of fire? Or the purr of a Buick Master Six compared with the clip-clop of old Charley down the pike? Or even the far-flung Pacific beside the pond at the bottom of Freemont Hill, which froze over each winter in time for Christmas skating? Nothing! What was good was what was gone. What was real was what didn't exist. What was present was what was past.

And even stranger than this real, though distant in time and space, world of Kentucky was the world of the Pilgrim Church. Stranger because even though we all inhabited it, and were its citizens by birth, we did not seem truly to dwell there. What did we *do* to show our citizenship?

There were numerous things we didn't do. In addition to the usual things not done by Christians, like murdering, stealing, committing adultery, taking the name of the Lord in vain, and so forth, as Pilgrims we didn't drink, smoke, dance, or play cards. But was that all it took? What did we *do?* We went to church two or three times a month, but, insofar as I could see, were uninfluenced by what happened there. (Usually nothing happened.) We made some contributions to the collection plate; Mother thought we should tithe, usually when family funds were the lowest, in the hope that the Lord, noticing the bread cast upon the water by the Murphys, would return it as cake. Mother read the Bible, or had Father, who liked to read aloud, read it to her. (This reading we children never heard. Father, caught Bible reading, stopped as short as he did when we came upon him fondling Mother; whether it was the subject matter or simply the fact of reading aloud that made him self-conscious I don't know.) We remembered the Sabbath enough, if not to keep it absolutely holy, at least enough to keep the garage closed, and to shut down the towing service. (Except in emergencies and for price and a half.)

But was this enough? Was this all it took? I didn't know what was expected of Christians, of the Pilgrim, or of myself. Or what I wanted. Something ennobling? Enrapturing? Self-obliterating? Transfigured by love? Did I want to preach to birds? Lick the sores of the leprous? To be absolutely loving? Even at twenty-four, no child, no virgin, with my own kind of hardness, I was not past longing. Not past feeling a loss. This was the eve of the birth of our Saviour. What did He save us from? (In the Murphy household this was never discussed.) Sin? We all sinned. Death? We would all die. Would anyone pray? Or read Matthew, Chapters 25 to 32? No one. Would anyone, like Marmee and her Little Women, pack baskets for the poor? No one. Were there any poor? We hadn't looked into it. "Give all and follow me"? Oh, no! The clothesbasket would reveal a fair and calculated exchange; the oven discharge a succulence in excess of need; the table speak of a prideful past, attested to by possessions.

At twenty-four I was already past (I judged) redemption; anyway, it hadn't happened yet. But at seven and again at seventeen I had made my try. Believing, even then, that a Pilgrim ought to *do* something, I got saved. It wasn't necessary. I was born saved, my parents being Pilgrims at my birth. But I wanted a hand in it myself. I didn't want it secondhand. I wanted my own vision, my own burning bush and cleft rock.

I went to the altar because I was afraid to go, and I was afraid to be afraid. I went because I was ashamed to go, and I was ashamed to be ashamed. I went because I pitied the preacher. I went because I pitied Jesus on His cross, to whom, because He had suffered (for me, it was said), I owed a little debt of suffering of my own.

Above all, I went (as I remember it) because I hoped by that

77

act, by that prayer, by that declaration, to satisfy a longing, so painful I felt it as physical ache, to transcend Tasmania Murphy and become one (in love) with all mankind: never again to envy Le Cid or be impatient with Marmion. I loved myself when loving; I knew the transporting bliss of complete self-forgetfulness achieved when I worked with hot cloths to cure Mother's headaches, or divested myself of my clothing for Blix, or went without lunches to buy Blackie a treat. I experienced the unnamable when I ran, at the close of day, up into the brown hills through a froth of sound (stirred up by disturbing the cicadas) to watch the sun go down behind the oil derricks.

I wanted by one act to nail it all down, guarantee it forever. One act was supposed to do it. After the second birth, the reborn supposedly became incapable of sin. I never lost my capability. For a short time at seventeen I really believed I had. First of all I experienced a euphoria of the same kind one has after having gone to the dentist, the euphoria that comes as the aftermath of the complete concentration courage requires. I mistook it for salvation. Evidently no one else did. No one, in my family or out, offered to watch and pray with me, to labor with me to keep the old Adam dead. And the rebirth of which I had on those evenings in the hills and in my acts of self-forgetfulness dreamed was never achieved.

Never forgotten, either. It was now seven years since my last try, at seventeen, to attain a perpetual state of grace. I had given up hope for it. It wasn't for me. Still, I had flashes of glory which kept me discontented with any other state. On Christmas Eve that thirst, undefinable, never properly slaked, made me, though relishing high jinks and joining in them, anticipating tamale pie and the surprises of the laundry basket, dissatisfied. This evening was as high and holy a time as our year could produce.

8

The day then, as we celebrated it, wasn't holy. I was more like Mama than I knew, I expect. The meaning of the day was reunion; and until Blix arrived the reunion was incomplete. I listened for Vurl's car in the driveway the way children listen for hoofs on the roof. Vurl was St. Nick for me that Christmas, and Blix was the Christmas present.

They arrived before supper, and I was first to reach the door to the screened porch.

"Welcome home. Merry Christmas. Love and kisses."

There weren't any kisses, of course, but we at least knew the words.

Blix had a sprig of real holly (not the red berries that grew in the foothills that we called holly) pinned to the lapel of her green corduroy jacket. You could always count on Blix to add to the occasion: to be the spirit of revelry at a party and the soul of Christmas on December twenty-fourth. She wore a scarf of cherry-colored chiffon tucked in the neck of her suit with just enough of it showing above the green to make you think of trees and ornaments.

Standing in the door to the screened porch she looked like "Home for Christmas." She should have had snowflakes swirling behind her, instead of the dingy, fading mustard of a Southern California sunset; she should have been holding an ermine muff, instead of a jar of spiced loquats.

Vurl was right at her heels with her suitcase. *He* didn't look like the spirit of Christmas; what he looked like was the spirit of football, in his blue sweater with the big gold block P and the three gold circles on his arm to show that he was a three-year varsity man.

I tried not to look at Vurl—for several reasons. For one, Mother (since my marriage, she had taken to trusting me with more and more of life's dark secrets) had told me four or five weeks earlier, "I can hardly stand that Vurl. He runs his hand through Blix's hair while pretending to have a conversation with me. But he don't know a word he's saying to me, because all the time he's talking, he's swollen up the size of a horse."

"Swollen up . . ." I started to ask, and cut off that question just in time. I didn't even start the next question, "How did you happen to notice?" Though I think now that Mother wouldn't have been offended. She would have answered honestly, "Because I've got eyes in my head." That's how you knew, all right, once you had freed yourself from the fixation of his big bold stare and had taken in some more of him.

That Christmas I didn't want *any* of Vurl; not the death-ray domination he loosed when he lifted the long-fringed lids of his big blue eyes or his equine qualities elsewhere.

Blix and Vurl had spent Friday, Saturday, and Sunday of Thanksgiving vacation in Brenner with Everett and me. They were undemanding guests. All they wanted was a chance to neck. I was having one of my bouts of side ache, and Vurl, as much to show up Everett as to give me a hand, wouldn't let me carry in wood, start fires, or even churn.

Blix wasn't much help about the house—at any time. And on this visit, between necking, repairing the damages of necking, and getting herself combed, curled, and made up in a manner to invite necking, she actually didn't have much spare time.

Brenner, and the whole of Southern California, for that matter, often gets 90° heat in November. It had been 92° on Thanksgiving Day, then 93° on Friday and Saturday. I kept doors and windows closed until four, then opened them to the outside, which was fresher, if not cooler. It was a listless heat. The leaves of the umbrella trees fell straight down. They lay like dead minnows at the foot of the trees. Any little breeze brought them momentarily to life. Towhees, slate-colored, held their wings away from their hot bodies. The baby beeves out in the corral bellowed in discomfort. The water, which dripped onto our burlap-covered cooler from an overhead tank, evaporated at once.

I was, in all seasons, a great mopper; more because I liked

80

the rhythmic push and pull of the mop and the slop of the water than because I was mad about clean floors. Vurl said I kept the wooden floor boards of the kitchen so continuously damp that he thought, whenever he came out there, that he was treading the deck of some wave-swept windjammer. He said he could feel the floor rise and fall beneath his feet. He asked me if I had any Mothersills' handy.

He came out to the kitchen at ten on Saturday morning. Blix was still in bed. Everett had run out of chicken feed and had gone into town to pick up a load. I had my big mop bucket in the sink, filling it for the first mop-up of the day.

"Hi, Tassie," said Vurl. "Swabbing down the decks again?"

"Again?" I asked. "This is the first time today."

I wasn't yet, at Thanksgiving, self-conscious with Vurl. He was a big handsome boy. There was no missing that. But he was Blix's, and, besides, I wasn't in love with him. I might have been, and still no "harm" have come of it, for I'd fallen into the habit of falling in love; and with that habit had developed the power and even the pleasure of hiding what I felt. I was like an Indian boy who can clamp a live coal under his arm and hold it there, smiling. Falling in love wasn't painful—the reverse—but it may take as much control to hide the exquisitely pleasurable as the exquisitely painful. Anyway, I thought of myself as that Indian boy, possessing something alive and burning, and giving no sign.

Falling in love appeared to me to be a special gift; I accepted the capability as I might have accepted a sense of smell suddenly heightened so that objects ordinarily scentless—hummingbirds, stones, ladybugs, clouds, tree bark, dust—became overpoweringly fragrant. If that had happened to me, would I have kept that pleasure secret, too? Perhaps. Perhaps I would have known that a woman who went around swooning over the fragrance of pebbles would be just as condemned as one who was transported by the sight of the assistant postmaster. Even though she had no intention of even speaking to Mr. Carmody, let alone touching him. Mr. Carmody was just my own pri-

vate red-hot coal, and he didn't have to do anything, and I
didn't have to do anything. Any more than a saint who sees
God has to *do* anything. He's done it already, the saint, I mean,
by having his vision.

Saints sought their visions by prayer and fasting. Mine came
to me unexpectedly and without effort. One vision faded; I forgot it. Another, unsought, replaced it. Without warning. Some
man or boy suddenly became luminous, every gesture enthrall-
ing, every tone significant. He could be a Dutch Boy paint salesman, passing through Brenner and sighted by me as I parked
the car in front of Short's Hardware. I would sit in the car and
watch him as Mr. Short came out onto the sidewalk to chat with
him. The Dutch Boy salesman would drive away, never again to
be seen by me. In which case, the "love affair" would be of a
week's duration, a matter of good memory and keen eyesight.

I'm not at all sure that "falling in love" or "love affair" are
the phrases I should be using. "Fall" is a verb and "affair" certainly suggests action of some kind, whether or not connected
with love. And there was no action in my "love affairs." "Love"
may not be the right word either. I certainly felt something.
And it really did seem to me a gift from heaven; as if additional
colors had been added to the spectrum, or sweeter songs given
to birds. What I experienced had nothing (I thought) to do with
Everett. Take away the cement contractor, the assistant postmaster (and time took them all), and I was no more and no
less a wife to Everett than I had always been. So it had nothing
to do with Everett, was no source of shame to him or me, or
matrimony; a pure gift, and I meant pure, pure as an emotion
experienced by an angel, all afflatus of the spirit without physical
expression, and without wanting any. Why would I want to do
anything about it? Any more than De Quincey, feeling the effects
of his glass of milky laudanum, would want to go out and work
off the dreamy ecstasy by chopping wood or pulling weeds.

My secrecy was partly good sense, partly preference. What I
felt was wonderful, but secrecy increased the wonder. Known to
me alone: the way to be fulfilled is to refrain; find satisfaction

82

in the *desire*. Secretly hungry, but not showing it, and not eating. Angry, but not striking. Amused, but not laughing. Sad, but not crying. In "love," speaking to the assistant postmaster, saying, "I want to send this first class"; waiting at the window to see him as he drives home from work.

It was a private system of courtly love; it was the worship of a do-it-yourself order in an invisible nunnery. It was a kiss without lips, an embrace without arms, a hosanna without sound. I was crazy. A young woman, two years ago, when asked "How are you and Paul?" answered, "Fine. We have three children. I am always in love." "With Paul?" "Oh, no. Other men." "What do you do about it?" "Not a thing, of course." I walked away from her quickly. The crazy attract the crazy, they say, but that craziness of mine was too long buried. It would be nothing but dust in my nostrils, and I didn't want to stir it up again.

Love, like Whittier's snowstorm, always came unannounced. That was one thing that made it so spooky and other-worldly. I didn't "develop" a crush on anybody. Some seed, unbeknownst to me, would be sown and from it a great scented flower would suddenly bloom in all my senses.

There was a young rancher—I can't even remember his name now—who used to supply Everett with baled barley. I had seen him a half-dozen times, I suppose, and had never consciously given him a thought. Then one Saturday Everett asked me to phone him and ask for an extra load of hay. In the midst of that phone call the transformation took place. His voice became "the voice." I prolonged the conversation just to hear it.

When the conversation was over (this is what makes my inability to recall his name so unexplainable) I remember sitting down and writing that hay dealer's name over and over again. I was enthralled by the look of its vowels and consonants. I think it was a name with a good many o's and u's in it, rich heavy sounds. Whatever the name was, I was enamored by the look of it written and the sound of it as I said it to myself. It was *his* name.

By the time he arrived with his load of baled barley I was too aware of him to even answer the door when he brought the delivery slip for me to sign. But I watched him. Hidden behind the curtains of first one room and then another, I moved from window to window noting his every step.

I was "in love" again. Or I was drunk, or having a vision, or felled by another bout of craziness.

Whatever it was, I welcomed it. There was a vacant place in my chest which such emotions filled. And in my nature there was a will that delighted to control such emotions. With the two working, one against the other, I was in perfect balance, fully (and fruitlessly) employed emotionally.

On that hot November morning when Vurl came across the floor boards to me, I was in love with no one, and hadn't been for a month or two. I thought falling in love might be something you outgrew, as you outgrew, with age, the ability to sit cross-legged or stay up all night. I had noted, but didn't mourn, the change, believing with Emerson in the law of compensation. What gift I expected at twenty-four would compensate for the loss of the ability to love, I don't know. At any rate, I wasn't in love, and was emotionally free to fall in love with Vurl—and no one would be able to see the least sign of my addiction. But whatever the power was, Vurl didn't have it for me.

My mop pail was full of water, and, before putting the mop in, I cooled myself by sinking my arms in the water, and then amused myself by looking at my underwater arms. Air, clinging to the hair on my arms, had traveled to the tips of the hairs and clung there like the milky berries on underwater mistletoe. Or they broke loose and floated upward so that my arms might have been two big fish, breathing.

I was moving my arms in the bucket, carbonating the mop water, when Vurl came to the sink. He leaned toward me and, without touching my body with his, circled my arms at the wrists with his fingers. He began very slowly to move the circle of his fingers upward, loosening all those trapped air bubbles. He worked as if this were his only purpose, and I watched intently. I watched as if Vurl's hands weren't his, or even hands, as if my arms weren't mine, or arms.

84

As this bubble-pushing neared its finish, I looked up from the mop bucket into Vurl's blue, flint-specked eyes. I don't know what he saw. But behind my eyes was the knowledge that without love, perhaps with hatred, it would be possible to face a man, possibly a monster—or a machine—or an animal (as a bird does a snake), and say, "Don't stop." Knowing that what was going on was brutal and impersonal; willing it, perhaps, *because* it was brutal and impersonal, to continue. I knew that if I didn't take my arms out of that bucket and out of the circle of Vurl's fingers before the last bubble was dislodged, I would die like any other land animal, sunk in water and deprived of air. I knew it, but I wasn't sure I didn't want it. But some movement of the mica specs in the lakey blue of Vurl's eyes turned me away from the idea of drowning. I decided to live on land and breathe air. Vurl, with my first movement, unlatched his fingers from my arms. Whatever you got from Vurl you would have to choose, perhaps even beg for. I took my arms from the water, and picked up my mop.

Vurl, calm as a Fuller Brush man demonstrating one of his products, took the mop from me. "Let me do that for you, Tassie." And I let him. He was mopping the floor when Blix, fresh and elegant, came to the kitchen door.

"Well, Tassie, I see you've found some use for Vurl."

I told her I had.

9

The dining room was reserved for special occasions, like Christmas Day. We ate our Christmas Eve supper companionably crowded together in the breakfast nook. We gobbled the delicious tamale pie, crunched the apples and walnuts of the Waldorf salad, prolonged the slow sweet slide down our throats of the rich plum pudding which Mother had steamed in Hills Brothers coffee cans and topped with lemon sauce.

Supper was over by seven. The minute it was finished, Blackie pulled the clothesbasket of presents to the front of the fireplace. Anyone who wanted to now had a final chance to see how his own contributions stacked up against what was being given to him.

Blackie made one more countdown and shake-up. Blix picked up three or four presents with her name on them, turned each slowly over, then put it slowly down.

She took my arm and led me into the dining room. "Tassie," she said in a low voice, "I haven't got a thing for anybody. Not even Mother. Or Marmion." She could have saved money from her allowance. Or even earned some. She knew I was thinking this, for she added, "I've had to spend every penny. On things I *had* to buy."

Things like expensive shoes and scarves, I thought. But I said nothing. I accepted Blix's need, her especial need, for pretty things, and I didn't blame her for it.

"I feel awful," Blix went on. "And I'm going to feel worse when I have to open my presents." I still didn't say anything. "Christmas came so fast this year," Blix added. "Didn't it seem fast to you?"

"It seemed slow to me. I thought it would never come." Blix looked so downcast, I said, "The stores don't close until nine. Let's go downtown and buy candy. Mother's fudge and heavenly hash'll be gone by morning. We need hard stuff for Blackie to chomp on. Candy can be your present to everyone."

"I don't have any money."

"I'll lend you what you need."

"Mother won't want candy—after making all that."

"I'll tell you what she'd like. You know how she loves sweet smells? I saw a box of Djer Kiss Dusting Powder, so sweet that the fragrance came clear through the box."

"How much was it?"

"One-fifty. I'll lend you the money."

"Could you really do it?"

"Sure I could."

It was the joy of Christmas, before I married and left home, recaptured. Town was ten blocks away, and I drove Everett's and my old open Buick. The stars were covered by clouds; it was warm; there might be rain tomorrow. The wind flopped our bobbed hair. I honked at kids who, because it was Christmas Eve, thought all traffic laws had been repealed.

We left the car like actors who have been waiting in the wings for their cues. But what parts were we playing? Who were we? Side-aching bookkeeper and penniless college girl? I think not. We were youth and the spirit of Christmas and joy to come. We let this shine in our faces and show in the rhythm of our steps and in the radiant carriage of our bodies. And our act was a success because we believed in the parts we were playing.

We were looked at; or Blix was. My walk was observed. I had developed, though not for that purpose, a walk that attracted attention. I developed it because I did not care to cover ground impersonally like an automobile or a wheelbarrow. I thought it a disgrace to walk the earth as if you didn't appreciate the experience. I had an exalted tread, a pace that declared the Glory of God and His handiwork, including myself. I don't know how I appeared to others: some glances were admiring, some merely amazed. But I was noted.

Blix needed no lope to turn heads. She was beautiful, with that lack of perfection which suggests vulnerability.

We turned off Palm onto Center, where the Kandy Kitchen was located. The Kandy Kitchen sold, at Christmas time, wooden tubs of hard candies: ten pounds for four-fifty, and with holly leaves stenciled on the sides and tops of the tubs.

Blix asked the price, and I said, "Let's get ten pounds."

The clerk, a red-haired lady we didn't know (they had in extra help for Christmas Eve), said, "You girls have got the voices of twins." We did have. The timbre must have been the same from the beginning, but the manner of speaking, like my walking, was acquired, and acquired first, I suppose, I being the older, by me. The manner was low, breathless, now slow, now fast; we intended to convey, first of all, that we considered the world a miracle, and second, that we, the speakers, might be pretty miraculous ourselves. Whether the effect intended was achieved or not, the manner was peculiar enough to cause instant recognition over the phone. Two words, and the listener knew it was one of the Murphy girls—though which one, until we identified ourselves, couldn't be guessed. When the saleslady remarked on our way of speaking, we felt the same pleasure movie stars experience when recognized.

Having acquired the candy, made a success of our speaking, and with only Djer Kiss to go and money still in my purse, I said to Blix, "Let's go have something to drink." Half of the Kandy Kitchen was an ice-cream parlor with round marble-topped tables and chairs with heart-shaped wire backs.

The Kandy Kitchen was crowded. Dozens of people like ourselves, suddenly convinced they weren't going to show up well in the big Christmas trade about to take place, were out in a last-minute attempt to strike a better balance. They had made it; their consciences were at ease; before they had to go home to sinks full of dirty dishes and living rooms ankle deep in peanut hulls, they would rest for a short time in a clean, well-ordered place. We found a table for three, jammed into a corner, a real box seat. We watched everyone—at least I did. Blix didn't notice, but I did, the man who was looking at her. This man watched Blix while the clerk made change for the three boxes of candy he had bought.

When he got his change, he thought matters over, decided to risk it, and made for our table. I knew what he would do: he would ask me if, since the place was crowded, he could sit at our table. Blix was the one he was interested in, but I was the one he would ask. I wasn't enough older than Blix to look like her aunt—or chaperone, let alone her mother. Did they just want to reassure me from the beginning that, though their interest was in Blix, they didn't intend to exclude me?

I don't know. This fellow, speaking to me as if Blix didn't exist, said, "Is it okay with you if I sit here?"

"It's okay with me. Blix?" Ordinarily, Blix, unless the guy was an obvious goop, enjoyed these chance meetings. I wasn't sure tonight. This fellow was no goop, but Blix didn't seem to

88

have much appetite for living, let alone adventure. She said in an impersonal, uninterested way, "We don't own the table." She returned to her straw and got the sound of an empty glass.

"May I get you another? You, too," the man said, politely including me. Blix said yes, I said no.

"We're due home by nine-thirty, at least," I reminded Blix.

Blix answered as if, though she knew her duty, it didn't appeal to her. "I know we are."

"If you need a ride . . ." the young man began.

"I have a car," I told him.

He turned to Blix. "If *you* wanted to stay longer . . . stores won't be closed for another thirty minutes. . . ."

I gave Blix a good hard ironic stare. Without me, where was her money for shopping? Blix stared right back, smiling. "Oh, Tassie," she said, "if you'll take my candy on home, there are some things I'd like to do. I'll be there in time for opening presents."

She wasn't, of course. And I had enough decency when there were exclamations of how sweet and gracious and thoughtful it was of Blix, in the midst of her studies and with all of her school expenses, to have remembered everyone, to keep my mouth closed. I was also decent enough to explain her absence. "Old high-school friend."

"Old male high-school friend," Le Cid said.

"She just got in with Vurl," Mother said. "I don't like the idea of her out with another boy before the evening's over."

"There's safety in numbers," Father said.

"She's only with one at a time," Mother said pertinently.

Opening the presents without Blix was flat. All of us liked to give Blix presents. She wasn't easily satisfied. It meant something to please Blix. She lived like an aristocrat. "Please me," she said; and it seemed a privilege to be permitted to try. With the exception of Mother, who worried about her, I was the only one, I think, who listened for the brakes of a stopping car.

Marmion was impatient to get through the gift-giving rigmarole and off to his date with Olive. Blackie was thinking about his presents.

Father tinkered with the radio when he thought no one was watching. He never gave presents to anyone but Mother. This year, perhaps tired of all that Hobhouse glass and china gracing holiday tables, he gave her a cut-glass compote dish.

I don't know what Le Cid was thinking about. Maybe nothing outside what was going on around that laundry basket. Le Cid had the gift of being with it. He was absent, or with it. He didn't divide himself, or the occasion. He, though marriage was the farthest thing from his mind, also had a girl, Honey Earle. He had no date with her tonight; and if his mind was on her, it didn't show.

Everett opened his own presents fast; and as soon as I had opened mine from him, a pink crepe de Chine nightgown and matching bed jacket, he went to bed. I didn't know when I would ever be able to wear the skimpy outfit. Not till summer, anyway. There was no heat at all in the second-story bedrooms of our ranch house. The downstairs had two wood stoves and a fireplace, and none of these were lighted in the morning. The price tag was still on the gown, $9.95. Charged at Goodman's. That wouldn't be paid until summer either. But I was no Blix. I didn't say, "Who'll pay for it?" or "Fine outfit for an igloo!" I said, "It's pretty as can be, Everett. Thank you so much."

Everett, with a fond pinch, said, "When a man's got a wife with a figure like mine's got, he wants to keep it in sight as much as possible. Day *and* night."

I knew what Everett was trying to do: prove himself a full-blooded racy fellow in company which frequently made him feel tongue-tied and pallid. I felt sorry for him and wished him success. But he missed the mark.

After Everett's pinch, and declaration in favor of nakedness (in his wife, of all persons), there was an embarrassed silence. I sided with Everett and against my family. I went with him to the hall door and took, without wincing, his ostentatious bottom slap, his final attempt to convince his audience of authenticity in

90

his role. It was a minute or two before feelings, which could not be expressed, could settle. But as soon as we heard Everett leave the bathroom and close the door to his bedroom, a repose, a geniality which had been absent, returned to the room. Le Cid stretched himself full length on top of the six-inch ledge formed by the back of the sofa pushed against the wall. Papa and Mama went to bed. Blackie went to sleep on the floor. I began to put the room to rights.

I finished my work on the Christmas disorder and stood in the midst of order achieved (as a painter never can stand in the midst of his picture), and was dazzled by the beauty that had emerged.

Le Cid, who had been silent on his ledge, smiled at me. "Transformed," he said.

"At midnight the beasts speak," I told him. It was quarter of twelve.

"There's one that won't," Le Cid said, nodding toward Blackie.

"Ah, Blackie's no beast."

"He's no angel."

"He's a thirteen-year-old, stuffed."

"He's your baby."

"Looks like all I'll ever have."

"You've got some years ahead of you . . . if you use them right, in that pink nightgown," Le Cid said.

"Don't be dirty."

"Is love dirty? I never knew."

Le Cid knew everything, and I knew it and didn't intend to argue with him.

"O Little Town of Bethlehem," I sang softly. "How still we see thee lie."

"Do you believe all that?"

"That Bethlehem was a quiet little town?"

"Away in a manger, no crib for His head?"

"I don't think the manger part matters."

"You believe in Jesus?"

"I believe there was a man named Jesus."

"Man? Like me?"

"You're no man yet. But not like you."

"You believe a father in the sky came down and planted a seed in maid Mary?"

"I don't think that matters."

"Pilgrims do."

"I believe in the example of Jesus."

"You don't follow it very well."

"Who does?"

"Me," said Le Cid. "Here I am right now, I'm Mary, you're Martha."

"I'm Martha all right. I'm doing all the work. But being lazy's not being Mary."

"That's what a Martha always thinks. Actually, I'm having religious thoughts."

"There's nothing very religious, or nice either, in talking about God's coming down to Earth to plant seeds."

"That's because you're a Martha—and a married one, to boot—and haven't chosen the better part, the way I have. What's wrong with planting seeds?"

I didn't answer.

"I forgot," Le Cid said. "You're married."

"That hasn't got anything to do with it."

"With what?"

I couldn't say with what. I put a couple more lemon sticks on the fire, and it blazed up green and yellow like cats' eyes. I turned out all lights except one bridge lamp. The clock on the mantel chimed, then struck twelve. Beanie, forgotten in a corner, gave a big snore.

"Now it's His birthday," Le Cid said, and made himself more comfortable on his ledge. "If they were put in a balance and weighed, the good deeds done because of Him, and the bad deeds done because of Him, I wonder which would outweigh the other?"

"He isn't responsible for the bad."

"He's not even responsible for being here."

"What do you mean?"

"Well, God didn't ask Him, did He? He couldn't, could He? Before He existed?"

"Jesus *was* God."

Le Cid opened his eyes. "So God just pinched off a piece of Himself and said, 'Piece, go down and get yourself crucified and reconcile Me with these sinful men.' That's why we sing 'Peace on Earth' at Christmas time, I suppose; 'Peace on earth, good will to men,' because Piece did that. Piece took a man shape; I guess He didn't have any choice about that either, considering where He was incubated, and He hung on a man-shaped cross, and Piece said, 'Father, if it be Thy will, let this cup pass from me.' But it wasn't Father's will. He said, 'Piece, drink up, because somebody's got to suffer and blood's got to flow, as atonement to Me for the sins of these mortals.' It was a pretty messy plan, besides being so painful for Piece, because more men had to sin in order to make the atonement a fact. But it was bookkeeping, if bloody. Man sinned. Piece suffered. So it all balanced out—in the minds of those who enjoy blood and judging."

My brother jumped from the sofa back. He made Blackie's stack of presents quiver; Beanie lifted his head. "But not me. Not me. O Jesus, good man and no Piece, not me. How could men make up such a bloody disgusting story? Want to worship such a God?"

Le Cid stood in front of the fireplace and bent backward until his long straight hair almost touched the flames.

"Watch out, you'll catch on fire."

"Okay. I'll be a burning bush."

"So I'll listen and worship?"

"Worship! That's what's so crappy about Christians. Because they love to kneel and kiss toes and sing hosannas, they have to dream up a God who wants to be worshipped with hosannas and toe kissings. And worse."

Don't you think there's anything beautiful about Christmas?"

"That virgin with a baby? That old man who didn't know the score? Those talking animals? That star that stalled? The big chase by mule back? The bookkeeping presents to match the bloody bookkeeping? 'My Piece bleeding for your sins'? Hell, no. I don't think it's beautiful. I think it's one of the worst examples . . ."

Blix opened the door and said, "Peace on earth!" which made Le Cid laugh. So we settled down to a second and private Christmas; and Le Cid was so merry even a Christian couldn't have guessed that he wasn't one of them.

My chief present for Blix was a pair of shoe buckles which fitted onto street pumps and changed them to evening slippers. I knew Blix had wanted them for a long time. She was shoe-crazy, and these buckles would make two pairs out of one.

Le Cid gave her something even better than buckles; and so far as I know she was never afterward parted from it. He gave her Housman's poems in a pretty green-backed illustrated edition. There wasn't any bookstore in Baranca. He must have gone all the way to Los Angeles to get it. Blix put the buckles on her shoes, sat down on the stuffed footstool Mother called a "humpy," stretched her feet to the fire, and turned over the pages of her new book. She read a line or two aloud. She wasn't a good reader, because she was too uncertain of herself. But Le Cid and I loved listening. There was only one poem she read through. She read it like a story whose ending she had to know; and because, in getting to this ending, she forgot us, the poem lived, and she was its heroine.

> *"Some lads there are, 'tis shame to say,*
> *That only court to thieve,*
> *And once they bear the bloom away*
> *'Tis little enough they leave.*
> *Then keep your heart for men like me*
> *And safe from trustless chaps.*
> *My love is true and all for you.*
> *'Perhaps, young man, perhaps.'"*

Blix read these lines with a kind of sad relish. But when she reached the poem's final line, "Good-by, young man, good-by," the relish was gone. She spoke those words herself, and nothing was left but sadness. She closed the book on her finger. She moved her feet so that the jet and cut-steel buckles sparkled with reflected light. I thought Blix, who never cried, was going to cry on Christmas night—Christmas day, it was now. I bounded up like Marmee in *Little Women,* and said, "I'm going to make hot chocolate. We're worn out. We're starved to death. We're dying for lack of nourishment. Man can't live by shoe buckles and poetry alone."

I gave Blackie a light tap with my toe to initiate the waking-up process, and he grumbled and flailed out with his arms. I kicked Beanie to create a diversion, and did. Beanie woke up, barking. I made the chocolate the way Mother did: I made it fast, I made it strong, and thick. I had it back in the living room while Beanie was still looking around for somebody to bite.

Le Cid sat Blackie up, and before he had had time for more than a practice bellow, shot a stream of the thick chocolate down his throat. Blix sipped slowly, but color came back to her face. Le Cid rolled the sweet stuff around on his tongue. "I don't know whether this is a thin pudding or a thick drink, Tassie, but it slides down smooth." When he finished, he hoisted Blackie to his feet and said, "Go to bed, Blackie."

Blackie was too sleepy to protest. "Don't put my things away, will you, Tassie?" he asked. I promised him I wouldn't.

"Piece on earth," Le Cid said at the door to the hall.

"Good will to men," I answered.

"You and Le Cid have a good time together, don't you?" Blix asked when we were alone together.

I nodded. "Blackie's a sweet bighearted bellower, too."

Blix said, "Marmion gave me a wrist watch for Christmas." She held out her wrist for inspection. "I guess Marmion's my favorite of the boys."

"He's your big brother and can do things for you the others can't."

"I don't see Blackie or Le Cid giving me a watch at any age."

I didn't argue. "Everybody loved your presents."

"No thanks to me."

"Don't think you won't have to pay for it."

"Who're you kidding?"

"Nobody. How'd you like your new friend?"

"He was kind of sweet."

"I don't know what you saw in him. If anybody came up to me like that, I wouldn't like it."

"Why not? Because it's not respectful or something?"

"Oh, I don't care anything about being respected."

"Well, why not then?"

"I wouldn't like *him*."

"Him? Why? You don't want to make the first move yourself, do you? Or *do* you?"

Blix had got hold of an idea that interested her. You could always tell when this happened because she tilted her head. Her hair slipped to one side, and she gave me the one-eyed look of a marksman with game in his sights.

"The moment anyone ever had a crush on you—or even liked you—you thought he was a nut."

"I think all crushes are kind of nutty."

Blix didn't pay any attention. "It doesn't matter *who*. That teacher at Asilomar who thought you were so wonderful. She would have driven you home—she was coming clear to Los Angeles anyway—and it would have saved the folks twenty-five dollars. And Aunt Amy. And that boy who kept phoning you. It's true, isn't it? If they fall for you, you think there's something wrong with them. If they fall for me, I think they're pretty bright. Andy fell for me. What's wrong with that? What's the point of being down on people who fall for you?"

I tried to think of a good answer to this.

"It's okay if you feel all right about it."

"Well, why shouldn't you feel all right about it?"

"It's like applauding someone who has applauded you."

"It's not. It's like going on doing whatever they applauded you *for*. Playing the piano. Or if it's Andy, being what he calls my 'own sweet self.'"

"That's pretty easy, isn't it?"

96

"What's wrong with 'easy'? It's easy to have Father on your side, because he's reasonable. It isn't easy with Mother because she'll box your ears one minute and praise you the next. Do you like Mother better because of that?"

"I *don't* like her better. I think Father . . ."

"You better hold your horses right there," Father said. Neither of us had heard him open the door. He had on Le Cid's gift to him, black-and-red outing-flannel pajamas. Usually he wore nightshirts Mother had made him out of flour sacks. I could remember him when what he wore to bed was even less dressy— his work shirt over his long drawers.

"What's going on here?" he asked. "One o'clock!" He walked over to the radio, snapped it on, waited, got nothing but silence, and snapped it off. "Wonder where that poor girl is now? Say, *you* two girls better get to bed."

Then for the second time in the last hour poetry was quoted. He was a queer figure to us in those pajamas. I thought him an old man, though he was only forty-six. I knew he was handsome, even then; hair Indian black, teeth Indian white and strong, flat stomach, heavy arms and legs. He was a surer reciter than Blix, less dramatic than Mother, less moving than either. But he had a good voice, he knew the words he was saying, and he understood their meaning.

"They told me, Heraclitus, they told me you were dead,
They brought me bitter news to hear and bitter tears
*   to shed.*
I wept, as I remembered, how often you and I
Had tired the sun with talking and sent him down the sky."

"You two will talk the moon down if you stay up much longer," he added.

He left without our having mentioned his poetry. If a subject moved us Murphys, we kept quiet about it—except Mother. I felt pity for Father; he had made us a gift and had gone away unthanked. The thanks, or at least the recognition, should have come from me. For Father had happened on that poem four years before while "helping" me with my course in Victorian poetry. He didn't know a thing about Arnold or Clough or Browning, had never heard of them, let alone read them, but he had the patience to hear me read them. After I had finished, Father had looked through the book himself and had read Cory's translation. It had meant enough to him to cause him at some later time to go to the pains of memorizing it. And he, with dead of his own to remember (unknown dead to me, though I was a repository of facts about deceased Hobhouses, Macmanamans, Griffiths), had wanted to say to his two girls, without the embarrassment and inadequacy of his own words, something about time's passing; and with time, those he had loved. He said it. He made his try. His girls didn't get it.

I excuse us now. You can't spring poetry, while standing in your Christmas pajamas, on young women of twenty and twenty-four without some preparation. You can't, unless you expect consternation, open your long-hidden heart. It's too revealing. As well walk out in your birthday suit and expect your daughters not to be surprised at what, up to that time, you have been at pains to hide.

Blix and I, after Father left, ignored the content of the poem he had recited and any reasons he might have had for reciting it. We talked about his recitation as if it had been a performance, meaningless as a handspring or a cartwheel.

"Father should leave recitations to Mother. She's the actress in the family."

"He's got the looks, though," Blix reminded me.

"But he can't thrill you the way Mother can."

"He can't thrill *you* because it's no feather in your cap to understand *him*. There's nothing for you to overcome."

"Overcome . . ." But I stopped. We were back to that again. I stood up. I was glad to have Blix feeling argumentative. Otherwise I couldn't have left her alone by the fire on our first evening at home together. I was drooping with weariness, yearning for bed and sleep. But I could not have gone if Blix hadn't sent me, or at least justified my going. If she had sat there, bent toward the fire, "Good-by, young man, good-by" at her fingertips, I would have had to stay with her. But stay up and suffer for the sake of arguing! I accepted the excuse she gave me, though it broke the pattern I had imagined.

10

I undressed in the dark. Everett was sound asleep and breathing deeply. The bed was a single one, in the curtained-off end of the back porch. Le Cid usually slept in it, but he was doubling up with Blackie tonight to make room for the influx. Besides the bed, the room contained a pine chest of drawers, one chair, and a table. I undressed slowly, anxious for sleep, but tireder than I was sleepy. I hung my skirt over the chair back, folded my sweater and underwear and piled them on the table beside Le Cid's books and papers. I wished the bed were larger. Everett's knees and elbows were sharp. He is kind of dry and twiggy, I thought. He is like manzanita, but not the right color. That thought, that fault-finding thought, brought back Blix's words. "You can't accept people who fall for you. If they fall for you, you think there's something's wrong with them."

I had thought of Everett at the time, but I didn't want to mention him. If he was an example of what Blix believed, the least I could do for Everett was to keep this knowledge to myself.

It was true he had fallen for me, at least to the point of finding out who I was, and asking for a date before I had ever seen him. I said "yes" without seeing him, because I had entered college two weeks late, knew no one, and wanted to go to the Uplands game. When he was pointed out to me the next day, I already knew, of course, that he had "fallen for me." I leaned out of the dorm window and watched him cross a footbridge and climb the little slope up to the library. June Gibbs, a black-eyed, hollow-cheeked girl from South Carolina, said, "That's Everett, your date for Saturday. Boy! Is he ever good-looking."

That's what everyone has always thought about Everett—except me. And "everyone" must be right. And, had I seen him before I knew he had "fallen for me," would I have agreed with everybody? Was that what soured me on Everett? What do I mean "soured"? I loved him, didn't I? Worked hard to win his proposal, his diamond, and his wedding band? So what do I mean "soured"?

Just as I didn't say anything to Blix about Everett, I hadn't said anything to June. I looked. I saw. A slender young man, five feet ten or eleven, was crossing a bridge in front of me. Neatly dressed. Too neatly? Shoes with cloth tops. Why should I find this upsetting? Why should I find toeing out unaccountably ugly? Thousands of men walk that way. His pompadour added three or four inches to his height, his collar three or four inches to his neck. He looked dapper. At seventeen, my ideal man, I suppose, had the build of a football player and the soul of a Byron. If that was what I wanted, Everett was disappointing, on sight.

I am still plagued by the question "How would Everett have looked to me if I had seen him first?" With no knowledge that he had asked me for a date. Was there in me, so early, something that made me relish irony? Some experience, forgotten, that made me forearm myself for disappointment? Say, "That's the kind of boy, all right, who *would* fall for me?"

I don't know. We went to the game in the back seat of the rented Reo, the faculty couple somehow maneuvered onto the jump seats, four of us wedged into the back seat. Everett had to put his arm around me; from thigh to ankle we were Siamese twins. That's what rented Reos were for. I had never before been touched by a boy, scarcely been touched by anyone, of any sex or age. A whole new sense was born that October afternoon in the Reo. Touch! I had never seen or smelled, tasted or heard, anthing like it. While it was going on I didn't want to see, smell, taste, or hear. In fact, I couldn't. Everett didn't *do* anything with his arm; it lay, an inert weight, across my shoulders. He didn't *do* anything with his leg. Exert any pressure or initiate any movement. But it was there, and the whole of my body, except for these points of contact, died, and I lived in them a life so disturbing my whole world was transformed; I was, pulse, body temperature, rate of respiration, all expectation. What did I care about a football game we lost 6 to 40? Or the carnival we went to afterward? Everett got dizzy on the Ferris wheel, refused to drink Coke or root beer because he thought carbonation effete. (Everett, for as long as I knew him, never owned a wrist watch. It didn't square with his rancher-farmer-cowboy ideal of himself.) In the photographer's booth, when we all had our pictures taken, he rested his chin on his tiepin and looked upward, so that nothing but the whites of his eyes was visible in the picture. But he had touched me. So I waited through Statue of Liberty plays and Ferris wheel nausea, and Delaware Punch and sheep's eyes for the touching to begin again.

And it didn't. Maybe I was throbbing visibly, because the chaperones got me and Everett onto the jump seats for the return trip, where there wasn't even a chance for my skirt to brush his trousers—let alone for aching shoulder and thigh to be assuaged by some more pressure. Neither of us would have tolerated the idea of a good-by kiss on our first date. That meant business, and though I, at least, intended business (by which I meant courtship and marriage), a nice couple knew that certain formalities should be observed before there were any binding transactions or exchanges of real property. But we did exchange what I felt to be an especially meaningful handclasp, soft but strong, moral but lingering, as we parted on the dorm steps. I felt it all night long.

So there I was. Blinded (perhaps) to Everett's real charms by the chance of his having declared himself first. Scornful of most of his attitudes and opinions. But bound to him. Determined to bind him to me by every device I imagined a sentimental and conventional boy would find irresistible. I wasn't much of a trap, so I didn't think I could afford to be tender. Efficiency was my goal. What bound me to Everett? Touch? If it was that which I found so irresistible, why did it never occur to me that the world was filled with touchers—that every man

101

jack of them, unless paralyzed, had that ability. It never did. Because his touch was the first, were touch and Everett inextricably mixed in my mind? And even more irresistibly in nerve ends and blood pressure and respiration?

If falling in love begins at nine, and dreaming, God knows how much earlier, and eight years pass without so much as a hug from your Mother (who loves with words not touch), let alone a nod from Prince Charming, and the flesh, ignorant as a leaf in the sun, trembles at dressmaker's touches, or shoe clerk's innocent fittings, what's to be expected when a man's hand and thigh (that's seventeen's definition of Everett's anatomy in the back seat of a Reo) make purposeful advances? What has been hinted at, the undisclosed secret, was all true. No wonder grownups wanted to keep it quiet. After one date I was madly in love with Everett. It wasn't love at first sight, it's true, but it certainly was love at first touch.

The power of the first! Something to be feared and dreaded. But how can it be feared or dreaded until its unsuspected power is known? And how known without experiencing? How can the unburned child fear fire? Or the child unlost dream of home? The power of the first. Does it exist for all? Or only for those who come to a first after dreaming and deprivation? Most feminine of traits, the opposite of the masculine impulse to explore and experiment, it binds the woman like bird lime onto the first twig where she settles.

Poor Everett! If I was a bird-limed bird, he was a bird-encumbered twig, and encumbered with a bird who, if she had wings, was determined never to use them again.

Thinking of these things I looked down on Everett sleeping soundly in Le Cid's narrow bed. I felt sorry for him. There was a good deal I didn't understand about the two of us, but Blix's speculations had set me to wondering. *Had* Everett, because of the chance of his "falling" for me, never really had a chance with me? I got into bed in a repentant mood. I didn't try to get my fair share of the space, but curled myself gently in and out of the sharp thicket of his elbows and knees and around the hard little burl of his bottom and draped my arms carefully over the soft bulge of his stomach; and before I went to sleep I made a Christmas prayer: "God help me to be a better wife to Everett."

I prayed with eyes shut, and after I had finished praying I kept them shut; but behind my closed lids I couldn't sleep. I had resisted sleep when earlier I had longed for it. Now resistance had become my habit. I was awake to every sound, to every movement, and touch. The long day of work begun in Brenner, the anticipation, the evening of excitement, had sandpapered my senses. My own breathing disturbed me. My own arm was a spear against my ribs as I lay cramped, spoon-fashion in the narrow bed. The rubber-and-sweat smell of Le Cid's sneakers, under the edge of the bed, filled my nose. I identified more slowly the smell of tobacco. There were no smokers in that Pilgrim household, except Blix, and she smoked only on the sly. Somewhere close by Blix was smoking.

I sat up slowly and carefully. This wasn't necessary—Everett was a sound sleeper. I looked through the screen that formed the top half of the wall against which Le Cid's cot was placed. Along the back-yard path, between the rhubarb plants and the guava bushes, with stops at old Bolivar's cage, only half-visible under the come-and-go light of a moon crossed by traveling clouds, Blix was walking and smoking. In pajamas and bedroom slippers, she moved soundlessly.

Why didn't I go to her? I did get out of bed. I did lean, as silent as she, against the screen to watch her. I could smell not only her cigarette but also Mama's Elmo, which she had been using. I knew she was troubled. Why else would she tramp a backyard path and whisper to a sleeping bird on Christmas Eve?

So there isn't the excuse that I didn't understand that she wasn't happy. I can't say, "If I had only known." I *knew*. And I stayed where I was. My feeling, at the time, or the feeling I permitted myself to recognize, was, "Blix wants to be alone."

The best that can be said for me was that I was bone-tired; the worst, that I was coldhearted. Perhaps it was something in between. In any case, whenever a decision not to act relieves us of effort, we had better ask ourselves if the purity of our motives hasn't been stained by laziness.

I watched. I sorrowed. I told myself, "Blix is upset, but she wants to be alone." I got back into bed. I slept.

11

Except for Pete I would have made the same mistake with Blix when she was here last July. And the circumstances being worse than they were on that past Christmas Eve, my memories now would be worse.

Pete saved me from that. It was the next to last evening of Blix's visit. The three of us had gone to our rooms early, nine o'clock, and, with daylight saving, scarcely dark. Towhees were still looking for crumbs on the terrace where we had eaten our supper. Cicadas were stitching their sewing-machine songs. A strand of saffron light still banded the western horizon.

"We are all tired," I, being tired, told myself. Across my desk all day had passed the complaints and threats of that faction which believed that the republic might be saved by censoring the public's reading.

Blix was worn out, I thought. She had had a day of discomfort. She might have shrugged off the discomfort, but its possible meaning she couldn't ignore.

Pete didn't look tired, but then, he never does. Good golfers are built to withstand strain. Nerves and muscles alike are smoothly padded. Not all golfers are as ruddy as Pete or have eyes as calm. But by and large they're not a haggard-looking lot.

Competition doesn't tire Pete. He enjoys the challenge of controlling position by means of propulsion. That's a sweet abstraction. But his day at the club hadn't been abstract or sweet. The ladies' team had been "hosting" the ladies from the Moon Valley Club. Pete doesn't look forward to these tournaments. They are made up in about equal parts of fashion show, gossip, gourmandizing, and golf. But he doesn't complain. They're a part of his job, and he likes his job.

I don't criticize these ladies either. It was once my ambition to be one of them.

After I had finished my work at the university and landed my first job, I was lonely, and, after eight or nine hours behind a desk, muscle-bound. I was accustomed to hard physical work: chasing baby beeves, playing basketball, racing a stack of wheats to an impatient customer. In my toy apartment the chances for muscle stretching weren't much better than behind my desk. No wood to carry in, no fires to start, no farmhouse kitchen floor to scrub.

This was before gyms were invented for women like me, before bowling became popular. I had never played tennis. The only swimming pool in town was inside a steamy YWCA. I was a good softball player, but the softball teams were made up of tough seventeen-year-olds, and at twenty-six I was, to them, in a class with their mothers.

I decided to take up golf. It seemed to me to be a sedate game, suited to my years. Nevertheless I was shamefaced buying clubs. Golf in Brenner had been considered ridiculous. If there were any players in Brenner, I didn't know them. Something was thought to be wrong with grown men and women who would walk up hill and down dale hitting a little white ball with a stick.

It was the up-hill-and-down-dale bit that appealed to me. I would have fine walks in the late afternoons across what was, even though called "a golf course," a nice traffic-free expanse of rolling hillocks. The ball would be the least of my worries. The ball, as it turned out, could not be so easily ignored. It was there, and because it was there I wanted to hit it, and in the right direction and with power.

Power I could manage. I could drive hard and with fair accuracy. But once on the green, that little white eye in the center stared me down. Near misses counted nothing. Near, close, clinging to the lip: worthless! It had to be *in*, dead center, and smack to the bottom. Faced with that requirement I blew up. I thought

105

about giving up golf as played by others. Someone long ago had made up these rules to suit *his* game. Why not some rules to suit *my* game? Disregard the putt. On the green and away again with a lashing drive.

The next step, I suppose, would have included further rules to suit *my* game. It would have permitted ball shifting, landscape altering, and a personal system of scoring. At this point Pete took charge of my nongame.

I had noticed him, of course. No club pro with a national reputation goes unnoticed on his home course. I thought from his looks that he was Irish. He was Portuguese, as Portuguese goes in this country. Some great-great-grandfather had had a Portuguese name. Pete's mother's name was Ross. I admired his powerful lazy-looking strokes. I envied, though I wouldn't admit it, the players who laughed and talked with him. And of course I avoided him.

Not because I had fallen in love with him, but because I was ashamed of my game. And in those years I was ashamed of myself, too. I was a failed wife and technical spinster. In my family divorcees were thought to be wicked, and spinsters, while morally untainted, were failed women. So there I was. And a flop at golf, too.

I'll never forget the first time Pete spoke to me. Nor what he said. It was a typical Central Valley steamy September afternoon. I had arrived at the number-three hole after two miraculous drives. I thought my luck must be changing. It is a rule of Grecian tragedy that its heroes must reach the heights before they fail. The drama is more poignant that way. Who suffers over the losses of those who have nothing to lose? I was no Greek hero. Surely my success off the green wouldn't have to be paid for by failure in putting.

Someone was sitting on the bench under the acacias, by the drinking fountain, someone who could see me. I had had to train myself to ignore onlookers—and I kept my eyes, as advised, on the ball. Besides, I really hoped that this time I wouldn't fail.

I failed.

After boggling around and ending up after four or five putts farther away from the pin than when I had started, I gave up. I didn't throw my putter or kick the ball or dig up the green. I did cry. Silently, of course, and with my back to my audience. My shoulders didn't heave. From the back I would be judged, I thought, to be admiring the distant buttes, already rising up rosy-tipped out of the blue of their long shadows. I *was* admiring them, they in their shadows, I in my tears.

I didn't hear Pete until he spoke. He's still very quiet. Why is it that big men are quiet, and that little men go through the world the center of a continuous clatter?

Pete said, "Don't cry, kiddie. It's only a game."

I've asked him how he knew I was crying. "I looked at you. Tears were running down your cheeks."

"You couldn't tell that from behind me."

"From behind you, I thought you had possibly had a stroke."

"I had had about twenty strokes. That was my trouble."

It was that "kiddie" that really melted me. I didn't give a big sob, or run over and bury my head in his shoulder. But I'd never been a "kiddie" to anyone before. Or even a kid. The four younger children were "the kids." I was the substitute mother. Kid? Kiddie? Child? Youngster? Little one? Baby? Babe? I don't think so. And I was big, too, remember, in addition to being the oldest. And now a bona fide divorcee and artificial spinster, to boot.

"Don't cry, kiddie." I think those are the most beautiful words I ever heard in my life. Full of pity. I know there are those who resent being pitied. Not I. I think the human condition is pitiful. The most beautiful line in the Bible to me is not "Lie down in green pastures," or "Underneath me are the everlasting wings," but "Like as a father pitieth his child."

Pete was my age, twenty-six, when he spoke those words; but compassion comes early to some.

I tried to answer him without embarrassing him with more tears. "I know it's a game," I agreed. "But it's a game I'm trying to play."

"Maybe you're trying too hard."

I thought he meant with too much physical force.

"I use psychology," I told him, wanting him to think that I was potentially, at least, a brainy player.

"Like how?"

"I can't putt. You saw that. So I tell myself, 'If you don't sink this ball your enemies will shoot and kill your entire family.' That really ought to motivate me. Oughtn't it?"

"Depends on whether you want your family shot and killed or not."

This shocked me. "Of course I don't."

"You'd better plan to save them by some other means than putting, then. By the way, who are your enemies?"

"No one. Anonymous. Made up to spur me on."

"Your family anonymous, too?"

"Oh, no! Father, mother, three brothers, and a sister."

I would have launched into an account of Murphy marvels but Pete asked one more question.

"Anonymous husband?"

He was looking at my wedding ring, which I had continued to wear. Partly because I didn't want to be thought an old maid. Partly because "unmarry" doesn't take place in the words of a document any more than "marry" takes place there. I didn't feel unmarried. Perhaps those who have never been properly married never feel properly unmarried either. There is too little change in their life.

"No. Divorced. My husband divorced me," I added, feeling it unfair to let him think that Everett was a man of reprehensible habits.

"Why don't you take your ring off then? You still carrying a torch?"

"No." I decided to tell the truth. Not the whole truth, but an authentic piece of it. "I don't like people to think I'm a spinster—at my age."

"I like to think you're a spinster," Pete said. "And I'd like you to think I'm a bachelor. It's true, too. Never been married."

108

This was a pretty fast conversation for me. Pretty real, too. I didn't know what to say next, so, fortunately, said nothing.

Pete said, "How about a lesson in putting?"

There was nothing I wanted less. I would be knocking that ball around the cup until the stars came out. I never could learn by watching someone else. But Pete's idea of a lesson in putting wasn't mine. He took my putter and lifted my ball off the green and to hell and gone—somewhere in the general direction of the Feather River.

"You could do that all right, couldn't you?"

"Of course. It's all I can do. But that's not golf, is it?"

"It's psychology. And you believe in psychology, don't you?"

I believed in mine. I wasn't sure that I believed in Pete's. What he said next was probably psychology, too. Even though he didn't label it.

"Aren't you thirsty?"

I was. Parched. Dehydrated by heat and all that miserable putting. Salted by the brine of swallowed tears. Feverish with conversation.

"Let's go down to the clubhouse and have a drink."

I didn't drink. Not hard liquor. But at the minute Pete meant more to me than temperance. I said, "Yes." When we get to the clubhouse, I thought, I can ask for lemonade or root beer.

At the clubhouse Pete said, "Something long and cool?" I said, "Yes." If it turned out to be alcoholic, I could take a sip or two for politeness's sake and ignore the rest.

What the drink was, I don't know. A Tom Collins, probably, pretty, stained with the colors of floating fruit. I sipped clear to the bottom of the glass. All I knew about the effects of strong drink I had learned at the movies: schoolmarms, after a few drinks, took off their spectacles and danced on table tops; country girls went willingly to meet a fate worse than death in a back room. I was no movie drinker. I became calmer and calmer. My hands stopped trembling. My throat relaxed. I no longer thought of myself as a failed wife and impossible putter. My family's well-being didn't hinge upon my putting—or my anything else. I had no enemies. I wasn't married. Golf was a game, and I was a lucky spinster. While Pete was at the bar reordering, I took off my ring.

When he came back, he noticed.

We were never engaged. I never "fell in love" with him. We didn't talk about marriage. We spent more and more time together; and the time apart was spent in soliloquies which rehearsed what we would say when next we met. We had a marriage of convenience. It would be more convenient to live together and to spare ourselves the sorrow of absence, the emotional waste of parting, and the irritation of continual transportation between our separated homes. We got a license to live together.

Pete delighted me. Just to see him and listen to him. The only other person who had affected me in this way was Blix. Pete and I hadn't the same tastes, any more than Blix and I. Pete's a hunter, which I couldn't and still can't understand. But he is a reader, too, which seems as natural as breathing to me. I've heard Pete tell friends, "Some men are attracted to women who are stacked. I fell for Tass because she carried the keys to the stacks."

Pete's too kind to say something like that except that he knows someone is pretty sure to come to my defense by saying, "It wasn't necessarily an either-or situation, was it, Peter, old boy?"

Pete always answers, "Speak for yourself, John. The books were what I had in mind."

It was Peter, the book man, who last July saved me from another do-nothing memory with Blix. The evening when I, being tired, decided that Blix, too, was yearning for rest.

Pete opened my eyes.

"Don't cry, kiddie" is only one string to Peter's bow. The other is, "Woman, don't give up."

Before undressing, I went down the hall to say good night to Blix. She was lying on top of her bed reading. At least holding a book in her hands.

"How can you see to read?" I asked.

She hadn't turned on her bedside lamp. The sun was down, and the little light left was additionally darkened by the bronzed leaves of the tall viburnum bush that shaded her west window.

"I don't want to read. Take this book away from me. It's getting me down."

She'd been down all day. She didn't talk about it, but she couldn't hide it.

When I left her I carried the book, opened, back to Pete's and my room. Pete took the book from me.

"Where'd you get this?"

"Blix."

"Have you read it?"

It was Baldwin's *Another Country*, and I hadn't, then. But I had read about it. "Negroes and homosexuality," I told Pete.

"And suicide," Pete said. "The best man among them kills himself. That's where Blix is now."

Pete put the book on my dressing table, and I looked at him in the mirror.

"Think it would be okay for me to go in to talk to Blix?"

"Sure. If you aren't too tired."

I was still sitting there on the dressing-table bench when Pete came back.

"Okay, kiddie. Off with the shorts and into something for the big city."

"The big city? I'm half ready for bed."

"Bed's later. Now it's the Persian Room and dancing."

"We've had dinner!"

"Who mentioned dinner? This is an evening for wine and women and dancing."

"Blix doesn't feel like wining and dancing."

"It's all she does feel like. You've seen that closetful of clothes she brought up. And all we've offered her is dinner at the club and pizza parlors with live music."

Blix herself came to the door. "Pete's right, Tassie. I'm nothing but a hypochondriac. Plus that damned book. The minute Pete said champagne and dancing I was cured. No one who gets cured by two words is very sick."

Pete, who was already in the bathroom shaving, stuck his head out. "Three words. Champagne, dancing, and San Francisco."

"Help me decide what to wear," Blix said.

It was like old times. I voted for an evening dress with a full skirt of smoky chiffon and a short sleeveless bolero covered with opalescent beads. It's the prettiest dress in the world for women built like Blix, women with slender arms, narrow waists, and ample breasts.

She wore gray satin pumps with buckles beaded in the same color and design as her bolero.

"You still like buckles?"

"You started me on them and I've never kicked the habit."

I didn't, last July, make the connection between Blix's talking to Bolivar on Christmas morning and Blix reading Baldwin in midsummer twenty-five years later. Blix didn't know that I had seen her outside talking to Bolivar that Christmas Eve. She didn't know that the December evening was tied to the July evening by my reluctance on both occasions to do anything. But with an understanding beyond knowing, she had associated the two by way of the remembered buckles.

That was the end of looking backward that evening. And there were no more forebodings about the future. The night was self-sufficient. I remember it as colors, the smoky grays and opals of Blix's dress and shoes. I remember it as form, round and shimmering, a champagne bubble perhaps. Like those champagne bubbles in "Wings" which rose out of the rounded bedposts before Buddy Rogers's intoxicated eyes. I remember it as sound, the foaming music and the muted leather-on-wood whisper of dancing and the subtly deepened and lightened voices of people whose purpose in being together is the present.

Pete can dance with anyone. Blix can dance with anyone. Together they were perhaps too perfect to be noticed: a wave goes curling over; long grass alternates silver and green in the wind; the movement of candle flame gives the shadow of a bowl of roses an indoor life on the ceiling. Not much heed is paid such natural grace. Pete and Blix were like that; but I paid them heed.

I can dance with Pete, not as naturally as Blix. More like the surfer who goes sliding down the wave than the wave itself; the element of failure is present. But with Pete I never fail.

An evening blossoms, and its blooming cannot be explained. Would Pete, Blix, and I have had, in our living room, with exactly the same music, recorded, and the same amount of champagne, and wearing the same clothes, the same evening? Impossible. Though to say that we had to drink, talk, and dance in public to achieve such happiness seems to admit the need for an audience. No, not *that* need. The same need that a partnering in dancing satisfies: an enhancement by sharing.

We didn't start home until after two. It was a night without fog, the stars as bright as the traffic lights. We were all in the front seat.

Blix said then, without explanation, what she was to enlarge upon three months later.

"If there weren't any more, if this evening were all, it would just about be worth it, wouldn't it?"

I was too happy and sleepy to answer. I squeezed Blix's hand to tell her I heard and agreed.

IV

The day after Christmas finishes Christmas without outside help,
but if a Santa Ana is blowing, it finishes it faster. That great
dusty rocking wind is obviously stronger than Christmas trees
and their tinsel. It sends Christmas paper, printed with holly
wreaths and Santa Clauses, just as high as butcher paper or week-
old Baranca *Bulletins*. It knocks over tricycles, blows lightweight
practice basketballs clear across town; it smudges the washings
energetic housewives, cleaning up after the holiday, have put out.
It reminds humans how rickety is the scaffolding of their special
days. All days are alike to the wind. The better the day, the better
the deed, with it, too. It brainwashes children who run outdoors to play in it; they forget whose birthday they were celebrating yesterday.

I walked out into the wind at three on my way to Dr. Brinsley's
office on the other side of town. Mama had made the date for me.
"Petty," she had said, "you can't let this side ache run on any
longer. It might be a growth." She made the date without a
word from me, figuring rightly that silence gives consent.

In those days I shrank from making any commitments about the future. What had happened to me, so long ago I could not remember it, to cause me to fear change? Why did I feel scorn for travelers, innovators, scene-changers, as people who couldn't take it? When had I, like the Stoics, decided that all happiness was centered in the self? When, in the past, had I banked on something, anticipated joy? Or love and understanding? And been disappointed? So that now even ordinary undertakings filled me with foreboding. I packed for the trips from Brenner to Baranca, which I loved so much, with heavy heart. Better leave well enough alone. Find fault with the present and the future will show you what real suffering is.

Mama's making the date for me absolved me from blame. *I* wasn't tempting fate. *I* wasn't expressing any dissatisfaction with the present or hope for the future. I was a good girl doing what my mother wished. I walked the cold windy streets with a light heart.

Dr. Brinsley had his own clinic, with two other doctors, I think, and his own hospital. This small-town medical center was lodged in a white stucco mansion which its original owners, in the hard times of the thirties, had found too expensive to keep up. It was called the "Baranca Sanitarium," and its residential aspect, white stucco urns with trailing geraniums, a fountain without water, an iron stag, whitewashed, made it appear a wolf in sheep's clothing. Bad things went on in there, and you knew it: amputations, births that went wrong, deaths from poison, self-administered; and all somehow worse because they happened in what had the appearance of a home. A good plain straightforward hospital that looked like a hospital would have been more reassuring.

Dr. Brinsley had something of this same deceptive appearance, though I knew and liked him. He looked like a hardware merchant, a good solid man with red hair going gray and a thick bristling scrub-brush mustache. He had delivered Blackie in Linda. He had come out to the kitchen to help me, aged ten, heat water; he had showed me how to make a boiled custard

115

without lumps. I had never before been to him for an ailment of my own, but he had operated on Mother twice and, though Mother refused to coddle herself, there were occasions when she broke down completely and Dr. Brinsley was called in. So Brinsley didn't frighten me, though no one in his right senses could enjoy the medicinal smell of the sanitarium or the sight of Dr. Brinsley's nurse, Miss Irene Irby. Miss Irby was a dark woman with red lips, black Gorgon curls twisting out from under her cap, and the ability to wear a starched white uniform like the skin of a diamondback rattler. If I had to have a nurse, I hoped I'd have a round motherly one, not Miss Irby.

Dr. Brinsley called me by my nickname. "Well, Tassie, about time you're coming to see me. Four years and no babies. What's the matter with you?"

"Nothing," I said. "I've been working, you know."

"Work fertilizes babies, far as I can see. The more a woman works, the more babies she has. That's been my experience."

"Maybe I don't work hard enough."

"Maybe. I doubt it. What's your trouble?"

"A side ache," I said.

"Show me where." I showed him. "That's not your side," he said. "That's your groin and lower abdomen." These weren't words I used, but I reminded myself that the human body was no more to a doctor than a broken-down auto was to my father. "Miss Irby will help you get undressed. Then I'll have a look."

Miss Irby took me into a dressing room and gave me a cold white smock to put on. When I was in it she directed me to a small room half filled by a high black leather couchlike arrangement. I say "couchlike" because it was only half as long as a couch and was equipped at one end with metal stirrups. No possible position I could imagine on it would be comfortable, and any way those stirrups could be used would be indecent. I couldn't take my eyes off that apparatus, but Dr. Brinsley, easy in its presence, put me in a chair and himself mounted the black leather mechanism, sitting on it jauntily, like a lady riding side-saddle.

"Well now, Tassie, how long's this side ache been bothering you?"

It seemed like forever. "It started two or three years ago, I think."

"Why haven't you done anything about it?"

"I thought it would go away."

"For two or three years you thought it would go away?"

Dr. Brinsley, who was a Sunday-school teacher in the White Temple Presbyterian Church, dismounted, and said prayerfully, "My God, my God. Hell and damnation, girl. Don't you have a lick of sense? What did you go to college for? Why, people had more sense than you have in the Dark Ages. Old ladies back in the Kentucky hills who can't read cat from dog have got more sense than you when it comes to taking care of their bodies. And your body is *you*. Don't you know that? It's not something you own, like a breadboard or a dish mop, and can get along without. It's you. And perishable. Didn't that ever occur to you?"

It had. I thought about death quite a lot.

"Get up here," said Dr. Brinsley, and he proceeded so directly and angrily, there was no room for embarrassment.

"Do you use douches?"

"I don't use any now."

"What have you used?

I didn't like to say.

"Tell me."

"Vinegar and cold water."

"Lots of vinegar and icy-cold water?" I said yes with my eyes. "During your periods too?" I said yes again. "If you didn't know any better than that, why didn't your husband do something?"

Everett had said that it was too embarrassing to go to a drug-store and ask for the things men used. Besides, it wasn't natural. But I was afraid to tell Dr. Brinsley this. I knew he wouldn't approve. I said, "I don't know."

"All right," he said. "You don't need to tell me. Now you raise your head a little and look down here in the lower left part of your abdomen. Do you see that?"

Dr. Brinsley was outlining with the fingers of two hands a mound, too large for him to completely circle.

"Didn't you ever see that before?"

"I never noticed it."

"Don't you ever look at your body?"

I started to say, "It's not much to look at," decided that sounded as if I were fishing for compliments, and said nothing.

"That," said Dr. Brinsley, making a circle around the protuberance with one disdainful finger, "is an ovarian cyst. Or possibly a uterine tumor. It's already the size of a grapefruit. You invited it with those douches. You encouraged it with your neglect. And now, by God, I've got to harvest it."

"What do you mean, harvest?"

"Operate. Cut it out. In one piece, if I can. Which won't be easy. Get it out of you, in any case, the best way I can."

"When?"

"The sooner the better. Sometime this week, certainly."

The sun had gone down when I left the sanitarium, but it wasn't dark yet. An afterglow, murky red in the dust-filled sky, smoldered in the west. The wind was still blowing, cold and gusty. You could feel the grit on your teeth if you forgot and breathed through your mouth. I walked slowly, not taking my last look at the world, for I had never been sick and did not expect to put up with any long-drawn-out period in bed as others, more inclined to invalidism than I, might do. But I was bewildered and angry.

Whatever Dr. Brinsley might think, I understood quite well that my body *was* me. And this being true, what did my body mean, or that part of it in my lower left abdomen mean, turning against me? It was civil war, wasn't it? And if I couldn't depend upon my own body to be *for* me, to wish me well, upon what or whom could I depend?

Now that Dr. Brinsley had shown me where "my growth" was, I could feel with my own hand its rise and fall as I walked. I am a lopsided non-mother-to-be, I thought: askew, awry, askance. I am pregnant with possible death. There is something wrong with

118

me. I am headed in the opposite direction from other girls my age. The organ to make babies is, in me, making anti-babies. It had never occurred to me when I was married that I wouldn't have children. I'd had a list of names since I was sixteen, and they were worse than mother's: Reverdy, Chapel, Satsuma, Concordia, Molloy. They in themselves were enough to scare off the stork without recourse to icy-acid douches suffered through in cold privies. But I didn't know that; and when Everett, after I began to work and felt that bookkeeping and pregnancy were irreconcilable, told me that he wouldn't think of going into a drugstore and making any inquiries, I remembered the old wives' tale: so by way of inseminations, sour and cold, I had conceived, not Satsuma or Concordia, but Growth. I, too, had, like other young women of twenty-four, my bulge, my by-product of marriage and sex: but birth and baby were not to be the harvest.

As I neared home I began to hurry, anticipating the comfort and sympathy I would receive there. *They* would assume half and more of the burden of my news. Mother, though shocked and sympathetic, would joke. "Best days of my life were spent resting in a hospital bed. A tumor? Nothing to it. Mrs. Thornwaite had one, and Dr. Brinsley snipped it off like a grape. Just think, petty, those side aches are a thing of the past."

Oh, I would be welcomed, reassured, jollied, comforted, kidded, petted, and fed! I hurried past windows through which I could see the still-lighted Christmas trees, toward home with its now empty laundry basket.

Everyone knew where I had been: to the doctor to see about my side ache. I pictured them as waiting apprehensively for the news. "Why doesn't she come?" "I hope it's not serious." "Poor girl, what an ordeal this must have been for her." I came in prepared to make my news easy for everyone, to spare them, to suffer silently. I came in the back way through the kitchen. Blix wasn't there. Out, I learned later, with Vurl. Le Cid wasn't there: at the library. Marmion wasn't there: at Olive's. Father, Mother, and Blackie were home, in the living room, huddled about the radio.

"The body of Marian Parsons has been found in an irrigation ditch southwest of the town of Carlsbad, in San Diego County. Her kidnapper and killer has not yet been apprehended. There are reports that he has been seen . . ."

"Mother," I said, "I had my examination."

"Just a minute, petty," Mother said. "They think they've found the murderer."

They hadn't, but they did have endless reports. Blackie, not very excited by rape, came over to the sofa, hoisted up Beanie, and sat down with the dog between us. We both patted Beanie, and sometimes, our pats coinciding, we patted each other.

I finally got to tell my news. But somehow, after murder and rape, after long postponement and many other words, it seemed less than world-shaking. I was going to have an operation. But thousands of people had no doubt received that same news that very day. Mother was as comforting and funny as I had expected her to be. Blackie said, "I'll come to see you every day." Everett arrived and said, "This doctor may not know what he's talking about. A lot of doctors are hipped on making operations. This is nothing to get upset about."

I waited up, hoping that Blix would be home early. She didn't come, and I thought, We live and die alone.

2

After Everett had personally checked with Dr. Brinsley, the operation was scheduled for Friday morning at eight. Dr. Brinsley convinced him that I had not been exaggerating, and that postponement might be fatal. Everett said he very much doubted this, but if I wanted to go along with Brinsley's verdict, it was all right with him. Everett left Tuesday morning for the ranch to look after the livestock and to take care of our milk and egg customers. He wouldn't be back to Baranca until after the operation; on what day, he wouldn't know until he found someone to do his work. This wasn't my idea of love and marriage: wife on operating table while husband takes care of livestock. But a good many of my ideas were undergoing change in this period; and I recognized, as well as Everett, that with the cost of the operation added to my loss of salary through sickness, someone had better be bringing in some money.

Once the decision to have the operation was made, I didn't have too many apprehensions. Decision itself was what upset me —and first Mother and now Dr. Brinsley had taken this out of my hands.

As a toothache lets up before a dentist date, so my side ache let up before the date of my operation. I had two or three delectable days. No early rising. No books that wouldn't balance. No eggs to clean and box when I got home from work. No milk to skim, and cream bottles to fill. No fires to start, meals to cook, dishes to wash. If this was invalidism, give me more of it. Only Blix, Blackie, and I were at home. Marmion had gone back to school. Le Cid was in Balboa visiting friends. Mother, who enjoyed cooking, and had in me and Blackie two of her most enthusiastic fans, outdid herself. A big pot of navy beans with dumplings as light as feathers floating on top. Pineapple upside-down cake. Cottage pudding, which was a layer cake held together by a thick rich chocolate sauce. Pot roast with browned potatoes and gravy that looked as chocolatey as the sauce that covered the layer cake.

When we weren't talking and eating, Blix and I went down to the Baranca library for books. We were permitted four books to a card, and by pooling the family cards we got out twenty-eight books. Enough to see me through at least the first week of hospital life. I can still remember some of them: *Now in November*, T. E. Shaw's translation of the *Odyssey*, *Scouting on Two Continents*, *Nazi Means War*, *Amiel's Journal*, Elinor Wylie's *Collected Poems*, *Tender Is the Night*, *Book of Talbot*, Giles's *History of Chinese Literature*, *Eimi*, *Foot-loose in the British Isles*, *Testament of Youth*, *Winner Take Nothing*, *The Shape of Things to Come*. We really reaped that library. Blix had no bookworm blood in her, but she was patient with me and enthusiastic on her own about some of Elinor Wylie's poems. "My love came up from Barnegat" I remember was one of them.

We came home from the library at dusk: the dying Santa Ana blew our hair in our eyes, but we were too laden with books to do anything about it. We walked, half-blinded, laughing with passers-by at our plight.

"Let's get someone to push the hair out of our eyes," I said to Blix.

"Let's ask someone to carry our books," Blix countered. "Then we can take care of our own hair."

We walked under the grape arbor, toward the lighted kitchen, laughing and talking. It was like a continuation of old times, before Blix's heart was stolen (if it was) and my interior (surely) damaged. And why shouldn't it be? Damage and break-age were recent. I was separated by only four years, and Blix by one, from coming into this kitchen every evening at dusk, with Mother busy at the stove. At that time, it was more natural for us to return to the life we had known than to move ahead into the strangeness of operations, and the miseries of love.

3

Mother was where we usually (unless she had a sick headache) found her at this hour. Sitting on her tall stool, rickety, in spite of the fact that Father had steadied its legs in a lasso of baling wire, stirring something on the stove. It was gravy again, this evening, made from the grease fried out of the pork chops. Four (when Mother made pies, she made pies) big raisin pies, seeping brown juice, were cooling on the drainboard. Blix and I headed for the living-room sofa, threw down our books, and exercised our aching arms. Blackie immediately grabbed *Scouting on Two Continents* from the pile and, when we went back to the kitchen, followed us like a sleepwalker, his nose already between the pages.

Something was wrong with Mother. I could see it in the slope of her shoulders, in the lackadaisical way she was stirring the gravy. It showed, whatever was troubling her, in the neat and careful setting of the table. She had set that table with rigid arms, without trust or spontaneity. When Mother was in good heart, she threw things at the table, too absorbed in life to waste time arranging china and cutlery.

"How do you feel, Mother?"

"Why, with my fingers, petty," Mother said, imitating her usual manner and avoiding a downright lie. Whatever she did with words, her body and face told the truth: trouble, dreadful trouble. But until after dinner, when Blix left for a girls' bridge party, Mother kept up her pretense that she knew no feelings except those her fingers gave her.

Dinner over and Blix gone, she did something unusual. She set Blackie to washing dishes; she snatched *Scouting on Two Continents* away from him and, when he set up his usual howl, gave him a smack that surprised him into silence.

"Now, Basil Murphy," she said, "you light right into those dishes. Your sister's a sick girl." Basil gave another hiccup. "There's not a thing wrong with you hard work won't cure, Basil. Dishwashing's too easy to turn the trick, but it's a start in the right direction."

She shut the door firmly on Blackie and, Burnham's book in hand, led me past Father and the evening paper through the living room and into Blix's room. She shut that door firmly, too, seated herself on the day bed (which Blix hoped gave her room the look of a study), leaned forward, and rested her face in her hands.

"Mother, are you sick?"

"I'm sick at heart," she said.

This is a sickness you can't inquire about. You can't say, or I couldn't, at least, "What makes you sick at heart?" Not to Mother. It's not like physical sickness. Probe, examine, and all symptoms of heartsickness may be hidden. All I could do was to stand ready and to wonder: Why was she sick at heart?

She was concerned about my operation, of course. But it didn't

123

make her "sick at heart." *Her* children didn't have serious diseases, and if by some mischance they did, they threw them off in no time. It was a mechanical affair, like a vapor lock in the Durant, mended in no time and better than before, no doubt. So it wasn't my operation.

Father made her mad, "mad as a wet hen," "drove her crazy," "provoked her," but he never made her "sick at heart."

Blackie could make her sick at heart all right; but it wasn't Blackie this time, or she'd have *him* out in his room, instead of me in Blix's room.

We might all be sick at heart if we knew all there was to know about Le Cid. But we didn't and we never would. Le Cid lived his own life. He was smart enough to keep it under cover and strong enough to have no need to talk it over. Le Cid lived with us like a man from another planet. Our weaknesses weren't his, and maybe not our sins either. Anyway he was never going to make Mother sick at heart.

Marmion? Was Marmion making Mother sick at heart? I didn't think he could. That left Blix.

I think I had known it from the beginning. It had always been Blix. Mother, I was pretty sure, had found out something "bad" about Blix. Now I, too, felt sick at heart—for Blix, for myself. Suspicion, condemnation, berating, suffering . . . my stomach began to contract. Hadn't Blix gone through enough?

I pulled out the chair from Blix's dressing table-desk and sat down. There was nothing to do but wait. The room was so Blix-at-twenty: chaos. Clean clothes tried on and discarded. Dirty clothes stepped out of and left lying. Shoes, magazines, coffee cups, half a sandwich. The room of a girl interested in clothes and boys. The room of a girl who did not live *there*, but only made preparations there, to live elsewhere. A complete contrast to my room as a girl. I *had* lived in my room as a girl. I did my preparing outside, seeing and hearing, and came back to my orderly room to try to give order to what I had experienced. My room was always as neat as a factory, ready to manufacture something, though what, I didn't then know. I began to

straighten out Blix's desk: get school papers sorted from magazines, bobby pins from paper clips.

The noise I made roused Mother. She looked up at me. "I
want you to see something," she said. She opened the door of
Blix's closet. "Come here," she said.

Blix's closet was her room, only more so. How could she walk
out of such confusion so immaculate herself? Out of my bandbox
room I walked all crooked seams and pinned-up straps and
flying hair. Out of her mare's nest Blix emerged a fashion model.
She was more unselfish than I. I cared about what *I* saw, not
what others saw. (This isn't quite true. I cared, but Blix said
I didn't care enough.)

Mother paid no attention to the things she had to step on to
get to the hangers that held Blix's clothes. She pushed aside
clothes until three garments hung by themselves, a coat, a bath-
robe, Vurl's big football sweater. Other things hung in a ram-
shackle any which way. These three were properly centered
and securely buttoned. Mother unbuttoned one at a time. Underneath each hung a pocketbook. Then, one at a time, she opened
the purses.

"Look," she said.

I stepped in closer so that I could. I don't know what I expected to find; something of the kind I did find, I think: a kit
for terminating pregnancy. It wasn't called that, of course, but
even I, ignorant vinegar doucher, understood the purposes of
castor oil, salts, viburnum compound, hot baths, and dilation. I
understood Mother's "sick at heart." I was sick there, or somewhere near there, in diaphragm and throat. Oh Blix! That she
had had this to bear, besides the knowledge, surely, of Vurl's
roving eye. Taking the stuff. Wondering. Worrying. Knowing
that Mother would rather have her in her grave. Talking to me,
but holding this back. Not trusting me enough. This at Christmas time, and giving no sign. Hair curled. Eyebrows arched.
Carrying the books. Laughing in the wind.

Mother closed every pocketbook carefully, carefully rebuttoned
all the camouflaging garments, carefully realigned the coat hang-

ers. Then she retrod the once-trod-on clothes, and I, following her, closed the closet door behind her.

"Blix must never know that I know," she said.

This was fine with me. If Blix had gone to all this trouble to keep her trouble secret, why hurt her by telling her we had, behind her back, spied it out?

"I think the stuff worked," Mother said. "I think she's all right now. Might be she didn't even need it and was late a day or two and got scared."

"How would she get it? How would she know . . ."

"Vurl," Mother said. The letters of his name were too slippery to spit out, but Mother managed to do so. "That horse? He's had more than one use for stuff like that or I miss my doubt."

I thought of Everett. Mother seemingly did so, too. "You don't know how lucky you are with a good husband. Tasmania, Blix must never know I know. She must have somebody left she wants to prove herself for. She must still think her father and mother believe in her."

"Well, don't you?"

Mother didn't answer me. Instead, she said, "Someone must talk to her. Someone must point out to that poor girl where actions like this will lead. Someone must tell her to cut that Vurl right out of her life, never see him again. Oh, petty," Mother said, "Blix looks up to you so. She told me just the other day you were her ideal. You are the one to talk to her. She'll listen to you."

I said, "How do I know anything about—her trouble?"

"You stumbled on . . . what she's got hidden."

"How did I stumble? I don't wear Blix's things."

"I don't know," Mother said. "You'll think of something. You always do. But someone she believes in must tell her how wrong . . . how low-down . . . someone she knows loves her."

"I can't do it."

"There's more in it than comes to the eye. This happening at this time, just as you go to the hospital. It can be your last word to Blix—before you go under the knife, I mean. It will have extra meaning to her coming then. I'm not going to say God gave you this misery so what you say to Blix will have added weight. But it has worked out that way. It's come at a time when she'll listen twice as hard. Want to please you twice as much. Oh, petty, you'll do this for your sister, won't you?"

I didn't say anything. I couldn't say "no" to Mother. Or Blix. And I couldn't say "yes" either.

Mother said, "I've put too much on you from the beginning. I've asked too much of you. Made you a second mother to the kids. What else could I do, sick half the time? Don't think I've forgotten *your* trouble. I make light of it, but I know an operation's no joke. But you're not in any real pain now. . . . And wouldn't you like to think this sickness isn't pure waste?"

I was weakening, speaking of the conditions now under which I would or would not talk to Blix. *I* didn't know it. But Mother did.

"I know what you're thinking, Tasmania. You feel like you'd be using your operation somehow if you asked Blix to throw away that stuff and to stop seeing Vurl. But you can't help being sick. The only question is, will you let the *chance* of what's happening to you now keep you from helping Blix? Don't you *want* to help your sister? Do you *want* her to go through all this again? She leans on you, Tassie. She looks up to you. Someone ought to talk to her. And you shouldn't make her suffer just because you think that it's not something-or-other, to speak up for the right, when you're on the verge of an operation."

"But that's one of the reasons you wanted me . . ."

"I said that Blix would pay more attention to you than usual, just now . . . and that's a fact. But it's not a fact that should keep you from talking to her. There's more at stake here than your dignity."

I could perhaps have said "no" if Mother had shown any signs of her old-time fury and hatred. She didn't . . . nothing but distress.

"What if it's too late? What if it didn't . . ."

"I think she's safe . . . now. I think so. But she won't always be so lucky, Tassie. . . . Do you want her to go through this again?"

Mother's great blue-green eyes were clouded. Her lips were colorless. The room was chilly; in spite of this her forehead was beaded with sweat. I could see the beat of her heart in the hollows of her temples. She sat down once again on Blix's bed and wrapped her arms in her apron. She was tired. While Blix and I had been chanting "My love came down from Barnegat," and tossing our windswept locks, she had been perched on her baling-wired, rickety stool, frying the pork chops, stirring the gravy: she had had her dreams, too. Not only virgin daughters and grandsons born in wedlock, but her *early* dreams: of a fair world, beyond the lace curtains (though she wasn't willing to give them up either), a fair world, in spite of the cruel verses of the hymns, where delight and loving-kindness flowered thick as calla lilies along the irrigation ditches.

4

Oh, I said "yes," to her. It was foregone. I said "yes" because I couldn't say "no." Maybe talking to Blix would or would not help her. But there was no doubt that Mother would be helped by a "yes." The sweat dried on her forehead the minute I said "yes." Her eyes cleared. "Oh, petty," she said, "I knew I could count on you."

I said "yes" to Mother but I couldn't say a word to Blix. I couldn't make a beginning. Say, "By sheerest chance I stumbled upon your anti-pregnancy kit, under your coats, inside your purses in the closet."

Mother arranged opportunities, encouraged talk, deplored postponement.

Finally, I had an idea. It was something I wanted to do anyway, so I had no trouble convincing myself that it was the right thing to do.

"Let's go over to the Normal Hill Apartments for the night," I suggested to Blix. "You take your car and I'll pay the expenses."

Blix agreed. She thought I wanted one last look at the city before my operation. She had never seen the Normal Hill Apartments, and the Biltmore or the Mayflower was nearer her idea of a fling in Los Angeles. I didn't have the money for such hotels, which she knew, but besides being cheap (the rooms were only a dollar), the Normal Hill Apartments excited me. They were like the ruins of a temple carved in the sandstone cliff overhanging a desert valley. They were to some degree actual ruins. They did to some degree overhang the street below.

When we finally reached the Apartments, I watched Blix fearfully. I wanted her to like them. They were my own discovery; I felt it was, in some way difficult to explain, strange and beautiful. The building was nearing its end; that was one of its fascinations. Another was that there had been no attempt to disguise what it had been, a rooming house for students who had gone to the old L.A. Normal. The Normal had been torn down; girls preparing to be teachers went to U.C.L.A., and the Apartments now housed shoe salesmen, librarians, old ladies. What the building looked like was a big broken-down bunkhouse of the kind the great, but disappearing ranches, Leffingwell, Bastanchury, Irvine, still maintained. You expected to see horse troughs, a dinner bell suspended from one of the olive trees. The olive trees told you what the place had been before it had become a part of the city.

"What do you think of it?" I asked Blix anxiously.

She liked it. I could see that at once. Not crazy about it, maybe, but captivated by its strangeness.

I knew which room I wanted, 215. I had been there twice before. We carried our own suitcases (there were no elevators or bellboys) down a long corridor and up a winding stair.

Our progress was noted and watched. And approved. At the Biltmore or the Ambassador we wouldn't have cut much of a swatch. Here we were pretty modish. We responded with our special somethings, our emotion-clogged voices, our knee-action gaits. A man older than Father asked Blix if he could carry her

129

suitcase. A woman as old as Mother complimented me on my handbag.

We entered our room like actors coming off stage, a pleased audience behind us. Blix liked the room. How could she not? It was large, clean, and threadbare, sparsely furnished: a Congoleum rug on the floor, its original pattern blurred to a soft mulberry stain. A double bed: the mattress a pad, the springs, chicken wire, but clean, with bedspread pulled as taut as an ironing-board cover.

It was pure bleakness; it was sparseness, unrelieved, an abstraction you could walk about in. People now travel hundreds of miles to find these qualities in the desert. We had them after fifteen miles, in the heart of Los Angeles, for one dollar a night.

"D'you like it?" I asked Blix again.

"I wouldn't want to settle down for life here."

We stepped to the window together. We may not have had the same thought but we spoke the same words.

"Well, here we are."

There we were, all right. Ailing in the same areas. Harmed by what should have healed. Dismayed by what should have delighted. Oh, what had happened to us? Where were the two high-steppers? The throb-throated talkers? The hair-tossers? The poetry-quoters? The wind-lovers? Were we demolished? Or only temporarily shattered and capable of being patched together again?

Blix wanted to try patching. "Let's eat at a nice place."

We didn't know, or I didn't know, any "nice" places. The only "nice" place I knew was Clifton's, a cafeteria with a waterfall, artificial stones, but real water and real ferns.

Blix hooted at this idea. "A waterfall! I'm not going to any cafeteria, even if it has a real ocean with real waves. I'm going some place where they have candles. And serve wine."

"Wine! Do you know where to find a place like that?"

"Yes, I do."

"Have you ever drunk wine?"

"What do you think I drink when I go out?"

Actually, I had never thought about it. But if I had, I would have supposed water.

When I didn't answer, Blix said, "Did John Everett make you take the pledge?"

"Of course not," I answered, nettled. What kind of a milksop did Blix think I was? "You find the place," I bragged, "and I'll drink as much as you do. It's a perfect idea. Eat, drink, and be merry, for tomorrow we die."

"Okay," said Blix. "I'll be ready to go in an hour."

It was impossible to understand, though I had often watched the process, how Blix *could* spend so much time "getting ready." What was there to "getting ready" besides wash, comb, dress, put on make-up? And with Blix, washing, as Mother often said, was a short horse and soon curried. Taking all the pains in the world, fifteen minutes was all I could manage to spend on "getting ready."

Once, disgusted with the uncertain blurry job I had done with lipstick on my mouth, Blix went to work on me with her brush and lipstick. She drew a perfect mouth, and filled it in with sure strokes. She stood back, looked at it, wiped it off. "For you, your way is better."

"In other words, a perfect mouth needs a perfect face."

Blix disagreed. "Who'd paint a door on a tree?"

This wasn't clear; but I didn't want it explained.

5

Blix's slowness in dressing often drove me crazy. But that afternoon I was glad for it. While she dressed, I would have time to visit the new library above which the Normal Hill Apartments rose.

I had, as usual, two purposes in the library that afternoon: discovery of books I didn't know existed, and the acquirement, if possible, of a specific book. I was an official card-carrying Los Angeles Public Library patron and I knew my rights: how many books, for how long, and so forth. I didn't expect much help, and, after decades in public libraries, didn't need much. The book I wanted was the recently published diaries of the brothers Goncourt. I wanted it because the brothers were literary and the book was a diary. In a diary, I was convinced, I got the writer's lifeblood warm from the vein. Pepys and Dorothy Wordsworth, Thoreau and Katherine Mansfield, set my teeth to chattering with excitement. None but the lonely heart, they say, keeps a diary. None but a lonelier heart, perhaps, reads one. The diary keeper has no one to speak to; the diary reader has no one who speaks to him. The diary writer is at least talking to himself. The diary reader is listening to a man talking to himself.

The catalogue showed that the library owned a copy of the Goncourt diary. I scanned both ways from the Goncourt's; scanned backward into the B's, the Brontës, and finally reached Mrs. Gaskell's life of Charlotte. I knew the Brontës, of course, but not Mrs. Gaskell. I took the book down. I began to read. I forgot all about the Goncourt brothers. I forgot my sister. I turned pages, picked up sentences. I left California for Yorkshire.

I read: "Weary with a hard day's work . . . a stormy evening . . . the wind is uttering a continual moaning sound . . . a household custom among these girls . . . to sew 'til nine o'clock at night. At that hour they put away their work and begin to pace the room backwards and forwards . . . up and down . . . often with candles extinguished . . . they talked over past cares and troubles . . . this was the time for discussing together the plots of their novels. Emily, that free wild untamable spirit, never happy or well but on the moors . . . Branwell resolved on stand-ing up to die . . . Emily, stronger than a man . . . simpler than a child . . . Keeper walked alongside the mourners . . . the day is windy, cloudy and stormy . . . I am trying to hope."

I walked to a table, reading, pulled out a chair, reading, and, still reading, sat down. Though I was no longer aware of reading or of words. I was living the life of the Brontës, high on the moors of Yorkshire in a house overlooking a graveyard; a house floored with flagstones and buffeted by winds. Cold flagstones,

132

bitter winds, damp sheets, pale curates, sickness unending: nothing to live on but the sweep of the moors, the bite of the senses, the warmth of the imagination. Weary, resisting, hoping. The day's work: bread kneaded, stockings mended, floors scrubbed, fires kept up. At night the pacing, the books and pens. The whisper of snow. The rustle of something neither snow nor wind. Oh, wild Decembers. Like Charlotte, I loved Emily. Strong as a child, simple as a man. Or was it the other way around? Take five years from me, Emily, I urged. I give you five years from my life.

6

Blix didn't even know I was half an hour late. Nor did she suggest that I try any improvements in make-up or dress. "When you're excited," she said "you look okay."

"Well, I'm excited," I told her. "I took a book out of the library for the first time in my life without checking it out."

"You mean you stole a book?"

"No. I just didn't check it out. I'm going to take it back."

"What kind of a book is it?"

I could see that Blix thought that it might be a book I was ashamed to present to a librarian. Something silly or off-color.

I held out the book. "A life of Charlotte Brontë."

Blix knew all about the Brontës even if she hadn't read Mrs. Gaskell. She had a kind of Heathcliff in her own life and like Emily she had an older sister.

"I don't know why you couldn't check it out."

I knew why. Because it would have been like getting a permit to pray, or a certificate for kissing. I wasn't going to have a librarian stamping down with her little mechanical clicker on a message to me from a hundred years ago about the right way for sisters to love and care for each other. But I couldn't tell Blix this any more than I had been able so far to deliver Mama's message. Why not? Emily and Charlotte had paced the floor together, nothing hidden. Sharing their dreams, confessing their fears. And I couldn't tell my sister so simple a thing as my reason for not checking a book out of a library.

Blix could talk about it though. *"You* may think you've just borrowed that book, but to the librarians you're a thief."

"Thief" was the very word I needed. It made me lighthearted. I felt as if I had risked something—for Blix. It was a breakthrough. If I could steal a book I could surely manage a few words of good sense and sisterly counsel. I left the Normal Hill Apartments with Blix feeling that the worst was over. We went down the hill and turned left on Sixth. Christmas was past and its remains looked tawdry, a festive table left uncleared and its clutter debasing the memories of the feast. The stars were out but their story had been told. No one would think of wise men and shepherds again for another year. The wine-and-candles restaurant Blix had in mind was down toward the Union Station, she thought. In a basement. The sign wasn't very conspicuous. We might miss it.

People turned their heads to look at Blix. They always did—for reasons other, I think, than that she was very pretty. She had a quality of yearning which required a response from passers-by to complete her. Passers-by did respond. Her movement along a street was the occasion for an emotional duet: yearning and response. She wanted, and they gave; and both felt better for it. Something lived, momentarily. Blix was the life the city streets had lost with the passing of Christmas.

In Pershing Square a great burly Negro, the color (and size) of a desert mountain at dusk, was singing revival hymns. Behind him stood a flour-white woman with her hand on his arm. Her eyes were closed, her lips moved. She appeared to be praying; the arm that linked her to him trembled. Did she give him power? Or was the flow of the current in the other direction? Was he her puppet, or she his? Or neither? Two together, one as alive as the other?

We had been walking along, aware of ourselves, of shop windows, of odd people like the Negro singer, thinking of what lay ahead of us.

Then we began to notice that there was something unusual about those who, with us, were walking down Sixth Street. A brisk stream of people in theater clothes moved together as if toward a known and common destination. Blix and I, brisk walkers ourselves, were, and had been for some time, a part of this procession. For a minute it was like either falling into a dream or waking out of one.

Blix said, "Tassie, what is it? What's happening?"

I didn't know, but I was accustomed, when asked, to finding answers for Blix. It was a part of my role as older sister. "They're all going to the same place."

It wasn't much of an answer. Where were they going? They were gay, laughing, animated; no one was tired or bored or worried. The women were perfumed. We could smell them. Their high-heeled slippers, black satin and gold kid, struck the pavement with the light clatter of rain. The women swung beaded bags and they wore pearls, or possibly even diamonds. Under their wraps of velvet and fur, there was a glitter of jewelry. The men were dressed in dark handsome suits. Their overcoats had velvet collars.

"They're going to a play," I told Blix. "Or to hear a speech. Or to a concert."

When we were in front of the Biltmore, Blix said, "Let's go with them, Tassie."

"Without asking them where they're going?"

"Without asking."

"This might be pretty expensive."

"We could beg."

"What do you mean, 'beg'?"

"Say, 'We've lost our tickets. We can't get in without your help.' "

"Okay. You say it and I'll back you up."

The minute we decided to join the procession, we became light-hearted. Abandoned, and possibly pregnant—if this was what Blix was—uncompanioned and ailing—and that *was* my problem—we didn't care. Young, daring. Blix was as well dressed as any, and far prettier than most. With my book (I hadn't been able to leave Mrs. Gaskell behind), I might pass for a student. No one expects students to have the money to dress for the opera. If that was where we were heading. That we didn't *know* where we were heading was the joy of it. Toward something good, we hoped. We were still optimistic. We still believed in secrets. Didn't we have to? If what we already knew about life were the whole of it, how could we ever hurry again? Take chances? Or laugh? There had to be more.

We *were* laughing. I was, anyway. At the end of the block, after we had passed the Biltmore, I put my arm through Blix's, in pure pleasure, and in order to keep from being separated. Blix's arm remained a little rigid. I read it like Braille: I was no substitute for Vurl. This was something that had not occurred to me. *She* could have done this with Vurl. He was the one, perhaps, who taught her such nonchalance. "Let's go where they go." "Beg, if necessary." My training was the opposite. Everett would have smelled, as we did, music or drama or lectures afar off, and bolted. And never have moved, destination unknown, toward any event whatever.

The column, of which we were now a part, paused at the Biltmore corner before crossing the street. We saw, at this point, our destination: the Shrine Auditorium. And by reading the marquee, we learned why we were going there: Madame Lucia Valzani was to sing.

Now a female singer, even a renowned one and a contralto, was not what we would have chosen. We knew nothing of music, and if the evening had to be musical, we would have chosen a male pianist with flying hands and tossing hair, or an orchestra, able to stun us with sound.

Madame Lucia Valzani was what we had, however, and she *was* worth looking at. Our eyes were better trained than our ears; we noted her lacquered black hair, her fine oval face, and her sumptuous bosom.

She began to sing, but for fifteen minutes or so, Blix and I heard nothing. We took in the wonder of Madame Valzani's appearance, of the auditorium, of the audience, of the fact that

136

we, the Murphy girls, brought up in the Linda Hills and more accustomed to cicadas than contraltos, were actually there. Finally, we became aware of the sounds Madame was making. We began to hear. Our overly conscious eyes ceded some territory to our ears. The sight of flashing sequins, the exciting idea of ourselves as concertgoers, dimmed. The songs Madame Valzani sang were not in English, so it was not the story we were hearing that moved us. By grace alone, by sound alone, a human voice entered and spoke to us in a language we understood but did not know.

We thought it was entertainment; it was not. We were too self-conscious to call it art. But it had art's concentration and firepower. It went in small, like a bullet, but once inside, it flowered like a dumdum. It went in the size of a song, then began to grow. It became a life; not a baby's simple life of sleeping and eating, but a man's life. Schumann's, Wagner's, Schubert's, large with an accumulation of joy and sorrow, even wisdom. It was sound. It entered our ears, but we felt it, too, in the same way that we could simultaneously hear and feel the wind, or the surf. And taste them, too: salt and damp, bitter and free. It was a voice that flooded the auditorium, there was no Mount Ararat of escape left for any listener.

Then, without notice, the great voice would dwindle down as thin as a needle shaft. I remembered Le Cid and his gnat. Thus it penetrated individual hearts. Blix and I were wounded and bleeding, but we loved our wounds. We were alive and suffering.

When the concert was over we were scarcely able to walk. But we *could* float. We were ennobled and enraptured. We found the restaurant Blix had in mind without looking for it. Blix's charm got us a good corner table. Blix faced toward the room, I toward Blix. She had on green again, not the corduroy suit, but taffeta; the green of the dress was reflected in her tawny eyes.

The restaurant was the most beautiful I had ever seen; "picturesque" and "romantic" were my words for it. It had brick floors, copper sconces, tables with red-checked tablecloths, candles in wine bottles. I placed my red-backed copy of Charlotte

Brontë's life on the table, the waiter lighted the candles, and Blix ordered: chicken en casserole and port wine. Port? At the time, I had no idea of the variety of drinks, or that one variety was more suitable for some courses and dishes than others. We had a whole bottle of port. We drank a whole bottle. I more than Blix, probably. I was always a greater eater and drinker than she. I don't know whether or not the wine loosened my tongue. It did calm my excitement. It acted as a sedative after the strong stimulants of Emily, Heathcliff, and Madame Valzani. It leveled me off to where speech was possible. I drank it like water, though in my opinion it tasted much worse; it wasn't until I went to bed, and found that when I turned over, my body rose ceilingward and hung there, delicately poised for a moment or two before descending, that I knew I hadn't been drinking water.

I knew of no way to begin my talk. I began bluntly and crudely, and even cruelly, though that was not my intention.

"Blix," I said, "I found your purses in your closet."

There was no reaction. For the moment, in the lingering excitement of the concert, in the pleasure of eating and drinking, I think Blix had actually forgotten Vurl. She didn't understand which purses I was talking about. She had many and she was always urging me to borrow one of hers and to leave my practical handbag, which she called my "shopping bag," at home. She looked down now at my nondescript bag. "Why didn't you take one?" she asked.

"I mean the purses you tried to hide."

When I said that, something came into Blix's eyes, something alive and shining, wounded, but trying to live. It was as if the whole of Blix, the whole of her life and her meaning to herself, at that moment concentrated in her consciousness, was visible in her eyes, visible there, and visibly dying and aware of who was doing the killing. I had read many times of the life-yearning of small animals cornered, awaiting death. That small, pitiful animal in all the concentration of its acceptance of fate lived in Blix's eyes—for one second. Then died. The light went out. What was next visible was shame.

138

Is shame the worst look we can bring into a person's eyes? Is fear worse? I have never been responsible for that, but I was responsible for shame, and that is very bad. Blix was ashamed of being "a girl in trouble"; and she was ashamed to have me know it. For there is no use in false modesty; in denying that up to this time, Blix valued my opinion.

So she knew what I meant. It was in her eyes. And since shame, I supposed, was what Mother wanted her to feel, as protection against the recurrence of such acts, I kept myself from comforting her. I longed to say, but didn't, "What the hell does it matter, anyway?"

Instead, I said, "I found the three purses you had hidden—and what you had in them."

Blix tried to be angry; she tried to manage some emotion, any emotion, to cover up or dilute the shame. The best she could do was to say, "I thought purses were private property." Before I could remind her of her many offers to lend them, she added, "What's in them, I mean."

I cannot recall the words of that conversation—for the very good reason, I suppose, that I have tried for so many years to forget that the conversation ever took place. On the matter of Blix's health—the harm that she could do herself; kill herself, actually, with such concoctions, and the taking of those baths and exercises—I was, I think, probably right. Though God knows that in giving any such advice a very sooty pot was calling a slightly gray kettle black. I think I was possibly on firmer ground, though I had no evidence, in calling Vurl a selfish two-timer and not worth her little finger. I was on agreed ground, anyway, in keeping her from knowing that Mother knew, and in suggesting that Mother counted on her.

I tried to do what Mother expected of me, which, in its crudest terms, was to say to Blix, "If you love me, reform." All the while letting her remember that I did this on the eve of a major operation.

I knew how much Vurl had caused her to suffer. I didn't preach purity to her. I preached health. "Is Vurl worth killing yourself for?" I stuck to one of Mother's points. "Have you thought that if Father and Mother found out about this, it would break their hearts?" This wasn't very honest ground; Mother knew, and, while sad and worried, her heart obviously wasn't broken, and obviously wasn't going to be. A mother's broken heart in pre-pill days was the best deterrent yet developed. I got away from Mother's broken heart and dwelt on the points in which I really believed. Health, Happiness, and Plain Good Sense. It would be just Plain Good Sense, I told her, to avoid the act that had resulted in her present plight. It would be just Plain Bad Sense to ever let that happen again. The best thing would be never to see Vurl again. But with the two of them in the same college, and with Vurl as prepossessing as he was, an occasional date might be more than she could resist. But the act. She could resist *that*. *That* could be abandoned forthwith. It would require nothing more than a little firmness with Vurl. The act could be abandoned with nothing but rejoicing; morality, health, convenience —all coinciding. A wife had duties. But *she* had no duties. She could choose her own pleasure, not Vurl's. And, in doing so, make sure that she would never again have to experience the past month's doubt and misery.

The shame, as I talked, went out of Blix's eyes; talk was easier. Her look now was curious, speculating. She seemed to invite me to continue. Perhaps she didn't. Perhaps the wine was more effective than I knew. In any case, I continued. This subject, the obvious Plain Good Sense of "never again until she was married and the act became her duty," was not a real Brontë subject. Anne, Emily, and Charlotte had not, I supposed, talked of it as they paced their firelit floor. But candles were burning for Blix and me. The subject *was* love and death, life and shame, a mother's trust and a daughter's dishonor. I loved Blix. Without falseness, without harping on what I didn't believe—"Mother's broken heart" or "my dying wish"—I was able (I thought) to bring reason and good sense to her attention.

Blix's look changed more and more. Shame left, pity took over. "Poor Tassie!" she said.

140

" 'Poor Tassie'?" I asked.

For a minute I thought she was talking about my operation. But she wasn't. I had given her leave to forget it and she had.

"Poor Tassie," she repeated. "You don't know what you're talking about, do you? You don't know a single solitary thing more than you did at twelve. Do you?"

7

On the day of Mother's funeral, the day Blix admitted that she had always resented me, I decided to tell her the truth about those three purses. I had kept Mama's secret for twenty years. I had not robbed Blix of "someone who believed in her." But death had taken that believer away, and Blix and I were alive. And perhaps she would resent me less if she knew that the talk I had had with her that night in Los Angeles was made to please Mama, and that the purses and their contents had been her discovery, not mine.

I thought over the pros and cons of my confession. I tried to imagine both Blix's and Mother's response to my telling. Mother had always cherished the idea of family unity: brothers and sisters together, loving each other. If the truth about the pocketbooks would draw Blix closer to me, Mother would be for it. "It don't matter what Blix thinks about me any longer," she'd tell me. "Why, petty, if telling Blix that I put you up to that talk will help you two girls, tell her! Tell her the night before the operation was my idea, too. Tell her I wasn't above doing anything to help her. Why shoot, I've gone to my reward. It's all settled, one way or another. And it won't mean much to me if my two girls are on the outs here below."

And Blix? Wouldn't she understand? Perhaps even pity? "Poor old Tassie. So you were only trying to be Mother's little helper. I might have known."

After Blix went downstairs, I dried my eyes, combed my hair, put on lipstick. I didn't want the messenger to offend, before the

141

message was heard. Blix was alone in the kitchen. Mother had been away from it for three days, but it was still her room entirely. Her bird sang in its cage in the bay window. The teakettle, one of those patented hissers, hissed on the stove.

Blix was at the round fumed-oak table (Mother had enameled it butter yellow) in the bay window. She had a cup of coffee and was looking at the morning paper. Before I could begin my speech, she began to read.

"Librarian Tasmania Murphy, in private life the wife of Pete Orcino, is in Los Angeles celebrating her successful attack on censorship in the state library. If you want to consult the 'dirty-word dictionary,' read *Catcher in the Rye,* or peruse the latest papers from the U.S.S.R., you can still do so in Sacramento, thanks to Tasmania's 'bastions of liberty' speech, in which she attacked as 'dictatorial' the right-wing effort to 'spoon-feed' the minds of inquiring Americans. Meanwhile, 'back at the ranch,' Pete is playing in the Thunderbird Invitational Tournament. If Pete has Tassie's luck, the Orcinos will clean up big this month."

Blix put the paper down. "Everything worked out just fine for your trip down, didn't it?"

Blix could do things like this. She knew perfectly well that I hadn't been in Los Angeles at all, and that any celebrating I had done about censorship was over and done with two weeks ago. She knew perfectly well that Pete's entry in the tournament was a matter of long standing, and that, in any case, there was no point in his hanging around, a second husband in a houseful of in-laws at a time of sorrow.

What Blix said, this insinuation that I had come south as much to receive plaudits as to mourn Mama, was an illustration of the fault she had confessed to me upstairs: the confession I had refused to accept.

I didn't understand that then. But I had learned to accept, as part of Blix's make-up, such sudden and inexplicable attacks. Sometimes they made me mad. Sometimes they made me cry. That morning, because I was intent on clearing up that misunderstanding of twenty years ago, I didn't attempt to explain or contradict her implications (which she knew were untrue) about my censorship speech.

"Blix," I said, "there's something I want to tell you. Something you don't know."

"There's a lot I don't know. You've chosen a fine pupil."

I ignored that, too. But Blix, who always knew what she was doing, knew what she had done and tried to make up for it. "How about a cup of coffee?"

"No, thanks. Blix, do you remember that trip we made to the Normal Hill Apartments?"

"Yes, I remember."

"Do you remember our dinner afterward?"

"It would be hard to forget."

"I want to tell you something about that. I don't know whether I should or not. But what you had to say about resenting me decided me. It came to me that what I said that night might have something to do with your feelings. You know I've never envied or resented you. I've always been proud of you. I always supposed it was the same with you."

"I've told you before," Blix said, "that what *you* feel, you're convinced everyone else will feel. You're proud, so I'm proud."

I ignored this. "Mama would hate your resenting me," I said.

"Mama hated quite a few things about me. Anyway, she's in her grave now. You and Mama aren't in cahoots any longer. You don't have to worry any more about what she thinks."

"I admit that we were in cahoots once."

"Once? All your life. For purposes of keeping me in line."

"I didn't know that you were out of line. Except once when Mama . . ."

"Let's leave Mama out of it."

"I can't—and tell you the truth."

"I'm not your board of directors. You don't have to tell me the truth."

"Maybe not. But, Blix, I want you to understand."

143

"What is there to understand?"

"I'm trying to tell you. Promise not to walk out on me before I've finished."

"I haven't made any promise to hear you out. I can walk out any time I want to."

With that threat, I plunged right into my confession. "That dinner was Mama's idea. And in spite of what you were going through, you did your best to make it what you thought it actually was: a celebration for me, before I went into the hospital. You talked about the good times we'd had. You made jokes. You analyzed people and their outfits. I loved you for it. But it made what I had to say harder to say. Finally I told you. A look came into your eyes I've never forgotten. Then it disappeared. I think maybe it was any love you had for me. Maybe it was then your resentment started."

Blix made a shadowy shake of her head. I went on.

"At least it didn't do anything to make it less. I thought I'd tell you the truth now, about that night. Mother showed me those purses. I had never suspected anything. She told me to talk to you, 'the night before I went under the knife.' To tell you that my last thoughts were about you."

"Were they?"

"Yes, they were. Mama may have put them in my head to begin with, but they were mine that night and they were about you."

I had expected everything from Blix except complete silence. The bird pecked away at the seeds on the floor of his cage. The refrigerator came on. The teakettle hissed. There was a slight smell of gas in the kitchen. Blix had her cigarette in her mouth. She inhaled slowly. I waited a long time for her to exhale.

She said, very quietly, "So Mother knew, all along."

"I don't know how long she'd known. But she knew about the purses."

"She knew something else. She knew your talk would stop me from ever seeing Vurl again."

"I didn't know that you never saw him again."

"Never again. Oh, I saw him at a distance a few times. But I was never with him again. In any way. Mother stage-set that little talk of yours just right. She should have been a senator. Or a general. Oh, she outthought us both. I wanted to be like you, Tassie. You don't know how I wanted to be like you. Strong, sweet, and clean; she knew that. She knew that would work on me as much as your 'going under the knife.' You didn't know that. But she did. And she couldn't tell you that, of course. So there you were . . . strong and sweet and clean . . . brave and gay . . . the . . . night before the knife . . . and your last thoughts were of me."

"Aren't you glad you broke up with Vurl? No matter how it was brought about?"

"Glad? I don't know."

"You know how he turned out."

"I loved him."

"Why did you pay any attention to what I said, then?"

"What chance did I have? You convinced that board that censorship was un-American, didn't you? I called Vurl the next evening after I took you to the hospital. I used to him all the words you had used to me. They were Mama's words, I suppose. Oh, I loved Vurl and he loved me, but that speech of mine did it. Of course he didn't know that I had heard it from someone who had only one chance in ten to live."

"One chance in ten? They didn't know it was that serious until they opened me up."

"Mother knew . . ." Blix began. Then she said slowly, "Anyway that's what she told me. Before the operation. One chance in ten."

We neither one said anything for a while. Blix emptied her cold coffee, poured herself another cup, lit another cigarette. Then she said, "Mama probably suffered hell the next day. She must have felt that her telling me you had one chance in ten made it happen. She had superstitions that way. She thought there was a power in words. If you'd died, she would've blamed herself."

"Did she blame herself about you?"

"You'd know more about that than me. She never blamed herself about Milt that I know of."

That was the first and last time I ever heard Blix say anything against Milt. If it *was* against.

Blix finished her coffee, stubbed out her cigarette. "My God, my God," she said. "So I threw over Vurl at the request of a dying sister."

"I didn't tell you I was dying. I didn't know that I *was* dying."

For a moment I thought I might see the young Blix again, the egg-thrower, the skirt-ripper. But that Blix had really died.

"You acted it," she said quietly. "You told me that if Mama ever found out, it would break her heart. And she already knew, and it hadn't broken her heart. And you knew it. Isn't that treachery? Isn't it?"

"I did it because I loved you."

"Loved me! You did it because you loved Mother."

"What's wrong in that?"

"What you loved was praise."

"From my own mother? Who doesn't?"

"You loved pleasing anyone. You still do. That's what makes you so good with the speeches."

Was it true? I couldn't answer.

"Now you've told me a terrible thing about Mother in order to win me over."

"I admit I want to win you over. But that's not so terrible either. And what's so awful about a mother's trying to save her daughter from a man who gets her pregnant, then risks her life with drugstore remedies?"

"Why didn't she ask me if I wanted to be saved? And look *how* she tried to do it. By lies. By using you. Can you forgive her that?"

"There's nothing to forgive. I understand why she asked me. And I told you because I hoped you would forgive me."

"Forgive you! Why, Tassie, you poor monkey's paw, there's nothing to forgive you for. Ever since you were a kid, you've been a poor blind monkey's paw."

146

I said, "Well, surely you can't resent a poor blind monkey's paw? Can you, Blix?"

Blix said, "Oh God, Tassie, don't try to clown your way out of it. Don't try to be funny. Don't try to make black white. Just face it."

I faced it. I had failed with Blix. What I'd said hadn't worked. And I didn't have anythig more to say. Or the strength to say it. Or to move. I sat there at the table, and the sights and sounds of the kitchen swept across me like a warm, but possibly drowning tide. I didn't want to be a person. Not the person I was, anyway. I'd rather be the sunlight on the yellow table, or the light wind rustling the leaves in the clump of eucalyptus down the street, or the creaking palm fronds. I looked at the cat on the washing machine on the back porch, and his yellow eyes opened wide to let me in. This was Mama's world. She had died, and I had betrayed her now, as I had Blix before. Always an approbation seeker! The kitchen's warmth and brightness narrowed and focused. The sounds fused. The cat wanted in. The doves called "home." The kettle's sound joined that of the palms. Blix was again hidden behind the smoke of cigarettes, one in her hand, one smoldering on her saucer. I heard Mother, in her springtime voice, which she never lost, say, "Petty, you took the blame for that for a long time. For as long as it would do any good. It's my turn now. I'll take the blame. You do what you can for your little sister. You be a mother to her."

Blix waved the smoke away with her hand. I saw her sandstone eyes and the curl of her soft mouth. She continued to fan; I was a person facing a person now, not palm, or wind, or sunlight.

"You're free for the first time, Tassie," Blix said. "If you want to be. You could please yourself for a change—if you ever knew how—if you haven't lost the habit."

I was a person alive, facing another living person. I knew that. But the echo of Mother's voice was still in my ears.

"But maybe you don't . . . and maybe you have," Blix added.

V

When Blix visited us last July we were still playing the game of hope. We weren't playing that game any more when I went to be with her in September. Blix was in bed, though not "bedfast." By electing earlier than need be some of the disabilities of her sickness, she seemed to make them a matter of choice rather than of necessity. Fate was not pushing her around.

There was nothing to tell a person who didn't know it that Blix was sick. Her skin was clear and bright. Her bones were too fine and too good to be harmed by any loss of weight. She was as careful with make-up as ever. She still wore her hair, though putting it up tired her, in her usual elegant French twist. She had bleached it for some years, and the desert sunlight, through the glass wall of her bedroom, gave it a hoarfrost sheen. She didn't, in the daytime, wear nightclothes in bed, but soft Capris with a variety of tops, more suggestive of beaches and ski resorts than sickrooms.

"I thought I might never see you again," she said very softly and somewhat wonderingly, the day I arrived.

148

I didn't know, and still don't, whether she meant that she thought that I wouldn't come or that she wouldn't be alive when I did come.

As in the past summer, when we had exerted a faith in the unseen to believe her well, now it took faith in what was not visible to believe her ill. Mother and I had always looked far more draggle-tailed in the midst of our colds and sore throats and headaches than Blix did mortally stricken.

Blix had cared very little for Mama's and my sickbed performances. But she had enjoyed a life of nearly perfect health, while Mother and I had moaned and groaned our way through a series of illnesses. We had told her that if *she* ever was sick, she would talk out of the other side of her mouth.

"I will never moan and groan," she had declared, "no matter how sick I am."

Mother and I would stifle our own moaning to predict, "Wait until you know what you're talking about."

Now she had waited, now she knew what she was talking about; but I never heard Blix groan: not awake or asleep; not filled with drugs or waiting for a shot.

On that first day with Blix, I arrived about noon. The timing of Blix's medications often let her sleep for a while after her lunch. Tired from driving, flying—and waiting—since morning, I, too, had a nap. The desert air, so much warmer than what I had left, made me feel that I was retreating in time, traveling backward. I had left autumn and moved into full summer.

Blix's and my relationship seemed to have moved backward to an earlier stage, too. Big and little sisters, again, helper and helped, again, useful and ornamental, needing and needed, loving and loved. I did not, on that first afternoon, grasp the meaning of our ease and happiness together. Happiness did not seem suitable under the circumstances. I thought I ought not to feel it.

But happiness was what I felt. When I awakened, Blix was still sleeping. I hurried to shower and dress before she woke up. The pleasures of desert living are heightened by perversities: to be living, not with nature, but in spite of it; to stand in a shower of cool water and look out into a hot and waterless land.

Blix was awake when I came in. She smiled, but said nothing.

"How are you, Blix?"

"Oh, I have a pain," Blix said. "But it's just an old shoe pain, one I can live with."

"Blix, would you like a glass of beer?"

I knew that she'd lost her taste for beer, but a glass now, with the shadows getting longer and day ending, would seem like old times.

She was willing, for old time's sake, to play-act. "Yes," she said. "This afternoon, I think I would like some."

While we were drinking, Dr. Reyes, without our hearing him, came to the bedroom door. It was his custom—I didn't know it then—to give one rap on the outside door and then enter, unbidden.

"What is this?" he asked, as he saw us. "A sickroom or a beer parlor?"

"Take your choice," Blix told him.

"I choose beer," he said, "naturally."

"Actually, it isn't an either-or situation," Blix said. "Here, you can have both."

Dr. Reyes was in his mid-thirties, a tall, melancholy-looking young man. He could flash a white smile now and then, but between smiles he looked troubled. Blix said he had a right to. He had seen troubles.

Dr. Reyes's mother had been a high-school teacher in New Araby, a town fifty miles from Oasis, where Blix lived. Dates are the crop in New Araby, and John Reyes's father had been the foreman at one of the big date ranches there. Ruth Ellis, the high-school English teacher, had fallen in love with the good-looking Mexican foreman and married him. She was thereupon fired from her job.

There are plenty of mixed marriages in the valley, though not usually between high-school teachers and Mexican foremen. The children of such marriages are Mexicans—and thirty-five years ago they were second-class citizens: segregated schools, swimming pools, theater seats. Ruth Ellis wasn't having any of this for her son. As a result, little Johnny Reyes, who wasn't accepted by the whites, and whose mother didn't permit him to play with the Mexicans, had a lonely life. And his looks didn't help him: a craggy Celtic face with a darker than usual Mexican coloring. The other way around would have been much easier for him: smooth Spanish-Indian face with white skin and blue eyes. That wasn't the way it had turned out, and little Johnny Reyes carried on with what he had.

Dr. Reyes was the man who first suspected Blix's malignancy. He hadn't performed the operation, but he had attended her in the hospital and since. The two of them had somehow surmounted the stereotypes of what is known as the "doctor-patient relationship." They liked each other as persons. Dr. Reyes, who had never developed a bedside manner, could be sarcastic and matter-of-fact—and Blix enjoyed this. It let her continue to exist as a woman.

Blix introduced us that first day. "Dr. Reyes, you haven't met my sister, Tasmania Orcino."

"My God," Dr. Reyes said, "what a name!"

"The name," I told him, "is not my fault. But the bare feet—and this ancient muumuu are. And I apologize."

"Don't apologize. I'm pleased to find a lady librarian out of her flat-heeled shoes."

"How long has it been since you were in a library, Dr. Reyes?"

"About ten years. I can buy my books now, thank God."

"While you were changing, the librarians were, too."

"Touché, Mrs. Orcino."

Blix laughed, easy with her old shoe pain, the nostalgic beer, the doctor she liked.

"What kind of beer do you want?" I asked.

"The brand doesn't matter so long as you hold me down to one glass."

He had two. When he left I walked to the car with him. I had promised Blix to talk to him.

"Sound him out," she had told me. "See where he stands. Find out how much we can count on him. We can plan our heads off, and he can wreck every plan if he wants to."

"Wouldn't it be better for you to talk to him?"

"I couldn't."

So that left it to me.

The carport was outside the kitchen door. Before opening the door, I paused. "I can never get used to the difference between the outside and inside temperatures," I told him. "I keep thinking that I ought to be able to *see* something that would warn me about the difference."

"Like the blind child who asked, 'What color is the wind?'" Dr. Reyes suggested.

I was surprised. "I suppose so. I suppose I think heat should have a red glare, like a furnace. Be recognizable before we see it."

It felt like a furnace, anyway, and the first shock was always delightful to me—like a plunge into cold waters—and with the same knowledge that what one was experiencing was terminable. What one enjoyed was neither heat nor cold, but the exciting awareness of the body's ability to experience.

I didn't know where to begin my conversation with Dr. Reyes. One thing I did know, and that was that he wouldn't be taken in by any fabrication of mine about being a story writer. I couldn't say to him, "Doctor, I am thinking about writing a story about a woman who is contemplating suicide. What would the attitude of this woman's doctor be?"

But I had to begin somewhere. "Dr. Reyes," I said, "if Blix should feel an unusual amount of pain, would it be all right for me to give her her pills a little oftener than you have prescribed?"

Dr. Reyes's eyes, I noticed, were bronze-colored, the color of grass in autumn at the bottom of an irrigation ditch.

He answered my question in a quick, harsh voice. "No. The time's specified in the prescription. Follow it."

"I was thinking about an emergency . . . some sudden seizure. I thought perhaps . . ."

"You don't need to think about that. Call me in any emergency. I'll decide on the amount of medication your sister needs."

Perhaps Dr. Reyes thought he had been too harsh. In any case, he went on more quietly. "If I'm too generous with the painkillers now, if I try to save her every pang now, I'm simply preparing a certain hell for her later on—when she's really going to need help."

"Dr. Reyes," I said, "Blix doesn't intend to go through that later hell."

Dr. Reyes gave no sign whatsoever that he had heard what I had said.

"I'll stop in in a day or two," he told me. "If you need me, phone. Office, hospital, or home. You'll be able to catch me one of those places. Or in between."

The minute I came back to her room after my first talk with Dr. Reyes, Blix said, "Did you ask him?"

There wasn't the least need, actually, for Dr. Reyes's opinion on that subject. I had come to the desert with all the information an experienced doctor could give me and there was no reason to doubt any of it. We did need, and had to have, some assurance that Dr. Reyes wouldn't try to send Blix back to a hospital, or saddle us with a twenty-four-hour-a-day nurse, or simply camp on our doorstep, prepared to undertake day or night rescue missions. But as to dosage, we didn't really need another opinion.

To Blix's mind, however, there was no authority like Dr. Reyes. She had followed all of his advice so far. She would like to have, if not his blessing, at least his approval of this final medication.

So I had to disappoint Blix: tell her no, I hadn't asked him.

"He has to know me better," I told her, "before he's going to trust me with any talk like that. He doesn't know but what my hobby may be the ruination of doctors. He doesn't know but what I may be a gossipy blabbermouth. He doesn't know whether I love you or hate you."

Blix objected. "He couldn't think that!"

"I didn't say he did. But relatives do hate each other. That's one of the reasons the laws are what they are. They're to protect you."

Blix gave me one of her big wide-open looks.

"Let the law look after itself," she said, "and I'll look after myself."

The second time I talked with Dr. Reyes, he was more outspoken.

"How many cases of terminal sickness of this kind have you known, Mrs. Orcino?"

"None."

"You're lucky. I've known hundreds and I've heard at least half of them say exactly what Blix is saying now. 'I'll never go through with it.' That's what they say at this stage. And they believe it. 'When it gets too bad, I'll put an end to it.' It never gets too bad. The smaller the amount of life they have to hang onto, the tighter they cling. Or perhaps the patient doesn't change his mind. He still doesn't want to go through with the pain. But he has postponed doing anything for so long he's lost the ability to act. They can't foresee that. I don't expect them to. But I have to. I'm the doctor for the whole course of their disease. Sure, I can make them fairly comfortable in the beginning. I can keep Blix comfortable now. And condemn her to hell later on. The pain getting worse and worse and the drugs getting less and less effective. I've got to foresee that. Is that what you want for Blix?"

I tried to defend myself. "Of course I don't want that for Blix. But she's one patient who'll do what she plans to do."

"Blix sick and Blix well are two different persons. She is, comparatively speaking, well now. I know what sickness does to a person."

"Not Blix."

Dr. Reyes refused to go around that circle again. I knew Blix. He knew sickness. We could grow hoarse repeating those statements. I came right out in the open with Blix's worry.

154

"Blix is afraid that an overdose might make her sick."

Dr. Reyes didn't help me. I wasn't going to be permitted to do any beating about the bush with him.

"An overdose of what?"

"Sleeping pills."

"I didn't know she had any. I haven't prescribed any."

"I know that. But she has them."

"How many grains?"

"One and a half."

"Three should be plenty."

This was a ridiculous answer. But before I could express any astonishment, Dr. Reyes went out into the heat, got into his car, and sliced away into the afternoon shimmer with surgical sureness.

When I told Blix what Dr. Reyes had said, she laughed. She was proud of him. He was going to be a hard nut to crack.

"He's no citizens' council," she said. "You can't talk to him about censorship and bring tears to his eyes."

"Maybe I asked a foolish question. At any rate, I got a foolish answer."

"You already know the answer, don't you?"

"I do. That's what I've been telling you. It was your idea to ask Reyes."

"Okay. You tried. Now he knows. What we've got to work on now is to keep him from being professional twenty-four hours a day."

2

The next time I saw Dr. Reyes was the night he taught, or tried to teach, me to give Blix a shot. That night, neither Blix nor I had any interest in trying to persuade him to give up his round-the-clock professionalism.

For a week or so after that, I slept in the bed next to Blix's. It was during this week that she discovered that she couldn't take

155

Numorphan and Seconal at the same time—the combination gave her frightening dreams; though once in a while the dream was simply outlandish. Even funny.

One night when I awakened her for a shot, she opened her eyes, smiling.

"I was dreaming about our Republican ancestors."

"That can't have been very gay."

"It was interesting. They were having a heartichoke."

I stopped assembling the hypodermic needle. "A what?"

"A heartichoke. You know, a Zanzibar."

"A Zanzibar?"

"You know what I mean. They have them all the time."

"The Republicans?"

"Both sides. A bill comes up that the other side doesn't want passed so they start Zanzibarring."

I knew then what she meant. If she was teasing me, I would tease her a little in return.

"If it's political," I said, "phone Milt. He'll know the word."

Milt had a phone in his office, which adjoined his bedroom. It had a different number from Blix's, and sometimes Blix phoned him for a chat. But not at three o'clock in the morning. The last thing Milt did before going to bed was to announce the exact time at which he would arise the next morning.

Blix got my joke. "The word has come to me," she said demurely. "It's a filibuster."

Blix wasn't the only one experimenting with drugs that week. I had to take enough Seconal to let me go back to sleep between shots, but not enough to prevent me from waking up in three hours. I never found an amount too great to keep me sleeping when my unconscious told me Blix's medication time had come. Bugles couldn't have awakened me more suddenly or completely. Drifting back to sleep again was a more difficult matter; no matter how many pills I took (and I had a limit beyond which I wouldn't go), the process was slow and chancy.

For a half an hour or so after Blix's shot and my pill, we lay, neither awake nor asleep, inhabitants of some world hard to

156

name: neither here nor there, neither now nor then. Because the place, if it was a place, and the time, if it was a time, were strange, we were free in it. We acted like tourists, capable of conduct abroad that would appall us at home; able, in the foreignness of our drugged half hour, to relive happenings never before mentioned.

It was an odd thing. More pitiful, actually, than odd. Here we were, sisters. We had had a mother. None of us tongue-tied. The three of us loving each other. All of us having suffered, having been confronted by perplexities, disasters, heartbreak. But not one had confided in the other, had gone to the other saying, "Comfort me, advise me," or even "Listen to me." Certainly not "Pray for me," as Pilgrim women of an earlier generation would have done. Why not? Oh, why not? Why never the arms outstretched? The shoulder offered for the other's tears? Or vice versa. Why did we suffer alone? Self-condemned to be childless, motherless, sisterless. Why?

Part of the Pilgrim discipline had lapsed, the comforting part: the praying and sharing. Part of it had persisted: the prudish part. Much of a woman's unhappiness has to do with sex. And since sex was the one subject which this mother had taught these daughters was unmentionable, we lived (with each other) our secret, unmentionable, frequently suffering lives.

But for drugs able to conquer pain and time, "Pilgrim" provides no obstacle at all. We were de-Pilgrimed by them; in the minutes before the pain let up, or the sleep set in, that job was done completely.

One night Blix concluded a confession, dreamily, even complacently. "I would have made a first-class whore," she said.

There has probably been more speculation on this subject by women than on all other subjects combined. Women might, perhaps, be divided into two classes: those who think they have an aptitude for this profession, and those who think they would fail at it. And of those who think they would succeed, there might be a further subdivision: those who take pride in the fact, and those who are ashamed of it.

Blix's statement combined pride and shame. I don't think she considered this aptitude on a par with a gift for composing poetry or even raising a houseful of children. On the other hand, I don't know that she would have traded it for either. Admirable or not, she did believe she had it; and, not one to harbor remorse or nurse vain hopes, she accepted it.

The Pilgrim in Blix had to be substantially anesthetized to permit her to make any such admission. Even so, it was a round-about way of saying something else, something even less admirable to a Pilgrim: "I found sex enjoyable." Brought up as she was, this had to be equated with whorishness. Another Pilgrim misconception, no doubt. She knew, and I knew, that this was what she was saying, and that she would have been the first to revolt against the hard-working whorehouse routine of any conscientious madam.

Before Blix had made her disguised confession (or claim) we had been talking about Vurl, murmuring about him, actually, in desert darkness, in drugged honesty, aware of approaching silence. The mind must move. When there is nothing to go forward to, it explores the past. The past is really almost as much a work of the imagination as the future. What really happened? How much has been forgotten? What, actually, was said? Why was that choice, and not another, made? Was there, in reality, any other choice?

"So it was Vurl," I said. This being my roundabout comment on Blix's roundabout statement about sex.

"Vurl," Blix exclaimed, "Vurl!"

There was far more surprise in her voice than there had been in mine when I heard her report of Zanzibarring.

"Vurl!" He might have been the Republican ancestor she had dreamed about. "I was madly in love with him. But making love! Oh, no. Whatever made you think that?"

What could I say? "He was so good-looking"? Or "You did succumb!" Or "You admit you were madly in love with him"? I said nothing.

"Vurl! He couldn't hold a candle to Milt."

Milt? Milt! Well, her Numorphan was stronger than my Seconal. Besides, Blix hadn't been brought up as I had, to be a model in speech and act, to her brothers and sisters. She *could* speak out, where I couldn't.

Still, I felt ungenerous, careful, self-preserving. Blix was willing to give herself away. She was willing to make me the gift of the life she had had. She was willing to open her heart to me. What could I do for her? What account reflecting no credit on me? What occurrence she wouldn't have guessed, about which she could ponder as the drugs took effect?

"Blix," I said, "do you remember that operation I had when I was twenty-four? At Christmas time?"

"I remember our talk the night before."

"I want to forget that. You knew the nurse I had. That gorgon-haired girl. We didn't think she was a girl then—she must've been thirty. Anyway, when I came to, I found that I had been split from navel to crotch. Up as far as possible and down as far as possible, as Mama used to say. The incision didn't heal properly, and that nurse—she married Dr. Nielsen later—dressed the wound each day. She had fingers like spider legs, long, thin, and brown. I thought she must have more than four on each hand. I thought they were hairy. They crawled around everywhere, very delicately. Still, she hurt me. I thought she intended to hurt. Maybe she didn't. Maybe it couldn't be helped. I don't know. Anyway, I moaned and groaned. Shed tears, even. You wouldn't have liked me.

"Then somehow I got the idea that she enjoyed the commotion I made. That the dressing wasn't a success for her unless she got some response from me. So I learned to keep quiet. I clamped my mouth shut, looked out of the window, pretended that what was happening to me was happening to someone else. The minute she leaned over me, brushing my face with her steel-wool curls, I went out into the garden and inspected the monkey puzzle tree. Why do they call them monkey puzzle trees? Do they puzzle monkeys? They puzzled me, and I was glad for it. My mind stayed outside trying to figure out their twistings and loopings while she roamed around my incision with her poisonous little fingers.

"I was out in the garden with my mind the morning she brought me back moaning. I didn't scream, because what I felt wasn't pain. In some ways it was worse than pain. In some ways it was an unendurable pleasure. Though that's pain, I guess. I actually thought I might be dying. If I could have moved, I would have risen up and hit that snakey-haired nurse. Not slapped her. Hit her with something hard, the water pitcher or the bedpan. I despised her. When she hurt me, I had hated her. But now I despised her.

" 'Is there something wrong?' she asked.

"She knew there was something wrong. She was responsible. You don't shiver and shake like that for nothing.

"A whisper was all I could manage. 'My wound,' I told her. 'You touched my wound.'

" 'That wasn't your wound I touched, you stupid girl.' She brought her face down near mine. I could hear her. I could breathe again. The sensation was beginning to drain away. Her hair which smelled like copper, was in my face. I thought she was trying to stamp me out with her eyeballs.

" 'Get away,' I told her.

"She stayed right where she was. 'That wasn't your wound,' she repeated. 'It had nothing to do with your wound. Do you understand?'

"I didn't. 'Don't do that again,' I warned her. I shut my eyes so that I couldn't see her scornful face. And all that hissing hair. She threw the sheet back across me and walked out. Another nurse took care of the dressing after that."

Blix said, "My God."

I said, "Well, that's something you don't need to feel resentful about."

"I told you all my resentment had disappeared," Blix said.

"Something at that time you wouldn't have resented."

"At that time, I didn't know. I couldn't have guessed. Who could?"

We both lay back against our pillows. "It would have been better," I said, "if you had been giving me little talks in those days, instead of me giving you little talks."

"You never asked for any. You never asked for anything."

It was the truth. I wanted to be a big giver. Independent as a hog on ice. "I was proud of what I could do without."

"You didn't even know what you were doing without."

"I was proud of that, too. I was proud of my ignorance."

Blix said, "I believe you were crazy."

"It's a pity you didn't think so then and institute therapy."

Blix didn't answer. I looked across at her in the starlit room. She had fallen asleep. I didn't sleep for a long time. After a while I heard coyotes calling from across the valley. Or that's what it sounded like to me. Only the old timers can tell how many and from where. Why is that call so beautiful? Loneliness, loneliness. Is that what it says? There's nothing beautiful about loneliness. Defiance? Self-sufficiency? Nostalgia? When the coyotes called, Blix and I remembered Linda. Do they take us back further than childhood? To the prairies? To the cave before the dog had come in to share the warmth?

Their crying always seemed a good omen to me. Better than a rainbow, which is simply an arrangement of colors. Coyotes are an arrangement of flesh and blood like ourselves. Oh coyotes! I suppose Noah, with his arkload of animals, had a pair on board. A rainbow was a promise better to him than any animal cry, however beautiful. I wanted to wake up Blix, who loved coyotes, to listen with me. I might awaken her pain, too. I let her sleep.

VI

If I say that Blix and I were never the same again after that long ago Christmas of my twenty-fourth year, I am surely exaggerating. I am not lying, though. It seems to me that we did change. I was changed by what happened to me in the Baranca Clinic. Blix had been changed by the need to buy those medications, by the need to hide them in those three purses, and, finally, by my outrageous sermon.

If we didn't change, then life itself began to change. Perhaps we didn't lose confidence in ourselves; but we did lose confidence in life. It occurred to us for the first time that we might not be fate's darlings after all. It occurred to us for the first time that life was not impressed by the way the Murphy girls walked, talked, or dressed. Not by the books we read, or by the kind words we spoke to our young brothers and to our old parents. It occurred to us that we had better develop a little strategy. If life, after all, was not a fairy godmother, but an old witch, we had better be able, if required, to shove her into the oven.

The strategies we developed were different. Blix had let her heart rule her head in loving Vurl. Okay. She wouldn't do that again. "The first question I'm going to ask a boy is, 'What's your bank balance?' I've been careless. I'm going to be careful from now on out."

My strategy was the opposite. I had been careful. Everett would have been approved by the board of deacons of any church. Same school, same religion, all that kind of thing. My head had approved of Everett. He was a careful girl's choice. I didn't actually begin to say, or sing, "Oh careless love." I didn't, by an act of will, embark upon a program of drifting and dreaming. But it appears to me now that some mainspring in my nature had been loosened during the time I spent in the Baranca Clinic.

2

In March of that year after my operation Everett began planning to dry apricots the following summer on a much larger scale than usual. He planned to buy apricots from other ranchers and to dry them, as well as his own, at our place. If he bought at low or even reasonable prices, processed the fruit economically and well, had the luck of a good market, and sold at an opportune time, he could make a lot of money. I didn't think that any of this would happen. I thought it likely that Everett would pay too much for the fruit, pick it late, dry it haphazardly, and sell it impulsively. I thought we would go broke, lose the ranch, and possibly end up in jail. And I didn't care. I just didn't care.

The need to advise, organize, supervise, had, however, left me. I had gone out of the business of foreseeing, forearming, fore-stalling. If, as a result of failure, Everett had to give up his dream of ranching and find himself a job as shoe clerk or Bible salesman that would be Everett's hard luck. Or maybe good luck. Who could say? At least it would be *Everett's* luck. I wasn't deserting Everett; but I was no longer directing, either. Somehow, my stay in the Baranca Clinic had excused me from that job.

Along in March or April, whenever it was that Everett first began to plan to run a big dry-shed, I also began to plan. This sounds contradictory for one who had given up foreseeing, fore-arming, et cetera. It wasn't. My plan was nothing but summer itself; for the first time in my life I intended to let summer *happen* to me. I intended to be with it. I was beginning to believe that being with it mattered more than anything else. Better be sick and suffer sickness than healthy and unconscious. My plan for the summer was to be able to say in July, "I'm in the midst of July." And when September came, to say, "Summer has passed. This is the fall of the year."

Unconsciously, though, I began to keep an eye out for summer while spring rains were still falling. That was wrong. While imagining summer, I missed spring. I don't remember a thing about that spring. Apricots bloomed, of course. The snow fields on Mount San Jacinto began to melt. The hills, I suppose, were blue with lupine and crimson with Indian paintbrush: I really don't know. I missed it all.

If summer was what I wanted, Brenner was certainly the place for it. It had summer the way the South Pole has snow. While I was dreaming about it, summer arrived. One afternoon toward the middle of May, I opened the front door and there, outside, was summer, heavy, warm, and fragrant. The umbrella trees had opened; there were cool umbrella-shaped shadows at their feet. Pepper tree leaves, so lacy they moved every time a hummingbird flew by, hung heavy and inert. No birds were flying. They all sat deep in the palm tree caverns, dozing the heat away.

The valley smelled like a country kitchen, wood range fired up and jam kettle bubbling. Cherries, apricots, peaches, plums: all had come to a rolling boil. The ripening vegetables had a bland, starchy smell, a man smell, as contrasted with the female smell of the acid-sweet fruits. I stood in the opened door and tried to identify individual scents. I failed. House smells were the only ones I recognized. Damp floor boards. Dust from recently swept ingrain carpets. The vanilla scent from a floating island pudding, cooling in the kitchen. I went back to my ironing. Dreaming was over. Summer had arrived.

At dusk I stood again in the doorway. The clouds of a summer afternoon had piled up behind Mount Tahquitz. They darkened as I watched. Then their scalloped edges were flushed with light, and I heard the distant rumble of thunder. The mountain storm of a summer afternoon had begun. There was not another thing to wait for. Summer was billowing up around me as rich and extravagant as I had dreamed: a sumptuous castle. I had planned to inhabit the whole of that castle: mount every stairway, gaze from every window, wave welcomes from every balcony. And here it was, complete. Turret on turret. Pennants flying. Drawbridges down. And I the sole possessor. And I couldn't walk in. It was too lonely in there, too inhuman. Heat records would be broken that summer. To whom, inside the castle, could I say, "Think of it! The hottest day since 1898!" Sunsets would vary. With whom could I discuss them? As, "Is this sooty enough for an African sunset? Pale enough for England?"

Could I no longer content myself by writing letters to Mama saying "Summer is here"? Couldn't I keep track of earliest and latest blossoms? Measure the girths of trees? Record the temperatures of bodies of water? I could. But the summer I wanted was more than a keyhole life. Summer was more than something to be experienced with thermometer and tape measure, recorded with fountain pen.

Where was some sundial of human hair in whose bleaching I could keep track of the passage of the sun-stricken days? Blix, Blix! I thought of Blix. I still feel the pressure of the screen door against my upper arm as that good thought came to me. "Ask Blix. Ask Blix." If only she would walk the zinnia rows with me, listen to the Mexican songs with me, speculate with me about the amount of haze mixed with crimson it took to make an "African sunset."

The bang of the screen door was still echoing in my ears when I took down the phone.

Blix herself answered. "Tassie? What's wrong, Tassie?"

We didn't make long-distance calls in those days just for the fun of talking. I had to reassure her before I could tell her my idea.

"Spend the summer here, Blix. Please do. We could have a lot of fun."

"I've put fun out of my life."

"You could make money, then. You haven't put money out of your life, have you?"

"Tell me more."

"Everett's going to be a big-time operator this year. There'll be all kinds of jobs."

"Cutting apricots? No, thanks."

"You could be a cutting-shed supervisor and see that the others do the job right."

"What Mother wants me to do is to find a husband. I'd be glad to be able to stop hearing about *that* for a while."

"Don't you want a husband?"

"Sure, I want a husband. But not just anyone. You got any good prospects up there?"

"Dozens. You can have your choice. Milt Hollister is only a half a mile down the road."

"Is he rich?"

"A rich, bald widower."

"A widower? How old is he?"

"Twenty-five or six."

"Any kids?"

"No."

"What happened to his hair?"

"His *hair*? Good heavens, I never asked him. It disappeared. Gradually, I suppose. His wife drowned. Caught in a rip tide at Newport."

"Well, that wouldn't happen to me. I can swim."

"Look," I said, "there are plenty of men up here. And you can have a job if you want it. But I'm asking you for my own sake, not yours. We could have a beautiful summer."

"Rich young hairless widowers! That's what would make my

summer beautiful. Guarantee Mama that I can land him, and she'll pay you room and board to have me. That's how desperate *she* is to get me married."

"Blix, I'm serious."

"Don't think I'm not. Or Mother. Here she is. She wants to talk to you."

There was a moment's silence. Mother drying her hands on her apron and running in from the kitchen. My dream was summer. It wasn't Blix's dream. Would I never learn that dreams can't be shared? Still less, imposed? Walking down a zinnia row. Keeping track of sunset colors. Remarking on heat records. Fine work for a disappointed Henry Ryecroft or stoical Marcus Aurelius. The old, the unmated, the timid, the resigned. Blix was a young girl looking for a man. Not resigned yet.

Mama wasn't either.

"Petty? What's this about Everett having a job for Blix?"

"It's a fact. In the dry-shed. She could clear two or three hundred dollars if she wanted to."

"Well, my gosh, what a godsend! Any place would be better for her than here. She's out every night with a different boy. Go, go, go. That's her whole creed and doctrine. Get away from this crew and make some money, too! And you'd be such a good influence on her, petty."

"Don't count on that. I'm reaching the dangerous age."

"Don't joke. Blix'll ruin her health carrying on like this. She ought to be married."

"I can't promise that."

"You'd help her. You'd be just what she needs. Have you got room for Blackie up there, too?"

"Do you want him married off?"

"It would be a relief. But who'd have him? No, I want him on a ranch and working. And earning his school clothes. Can Everett use him?"

"Sure. He'll need more workers than he can find."

"I don't want to impose on you and Everett. Saddle you with Basil and Blix both, if it don't suit."

"It's suits fine," I assured Mother. "It makes my summer."

It did. But not the summer I had dreamed of. Though I can't honestly say that I wasn't with the summer that happened.

Blix and Blackie arrived at four o'clock on a Saturday afternoon.

I had expected them sooner. I thought they'd start early to avoid driving in the heat of the day. But Blix was always a slow starter, an evening girl. I heard her Model T coupé turn in the driveway. There was no mistaking it. It was made up of loose parts; each kept its own time, and played its own tune. I couldn't see the car until it passed the kitchen windows; and all I could do then by way of greeting was to shout. I was busy with something that couldn't be dropped.

3

Blix and I, twenty-five years later, talked about her arrival that distant summer day at the ranch in Brenner.

In our nights of frequent waking and short, drugged sleeping, we had discovered that certain memories were gateways through which we could enter the past. Not all memories were gateways. Some proved, unexpectedly, to be walls; and some of these walls, in addition to barring entrance, were flinty and hard, studded with glass and nails. I slammed Blix against such a wall once.

My intention, I believe, was good; though it seems to me now (undrugged, unsleepy) to have been at the very least stupid, possibly sadistic. Jesus, Jesus! I offered that intelligent woman on her deathbed the wicked comfort of, "Look how much worse it might be. Look what others have also suffered!" What kind of solace is that? Ask someone burdened by fate to contemplate the greater burdens fate has imposed on another? Nevertheless I did it. I showed her the picture of "how it might have been," complete with details. I told her of the death of our father's mother.

"They had moved to a mean, dirty little house set deep in a lonely woods," I told her. "On a muddy lane off the main road.

168

It was the fifth move that year. There was no one near that she knew. No friends. No relations. No money. Bedfast. In pain. She wrote Father: 'If I had two dollars I would invest it in a bottle of port wine. Joel' (her youngest son) 'writes me that he knows a woman with my trouble that two bottles cured.' "

Blix said very low, "Don't," then she turned away from me to face the wall.

Our grandmother Lavinia Murphy had Blix's "trouble." She never got the two-dollar wine. In two months' time she was dead. She would have died, wine or no wine. What had made me think that an account of the lonely, ignorant, poverty-stricken death of Lavinia Murphy would cause Blix to say, "Hurrah! I'm better off than she was."

This was the worst I did. Slowly, making mistakes, we learned which were the "gateway" experiences, the experiences by which we could enter the past. They had one characteristic in common: they had to be experiences of love, of joy, of delight. Once inside, we might move on to happenings of any kind: ludicrous, painful, selfish, wicked. This didn't faze us. If the start had been right, we could tolerate them. They were a part of life.

One miserable night, or one night that started miserable, while the infection, which later cleared up, still plagued her, Blix awakened and said, "Gosh, I think I'm well." She wasn't but the antibiotics had suddenly taken hold. She felt convalescent, herself again. As late as that afternoon, every sign pointing downhill, Milt had said to me, "I don't see anything for it but that handful of pills."

I had walked quickly away from him. With "that handful of pills" I was more deeply involved than he; but, like any other hypocrite, my mind was unwilling to face the word for the act. Now, only twelve hours later, Blix was lighting a cigarette, looking about her room with relish.

"You fed me with a spoon while I was sick, didn't you?" She spoke like a child who says, "I remember it snowed on my second birthday." Something dreamy, long ago, and remembered with wonder.

"You wouldn't let me feed you much," I told her.

"I'm hungry now."

Few words have made me happier. "What? Tell me what?"

"Clam chowder and coffee ice cream."

The clam chowder, thank God, was easy to make. Coffee ice cream is even easier: vanilla ice cream with instant coffee stirred in it. We had a feast, a festival, a resurrection. A bright night, still and clear, no coyotes, the rest of the valley asleep. Blix was talkative. Not about the days she'd just been through, or the days yet to come. The past of past years, not the past of past days. She knew the entrance doorways as well as I, though we never spoke of them as such to each other, or even admitted they existed.

4

Blix began our talk of that past summer in Brenner.

"It was her earrings that made her so darling, I think," Blix said. "And being naked. The two together."

Blix didn't have to say another word. We knew whose earrings. We'd used those earrings before. They were a proved gateway.

When Blix and Blackie came into the kitchen that hot Saturday afternoon in July, they saw at once why I hadn't been able to run out to greet them. I had a Mexican baby in the sink, giving her a bath. She was naked, of course, except for her earrings. I would have taken them off, but her ears were pierced, and I didn't understand how to unfasten them.

"I've always thought," Blix said, "that that baby was the most beautiful child I've ever seen."

"Not more beautiful than Sara." Sara was Blix's daughter. Perhaps tonight the earrings would be the gate to Sara.

But Blix's thoughts didn't move in that direction. She continued to talk of Josephina Sanchez, the child I had been bathing.

Josephina was two years old, brown by nature, but a coating of dust and apricot juice usually gave her a pink-stucco tinge. When I finished washing her, she was brown again. I sat her on the sink board to dry her; and drying, mixed with peek-a-booing and snuggling, took some time. Blix didn't leave, but she herself did no fondling, made no baby talk.

Blix once told me that she had never been at ease with children, that she had not felt comfortable with her own daughter. "I was always self-conscious with Sara. I never could think of anything to say to her."

This was easy to believe. Blix talking to Sara sounded like a Republican senator attempting to converse with a sparrow. The senator's predicament was more understandable than Blix's. *He* had never been a sparrow. Blix had once been a child; or, having had a child's shape, we had taken her to be one. Who can tell about these things? It is true she had always aligned herself with her parents, not with sister and brothers. "Us and the kids," she'd say to Mother and Father. And all kids, even her own child, remained strange to her. Once when she said she hadn't been a good mother to her daughter, I tried to reassure her.

"Sara," I reminded her, "was a very special case."

This, whether or not it reassured Blix, was God's truth. Sara was a female Le Cid, which is infinitely more special than being a male Le Cid. She was a mathematician, a physicist; she had a high-bridged nose, plum-black hair, and Blix's big, slant-set eyes.

Blix agreed about Sara's being a special case. "Sure, I know. How many kids have an I.Q. of 185? Or eyes that shade of violet? But it wouldn't have made any difference if her I.Q. had been 90 and her eyes pale blue. Kids make me uncomfortable."

"Like a cat with a dog?"

"Oh no. Nothing like that. I'm not mad at them. Or scared of them. I just don't feel comfortable with them."

"Blix," Sara once told me (Sara called her father and mother, by their request, "Milt" and "Blix"), "never kissed me after I was ten years old."

"Not when you got your degrees? Not when you were married?"

"No, never."

I didn't ask Sara why. I never asked Blix why; and I don't *know* why. Was it part of her decision to put head over heart? Was she soured on touch? Or children? Or Milt's child? Was it a part of her dislike of demonstrativeness? Of Mother's uninhibited groans and belches? Blackie's bellowing? My exuberance? In any case, she didn't change. Before asking me to stay with her, Blix had made me promise that there'd be no tears, no moans, no sighs. "I couldn't stand it if you cried."

Though Blix had kept her distance when I dried and dressed Josephina, she went with me to return the baby to her mother. The Mexicans had set up their tents in the apricot orchard west of the house; perhaps a hundred people, counting the children, were living there. It was like walking through a Mexican village. It *was* a Mexican village. Fires were burning, suppers cooking, goats blatting. Mexican men, through with work, were washing up at the weir box. Others were playing their guitars and singing. Handsome Domingo Garcia played his violin. Children ran up and down the tree rows, shouting at their evening games. All girls over twelve had put on their best (transparent georgette blouses and high-heeled patent-leather pumps, if they owned them) and were parading amid the bean pots and campfires in a Brenner version of the *paseo*.

I put Josephina in her mother's arms. Mrs. Sanchez was a widow with seven children, all of whom, with the exception of Josephina, worked. The oldest son, Manuel, was in charge of sulphuring. Manuel, stripped to the waist, from his evening washdown, came to the Sanchez tent while Blix and I were there. Wet and dripping, he was smooth and sleek as a seal. He was part Indian, of course, but there wasn't a thing of the local Sobobas, who were a pudding-faced lot, about him. His nose and jaw line had come to him from Spain with Cortez. Only his color was Mexico's contribution.

I was in love with Manuel. I didn't know whether Blix knew it or not; in any case, I didn't want her to know it. Before, I had never been ashamed of being in love. True, I didn't talk about

172

it. Any more than I talked about John Keats's death. Or what I would wish for if given three wishes. But I wasn't ashamed of it. I didn't feel like an unfaithful wife. Or even a wife hoping to be unfaithful. I didn't, I suppose, coming right down to it, feel like a wife at all. What I felt in those previous "love affairs" was a schoolgirl infatuation for a storybook hero. The difference was that I wrote (with my heart) stories about heroes who were real. And I was real, too. Not a substitute for anyone. Not Fanny Brawne or Cathy Earnshaw. I was Tasmania Murphy, my own heroine. And if my storekeepers and bus drivers and track stars were no Sidney Cartons or Heathcliffs, they, at least, had more than ink in their veins. (Though at this date I can't see that it really made much difference.)

It did then. What a real person felt for other real persons I considered real. And the secrecy enhanced it. I was love's secret agent; and no one guessed it! I inhabited a magic world. Far from being ashamed of what I felt, I rejoiced in it. I possessed an unexpected treasure. I lived in an invisible world. A resolve to "be with" summer could have been made only by someone trying unconsciously to break away from unreality, to try the unusual experience of living where he was, a real part of a real season.

What I felt about Manuel was what I felt about that particular summer. I hadn't wanted to "be with" other summers. Any more than a child with a make-believe playmate wants that playmate to materialize. What he loves is make-believe, not playmates. It was the same with me. Or had been. My world of love had been a childlike world. My discontent with it was a sign of growing up. Was I beginning to be ashamed of leading a life of make-believe? I'm not sure. Anyway, I didn't want make-believe with Manuel. I wanted to be with him, talk to him, touch him. Such desires I knew were shameful. And I wanted to hide them from Blix.

First of all, I was supposed to be an example to her. And a married woman yearning after her husband's sulphur foreman is not exemplary. Secondly, only six months ago I had been preaching red-hot non-touch sermons to Blix on the subject of her and Vurl. True, I didn't know what I was talking about. That hadn't kept me quiet. Sometimes you don't know that the house you live in is glass until the stone you cast comes boomeranging back. Maybe that's the actual reason you threw it. Something in you was yelling, "I want out." The life you saved, as well as the glass you shattered, was your own.

Apart from shamefulness, there was the craziness of it. That might have hit Blix hardest of all. "How crazy can you get!" A case on a Mexican apricot worker, the chief support of a mother and six younger brothers and sisters. I knew the questions Blix would ask. "Has he any decent clothes? Would you ride in that broken-down truck of his? Would you take all the kids along? What would you use for money? What could you talk about? Don't you care anything about what John Everett would think?"

If I answered any of these questions truthfully, I would give everything away. Truck, money, kids, talks: I didn't care. As to John Everett, there was no problem. I could've told John Everett all I felt, and he would have laughed merrily. If he hadn't taken my conversations with God seriously, what would he think of my wish to know a greaser? Silly. Nothing he couldn't put an end to. "Who do you think you are? Ramona? And Manuel's another Alessandro? You've been reading too many novels. Come on up to bed and I'll give you the cure."

That's what he would have said if I'd told him. As it was, he didn't say anything about The Cure or anything else. He went off to bed every night very early. He yawned at the supper table; he yawned and stumbled all the way up the stairs. He had begun to fear that he had bitten off more than he could chew. Dried-apricot prices were not holding up. If he failed to pick fruit at its prime, to dry and sulphur it perfectly, he might easily finish the summer bankrupt, owing the ranchers he had bought from, and with tons of unsalable dried fruit on hand. He was up at daybreak. He made a real effort to determine at which ranches fruit needed picking. It went against his grain to be anything but the bountiful *padrone* to his Mexicans, but he

174

was firmer with them than he had ever been before. Rotten cots, even overripe cots, were to be discarded by the cutters, not plopped down on the trays, with seeds thumbed out. Kids were not to relieve themselves against the stacked trays of cut cots. Checkers were not to check their girl friends' boxes twice. Pickers were not to shake trees of well-ripened fruit. The chances of getting a poor dry were endless; and Everett, working to prevent this, was worn out by the end of the day. After supper, he would go into the living room, stretch out on the wicker settee, and open the week's *Saturday Evening Post*. He never did more than open it. The very sight of the print put him to sleep. It lay opened across his chest, a pygmy pup tent, from each end of which Everett, eyes closed and stockinged toes twitching, extended gigantically. Unlike Blackie, Everett did not resist being awakened. He opened his eyes easily and, though he stumbled, climbed the stairs docilely. Once Everett was in bed, Blackie and I were ready for an evening with the Sanchezes.

It would still be light, a hot summer dusk, supper fires quenched, cicadas and Mexican babies crying, guitars plaintive. Later, lights would go on in the cutting shed, and cutters, between seven-thirty and ten, would turn out as much work as they had between one and five. But at dusk there was a respite. At that hour it was cooler outside than inside. Doors shut all day were opened. The house exchanged its smells of applesauce, fried potatoes, and newly ironed clothes for wood smoke, chili, and the pungent brandy scent of rotten apricots. There were shadows in the corners of all rooms. A mockingbird, too hot till then to utter a note, imitated Domingo's downward-sliding trill, liked it, and tried again. It was then Blackie would say, "Let's go out and talk to Manuel about boxing, Tassie."

"All things work together for good for those who love the Lord," Mama used to say humbly and reverently when some of her own sacrificial energy had paid off. The saying was a charm, really; an incantation used to convince the Lord that His creatures weren't giving themselves credit for what was really all

His doing. That saying would be a good deal more true if it stopped short of "the Lord." All things work together for good for those who love.

When Mother proposed that Blackie, as well as Blix, spend the summer on the ranch, I saw the summer I was longing to "be with" vanish. Heaven knows, I doted on Blackie, but with Blackie on the ranch, what I'd be "with," I feared, would be cook-stove, skillet, and washboard.

I doted on Blackie; he was a man for all seasons, but *which* season was never very clear or important. And what I wanted that summer was summer. Not knowing yet that Manuel would be my summer. Only my love for Blackie had made it possible for me to answer Mama's proposal with enthusiasm. "Of course. I'd love to have him," I had told her.

So my love brought Blackie to the ranch; and once there, he became love's unwitting servant, providing me with excuses to be with Manuel.

Blackie was mad about boxing, and the minute he heard that the Mexican in charge of sulphuring was Manuel Sanchez he gave a whoop.

"Kid Sanchez! What's he doing here?"

"Working!"

"Working! What's he working for? He could be middleweight champ."

Blackie was a boxing fan. He knew the histories of boxers, had memorized their statistics, could demonstrate their styles. He'd seen Manuel fight at the Pico Arena. He knew all the fights he'd been in, who he'd knocked out, and in what round. He was an authority on Manuel's specialties. Manuel was a boxer with a punch, the best and rarest combination in the world, according to Blackie. Sluggers usually hadn't any skill; and the ones with skill lacked a punch. Manuel was a killer, but a stylish one. He had a k.o. punch, but he enjoyed fighting. He took a cat's good and graceful time for the kill.

It never occurred to Blackie that I wasn't as fascinated listening to explanations of jabs, hooks, uppercuts, and kidney punches as he was; that the old one-two wasn't as endlessly interesting to me as to him. He thought he was doing me a favor, inviting me to go with him to his boxing seminars. He was, of course. Josephina provided some excuse for my going out to the Sanchez tent, but I could see Josephina all day long when Manuel wasn't there.

Blackie sometimes asked Blix to go with us. But Blix didn't care for boxing. Or Manuel. And she had no intention of spending a hot evening sitting on a field box in the midst of dust, beans, and kids, listening to Manuel, at Blackie's prompting, re-fight his fights.

"You get Domingo to play his violin, and I'll go with you, Blackie," she told him.

But Blackie wasn't interested in violin playing and I wasn't interested in the handsome Domingo, so we never made the switch. Once in a while I said no to Blackie's invitations. But I didn't have to do this often. Blix knew that where Blackie went, I went. But she was no dunce; and she would have a hard time convincing herself that love of Blackie alone would make me endure so much prize fighting at second hand on sweltering evenings.

I hoped she didn't notice the dresses I put on for these orchard refights, dresses of a kind I think don't exist any more: "summer dresses" of voile, organdy, dotted swiss; dresses ruffled, tucked, trimmed with rows of ribbon and lace. One yellow dress, I remember, had twelve rows of lace at the hem, eight at the scoop neck. I remember easily; I had laboriously sewed all that lace on. The dress had been a part of my handmade trousseau. Another, a lavender voile, had swinging panels, encrusted with rows of violet ribbon. They were no longer new dresses. Their average cost, homemade, was probably $3.98. But they were not apricot-orchard or cutting-shed dresses, either. They were dresses that made me as pretty as possible; that said, "Woman"; dresses that said, "The day's work is over." I was aware, as I walked with Blackie to the Sanchez tent, of the soft sibilance of those full skirts rustling about my knees. Aware of a neckline scooped low

177

enough to show the first rise of bosom, of puff sleeves displaying rounded arms, of the scent of Yardley's violets. All of these awarenesses I added together, in an attempt to sum up for me something, some question still unanswerable, some yearning unnamable, and for which I wanted an unknown response.

Manuel was always waiting for us. If he had to be looking after the sulphuring, he would leave word that he would stop by whenever he had time. I took heart from this. Other Mexican young men went into town after work, or sat drinking a concoction they made out of overripe apricots and near-beer. Or they went deep into the orchard with the high-heeled girls. But Manuel was always either at his tent or working; he was always washed, combed, in a clean shirt, a shirt he had laundered himself. I knew. From my bedroom window I could see him, early in the morning, washing it. He hung it on one of the guy ropes of his tent; by nightfall it was dry, unironed, but fresh and clean.

It occurred to me, of course, that Manuel, having been a boxer, might enjoy talking about himself and boxing even more than Blackie enjoyed listening, that he would have turned up as faithfully each night if Blackie's sister had been Blackie's grandmother. It occurred to me that Manuel, knowing which side his bread was buttered on, and hoping that there might be a winter job for a good worker, was more interested in his boss's response to him than the response of his boss's wife.

Such thoughts crossed my mind. I didn't let them linger. They belittled Manuel. It was not necessary, in order to inure myself against disappointment, to attribute vanity and self-seeking to someone else. I choose to believe in the reality of the goodness that I felt, to believe in the closeness, beyond words, that I experienced as Manuel explained and illustrated boxing techniques to Blackie. He often looked at me. His look, it seemed to me, was like the one I gave him in return: grave, fond, and admiring; though what he could admire about me, except that I wore pretty dresses and was good to his family, I didn't know. Manuel possessed that teeter-totter combination of tenderness and toughness that provides just the tension emotionally a woman desires.

178

She wants and admires both, will follow either, but a balancing of the two holds her. So there was Manuel, the boxer with a k.o. punch who had given it all up to be a father to his six brothers and sisters. And there was I, late admirer of postmen, tempest-tossed by grocers, susceptible to schoolboys. It was summer and I was with it.

Workers handsomer than Manuel were camped in our apricot orchard that summer. Mexicans, delicately boned, liquid-eyed, with silky down-drooping mustaches; blocky toro boys with obsidian eyes, who once had used the obsidian knives on the old sacrificial altars. Manuel was neither of these: a young man of medium height; on the stocky side; brown, not black, hair; a mouthful of white, though crooked, teeth. But possessing that irresistible temperamental teeter-totter.

Blix was with me all that summer, free to see all that there was to be seen. But she had a real, not an imaginary, courtship on her hands; Milt Hollister was providing more interesting things for her to do than to listen to her kid brother, her married sister, and an ex-boxer talk prize fighting. And I didn't tell her a thing. I had the habit of silence. My daydream love affairs had been too unreal to talk about. By talk, I would have destroyed them, even for myself. Watching with burning cheeks a grocer put potatoes in a sack! Had I mentioned that, the sound of my own words would have made me laugh. How ridiculous! I couldn't speak about Manuel for the opposite reason. He was too real. A word would tell what I really felt—and I was ashamed of what I really felt. I could and did talk to Blackie. He thought my passion for Manuel was a passion for boxing—a passion he considered natural.

VII

During our autumn nights of alternating sleeplessness and drugged sleep, Blix and I often spoke of that long past summer. We had been in it together. But at the time, we had been tongue-tied. Or unobservant. Or bashful. Now in our nights of pain and joy, we made each other gifts of what then we had withheld. Sometimes, in the midst of talking, insights, as new to speaker as to listener, came to us. We were mutually amazed. Silenced. How could we have been so blind so long? Illuminations denied us in the far-off summer became our autumn rewards. We didn't seek them. That would have invalidated them. They sought us. Oh, they did. They came rushing. They shook us with truths palpable, but unimagined. "So *that* was it." "*That* was what he was trying to say." "*That* was what I really wanted."

Blix would narrow her drug-dilated eyes. She would take a sharpshooter's bead on a truth momentarily glimpsed: was it real? It was real. It was God's truth, some years delayed, but sure as shooting now. She would lean back against her pillows, smiling. In the midst of death we had discovered instant life. Formula: mix the memories of two people around a single past event and reconstitute with nighttime knowledge. We didn't create something that never was: we created persons, able at long last to see what had actually been.

All of our illuminations weren't mutual. We achieved some solo. Blix, for instance, had no need to learn that a hard death isn't made easier by hearing of a harder one. It was in the midst of my account of Grandma Murphy's death, in that lonely house in the dark woods, that I learned this. Never since have I tried to solace a man torn by dogs with reminders of Christians and lions.

Some discoveries, perhaps mutual, perhaps not, were never mentioned. I rediscovered clowning. It is the means by which we are able to contemplate tragedy without tears. It wasn't a new act for me. I had been a great clown when young. My life, growing happier as I grew older, had less need of the act. When I was young, the only differences between me and Chaplin were sex, size (I was larger), a mustache and money. Chaplin was paid in money; I was paid in attention. I was paid in the greatest prize of all: irresponsibility. I could take the coward's escape: say it, then disavow it. "Hey, you didn't take me seriously, did you? For heaven's sake! I was only kidding."

For Blix's sake (I thought) I took up my clowning again. The insights of another decade may reveal that my clowning then, as earlier, was a clown's escape. Coward's, I meant to say.

One real insight, though, was that life is actually funny, downright tragically absurd.

"Side-splitting," Blix said, "though what I've been is belly-split, not side-split."

The comic can't be manufactured for however good a purpose. You can shed a false tear and fool yourself. The false laugh won't even fool a listener. The comic is inherent; otherwise nonexistent. It can't be laid on. During our long autumn dialogue, Blix and I laughed a lot. Not loud, not loud. "White on the winter night, your breath is cloud." We knew that. But when the paroxysm of laughter grabbed our stomachs, we didn't hold back on anything.

So we laughed in the night. Had funny insights, were happy. Were amazed to be happy. "How can this be?" we asked ourselves. We didn't "look on the bright side." After my horrible story of Grandma Murphy there was no more saying, "Things could be worse." I pretended nothing to spare Blix, nor she me. When she told me that she didn't want me around if I was going to do a lot of crying, she wasn't thinking of the wear and tear on me, but on her. Neither Blix nor I believed that this life was a preparation for another. This was it. A sleep would round it off; and sleep was not far away.

Still we laughed. We remembered. We listened to the wind and the coyotes. We turned on the TV. We had callers. We discussed them. We ate and commented on the quality of the food. He scanned headlines. We were amazed by early rain, delighted with Dr. Reyes, disgusted with get-well cards.

"How can it be?" we asked. "How can it be?"

We talked about it. Our happiness was strong enough to bear looking at.

No more resentment. We knew that.

A return to the pattern in which we had grown up. Big sister, protective; little sister, dependent. Youth, in that. Dailiness. The time being short gave us time for each day's events. We weren't getting through today for the sake of tomorrow.

The gains were all chiefly mine. I knew that. They were gifts Blix gave me. In the first place, I wasn't dying. That wasn't her gift; and yet by dying she enhanced my living. We both knew that. In her bed, she pointed out to me pleasures I took for granted: running and jumping. Breathing. Blowing my nose. Seeing the dark come down.

There was another gift she made me. I had discovered earlier, with Mama, the power complete physical devotion has to bless. There was not, with Mama, or anyone else, an iota of the nurse in me. Schoolmates who dreamed of being nurses filled me with distaste. They seemed to verge on the unwholesome. Perhaps it was this very distaste, conquered, that made my care of Mama so transfiguring.

She was often ailing; painfully at home, desperately in hospitals after serious operations. In the hospitals she was always at loggerheads with everyone; with the possible exception of some handsome young doctor with a sense of humor. A hospital by definition is a place where when they make tea, water results. This went against Mother's grain. So did hot-water bottles half-filled, toast half-cold, and nurses halfhearted. *She* went against the nurses' grain. They dearly loved a quiet sufferer, a patient who swallowed without protest whatever was handed her, who would suffer rather than ring for a bedpan, who, when asked, "How are we feeling this morning?" never told the truth.

Mother did none of this. In sickness she did not become a different person. Never subservient in health, in sickness, irritated by pain, she became less so. She lifted the covers and gave indifferent nurses unexpected and galvanizing kicks. If a bedpan wasn't forthcoming, she moaned, groaned, and shouted.

"Isn't she deft," Mother said to me, syrupy-sweet, of a nurse bumbling about her bedside.

"Did she call me daft?" the nurse demanded, getting the drift, if missing the word.

So I was often Mama's nurse. With nursing, as with summer, the only criterion is, "Are you with it?" At the patient's bedside you cannot lead your life. If you are to have any life at all, it must be his. You must become his hands, his feet, his ears and eyes. Suffer with him, if not for him. The stinks, the sweats, the complaints, the horrid sounds. Be with them and emerge sanctified. Not because of unselfishness. Or love. Or devotion. Because of concentration. Concentration blesses. That's the power of love, crime, and creativity. And nursing also if practiced to the point of sweat and self-forgetfulness and identification.

Eased by my efforts, Mother sometimes held out her supple long-fingered hand. "Oh, petty," she'd say, complete understanding of what you'd done in those words.

Whether she spoke or not, I had blessed myself with my act. Two people united in an act of love; the calm that follows is pretty much the same, whatever the act.

183

Mother didn't change so long as she had breath in her lungs.

Once she wrote me, "My poor dear Tassie." (There was nothing wrong with me.) "I feel like I've had a breast carved off." (She had.) "Woe is me. My meals are brought to me. My medicine is poured out and put into my mouth. My kinfolk have failed me and my familiar friends forgotten me. They that dwell in my house count me for a stranger. When knickknacks and tidbits are brought to me they eat the edibles and give me the others. Yea, and though get-well cards give great pleasure, yet crave I the edible tidbits—or at least to see them. Yea, curiosity eateth me like as a cat devoureth a mouse.

"I am stripped of my glory and destroyed on every side . . . especially the right front side.

"My sighing cometh before I eat and my roarings are poured forth like the waters, for the thing I greatly feared hath come upon me. I was born not for safety, neither have I rest. Know ye I am down and out. Doth the wild ass bray when he has fodder? Or loweth the ox when the grass is under his nose?

"Therefore I will refrain not my mouth, for my nose was blistered with anesthetics and my fodder is withheld. When I lie down I say, When shall I rise and the nite be gone? And I would be full of tossings to and fro until the dawning of day if it didn't hurt me so badly to toss.

"I am full of codeine and would I were out in the woods and covered with a tarpaulin."

Thus with Biblical rhythms she rocked her pain to sleep and dreamed of finding ease in the woods of her childhood, woods that didn't exist in Southern California.

What's your reply to a letter like that?

Or to a phone call like this?

Father: Your mother is wandering in her mind.

Tassie: What makes you think so?

Father: She says she is seeing things.

Tassie: What kind of things does she see?

Father: Nitwits. She says she is surrounded by nitwits.

Tassie: Who is there?

Father: No one at all. Not a soul but me and the doctor.

I smiled. It was a cheerful report. Mama was in her right mind and absolutely herself. But what's your reply to a phone call like that?

On a cold January night at the beginning of her final illness she arose in the middle of the night and lighted, on the lip of the gas heater, a fire of newspapers and pine kindling. She managed it well, and warmed herself without bothering anyone. In the befuddlement of a stroke's aftermath, she had forgotten that the wood fires of her Kentucky girlhood had been replaced by gas. And she had been comforted as well as warmed, no doubt, by the sight and smell of a wood fire.

The unimaginative healthy asked only: "Why didn't she light the gas?" Prophesied only, "She'll burn the house down." Blamed themselves not at all for failure to keep an invalid's room warm.

Placed finally, for such reasons, in a place neither homelike nor restful, and for these reasons called a "rest home," she turned her face to the wall, and never again looked out of the door through which she had been led to her betrayal. Too diffident to express her religious yearnings, she had neither Bible nor preacher to comfort her. A horse in his stall dies surrounded by more of what has given his life meaning. Once, filled with some kind of momentary intuition, I recited to her a poem I had learned as a girl: Whittier's "I know not where His islands lift their fronded palms in air: I only know I cannot drift beyond His love and care." The words soothed her. Her hands unclenched; the lids over her eyes relaxed. She lifted a finger and kept tremulous time to the marching beat of the verse. I said it through twice. As I began for the third time, she opened her eyes and gave me her old green-eyed look of lively scorn. "Don't you know anything else?" she demanded tartly.

I dredged my mind for something Biblical, and found more than I had ever known was there. Mother, though I was neither ordained nor accurately Scriptural, accepted me as a substitute better than nothing.

The last time I saw her, three days before her death, she mistook me for her own mother.

"Mama," she said, as I entered the room.

"It's the other way round," I told her. "You're the mama, not me."

Her look was both mischievous and shrewd. "It doesn't matter much which way it goes, just so one of us is."

The death of her body didn't trouble me greatly. Her body was sixty-three years old and worn out. The dust of bodies layers the earth. Mice and mosquitoes are killed in every home. Children are run over. Hunters travel thousands of miles to get a good rack of horns. We weigh down our tables with the flesh of the meek and the frolicsome. Dust to dust is the appointed round of flesh. But what about dreams? What about the dreams of Maude Hobhouse? What I mourned when Maude Hobhouse died was the death of her dreams. Built of love and fear and misinformation and talent, she'd raised a tower of dreams; and was still at it when she died. It was an edifice I was at home in, and a home I lost when her fabrications ceased.

Blix, unlike Mother, was easy to care for. She was not completely bedfast; she wanted no recitations of John Greenleaf Whittier. I could not achieve sanctification by sweat with her. But I had the same bedside happiness. Some war was over, some peace achieved. Was it a war I had lost? Had I accepted enslavement? If so, enslavement was what I'd always craved. Nothing to be proud of: the goal of masochists; the pulse-quickener of enamored women. But inside of this enslavement, if that was what it was, I found freedom. Freedom from choice. I had a nun's happiness. My vocation enveloped me.

Of course I wasn't relinquishing much. Pete was more or less lost to me at that time anyway. I never followed him around to the tournaments. I had a leave of absence from my job. About the only thing I no longer had time for (or interest in) was the history of the Hobhouse family, begun ten years before Mama died as a present for her. I had kept on with it, partly because I thought she'd be pleased to have it completed, partly because I was mulish. And possibly because, as Blix had said long ago, I had a yen for the unobtainable. The past is a mystery. We can

186

never recover even a part of it, absolutely. The present surrounds us. Anyone can take an easy handful. For that reason I undervalued the present and pursued the past.

In Blix's room all that changed. In Blix's room I saw the present becoming the past. I saw that departure was more mysterious than the departed. I saw that what had vanished (all those Hobhouses) was easier to reconstruct—who's to contradict you? —than the present. Blix, on her bed, with make-up, French twist, and time bomb ticking away inside her, was far more of an enigma than any Hobhouse I could "re-create." The puzzles you make up, you can solve. Miss Historical Hobhouse would in large part be made up by me. Blix was no creation of mine.

It is unexplainable. Blix, dying, reconciled me to the present. Death canceled out all the blandness, all the banalities of the present. Its silence smothered the hum of air conditioners, refrigerators, jets, automobiles, power lawn mowers, electric can openers, and carving knives. Was death then what I cared for? No, life. Life is so much more dangerous and uncertain. Mama's Hobhouses, moving westward, had lost their meaning for me. The frontier was right there in Blix's room. She was the only explorer I had ever seen. She was going to cross a river deeper than the Missouri, wider than the Mississippi.

Blix didn't worry a whit about poor Pete, three strokes off the lead in the Portland Open. She didn't worry about my job. She did worry about Hobhouses. She considered them my peculiar concern, a grail I had chosen to follow. She didn't want to be responsible for my defection.

I couldn't tell her that I had lost my taste for those old-timers. That would have made her feel guilty. Made her feel that she had robbed me of something I held dear. And how was I to explain to her what I didn't understand myself? "Your dying has reconciled me to the present"? How could I say that? I couldn't.

I said, "I would never have thought I could be happy here . . . now, doing just what I am."

Blix answered, "Me, too. Isn't it strange?"

Stranger for Blix than for me, of course. I wasn't dying. In my

187

prison I had found freedom. In hers she was awaiting, after suitable torture, execution. Only, that was the point. She didn't propose to be tortured or to keep her date with the executioner. What Blix was planning was an escape. Because, when she had written me saying, "Sister, dear sister," I had answered, "I am with you in this all the way." I was with her in planning the escape. Plotting is perhaps the better word. Dr. Reyes was the only one we hoped to win over. There were plenty of others who had to be outwitted. Blix had been condemned. Almost everyone wanted to see that the sentence was properly carried out.

Everyone except Pete, Milt, Le Cid, and I. "The hell with the others," Blix said when we discussed them. "It's my funeral."

So we planned, plotted, organized, lied. The supplies were laid in, the risks calculated, emergencies, to the best of our ability, foreseen.

"We'll outfox them, won't we, Tassie?"

I thought we would. We were like those prisoners in *The Bridge Over the River Kwai*. We were so busy building the bridge we had no time to worry about who, finally, was going to use it.

We never talked about it, but this may have been the chief reason for our happiness. We had a future to plan for. Planning, we lost sight of what this future was. Also, in addition to the pleasure of planning, we experienced the downright mean satisfactions of craftiness and defiance. We were putting something over on quite a few people. This gave Blix a lot of satisfaction. She was choosing. She was not a victim.

The first thing Blix said when I saw her in the morning (I awakened later than she did) was, "Are they still there?" That was the second thing, actually. The first was to send Vida, the day nurse, off on some errand. Not until Vida had gone could Blix ask me that question. Those pills meant everything to her; and it was Vida's duty as a dedicated nurse to smell them out and confiscate them. Vida was no match for Blix and me, though.

"Our only trouble," I told Blix, "is that we're going to hide these pills someday in some such far-out place neither one of us will be able to remember where."

We always remembered, though; and they were always where we remembered them.

Recently, talking with Pete of those nights of hiding and mornings of looking, he surprised me by asking, "Wouldn't it have been more logical to put those pills under lock and key and have been done with your games of hide-and-seek?"

The question surprised me for two reasons. First, because such an idea had never at the time, or since, occurred to me. And second, because Pete is usually more understanding than that.

What did logic have to do with what was going on in that room? And how many games did we have left to play? As well suggest to children playing blindman's bluff that they could find each other more easily if they took the blindfold off. They don't want it easy. Blix didn't want it easy. There were very few ways left, except in the endurance of pain, in which she could demonstrate her powers. Fooling the bright-eyed Vida was one of them. She was not yet ready, she who had always driven too fast, smoked too much, and danced too long, to live without risk. Life had been lived with risk. Death, which is life's last act, she would move toward precariously.

"Perhaps," Pete said, "she really wanted the pills to be found. Perhaps she really wanted to be spared at the final moment. She, strong and willing—but the pills nowhere to be found."

"I think," I told Pete, fumbling to explain an act that had at the time seemed to me to have no alternative, "that Blix was willing to give the other side a sporting chance. If they had the power and luck to win, okay. But I could never have said to Blix—even if the idea had occurred to me—and it didn't, 'I'll just lock these pills up, Blix, and put an end to our hide-and-seek.' I couldn't have done it. There was too much that was inevitable in that room. Too little that we could control."

"You could've controlled those pills absolutely," Pete said, "with a little better planning."

"'Absolutely' was what we didn't want. We wanted a taste of victory fresh and *not* inevitable each day."

189

Pete said, "I wasn't actually criticizing you girls, you know."

"Yes you were. You were criticizing us for not being men and not being well and not sizing up the situation objectively. My God, Pete, how much golf would you play if the whole situation was cut and dried?"

"Golf's a game, not a matter of life and death."

"Life and death was the only game we had. And we played it. Inside a chanceless pattern we took some chances."

I don't know whether Pete ever really understood or not. Even after I'd explained how it had really happened, he kept thinking of more sensible ways of taking care of those pills. Locking them in my suitcase, for instance, even though he knows I don't have a suitcase key to my name. And knows, or should know, that if they had been locked there, we would have played the same game even more hazardously with a small easily lost key. There is something terribly circumstantial about even the best masculine mind. Like Papa, more interested in the radio tubes than in any word or song it might produce. In any case, whatever we should have done, what we did was to hide those pills in a variety of places in Blix's room. Actually, with her there constantly, the biggest risk we took probably *was* losing them ourselves.

We never did; and once they were located, we went over the Escape Plan. Refined and embellished it. Tom and Huck couldn't have been more excited planning their trip. Big river ahead. Raft to equip and launch. Authorities to hoodwink. Extreme danger. Unimaginable adventures. All, Blix's gift to me. She, the daring Huck. I the go-along (and only part-way) Tom.

"Except for Dr. Reyes, we haven't any problems," Blix said.

I didn't say anything. I knew he was our problem but I didn't have any solution.

"He's your problem," Blix added.

"How's he mine?"

"You know he's not going to talk about this with me. It's not a thing a doctor does with his patient."

"He hasn't shown any inclination to do it with his patient's sister."

"It's you or no one," Blix said.

For a long time I thought it was going to be no one. What more could I say to Dr. Reyes? (Dr. Reyes called Blix, Blix; and me, Tassie. But we never called him John, let alone Johnny; he was far too dignified and intense for that.)

2

Occasionally Dr. Reyes reversed his schedule: visited Blix on his way to the hospital instead of on his way home. When he did this he wasn't tired, but he was hurried, with dates awaiting him that couldn't be postponed in the way, homeward bound, he could postpone dinner.

On these morning visits he often brought Blix flowers from his own garden, flowers he grew himself. He was proud of them. One morning at the beginning of October, after his usual perfunctory knock, he came striding down the hall to Blix's room, bearing a great armload of desert roses, sun-blasted and sand-pitted. There was nothing amiss with their color, though. Saffrons and yellows and bronzes. Or with their warm cinnamony fragrance.

"They're a little wilted," he told Vida. "But you put them in a big jar of tepid, not cold, water, and they'll come out of it in fine shape."

After Vida left, Dr. Reyes told us the most he ever had about his life.

"A doctor with an armload of roses. Grown in my own yard. Beside my own pool. Looked after by my own gardener. You can't have it much better than that, can you?"

He wasn't bragging. He wasn't even rejoicing. He was simply summing things up, holding in his mind's eye his past and his present.

He tried to tell us how it had been: hard enough for any poor boy to find the money for a medical education. Almost impossible for a Mexican. " 'Who'd hire a Mexican doctor if you did get licensed? Except another Mexican. And they don't have any money to pay.' My own father said that."

"What did your mother say?"

"She said, 'You can do it.' I made it hard for my father and mother. When she encouraged me she seemed to my father to be against *him*. Against Mexicans and for whites. She seemed to him to be encouraging me to take a stand against him."

"'Mexicans and whites,'" I said. "Don't talk that way, Dr. Reyes. As if we weren't all human beings together."

"We don't live that way, Mrs. Orcino," he said with unwonted formality, "and you know it. We'd better learn to face the way we really live with words. 'Mexicans *and* whites.' We live that way even now. Better than when I was a boy, but still that way."

"But the pool. The gardener. The roses. Your reputation."

"Okay," said Dr. Reyes. "My reputation. My skill. My training. My license. Take those away and what's left? A peculiar-looking greaser. I'm back where my father was, climbing those date trees."

I'd always admired those men on their fifty-foot ladders.

"That's not so bad," I argued.

Dr. Reyes said, "It's bad if there's something else you can do and want to do and would be better at. I don't want to climb ladders. Washing dishes isn't such a bad job. You want to have to do it because you're the color of a dishwasher?"

"No," I told him, "I don't. I'd fight it. I was praising your father, not defending a system."

"He was part of the system. The system said my mother, who was a good teacher, a high-school teacher of English, couldn't teach any more. Just touching a man the color of my father took away everything she'd learned at Stanford and in the classroom. I'm better off than she was. No one can fire me. I'm licensed to practice medicine. And as long as I'm good at it, and hang onto that license, no one can stop me."

Okay. We knew what he was saying: "Look what I have at stake."

We knew what he had at stake. He didn't have to talk about it. We didn't want him to talk about it. People can change if they aren't bound by the memory of some earlier inflexible declaration of policy. We didn't want Dr. Reyes making any declaration of policy. When the time came we couldn't believe that he wouldn't be with us.

After Dr. Reyes left, Blix said, "Who does he remind you of? Someone we knew somewhere?"

"Domingo," I told her. "The violin player at Brenner."

Blix gazed backward toward that lost summer, backward and backward until she saw Domingo. "Yes, but Domingo was a little la-di-da. I bet he'd faint at the sight of blood. You should see Dr. Reyes at the hospital. He had those nurses going tippy-toe."

"His mother must've been quite a woman."

"To marry a handsome Mexican?"

"She probably knew what she would have to give up. For the handsomeness."

Blix looked at me. "I suppose she did."

A week later Dr. Reyes stopped in, as was more usual, on his way home from the hospital, too tired, he said, for beer.

"Blix," he said, "someday you're going to have to let me make a little examination. One finger," he said, holding up a stubby forefinger, "one minute, is all it will take."

"What good would that do?"

"It would do you the good of letting me know better what kind of medication you need."

"I can tell you that without an examination. More."

"How many shots did you have last night?"

"Three."

"The third was a little heavy," I said.

"Four was what I really needed."

"You really don't need a doctor, do you?"

"Not if you'll sign me some blank prescription forms."

"That's the way I make my money."

I walked Dr. Reyes through the house to the kitchen. He paused to look out of the window over the sink. A covey of quail had come out of the shade of the greasewood to hunt food. They were as thin and brittle as feathered sticks.

"What do they find to eat?"

193

Dr. Reyes didn't hear me. Perhaps he didn't even see the quail.

"She's got a low threshold of pain," he said. "I know that. I'm the same. I understand her. But the medication's got to be spaced. She'll pay for it later on."

We were back where we'd been before. I didn't think there was any point in my reminding Dr. Reyes once again that Blix wasn't planning for a later on. He expected me to say it. He looked at me, expecting it. I didn't say a word. He had to argue with himself.

"I've got to think of her," he said.

I nodded.

He turned away from the window, climbed onto one of the stools at the breakfast bar. He supported his head on his hands, and his black curly hair, too long, sprang upward through his fingers. He needed a haircut—and it would have been easy to have given him one. Clip down to his fingers.

"Any beer over there?" he asked, nodding toward the refrigerator.

There was. I poured him a glass. It was two thirds empty when he put it down.

"That's good stuff. Aren't you having any?"

"I'll have some later with Blix."

"I thought she'd stopped drinking."

"She pretends a little—for me."

"When Blix's weaker, she'll have to come back to the hospital."

"There's no law about that, is there? The undertakers have things organized so that you have to be buried from their parlors. There's no law about being sick in hospitals, is there?"

"Law? Of course there's no law. You'll want her there yourself."

I didn't say anything. Dr. Reyes said, "Was that the last of the beer?"

I poured him another glass. "You've got a nurse here now. Your hands aren't as free as they were."

"Don't worry about Vida. She's been taken care of."

" 'Taken care of.' You talk like a gangster. You planning on machine-gunning Vida?"

"Don't worry about Vida," I told him again.

He told *me* again, "I haven't prescribed a thing in any quantity that's going to be useful to you."

"I know that. You've been very ethical. Very careful. We don't blame you. But there's nothing you can do now, is there?"

"Rob you, do you mean? Turn you over to the law?"

"That's what I mean, I guess."

Dr. Reyes poured the rest of his beer into his glass, built up a fine creamy head, then stared at it without drinking.

"They all think they can do it," he once again reminded me.

"I'll be with her. I can help her," I told him.

"The helpers are all convinced they can help, too. In the beginning, anyway."

He finished his beer, and left without saying another word.

I went to the refrigerator, got a bottle of beer for myself, sat down on the stool Dr. Reyes had vacated, and drank from the bottle.

3

On Friday of the second week of my stay with Blix, she had said to me, "Tomorrow night's the right time."

I was in the bed beside her when she said that. With those words there was a pause in everything: the wind, the hum of the air conditioner, the flow of my blood. Planning for the future is one thing. Saying "Tomorrow night" is another.

After a while I said, very casually, "Why tomorrow night?"

"Everything fits. Sara's coming for a visit in the afternoon. Milt leaves early Sunday morning for that convention in San Francisco. Dr. Reyes never comes on Sunday. The timing's perfect."

" 'The timing's perfect'!" I could breathe again. I could hear again. " 'The timing's perfect'!" I was outraged. "What you're proposing is nasty. I'm with you in this. You know that. But I'm not with you in anything planned simply to make things convenient for Sara and Milt. A slick bit of timing. My God, life is all we've got. There are various good reasons for parting with it. You've got one. But if all life has meant to you is arranging what's convenient for Milt and Sara, the hell with it. I'm going home. I prefer arranging what's convenient for Pete.

"Anytime you tell me 'I've had it,' I'm with you. But don't make life trivial. I had enough of that in my own life. I threw a lot of my own life away.

"I don't know when or how I'll die. But it's not going to be for an auto dealers' convention. Or the convenience of any visitor. Daughter or no daughter. Our lives haven't been perfect. One way or another we've wrecked quite a lot of life. Left quite a bit of it unlived. Let's finish up in some kind of style. Part with it, yes. We've all got to. But not for something convenient."

The light had been turned off. Blix snapped it on. She lifted herself on one elbow and stared at me. "You mean that, don't you?"

"It wasn't a fairy tale."

Blix said, "Tassie, I was thinking as much about your convenience as Milt's or Sara's."

I saw that this was probably true.

"Blix," I said, "make me one last big gift. Let me believe that I value something more than my own convenience. Could you do that?"

"I could try."

"I'm not very proud of myself with Mama in her last days."

"I never thought of this as mixed up with your pride."

"It is, though. You know that."

"How am I going to know when the time comes?"

"Your hand will know."

"My hand?"

"It will reach out for that bottle. It will know. It's not doing that now, is it?"

"No."

"This was just a scheme of your mind. Just a little plan mapped out like a crossword puzzle."

"We've got to plan and scheme. You know that."

"We've got to plan and scheme to be ready when your hand reaches, that's all. When you were born, nobody set an exact date. It was going to happen; they knew that. Some preparations were made. And when your body was ready to come, it came. It got some help. But it knew when it was ready. It will know when it's ready to leave. We'll be prepared. We'll help it."

"The doctor won't help us now."

"We don't need him. Babies are born without doctors. People die without them."

Blix held out her small, long-fingered hand. She opened and closed it. "My hand will know?"

"It will. Without your giving the matter a thought, it will reach for the pills."

The idea pleased Blix. "I would have to make it reach now," she admitted.

So she stopped worrying about "the time." When the time came, her hand would know.

So for a while the life she had was a gift. She had renounced it, and it had been returned to her. She had a week of unbelievable ease. She sat out on the *lanai* and ordered rearrangements of furniture and plants as if she'd be out there every afternoon from then on.

A week after the Saturday that was to have been "the time," she watched the season's new television shows. Most of them were pretty terrible. "I never expected to see a one of these," she said wonderingly.

Every leaf, shoestring, cup and saucer; every fly rubbing its legs together. She looked at them all. I think I know what it was like. After the Christmas tree had been stripped of all presents, you find way in the back, under the lowest branches, a final unexpected gift. It outshines all the others. Blix's unexpected gift was life. And I sat beside her, the life-giver. I had said the words that had given her new TV shows and shoestrings. Yes, and coyotes and wind and sand-pocked roses and trembling caramel custards.

I was happy. I was Godlike. Who besides God had ever been able to make such gifts? It was happiness. It was also power.

Talk about Big Brother. Big Sister can be dangerous, too. A live-giver, a life-sustainer. How small a gift of that kind would finally satisfy me? "She took a sip." "She smiled at me." "She had a normal bowel movement." "She opened her eyes. I'm pretty sure she knew where she was."

Would I become an addict? Unwilling, unable to part from the invalid whose life I sustained? Was that what Dr. Reyes had been telling me? Had I been wrong in thinking that my problems, unlike his and Blix's, were purely technical? His Oath would tell him what to do. Blix's hand would tell her. What could I rely on? No Oath. No pain to prompt my hand. And a growing relish for my role as the great good giver of all things.

"She smiled, she smiled." (I made her smile.) Could I part with that? Could I part with her?

4

Like Dr. Reyes, I drank a second beer. A milky ribbon of sand, down on the floor of the valley, was growing larger. The wind was already blowing down there. Before morning we would hear the dry clatter of palm fronds and the scrape of sand against our windows. The stub-tailed cat had crossed the road and was stalking the quail. If he caught one, what would he have but feathers?

If Dr. Reyes had seen hundreds of patients change their minds, he had also doubtless seen the relatives of hundreds of patients change theirs. Was I already changing? Would I urge Blix again and again. "This is not the time. Wait until your hand knows?" Until her hand knew nothing? Neither pain nor the will to end pain?

I put the beer bottles in the garbage pail. I rinsed the glasses. When I went back to Blix she said, "You two had a pretty long talk."

"It was a two-bottle day. For both of us."

"Did you get him to make any promises?"

"I didn't try to."

For a minute I thought about telling Blix exactly what Dr. Reyes had said. And exactly what I feared about myself. But I didn't want to disturb her confidence. Her confidence that she would know when the time came; and that when the time came I would help her. That was probably my best gift to her.

"Didn't you talk about it at all?"

"Not in so many words."

"What if they don't work? What if I begin to come out of it? What if Dr. Reyes comes by and tries to rescue me?"

"You won't. He won't."

"What if I do?"

"I've got a plan."

It was a plan I had gone over step by step. Its dangers were so real to me that I couldn't breathe very well when I thought of them. Speaking of it made my heart race. Since Blix was worrying, I thought I should tell her.

"If you showed the least signs of coming out of it, I would pick you up and carry you out to the car."

"Could you do that?"

"I could drag you, if I had to. But I can carry you."

"What if it's daylight?"

"That won't matter. I could see a car coming from either direction. The wall hides the carport from the neighbors. But it will probably be night, or toward morning of the first night."

Blix, understanding what I had in mind, said, "They could hear the car running next door."

"All they'll hear is the car driving out. If they hear anything."

"Where will we go?"

"On the road to Snow Peak there are a lot of unpaved roads off to the left. You've seen them. One goes about two miles into a wash. Somebody tried to sink a well there once. That's where we'll go."

"There might be some parkers there."

"We'd be some more parkers. Or go on to another road I know. When we get to the right place, I'll connect the hose to the exhaust."

"Where'll you get the hose?"

"I've got it. It's in a gunny sack in the garage right now. It fits exactly. When it's connected I'll go over and sit on a sand dune and smoke."

"What if somebody comes?"

"What for? Nobody but parkers will be out at night. The car will be running to keep it warm. In the daytime I can see any car that turns off the road."

"What if someone wanted to steal the car?"

"No one will *get* there without a car. What would he want two for?"

"What if he wanted women?"

"I'd be on the dunes out of sight. And you wouldn't care. But we're being romantic. None of this will happen. Finally I'll drive the car back, leave you in it, the engine running, and go to bed. The neighbors or somebody will discover you. I will have been sleeping since I gave you a shot at one. You're strong enough to have gone out there and started the engine. Or I can leave you out there at the wash and walk back. I don't think any of this will happen. What will happen is that you'll go to sleep here in this bed and not wake up."

5

That night we both woke up at one-thirty, the wind slamming itself around the corners of the house and blowing the sand against the windows. The wind probably awakened us.

"Your next shot isn't due for an hour," I told Blix.

"I'm all right," she said. "I can wait."

I hunched the pillows up under my neck. I wouldn't go to sleep again before two-thirty. I kept quiet, because the time for talk was after the shot and the food and the cigarette—as we were drifting back to sleep. I didn't hunt for sleep now, or expect it; only for what was tranquilizing. Mother once told me (trying, by hearing the report, to understand it herself) that when she returned in memory to a house, that house was not her parents' home but her grandparents'. She wondered at this. Hadn't she been happy as a girl at home? Why did she want to return to her grandparents' spring and well? To their books and window seats? Why, in memory, was the water sweeter there? And the view broader and the books wiser? In actuality, it was not so.

My problem was similar, though even less understandable. I knew *why* I wanted in the nighttime to go back to houses and landscapes. It quieted my mind to see objects and not to hear sentences. I wanted to put all words out of my mind, and substitute for them, images. I wanted to stop thinking about; and to do. Or be. The difference (inside our heads) between age and youth is this: when young, we daydream. Words do not then separate us from experience. We move in our thinking among people and objects, acting. We may speak to others, but we don't talk to ourselves about others. We think like poets when we're young. Again, our night minds are no longer able to take us on these wordless tours, into these wordless encounters. With words we recall what has passed. The shape of tomorrow is sentences.

I had a ritual which released me from this rat-a-tat-tat of syllables. A ritual which aped youth's daydreaming; a ritual which was wordless. I approached a house where once I had lived. I got out of the car. I gathered up an armload of wood on my way in. I started a fire in the kitchen range. My hand reached for the forgotten lever that sifted ashes down into the ash box; for the key that adjusted the draft in the stovepipe. Step by step, door by door, cupboard by cupboard I made my way through a house I had not been in for over twenty-five years. Nothing was called by name. I returned to my senses. I smelled, touched, saw. My remembering mind was empty of all words. I characterized nothing. Men, wooing sleep, count sheep. I wanted nothing so wordy and rational as numbers. I *became* a sheep; I moved silent, not simply unspeaking, but without a word in my mind. Somewhere in the midst of this ritual of return, I always fell asleep.

So I knew why I made these tours. What I didn't know was why I made them *there*. There, in that house where I had been unhappy, silly, stupid, sick, overworked. The house where Everett and I had parted. Parted? Well, yes. Though I was parted from Everett in the way that dust is parted from a broom. I was pushed out. Not even gathered up on a dustpan. Thrown to the wind. So why *there*? Like a fish to sweet waters? To that ugly house of misunderstanding and falseness and pain. The wordless hour of starting fires, serving meals, picking flowers, *there*? I don't know. Since the purpose of these nightly tours was to escape words, I didn't, in the midst of them, ask "Why?" And even now, when I've used words to set forth the experience and am capable of analyses, I don't know why.

There were never any people in that house when I returned to it. I did not go back to be with persons. I went back to solitude; to rooms and the furnishings of rooms, to certain enjoyable motions with brooms, spoons, stove pokers, mops, dishtowels. The telephone never rang. A car never pulled up in the driveway. I inhabited a cave before the dawn of language.

I was there the night Blix and I were awakened by the wind-driven sand against the windows of Blix's bedroom. I was not seeking or expecting sleep that night. Blix knew I wasn't asleep because of the way I was lying half propped up against the head-board. Nevertheless, just in case I had dozed off she spoke in a voice so low that for a second I thought my resolve to be word-less had failed me.

"Tassie? Why do you think I married Milt?"

"Blix?"

"I'm all right. I was thinking about me and Milt. Why did I marry him?"

She would never have asked me "Why do you think you married Everett? Or why did you marry Pete?" That was my business. But her marriage was her business and she could ask me to speculate about it if she wanted to. It wasn't a dangerous question either. In the first place, I didn't know why she had married him. In the second, when had either of us ever wittingly told the other a truth that hurt? Not that we lied.

To answer her question I had to use words. But I didn't have to leave that ugly ranch house in Brenner. It was there in the summer of partings and failures, of infatuations and marriages that Blix had been wooed and had made her decision.

Sand on the windows; Seconal in the veins; the purr of the electric clock; the clatter of wind-blown shutters. The persons we speculated about were ourselves. Or had been. They had done these things, said these words. It was tantalizing not to know why. And to remember that even at the time of the happening, we didn't know why.

"You always have said," I told Blix, in my drug-rough voice, "that you married Milt because of his money."

"I said it partly to tease him. Because it was such a good joke on me. The minute I married him, he didn't have any. Do you think I hurt him by saying that?

"I think he thought it was cute."

"The way, if he'd married me for my beauty and I'd got smallpox, it would've been cute for him to say, 'I married her for her beauty'?"

"He got back the money."

"But did I marry him for it?"

"He had more than money. His looks . . ."

"He wasn't handsome."

"Striking. Bald, and eyebrows thick as mustaches. And hair billowing out of his shirt. It whetted your curiosity."

"And a widower."

"That whetted your curiosity, too, didn't it? He had won one woman. Been a bridegroom. Had a wedding night. Stood by an open grave. He was a man of experience. He wasn't going to tremble at the touch of your hand just because it was female. If he trembled, it was because it was *your* hand. Isn't that true?"

Blix said, "I could make Vurl tremble. He wasn't a green schoolboy."

"Anyone could make Vurl tremble. He was as impersonal as a dowsing rod. Milt was never a woman chaser. And there was another thing you liked about him. I remember the first time I noticed it. We were at his house and you got a glass of water from the water cooler, drank half of it, and poured the rest back into the drain pan. Milt came over to you and said, 'That water costs money. Try not to take out more than you need.' "

"I remember that. I've never forgotten."

"Why?" I asked.

"It was so bold."

"Bold?"

"Like saying, 'Where's the toilet?' instead of 'Where's the bathroom?' It was sexy." Blix declared.

"Sexy?"

"He mentioned the unmentionable. It was exciting. You know how we were at home. The less we had of anything, the more Mama would urge, 'Have another helping.' Milt would have said, 'Go slow on that. That's all there is.' I thought it was sophisticated. I couldn't get used to bragging about how little something cost. Or saying, 'I'm overdrawn.' Or 'That's too rich for my blood.' We were poor and tried to hide it. Milt was rich and tried to hide it."

"He succeeded pretty well. Remember the salt?"

One evening in that hot summer of wooings and partings Milt came to dinner, carrying a pound bag of Morton's salt.

"I've got something wrong with a wisdom tooth," he said to me. "I've got to keep it warm. Will you heat this for me?"

He handed me the bag, and I put it in the oven with the biscuits and served it to him, piping hot, along with the fried chicken and mashed potatoes. He held the bag to his jaw with one hand, and ate with the other. Everett, Blackie, and I watched in astonishment. We would all have died rather than have gone courting, salt bag clapped to jaw. Blix watched in admiration. Why? Why? The experience of honesty in a false world? Honesty, particularly when you're unaccustomed to it, has a strange, bittersweet flavor. Intoxicating. How much of it can I take? You see what's been invisible before. How much more do I want to see? What do I want to see? Joy, saintliness, sacrifice? Bestiality, cruelty, bigotry? There's an endless variety—all real as rain. But what's so appealing about watchfulness with water? Home-heated salt bags instead of store-bought oil of cloves? Hasn't honesty more endearing revelations? What responds? Masochism? "You take and I give"? Or does something fit? Is there correspondence? "We take together."

Did something fit? I didn't know. Perhaps I didn't want to know. I didn't intend to add that question's answer to the cold nighttime scrape of sand across the thin membranes of our listening ears. I made the roll of the pillows against the back of my neck harder and smaller. I lay in the unsleeping clarity of a Seconal aftermath, in quiet and even pleasure, contemplating unanswerable questions, enduring conflicting emotions: sorrow and felicity, ignorance and insight. The wind bloweth where it listeth.

Did something fit? In every marriage needs are answered. And if the need, which in the beginning was childish and simple, becomes more complex, the answer, which in the beginning was so satisfying, may become more and more partial.

In the beginning, all Everett needed to be was young, male, and able to read and write. I asked for nothing more; and I'm not at all sure that in a pinch I wouldn't have overlooked the last two requirements. Poor Everett didn't have a chance. I was powerful as a python. I led him on with a serpent's skill to kisses in rainstorms under honeysuckle bowers. I elicited irrevocable answers to loaded questions: "There's one thing you've never told me."

"I love you."

"Shall we wait until I've graduated to be married?"

"I think we'd better."

Everett could no more resist saying, "I love you; marry me," than the piano string, struck by the hammer, could resist its built-in response. I didn't know enough then to know that the response was all I wanted. Or, rather, the knowledge that I had the power to elicit it.

Poor Everett. Poor Milt. Everett said, "I love you." Milt said,

"Watch the water." Both were gone geese with these words. Blix and I, too, I suppose. Though I escaped. Escaped? Escape and expulsion are two different matters. I was expelled by an act, though neither performed nor accepted as such, more loving than any Cure.

6

My autumnal visit with Blix began with a telephone call of mine to her. A year after her operation she had gone to the clinic in Los Angeles for further tests. I had put off the call, out of fear, until the day after her return.

Blix answered the phone. Blix's voice had always been a chord, a subtle mingling of notes. She was dappled, eyes flecked, hair tawny; and she was dapple-voiced, light and dark alternating. There was no need for words when I called her. Her voice told me everything. All the notes were there, but uncertain in their relationship to each other: a handful of arrows shattered, but bound together.

"I'll write you," she said.

I don't know what I said. Perhaps "Tell me now."

She said, "There's been a recurrence, inoperable, a matter of time."

The arrowy voice, with its twang of bow cord and reminders of feathered flight, held together firmly enough to say those words.

"Shall I come?"

"It can't be too soon."

The whole of our living is a war we are going to lose. But in a long sickness, battles are sometimes won. Then, not only is relief felt, but joy, power, even invincibility. Cowards may die many deaths, but the doomed experience many resurrections.

The night of the wind-blown sand, the night Dr. Reyes had set me to wondering whether it might be my resolution, not

Blix's, that would fail, Blix experienced one of these resurrections.

It was almost three when she snapped on her light. She had waited the full time for her shot—and a little more. I was out of bed while the click of her light was still in my ears.

"Blix?"

"I'm all right. But the damned thing's acting up."

She had a good many names for the "damned thing." Inside her, at the base of her spine, it was invisible. But she saw it clearly: shapeless, though far from bodiless; something like a science-fiction blob. If it had been a science-fiction blob, a Satan bug from outer space whose function it was to attack humans, she could have endured it better. But this was a Satan bug from inner space, her very self, her own dear body, by means of which all she had experienced had come to her.

Once, she asked me, "What if one of your hands kept trying to strangle you? And couldn't be cut off. And you knew that sooner or later, it *would* strangle you. A part of your own body, turned against you. Wouldn't you hate it? That's the way I feel about the damned thing."

"Have you waited too long for the shot?"

Blix didn't answer. I think she was afraid that if she opened her mouth a moan might escape.

By this time I could give shots as well as Dr. Reyes. As I pinched together the flesh of her upper arm, the power of the nurse came over me: I was the technician, the comfort-bringer, the one depended upon. The shot, as always, was followed by a variety of pills. That night they proved very strong medicine. Or else the damned thing was unusually weak. I could see the pain leave Blix. It crept back inside its parent. The damned thing didn't die because of this invasion, but it was knocked out. It had no strength for attack. All it could do was maintain itself. The furrow between Blix's eyes became shallower. Her mouth relaxed. She didn't mention what was happening. She didn't want her luck to be noticed, and maybe spoiled, by fate.

All she said was, "I'm hungry."

I named the usual nighttime treats.

"Coffee ice cream. And a glass of hot malted milk," Blix decided.

"A miserable combination. Narsty."

"It's what I want."

Blix was back, and herself again. She knew what she wanted and said so.

When I returned with the food, she was out of bed in bra and panties. Blix had never fought her sickness, never tried to live "as if": a woman doomed, but dining out; driving her T-bird; dancing with tears in her eyes. She didn't wait for things to be snatched from her. She said her good-bys with dignity, made her bedroom her world, bedclothes her costume.

"What are you doing?" I asked.

"Dressing," Blix answered calmly. "Hand me the pink Capris and sweater, will you?"

I put down the food and found what she wanted. She stood, before dressing, looking at herself in the full-length mirror.

"Stork, stork," she hissed, and turned quickly away.

She hadn't lost much weight, but there had been a shifting of weight, so that her trunk appeared heavier than it should. She dressed very carefully, sat at her dressing table to give full attention to make-up and hair.

Sara, a week or two earlier, had asked me, "Do you know what Blix would like?" "No," I told her. "She would like, she says, to have had her hair done, be made-up, perfumed, and in her best dress when they find her."

"It's her idea, for Milt's sake, that no one know she didn't die of natural causes. If she wants that, she'd better be in her bedroom in her nightgown."

"Oh, she knows that. That's why she won't tell you. She says, 'Tassie would talk me out of it, if I told her.'"

"I won't talk her out of it if she's changed her mind about 'Leading Citizen's Wife a Suicide' hurting Milt. And Papa. That's the only argument against it."

"She's got the idea you think dressing up like that would be silly."

"I'm just slovenly, living or dying. If Blix wants a well-dressed exit, it's *her* exit. I'll help her. She can wear anything she wants to."

"She doesn't really want to—under the circumstances," Sara said. "But if she had only herself to think of, that's what she'd do."

The pink Capris had stovepipe legs. The sweater was a light but bulky mohair, embroidered with a spattering of white daisies. Blix put on white sandals and picked up a matching white clutch.

"What are you going to do, Blix?"

I don't think she knew herself until she answered me.

"I'm going outside," she said. "I'm going for a short walk. Then I'm coming back. And when I come back I want you to let me in."

"The door isn't locked."

"I don't mean, 'let me in.' I mean, invite me in. Welcome me."

Invite? Welcome? It was her house. What was she doing? Practicing ghosting?

"I want to come back like a stranger," Blix said. "Or try to. I want to see the house for the first time, once again."

Bulky sweaters and Capris make storks of everyone. Blix was a fashionable figure when she went out into her Japanese garden. I slid the door open for her. The garden was protected on three sides by walls and on the fourth by a fence. Even so, the wind eddied there, cold and dry. A dusty buffeting night. Nearer day than night, actually, but no sign of dawn yet. Everything perfectly visible in spite of that. Big stars, hard and glaring like automobile headlights, a lopsided, bleached moon, white sand. Blix walked through the garden without pause until she was opposite Milt's bedroom. She stopped there. Was she listening to him breathe? Did she think about awakening him? Saying, "Let's take a walk in the wind, Milt"? If so, she decided against it. She opened the garden door and passed from my sight into the carport which connected house and garage. I went into the living room, where, through the glass wall, I could see the street in both directions. Blix crossed the street. She did so, I think, in order to have a stranger's view of her own house.

The sleeping pill I had taken when I brought Blix her food (I wanted to be sleepy when she finished eating) gave me the sensation of being two persons: a sleeper who, though sleeping, lived in what was not a dream.

The transplanted olive trees in front of the house were built for wind: their lacy leaves were unresisting; their short gnarled trunks anchored them strongly. The hedge of denser oleanders, taking the wind broadside, heeled over like a boat. The wind was an old story to the palms. Their dry clatter was almost as old as its blowing. Down on the floor of the valley the ribbon of dust and sand had become a river.

Blix turned away from her own home to look at that river of sand. She knew it well. She had swept it from her floors, brushed it from her window sills, eaten it with her food.

She leaned into the wind as she walked. If it had stopped suddenly, she would have fallen forward.

She went down the street as far as a house brightly lighted, at four in the morning. There, turned toward the house, arms folded against her chest, she paused. What did she see? Sickness? Quarreling? Drinking? Preparation for an early journey? Whatever it was, she watched and watched. Whatever it was, sorrowful or ugly, it was life. It was what she was losing. Did she think, This will be my last look into the story of someone else's lighted room? She started to leave, then turned back. Perhaps it is easier to give up your own life than someone else's.

Finally, the wind at her back now, and hurrying her, she began her homeward walk. She came slowly in spite of the wind, determined to take her time. She lifted her head, gazing at what I couldn't see, the somber wall of mountains behind the house.

The drug, the wind, the unexpectedness of Blix's leaving the house confused me. Were we both ghosts? Was this a visit, in afterlife, to a former habitation? Was this the past, repeated? Poor towheaded tyke, walking, walking in the gusts of a long-past Santa Ana? Would I go to a piano and once again play the "Barcarolle," which said, "Observe me, dutiful, loving and helpful?" Was this Mrs. Kilgrew's faith put to some final test? "Disease is error." Had Blix sent down a ray from her believing mind, lethal to the damned thing? Was she free now of her bed? Could she pick it up and walk?

She looked toward her own home. I left the window. I didn't want to be a spying hostess. The sage greens and Chinese reds in the living room made the statements planned for them by the decorator. A picture was revealed. I wasn't sure its name was home. It was as deliberate as "Whistler's Mother." It was a place for the eyes. It took for granted that living is mostly looking. I moved, light-bodied, Seconal-alienated, away from the front of the house. I turned my back on the road down which Blix was walking. I faced the Japanese garden, where nature, treated like furniture, composed another and weatherproof picture. Above the garden were the mountains. They could be scaled, but not changed. In a temporary house I stood between mountain and desert, reflecting on the shortness of time before I, too, would be part of the burden of dust blown by that timeless wind.

Blix didn't, as I had half expected, ring the doorbell. I heard the door open, and after a little I turned to face it. Blix had her minute in which to catch the room unawares, to see a strange room with a stranger's eyes. But this was play-acting and slightly pompous, not a role Blix could maintain for long.

She closed the door behind her and smiled at me.

"Where's the ice cream?"

"Melted, of course."

I thought that she, who never shed a tear because of pain, might cry now for lack of what she'd counted on.

"There's more," I told her. "Lots more. A half-gallon. We can eat all night."

"Will you eat, too?"

I didn't, usually, but this wasn't a usual night. "I don't intend just to watch you."

She had cried once. From pain, I thought. In the kitchen, stirring the powdered coffee into ice cream, I remembered what Blix had told me on the evening I had persuaded her that her hand would know when the time came to reach for that plastic container.

She had cried the afternoon before. Some fierce pang, unaffected by shots or pills, had gripped her. She had gotten out of bed and folded herself, crying, into the position, knees and cheek to floor, that newborn babies, remembering a lost ease, take when sleeping. She had stayed there, without ease, unsleeping, silently crying. When she did get up, a tear-damp spot, large as a puppy's wetting, was left to gray the white carpet.

The next day, persuaded that her hand would be knowledgeable, she said, "Tassie, do you know why I cried yesterday afternoon?"

"Because you were hurting," I said.

"I was hurting, but that wasn't why I cried. I cried because I was happy. I was glad to feel the pain get fierce. It would help me to want to do what I had to do. I didn't know about trusting my hand then. I thought I'd have to be given a shove—and this was the shove I needed. The pain didn't make me cry. The happiness did. I thanked God for the pain."

Blix was still in the living room when I came back from the kitchen with the food. She surprised me by saying, "Let's eat in here."

I put the tray on the coffee table. The ice cream was good, strong, and bittersweet.

"Blix," I asked, "do you remember the funny ice-cream fad you brought to Brenner the summer you stayed with me and Everett?"

"Ice-cream fad? I remember a lot about Brenner that summer, but if there was a funny ice-cream fad I've forgotten it."

VIII

There hadn't been anything funny about it at the time. Not to us involved in it, anyway. Something ludicrous, yes. But that only added to the misery. To know that what you're doing is ludicrous, to hate being ludicrous, but unable to stop.

Talking to Blix all those years later, the whole summer was funny, too sad for tears. The ice-cream episode, funny as a crutch. Exactly that funny. A story of accidents and cripplings. Some of the story, which started with melon à la mode, Blix had never heard before. I told her partly to make her laugh. Partly, since she was short-changed on future, to give her more past.

"Don't you remember," I asked her, "that you took cleaned cantaloupes to the Tahquitz Confectionery that summer and had ice cream put in them?"

"No. I think you're making it up."

"How could I make up anything like that?"

"What I remember about that summer is Milt."

"What I remember is Manuel. But your cantaloupe caper was what gave me a chance to be with him. So I remember the cantaloupes, too."

This was the first time I had ever stepped out of my role of elder sister to Blix. Admitted I was no example. Mentioned the name of a man not my husband. Mentioned Manuel's name. A kind of sick emptiness filled me as I did so. I was saying good-by to a part I had played for so long that without it I didn't know who I was. No. I knew who I was. But I didn't know how, publicly, to be the person I was. Face to face, I knew my own self. But I had never let Blix face me.

The craze that Blix introduced to Brenner that summer was a mild one, well suited to a Pilgrim campus, where it had started. There the college kids had taken cleaned cantaloupe halves to the local ice-cream parlor and enjoyed cantaloupe à la mode at cut prices.

Everett had a patch of small but flavorsome melons out beyond the chicken houses. Blix cleaned a half a dozen of these one morning, kept them in the cooler all day, and when Milt came over that evening proposed a trip to town to get them filled.

Milt wasn't able that summer to deny Blix anything, not even her request that Blackie and I go along.

"Can Manuel come, too?" Blackie asked.

"Who's Manuel?" Milt wanted to know.

"Everett's sulphur foreman."

"A Mexican?"

"Sure."

"He won't want to go then," Milt said.

But he did. And Milt, with his twosome already ruined, didn't really care how many more crowded into the back seat of his Packard. Blix was up front with him. Blackie, Manuel, and I and the twelve melon halves were in back.

I sat in the middle between Blackie and Manuel. I didn't have to talk. Blackie took care of that. I was left absolutely to feel. Shoulder to knee to ankle, there was no possible way I could avoid touching Manuel. Fate doesn't often make you gifts like that.

The trip to town was over in a minute, of course, and the melon eating didn't take much longer.

214

Manuel paid. Milt would have, except that he saw that to do so would hurt Manuel's pride. Besides, leaving Manuel tied up with change-making, and Blackie eating his last half-melon to the rind, and me waiting for the two of them, gave him the opportunity he wanted.

When Manuel, Blackie, and I stepped outside the confectionery the Packard was gone.

Milt hadn't abandoned us to much of a hardship. Home was a mile and a half down a black-topped road lined with walnut and apricot orchards. The orchards were full of campers. The supper campfires were out but the sweet smell of the evening wood smoke was still in the air, mixed with the sharp brandy ferment of overripe and rotting apricots. The night had cooled off. The tree leaves were fluttering with a rainy sound.

There is no good way for two people to touch, when walking, without being linked, without a matching of rhythms. Attempts to touch without linking, turn out to be nothing but bumps. The intent may be love, but the body, walking, is a mechanism; and the touch of another unsynchronized mechanism is nothing but unlove to it.

Manuel knew this. He offered me his arm. He didn't know how to do so; or I to accept, for that matter. He didn't even know what to call me. Mrs. Henshaw. Tasmania. Tassie. Blackie's sister. He never once in my life spoke my name. In his life, maybe, but never in my hearing.

We walked in silence. Our footsteps, we being light-footed, made soft light sounds on the asphalt, muffled like the sound of fruit falling onto plowed ground.

We made our own music, and we kept time to it. I was almost as tall as Manuel. I managed to equal his stride; perhaps he shortened his a little for my accommodation. Unlinked, when we reached home, the harmony of reciprocal action ceased. We became what we were. Brother, sister, Mexican fruit worker. Blackie was too sleepy to provide us the bond of boxing. We parted quickly.

Everett was sleeping soundly. I went to the window without

thought, following a habit of star-gazing before sleep. Below me was Manuel. There was no mistaking him, in the wash of pale starlight. He sat on the stump of an umbrella tree which had been cut down because its roots were robbing the first rows of the orchard.

He looked up. I looked down. There was no throwing of kisses, no waving, no whispered word. I knew he saw me. There was a movement in the long-torsoed upper half of his body: no more than a deep breath, possibly. I leaned my elbows on the window sill and gazed down. Manuel gazed upward. So we spent the night.

"The whole night?" Blix asked.

"All of it. Till daylight."

"Weren't you dead next day?"

"Too tired to move. But what do you expect after a night of love?"

"I expect more *in* the night."

I said nothing.

"And I was right there, down the hall from you that whole night?"

"So far as I know, you were. I wasn't giving much thought to you that night."

"Or me to you." After a little she added, "It would really have been better for me to have been the older sister, wouldn't it? You needed more advice than I did."

"Maybe being the oldest would have *made* you me."

"I don't think so. But it would have been better. I would have been authorized to help you, then."

"I'll tell you something you did that summer to help me. Do you remember the dance Everett had for the Mexicans?"

As the apricot season progressed, Everett began to care less and less about trying to keep the cost of operation down. He was going to go bust anyway. Why not go bust with a bang?

He had always been freehanded with his help. He had already bought a couple of truckloads of watermelons for his cutters.

When things got worse, he bought another truckload and planned a dance as well. The dance didn't cost anything—the Mexicans provided their own music—except a broken-down crew of workers the next day.

The tables and benches were moved out of the cutting sheds. The earth, by now a smooth cement-like mixture of dirt, Nehi, and squashed apricots, formed a fine dance floor. The music was Mexican, that peculiar blend of whine, fire, and sweetness. Occasionally, the musicians played old American hits: "I'm Sitting on Top of the World," "Show Me the Way to Go Home," "Baby Face."

Everett didn't dance. Milt, who was running a dry shed of his own, couldn't be there. I couldn't dance—except solos. But Blix danced with everyone who had the nerve to ask her—but most often with Manuel. Manuel turned out to be an extraordinary dancer. Blix seldom had partners her equal. That night she had one. She was wearing a white silk pleated skirt, a white silk hip-length blouse, and a long fluttering blue-and-green, sea-colored scarf. Her skirt opened up like a ballerina's. Her scarf stood out as straight as metal. In any other crowd the dancers would have stopped to watch them. The Mexicans wanted to dance, not watch.

I still think Blix and Manuel were the best "ballroom" dancers I've ever seen. I still think this, though I now know what I saw in Blix dancing: I saw my own unexpressed femininity and grace, my own invisible fire and beauty, given expression. I even believed that Manuel knew this: that he didn't think of himself as dancing with a beautiful and gifted dancer, but with my spirit. It is unlikely that this is true. I didn't feel a second's envy or jealousy. Just pride, pride, pride. And joy. Blix expressing with Manuel that part of me which was undeveloped. Or suppressed.

"What was the dance they were all dancing that summer at Brenner?" I asked Blix.

"I don't remember."

"You were dancing me, that night. I know that, anyway."

2

The melons à la mode, the dance, Blix remembered. The peach-pit necklace, like the all-night tryst, was news to her.

It was a summer of courtly love for me and Manuel: nothing but gifts, symbols, and gestures. The lady's honor untouched. The knight's fidelity proved. It was put together out of uncourtly materials: instead of tournaments, evenings talking of boxing in the Pico Arena. Instead of candlelit meetings in chapel or high hall, vigils on stumps and bedroom chairs. Instead of songs and ballads, dancing in the cutting shed. Instead of a gift of silk or a trained hawk or a palm from the Holy Land, a necklace made of carved peach pits.

How he did it, I don't know. Everett burned the necklace before I had a chance really to look at it. I'd seen baskets carved from peach pits before, one half the pit forming the basket, the other half cut away to make the handle. But that was the first and last necklace I have ever seen, handle looped through handle to form a chain of rosy whorls and wrinkled openings. Hours of cutting and gluing had gone into it.

The apricot season is only six weeks long. Any six weeks, unless you are sick or waiting for a letter that doesn't come, is short. Six weeks of love unexpressed is shortest of all. Short as the fall of a leaf from a tree in still weather. The last chance is gone. The pain of the word, turning in you, that wanted to come out is stronger than ever. The eyes ache from trying to carry messages forbidden the tongue. It is like a prayer unsaid. There is the puzzle, too. The mystery. Unrequited love can be dealt with. "He doesn't love me." You don't blame yourself for that. You bear it. You did your part. But love neither expressed nor denied, possibly imagined? Nothing resolved there. A lifetime can be spent imagining might-have-beens.

Whatever my state, the apricots had blossomed, set, ripened, been picked, cut, and dried. There were no might-have-beens for them. The season was over. Many of the apricot leaves were already yellow and on their way to orange. When a breeze stirred, they fell, turning as they went to earth like coins caught in a current of water.

The Mexicans were packing their trucks, collecting their kids, getting their gear together. Heading home, or to the northern peach orchards. It was finished for them. What they had come to do they had accomplished.

Everett was finished. The bottom out of the market and dropping lower. There was nothing to do but sell what was salable, give up the ranch, pay what he could, and hope for the best.

Blix was engaged. No ring, because she wouldn't have the diamond that had belonged to Milt's first wife, though Milt said, "The stone doesn't know the difference." Blix took it, but she wouldn't wear it. "I'll sell it someday," she said. "It won't know the difference about that, either."

This didn't sound very romantic to me. But that summer I had become less oracular about love and romance. The Sanchezes loaded up on Saturday night, and Blix wasn't around to be my stand-in for a ritual farewell. Blackie had gone to the movies. If I wanted to say good-by, I'd have to say it all on my own and without help. I wanted to say good-by too much to go out there in the finished orchard and pretend that Josephina was the object of my farewells. Not that I didn't want to cuddle and squeeze her. I did. I missed the feel and taste of her brown soft warmth, missed it too much to let it be, as I had when summer began, a means for something else.

Sunday morning was Sunday bright. Still and quiet. The air, though there would be plenty of days of 110° heat before the October rains, had already turned the corner toward fall. The sad clear air of a season ending. Blue sky, a million miles overhead; brown earth, for the minute dry and dead as ashes. In between, the living was hushed. Half the Mexicans were gone. There would be no more singing in the morning, no more bird-jabber from the children as they awakened talking. No more evenings of wood smoke and guitar music. The electric lights would burn no longer at night in the cutting shed. The season was over, the debts were incurred, the winter was coming.

On Sunday morning I went downstairs so that I could see the Sanchez truck as it passed the front of the house. One more vigil, and my last. I heard it pull out of the orchard and I couldn't help smiling when it came into sight. It wobbled with its weight. Stove, tent, bedding, the Sanchez kids, a goat. All except the kids and the goat lashed on in a lumpy mountain. The kids sat on the lumps. Manuel, his mother, and Josephina sat in the cab. In front of the house Manuel stopped the truck, got out, and came up the walk. I could not believe what I saw, because it was what I wanted. If I had seen him thumb his nose at me or throw a rotten apricot at the house or drive past without a look, that I would have believed. What I couldn't believe in was my luck— and I was having some. I thought about running. Not toward Manuel, but away from him. Stop while I was ahead.

Dreams go by contraries, don't they? Dream of a wedding and go to a funeral? This was something I had dreamed of. But Manuel came right on up the walk and into the house as if he'd never heard of the law of contraries.

If I said a word the whole time he was there, I can't remember it. He was holding the peach-pit chain in his hands, though until he reached me, I didn't know what it was. When he reached me, he said, "I've come to say good-by and to give you something I made for you."

Then he held up the necklace of carved peach pits, and I inclined my head and he hung the chain around my neck. It was lighter than it looked and rougher. I remember thinking, as it settled into place, My neck will bear the marks of this. It hung halfway to my waist. I lifted it with one hand and was dazed, knowing the hours of tedious work that had gone into it. By him for me, while I had dreamed and wondered and given Josephina baths.

Then, more to separate our mouths, which would soon be kissing, than anything else (I think), Manuel went down on one knee. I might know about courtly love. He didn't. He wasn't pay-ing fealty or taking any oath of allegiance. He was doing *something*; he had to do something, and was trying to keep what he did within bounds. I also had to do something. I bent my cheek to his hair, heavy and silky, smelling of smoke and apricots and Lucky Tiger.

It was in this ridiculous posture that Everett found us. Or found us actually coming out of it, for I had heard his footsteps approaching. Perhaps the coming out looked worse than the original posture, suggesting, as it might, a kissing and clasping that had never happened.

Manuel, on his feet by the time Everett reached us, simply held out his hand, which Everett took, shook it, thanked Everett, and said he hoped to see him again next year at apricot season. Then he went calmly back to his truck and calmly drove off. All the kids waved and shouted *"Adios."* I waved and shouted *"Adios."*

Then there was a great silence and a great emptiness. Finally Everett lifted up the necklace.

"What's this?" he asked.

"Peach pits," I told him. "Carved peach pits."

"He carve them?" he asked, nodding in the direction the Sanchez truck was traveling.

"Yes."

"Well, you don't want that," he said, and gave the necklace a jerk. It didn't break easily. I could have lifted them off. I could have said, "No, it's mine. Let it alone." Instead, I stiffened my neck. Everett jerked, and the chain parted. He threw it into the fireplace, into a fire laid, though it was summer, for appearance's sake. Then he lit the fire. That was my big chance. Stick my hand in the flames and rescue what I valued. I didn't do it. A single basket, when Everett jerked, had rolled unnoticed by him under the library table. I told myself that numbers didn't count. One basket could speak of love as truly as twenty. After Everett left I rescued it and put it in a box I kept for treasures.

IX

Next day Everett suggested that we go to the beach on a camping trip. The beach was near. It was cool. In another week we'd be cleaned out, so we had nothing much to lose in the way of money. The ten or twenty dollars we'd spend on the trip wouldn't be a drop in the bucket of our debts. I told Everett I'd go. I wasn't crazy about camping trips. A camping trip for Everett, maybe for all men, represents man's conquest of nature worked out on a personal scale. Everett hadn't licked nature as a rancher. Nature had licked him. He hadn't licked nature as a husband. He hadn't even discovered it. His wife was receiving peach-pit gifts carved by a Mexican hand. There was not much left for him to try his mettle on. So he proposed camping.

We were lucky, in mid-August, to find a secluded camping spot. We waited to move in while another family moved out. The beginnings of a cave had been carved out of a natural indentation in the sandy overhang of a ten-foot bluff on the far side of Balboa Bay. It was nothing but an eyebrow really, but that wall at my back was all I needed to feel at home. Blix and I had played house in spots like that back in Linda; rooms outlined by pebbles, flower petals on the table for food, and grasshoppers and stinkbugs corraled in stone stables for livestock.

Everett, in camping out, became an imitation pioneer. I became an imitation little girl. The quilts we brought with us made a pretend bed, the grill a pretend stove, and canteen a pretend water faucet. I outlined the magazines and books with shells to make a pretend library table.

Our pretend front porch was the bay, which was not pretend. It was the bay. It was water of varying color and unceasing movement. Even in the early morning, when a lid of white covered it, there were those tremors beneath the lid which in the eye of a sleeper betray dreams. At night the sand under our Kentucky comforters shook with the impact of the big free-running breakers, pounding against the ocean beach a quarter of a mile away. They growled, with the same sound I had heard in Linda of oil wells coming in. Both sounds frightened me.

If camping was what you wanted, or the sea, we had no reason to complain. There was no fog. The sun came up uncovered. The alternations of hot sun prickle and cool salt spray awakened us, so that we felt that we had been only half-alive back in the unvarying heat of Brenner. The cooking, though not the posture —bent over a grill on two stones—was easy. There was not much to cook: eggs, bacon, beans, potatoes. Gulls made our acquaintance and waited for handouts. In late afternoon the clouds piled up like castles; and the sun, going down, first gilded them, then dyed them the purple and black of overripe plums and figs.

Happiness, if camping could give it to you, was there. It wasn't there for Everett. He still believed in the effectiveness of what he called the Cure for me; but it was plainly not proving effective for him. The Cure was, actually, during that week, of more satisfaction to me than to Everett. It was still something for my stoicism to endure. Everett enjoyed camping because, through it, he conquered nature. But nature in our sand cave, potatoes boiling on the grill, and *Scattergood Baines* on the library table didn't take much enduring. The Cure, however, took as much endurance as ever; and there was satisfaction in the possession of a technique of being elsewhere. Pitiful way to live; but human beings must feel something: ecstasy or fury. I chose to feel pride, a rigid deadly sin. Pride in endurance, in calmness, in secretiveness, in irony.

Pride was perhaps what Everett wanted, too. Something or someone to conquer. But the camping was too easy and the woman was too complacent; and the memory of the summer failure too raw to be erased by small successes.

Everett was trying to find a substitute foe when he suggested that we rent a rowboat, and let the money it cost be hanged. I agreed with him. I felt sorry for Everett. He had worked like a dog all summer, and the winter that lay ahead of him was one of more work—with debts added to the burden. A boat for a week cost only $1.50. If he thought rowing would help, I would row with him.

It did help. It helped us both. We set off across the bay in mid-afternoon. The water resisted us, and the wind, blowing inland, pushed curling whitecaps against our blunt-nosed boat. We worked at it together, sweating and pulling. The boat, our own power conquering the forces of nature, moved toward the ocean side of the bay. Car and cave became smaller and smaller. Bed and stove, library table and store of groceries disappeared completely from sight.

We beached the boat on the strip of sand that separated bay from sea. The town was built at the far end of the bay, on the ocean side. We walked along the glistening surf-packed sand into town. After three days of nothing but our own closed faces, a town, particularly a vacation town, was a miracle. We had forgotten that people lived like this. We had forgotten people. We had forgotten (I had forgotten) living as pleasure and not as symbol. Where a kiss was a kiss and not a Cure; and a Cure *was* a Cure and not an occasion for pride. We were Adam and Eve come back to an Eden we had never inhabited.

Crowds of young people, almost our own age, brown and laughing, strolled the boardwalk, sat on stools at counters, near-naked in their bathing suits. They played ukuleles, drank beer, drank Cokes; they yelled, screamed, sang, hugged, kissed. *They* had no pride. They yelled at passers-by. The girls had slave bracelets on their ankles and monkey kisses on their necks. (I once made a false monkey kiss with ink on my neck. It looked like what it was, Waterman's Royal Blue, and not a kiss by man *or* monkey.) The boys had sweaters tied around their waists. They were glazed with sand. None of them had ever heard of apricots, feed stores, cows, Cures, peach-pit necklaces.

Everett and I weren't so much cave dwellers transported to the city as one generation (our grandparents) looking at another generation. We spoke the same language as the people around us; yet if we had sat on a stool next to one of these couples, what could we have said? We were not even visible. We had erased ourselves, somehow. Not crazy, peculiar, or different. Invisible. If we bumped into somebody, would he feel it? If we asked for a Coke, would we be served? We clung together. We were a few years older than these young people. That didn't trouble us. What troubled us was that we were strangers to the world in which they lived.

We walked the sea-front street, up and down. We didn't speak a word to anyone or spend a nickel on anything; and when we got back to our boat we were glad. Rowing was work and opposition, something real and familiar.

Our camp, however, looked make-believe. It didn't have even a grasshopper, stinkbug life. Across the bay was something more difficult and exciting; it might not give pleasure, but it had to be tried.

I cooked us a special supper that evening. I fried bacon. In the bacon grease I fried cubed boiled potatoes. Into this mixture I stirred four eggs. It was a marvelous dish. We were hungry from all that rowing and observing. Eating alone provided some of the happiness the Cure was supposed to bring.

"We should've bought a couple of bottles of Delaware Punch," Everett said. "This is a real feast."

I felt close to Everett. We had rowed together, made it to a strange shore, and been drawn to each other in our estrangement from everyone else. Everett praised my cooking.

"Let's go back again tomorrow," I urged.

Well fed, and with a plan for the next day under our belts along with the bacon, potatoes, and eggs, we went to bed contentedly. The sea rocked us; our quilts covered us.

Everett didn't use the word Cure, and I didn't feel scorn and pride. I thought of the two of us with compassion. Babes in the wood. Quilts instead of leaves. Each the other's only comfort. A house outlined with shells and pebbles. Built on sand, too, but I didn't think of that. I felt like saying some old-time prayer. "Gentle Jesus, meek and mild. Here I lie a little child." But I went to sleep before I could pray.

2

We had decided on the proper time to start our trip next day and we made ourselves wait until that hour came. We wanted to start earlier. The visit to town had become in our minds half-party and half-test. The test was to see if we could become one of those singing, eating, kissing young people. If we passed that test then the party began.

We wanted (or I did) to dress like the boardwalk crowd. All we could do was to put on the best we had in our suitcase. Everett's best was ice-cream pants, black-and-white suède shoes, and a red-white-and-black-striped regimental tie. He wore his suit coat with the pants. I thought he had a resort look. A front-porch look was the best I could manage. Another trousseau dress, lettuce green voile with a six-inch moss green belt of satin at the waist. It should have been at the hipbones. Or, better still, nonexistent. White buck shoes. A matronly purse.

We rowed carefully so that we wouldn't arrive bedraggled. We tried to calm ourselves down on the way over. Going out to dinner and a movie? What kind of a feat was that? Thousands of people did so regularly. Thousands of people were mountain climbers, opera singers, and pearl divers, too, but their success didn't incline us to climb, sing, or dive. We *had* gone to the movies in the four years we had been in Brenner, but we had never once "gone out to dinner."

This was my first trip to any town except Brenner or Linda since my Christmas visit to Los Angeles with Blix. Just remembering that December evening promenade relieved me of some of my qualms. Why had Blix and I been full of swagger there? What if Blix had been with me now? Would trial become adventure?

"Where'll we eat?" Everett asked.

Well, *there* was one difference. Blix always knew where to eat.

We looked at menus tacked outside restaurants. The food was expensive and had names we couldn't pronounce. Murphy bravado could have brazened it out, but Murphy bravado was something, with Everett, I tried to soft-pedal. Everett moved us on from one restaurant to another. The farther we got from the sea the farther we got from seafood. We settled for strawberry waffles in a waffle shop. The Waffle Shoppe was hot, with hundreds of glazed eyes staring at us from the varnished walls of knotty pine. The waffles were pine-colored, but flabby under a watery smear of crushed strawberries and whipped cream that came out of a jar labeled "Fluffo."

Seafare was what I had imagined, and this food was so land-locked I wanted to cry. Where was the taste of iodine? The wind off the sea and the sandy ones jangling their slave bracelets? Stroking ukuleles and bodies indiscriminately? We were lost between two generations, and neither generation wanted to claim us. We were young to the oldsters, old to the youngsters, and pleased nobody, including ourselves.

We were homeless.

The movie was better. Better for me anyway, because I had wanted to see it: a picture that simultaneously gratified desires and satisfied snobberies. Everyone agreed that *Arrowsmith* was a great book and Helen Hayes a great actress. That took care of the snobbery department. Ronald Colman was a beautiful man, cultured but passionate, fire under control, but barely. He didn't have to be in a great play to be enjoyed.

As it turned out, the great moment of the picture wasn't his, but Helen Hayes's. We watched her, unselfish, devoted, misunderstood, pick up, then light, the cigarette onto which we had seen, earlier, Dr. Arrowsmith's death-dealing serum drop. We cried out to her with every indrawn breath, "Don't do it. Don't do it." She did it anyway. She inhaled deeply. We recognized in her act the chanciness of life. We saw how life hinges on small things and luck takes precedence over design. At the very moment of our happiness the seeds of death are sown. The short time allotted us is shortened still more by fate.

"Don't, don't, don't," we called to her. "If you do that, you'll die."

She couldn't hear us. She filled her lungs with death. She died.

Everyone walked out of the theater saying to himself, "Live while you can."

After "Arrowsmith," after chance, death, and defiance, how could we get into a boat we had rented for $1.50 a week, and row back to a semicave of counted bacon strips and carefully graduated pebbles? Where were the chances we should be taking? The dream we could die for? Oh, Martin Arrowsmith, where are you? Oh, Sinclair Lewis, define our problem!

After a movie, a couple should saunter. Everett wanted to saunter. He saw himself as the compelling lover, the man on whose strong arm a clinging woman depended. I didn't want to saunter, I couldn't saunter. I wanted to hasten. Fate was at my heels and the time was short. Hasten, hasten! Everett? Everett! My God, I was Hester Prynne, Jane Eyre, Cathy. Where were Heathcliff and Rochester? Not at my side. Hasten, hasten in their direction.

I wanted to please Everett. So I acted the part I knew he wanted: the sauntering woman.

Day was over, but it was not quite full night. It was a hovering time of ambivalence, some light, sand-yellow, still in the western sky, but dark enough to show the flash of phosphorescence on

228

the lips of the breaking waves. Everett and I had given up all hope of being accepted by those whose skins were bronzed, who sang, who could have worn seaweed without self-consciousness.

We were outlanders, hayseeds, and, though the word hadn't yet been invented, squares. We had sharp corners. We couldn't roll with the crowd. We took a stand. Our dimensions were visible.

And the other squares, the middle-aged diners down there in the Waffle Shoppe? It had been a look into a mirror that foretold our future. Young people train themselves not to see the middle-aged. (The elderly are so remote they are invisible without effort.) And without such training, who would have the courage to persist into middle age?

When it goes against the grain, sauntering is more difficult than hurrying. But I sauntered. The night was unusual for the beach: warm, no wind.

In the way married couples have of reconciling each other to failure, of giving each other reasons for not trying again, Everett and I praised the waffles, the movie, the weather. Everett said he hadn't seen a prettier dress than mine. I said I hadn't seen a snappier outfit than his. We pitied the people sweating in Baranca and Brenner, while those who had planned better sauntered by the seaside.

We sauntered toward our boat, going the long way around, following the curve of the bay. Before we came in sight of the dance pavilion we heard the music of the band. The sound came to us over the water, and the water gave it some magic earth could never have conveyed.

We had to look up to see the "Balboa Ballroom," which was built onto a wharf standing high above the gently lapping water on its forty-foot piers. It was a beautiful sight, its beauty doubled by the reflections below. Mirrored in the glassy darkness, the Japanese lanterns rising and falling with the movement of the water appeared to be keeping time to the music.

Young (though we didn't know it), a summer night by the sea, the sound of the sea and music mingling in our ears. We heard the beat of the music and saw the dancers respond to it. What was the music? We didn't know. The dance? A mystery to us. What was the longing, unsatisfied, in our narrow but growing hearts, which the sea and the music stirred so painfully? Nameless. But we were bound to satisfy that nameless longing or die.

As we came closer we could see the delicately tapping fingers of the horn players, the curved shoulders of the violinists, the vigorous, but voluptuous strokes of bass fiddlers slapping their big wooden women. The piano player roamed up and down the keyboard, lacing all the other sounds together with the in-and-out shuttle of his flowing notes. It was the first dance band we had ever seen. We knew they existed. We had heard them on phonograph records. But we had never seen one.

To reach our boat we had to pass under the wharf. The main entrance to the ballroom was above on the street side, but there were stairs leading up to the dance floor from the bay rim where we stood.

At the foot of these stairs I stopped. I put my hand on one of the heavy piers that supported the wharf. I closed my eyes and *felt*, as I had seen Helen Keller do in pictures, the surge and pound of the music.

"Feel," I told Everett.

He didn't care to be seen feeling a barnacled pier in plain sight of any passer-by.

"Shut your eyes and feel."

"Why?"

"To feel the music. Feel and hear at the same time."

He took his hand down. "I can hear it. That's enough. I don't need to feel it shake a piece of wood."

Shake wasn't the word exactly. What sound waves do to the eardrums, the vibrations inside the wood did to the marrow of all my bones. I heard all over. My sauntering resolutions were broken by what I heard. What I had controlled with slow steps and well-chosen words came alive again.

"Let's go," I urged Everett.

"Go?" asked Everett. "We are going. You're the one who's slowed us down. Feeling wood."

"Go to the dance, I mean."

"We can't dance."

"We've never tried."

"I have."

"There're so many people up there. No one would notice us. They're people up there just walking around in time to the music."

"You wouldn't be content with that. You'd be doing a jig. Or a highland fling, or something."

"Everett, I wouldn't. I've got some sense of what's proper. I want to dance with you. I want us to dance together. I feel like that's what we came for."

"I don't."

"We could learn. We'll never have a better chance. Here in a crowd, where no one knows us."

I went up one step and Everett followed me. I went up another.

"I don't think people are supposed to walk up these stairs."

"What are they here for?"

"Exit. In case of fire."

"There's a man up at the top taking tickets. I saw him."

"We don't have any tickets."

"Selling them, I mean."

"We don't have money to throw around."

"A dollar. A dollar at the most."

We went up two more steps.

"What makes you think you can dance?"

"I can feel the music."

"I can't."

"Feel me." I put Everett's arm around my waist.

"You feel pretty good."

"I'll feel even better dancing. A me you don't know a thing about."

We were still climbing. "Did you ever dance with anyone else?"

"Yes."

Everett stopped. I kissed him on the cheekbone. "Blix. Le Cid. Le Cid said I was terrible. But it will be different with you."

"Why?"

"You're not my brother. Le Cid was my little brother. I hauled and pulled him around. I want you to lead."

We were one step from the top, and could see the whole dance floor. I remembered the emotion of the revival meetings. Something in the music and the dancers called to me in the same way. Only here, you could not dance alone to salvation. You had to have a partner. I was as certain as could be that if Everett and I would put our arms around each other, we would succeed. We would be dancers. We would get better as we went along.

We were on the last step.

"I've got the dollar if you haven't."

We were face to face with the dancers now. All ages. All skills. Walkers, trotters, joggers, bouncers, gliders, leapers. Men's faces were buried in partners' soft hair. Women snuggled close. Put a sheet over them and what they were doing would look wicked. I had wanted to hurry and had managed to saunter. Now I wanted to dance, and inside me, though my feet were stationary, I *was* dancing. If Everett would only companion me here, I thought, our lives might change. Take me, glide off with me, lead me. Share this marrow-melting rhythm.

I didn't take the dollar from my purse. If we danced, Everett would have to lead.

We stood at the top of the stairs, nothing between us and dancing but one dollar and willingness. It looked easy to me. It was a merry-go-round. Get on, and the merry-go-round would dance *us*. There wouldn't be any question of our having to perform. We would be carried, *swept* to a conclusion, gold rings as prizes and trumpets blaring in our ears.

The dancers circled past us, young and old, agile and awkward. A Mexican couple whirled by, gyrating so furiously her outspread skirt touched me. She smelled like red roses. He was doing double time, two steps to the beat.

Everett followed the couple with his eyes.

"I suppose you'd like me to dance so that you can pretend that I'm Manuel."

I had no intention of pretending that Everett was Manuel. I was already, though, and I knew it, pretending that I was Blix, graceful, seductive, alluring. If I did what Blix did, wouldn't I be Blix?

How could I tell Everett this? "I would like to dance like Blix —with you," I said.

What was wrong with that?

Everett said, "You couldn't do that without her partner."

Everett turned and started back down the stairs. I didn't move. The ticket seller evidently thought I wanted to go in alone.

"Sorry, miss," he said. "No tickets to ladies without escorts."

When I remained silent, he decided I needed simpler language. "Sis," he said, "you can't dance without a man."

I knew that. I went down the stairs. Everett was waiting for me at the bottom.

3

The prophetic sparkle of autumn, which had come earlier to Brenner, invested the water and air of Balboa next morning. The inland garden softness of the night before was gone. The bay was still blue, and the wind-blown, watery ridges looked sharp enough to draw blood. The sand glittered with minute glassy igloos.

Before we were up, Everett said, "Let's go to town and have pancakes for breakfast. Let's row over and spend the day there. Let's not plan anything—just go and take it as it comes."

I thought: Why not? The third time's the charm. Flyers who crash must fly again at once. If we didn't return to town at once, we might never have the courage to try again.

With no plans for the day, we put on our everyday clothes. Me, a blue pleated skirt, white blouse, sneakers. Everett, khaki pants, white shirt, work shoes.

The bay was bluer than the sky that morning, and we rowed hard because we were hungry and in a hurry to reach food. Though he didn't say so, I knew that Everett was sorry that he had walked away from the dance. For no reason, actually, but fear. He cared about the figure he'd cut as a dancer. I understood this. I was the same way myself. Only I had believed that in dancing I would forget the figure I was cutting.

Everett hoped that he would be given another chance; he hoped some challenge would come up that he wouldn't walk away from.

We crossed the bay in jigtime, beached our boat, and took the ocean way to town because it was the quickest route to food. It had been a long time and a lot of emotion since those strawberry waffles. I was so hungry I considered eating a piece of kelp. I felt empty and fragile as a shell. If a wave caught me I would ride out to sea like a bubble.

We passed a fruit stand, and I bought two Valencia oranges, thin-skinned and waxy. The feel and smell of them reassured me. They were a promise to my stomach that if the worst came to the worst, food was at hand.

Everett said, "You're not going to eat those out here on the street, are you? And spoil your breakfast?"

"No," I said. Though I thought that eating one, then, instead of spoiling my breakfast might keep me alive until I had some. "I thought we might have a picnic lunch on the beach at noon."

Everett liked that idea. It would be camping out on a miniature scale.

We were lucky about breakfast. We found almost at once a place that suited both of us. Hungry as we were, we weren't choosy. This place had food, looked inexpensive, and was so near the beach that spray from the big waves touched our faces. The place was windowless—a kind of shed, really. Roof, floor, and the waist-high wall of a porch. Tables were attached to the wall on one end and supported by a single leg on the other. The diners sat on benches. The food had to be good, since there was nothing else, except it and the ocean, to attract diners.

Everett and I had to wait for a table. There was no head-waiter, and people, like autoists at crossroads without stop-and-go lights, decided for themselves when their turn had come. Everett waved people ahead who had come in after us. At crossroads these tactics confused motorists. But here, though startled, no one was confused. They made for tables. It was *noblesse oblige;* unusual, but recognizable. I wished Everett would wave me to a table, but I kept my mouth shut. I was determined not to repeat the night before. "Let's hurry. Let's dance. Let's eat." The diners were a mixture: kids, Waffle Shoppe customers, ukulele players; dogs rambled around the sandy floor. Gulls perched on the railing beside tables ready to snatch a bite from any un-guarded flapjack. People were here because they were hungry. It was too early in the day for them to sort themselves out to fit subtler classification. They were just hungry; and the big man in undershirt, chef's tall white hat, and red bandanna kerchief entertained them by keeping eggs, sausages, potatoes, and pan-cakes in the air like a juggler.

A man behind us, independent as a hog on ice, refused to be beholden to Everett. "Your turn, buddy."

"We're in no hurry," Everett answered courteously.

"If you aren't eating, get out of line."

"We're eating," I said, all my patient Griselda resolves giving way at once.

Everett, hungry himself, didn't have a word of rebuke for me. We found a table on the ocean side and had gulls for company. I put my two oranges on the table for decoration and thought, I am happy.

Our waitress, a freckled twenty-year-old, gave us water and said, "We're shorthanded. You may have to wait, but I'll take your order."

We both ordered the same meal: two eggs, coffee, a stack of hot cakes. The promise of breakfast affected my tear ducts. The prospect of a reunion with food made my hands tremble.

"It smells wonderful," I told the waitress.

"Dad's a good cook," she said, as she wrote up our order.

"And he's fast," I said.

"Fast and good."

When she left, Everett said, "Dad would be better off if his daughter talked less and did more."

"It hasn't hurt his business," I said.

I had no intention, actually, of eating the orange. I began to peel it unconsciously, the way you yawn or smile. I wasn't looking at the orange or even thinking of it. I was watching the track made in the sandy floor by a baby crawling after a puppy. I was listening to the surf, the kerboom of its arrival, the long suck of its withdrawal. I was smelling bacon and sausages. I was thinking of the freckled girl and her job and wondering if she had only a summer job and went to school in the fall. I thought I would ask her when she came back. I was smiling. I felt at home in a family world, but a world with a sea view.

I had to look at my hands to see what Everett was talking about. "You don't peel oranges at restaurant tables," he said.

"Who doesn't?"

"No one. No one with good manners."

"Why not?"

"It doesn't look nice."

"Some places it might not. But it's okay here. Nobody cares."

"I care."

I couldn't believe it. I just couldn't enter into Everett's mind. The trouble was, I was feeling jolly. The waitress's freckles, Dad's juggling, the crawling baby, the booming surf: they took me out of my tight world of failures and resolves. And food, the smell of food! And the feel of the orange in my hands, and the anticipation of the sweet squirt of its juice in my mouth! I spoke out of my jolliness to Everett. I didn't take him seriously. I joshed. I also exaggerated, something else he didn't care for.

"Care? They wouldn't care if you cleaned a chicken here. You could mash potatoes here and no one would notice."

I put a section of orange in my mouth. It made me drunk with good humor. I held out a section to Everett. He tried to stare some good manners into me. He stared playfulness into me instead. I leaned across the table and placed the orange section against his lips.

"Come on, Adam. Try it. Fruit of the passion tree."

Everett looked disgusted. He gave my hand a little bat, and the orange section dropped to the table. I picked it up, put it on top of the railing. A gull flew away with it.

Everett, without a word, got up from the table and walked out of the dining room.

4

When the waitress brought our order I told her my husband wasn't feeling well, but that I could eat both orders. I couldn't even eat my own. The food I had looked forward to as a banquet was dry as bread crumbs in my throat. It would hardly go down. This meal which was to have been a beginning again was another failure. Poor Everett, wandering starving along a windy beach while I cut into a trembling stack of hot cakes and broke the crisp crust of a delicately browned pat of hashed browned potatoes.

Every act of mine since I had arrived at the beach had been selfish and self-centered. Look at the husbands who gambled, drank, cursed, ran after bad women, and got into fist fights! Where would I find another high-minded clean-living boy like Everett? What was wrong with me, anyway? A meal he had planned for our pleasure, and I had driven him from the table with my indecorum!

Find Everett! Ask his forgiveness. Beg for one more chance. Promise reform. Half of my breakfast and all of Everett's was on the table when I paid and left. There was no reason now not to hasten. I ran down short streets which dead-ended at the beach. I hastened, panting, up streets which petered out in keystones in residential sections. I walked the aisles of grocery stores.

Everett might be buying cheese and crackers to eat on the beach. I looked into hardware stores. Everett might be inspecting rakes and hoes.

Once, leaving a drugstore, I was sure I saw him following me a half a block away. My heart, which had been painfully crowding my chest, went back to its normal size. I could breathe again, swallow again.

"Everett, Everett," I called before I thought. Yelling in the streets was nothing that would endear me to Everett. When I reached the corner where I had seen him, he was nowhere in sight.

I don't know how long I ran or where I searched. I darted in and out of stores; I recognized streets I had been on minutes before. Separated from Everett I was homeless. Without him I had no purpose in being. He was the unfavorable wind against which my stance was canted. Alone, the sound of the sea frightened me. Strangers were menacing. With Everett by my side I could be a bold public peeler of oranges, a secure fantasy-lover.

My panic was increased by the tantalizing glimpses I had of him at a distance. I turned a corner and crashed into a man.

"Everett," I cried, thinking I had found my husband. The man turned on me with a strange angry face. A block away, a man with a high pompadour paused, to watch *me*, I thought. My sight blurred with tears. Everett's heart had softened; he was waiting for me. Before I could catch up with him, he turned into a five-and-ten. Inside the store there were no male shoppers to be seen.

"Where is the man who just came in?" I implored of a saleslady.

The saleslady looked around. "There is no man here," she said with the weariness of those required to speak the obvious.

"I saw Everett come in."

"Of course you did," she said soothingly.

I saw that she would agree with me if I said that the man had had wings. I went outside.

Sparkling morning of summer by the sea. Where had it gone?

I could run no more. I was like a man lost in the forest and running in circles. What I had always known would happen had happened. I had been abandoned. I was truly orphaned. I couldn't, like Blix, say, "Hello. So long." "Don't leave me" was my only cry.

I needed a place to hide, and in my runnings up and down I had seen a church with an opened door. The church didn't, like Everett, appear and disappear. It was where I remembered it, and the opened door wasn't an illusion born of my need. The door was truly open, and it stayed open while I walked through it.

It wasn't a Pilgrim church but I didn't care about that. Or about the flutter of candles and the glitter of crosses and drops of blood from the wounded heart. I did care about the women kneeling, murmuring their prayers and softly shuffling their beads. I had no ritual that would make me one of them. I wanted neither to intrude upon them nor to expose myself.

I saw exactly what I wanted. At one side of the church were those cubicles whose purpose I knew, and knew that at this time of the morning priests wouldn't be hearing confessions. I opened on my first try the wrong door of the three available to me: the central space with its seat for a listening priest and the grille through which he listened. I shut that door quickly. I would no more think of occupying a priest's domain than of mounting a pulpit. My place was where the sinners confessed their faults.

The minute I stepped inside I was comforted. There was a kind of little platform to kneel on, and I sank onto it as naturally as if I had been doing so since childhood. I stopped crying. At first I said nothing. Then I began to speak to the grille as if it actually could hear, was sympathetic and holy, the living ear of God. Did some play-acting enter into it? Because I was in a confessional did I play the part of a penitent? I don't think so. I would have prayed in a telephone booth. Privacy was all I needed.

I asked God for his help. "Dear God," I said, "I have been a bad woman, thinking only of myself. I do not try to please my husband. Please help me to love my husband as I should. Oh God, make me love Everett. You can do it, God. He deserves to be loved. If I truly loved him I would not do these things to displease him. I have driven him away with my hard heart. Make me love Everett!"

I don't know for how long I ran on. I didn't ask God to send Everett back to me, because I didn't think that until I had a change of heart this would do any good. I would just drive him away again with some unloving act. I took all the blame onto myself. Everett was good and I was bad. "Oh God, make me love Everett as he deserves."

With the first sound from behind the grille I stopped praying. I could play at confessing, alone. But confession was a holy sacrament, and I had too much respect for all things religious to make a priest a part of my game.

When the door of my cubicle opened, I looked up expecting to see a priest. At first I thought I was looking at a priest who looked like Everett. It was the other way around.

It had never occurred to me that Everett would find fault with what I had been saying—if he had heard. What I felt was wonderment at his being there at all—and relief that we were reunited. I hadn't asked God to send Everett back to me, but God knew what was in my heart.

Not Everett. Or maybe he did.

When I said, "Oh, Everett, how did you find me?" he answered, "I followed you, and now I am through following you. For the first time I've heard the truth. You have to ask God for help to love me."

I said, "Don't you want me to love you, Everett?"

"I did, but I don't any more. I don't want anything that doesn't come naturally to you. I don't want anything from you you have to pray for."

"You never liked me to pray. Even when it was silent."

"You were probably asking God to give you the strength to love me all along." He spoke bitterly. "There are women who pray that their husbands love them. Why don't you pray that? Why don't you ask God to make me love you?"

The answer was that it wasn't necessary to ask God for what you already had. But I was too polite to say that and I couldn't think of anything I could say. I was still on my knees, and my neck hurt from gazing upward at Everett's face of stony fury. But I couldn't lower my eyes.

Everett said, "Well, you aren't going to have to ask God's help to love your husband any more. You don't have a husband any more."

With that, Everett closed the door of the confessional. He didn't bang it as he did doors at home when he was mad. He closed it quietly, as if he were sealing a tomb.

I heard his footsteps as he left the church. I didn't believe what he said, that I no longer had a husband. But I made no effort to follow him. I rolled the remaining orange, which I still held, around in my hands. It was the cause of all my sorrow. If I hadn't bought the oranges, I couldn't have peeled one at the table. If I hadn't peeled an orange at the table, Everett wouldn't have run away from me. If he hadn't run away from me, I wouldn't have gone to the church and prayed. And if I hadn't prayed, I would still have a husband.

When I left the church, the midday light, reflected from the sea in wounding shafts, half blinded me. I walked very slowly, my eyes on my feet. I went to the boat, sat in it and waited till sundown, hoping that Everett would come. No one came. At dusk I went back to the place where Everett and I had eaten breakfast. I thought Everett might come there. We would order the same food. I would, as before, start to peel the orange I still carried. Everett, as before, would ask me not to peel it. This time I would listen to him, put the orange down, say, "I'm sorry." I would take the road not taken that morning, and a different life would lie ahead of me. We would row home in the moonlight to our pebble house and our ancestral bed.

He did not come.

The freckle-faced girl remembered me. "Where's your husband?"

"I lost him."

"Permanently?" She was joking.

"It looks that way," I admitted. "I've waited for him all day."

How sorrowful did I look? How abandoned? Sorrowful enough, abandoned enough for her to tell her father.

In a lull between orders he came to my table.

"Mind if I sit down, sis?"

He was plump from eating his own good food and, at the same time, muscular from running from one end of the stove to the other, keeping the pancakes in the air, the bacon sizzling, and the eggs half sunny-side up and the others once over easy. He was bald; face and scalp were both a rich kelp color, whether from hot sun or hot stove I didn't know. I wasn't accustomed to talking to strangers, but this stranger was cooking my supper for me, and this made him a kind of host.

His name was Clyde Fetters and his daughter's name was Lucy. The inside muscle of each upper arm was tattooed, the sign to me of a wild and roving fellow, but his face, except for the kelp coloring, was a composite of all the illustrations that have been made for St. Nick; the same twinkling eyes and nose big enough to lay a finger beside. It was hard not to trust him, and I wanted to trust someone.

"Lucy says you've lost a husband."

I could only nod.

"Have a spat?"

Nod again.

"What's the trouble?"

"First, I peeled an orange in here this morning. At this very table."

"What's wrong with that?"

"Everett asked me not to and I kept right on. So he left."

"That all?"

"No. Next I went to church."

"That's nothing to quarrel about."

242

"Everett heard me pray. I was in one of those booths and he got in the middle one. How could he get there without my hearing?"

"Search me. I've never been in one of those boxes. Side or center. Don't Everett care for praying?"

"I asked God to make me love Everett."

Mr. Fetters sucked his teeth. "That puts a different face on the matter. Don't you love Everett?"

"Not enough. I wouldn't have put peeling an orange ahead of his wishes if I did, would I?"

"If he loved you, I reckon it wouldn't have mattered."

This put a new face on the matter for *me*. What if Everett *didn't* love me? What kind of a Santa Claus in reverse was this mahogany-colored St. Nick? Taking instead of giving; and by his taking, leaving me light as a feather, about to float in a minute to the top of the world's highest Christmas tree. There to sing like a mechanical angel, "Peace on Earth." Oh, Le Cid! Piece on Earth.

Everett had left me. It had never occurred to me that Everett didn't love me. I had supposed that he left me because he thought I didn't love him. If he didn't love me, that did put a different face on it.

Mr. Fetters saw my confusion.

"What's your plans for the night?"

Until he spoke I didn't have any.

"Eat some supper," I said, "and row back to our camp."

"How're you fixed for money?"

"I've got five dollars."

"That won't last long."

"I can work. If Everett doesn't come back for me."

"I'm shorthanded. How about waiting on tables?"

"I never tried it."

"Try it."

I tried it that night and could keep up with Lucy. I rowed, frightened of the night and the dark water, back across the bay to our camp. If Everett had been there I would have clasped him

243

thankfully and tearfully. He wasn't there. Nor was the car. I lay sleepless on the sand and saw myself living henceforth under culverts, a female hobo, derelict and abandoned.

In the morning I rowed back early to the Fetter Fish House. In addition to waiting table I started work as an assistant fry cook. I was good at it. Why shouldn't I be? I'd been flapping pancakes and frying eggs since I was six. I didn't have to make any big decisions. I worked from day to day. And, half expecting Everett, spent every night in our camp. He never came. At the end of the week I moved in with Lucy. At the end of the summer I went up to Berkeley with her, was enrolled as a graduate student, and employed as fry cook in a café owned by Mr. Fetters's uncle.

After the divorce I never saw Everett again.

Blix did, though. She kept in touch with him through all the years.

Blix never told me so, but I think she felt that she and John Everett were to some degree fellow sufferers. She, too, had had to live with me when I was young and righteous.

She attempted, once or twice, a report on Everett's subsequent marriage and success. I didn't care to hear. Not because there was any pang in hearing, but because, after I was married, really married, I mean, I couldn't bear for a long time to be reminded of my misspent youth.

If Everett had abandoned me in a zoo, would I have become an animal trainer? In a movie, an usher? He walked out on me in a restaurant, where the daughter was a student and the owner the cook. So I became a fry cook, a waitress, and later a student. The form I took was imposed from the outside—as it had been with Everett. But I didn't have to pray for help in my new undertakings. Though I missed Everett. I missed the strange unreal world in which I had lived: the world of love dreams, and dream Cures; the world of irony in which knowledge was unexpressed and acts were misinterpreted.

On cold raw nights when the foghorns were hooting, I'd press

244

my cheek to the dark glass of the window of my one-room apartment on Grove Street and think about calling Everett. "Everett, I will never again peel an orange you don't want me to peel." I could promise that, all right. Could I promise "I will never again pray God to help me love you"? And Mr. Fetters's further explanations of Everett would come back to me and keep my hand away from the phone. "Why, sis, if Everett had loved you, he would've thought orange peeling the cutest trick in the world. He'd of prided himself on having the hungriest wife in the world. Everett didn't give two hoots in a hot place about you, kid. He like as not never even seen you. His idea of a wife was something else. The only times he seen *you* was when who you was got so far out of line from his idea of a wife that he couldn't help but take notice. You're a real fry cook, sis, but you weren't never any more than a make-believe wife. And Everett seen through that. More power to him."

More power to him. At that window, thinking of phoning, make-believe sometimes seemed to me the only life I'd ever succeed in. But I never phoned. I had climbed out of a prison. Tom Thumb–sized myself and the prison no bigger than a milkweed pod. Maybe. And climbed, the wrong word. I hadn't climbed. I'd been kicked. Get back in, and I might never have so much luck again. I was lonely, and the loneliness was real. Scared, discouraged, bereft now of all make-believe love affairs, and the solace of real irony. All Everett's gifts. I took my gifts to bed with me and went to sleep to the foghorns' hootings.

X

Blix was outside only once again after that night of walking and talking. She could have gone oftener. In her place I thought I would have. Sentimental trips. "One last look." The new moon, an African sunset, a road runner.

Dying, like living, is a performance. Since it will be required of each of us, we can't help comparing our possible performance with that of others. Though all comparisons are probably invalid. We are not, sick and well, the same persons. The man who in health thinks about his death is thinking about the death of a stranger. The healthy man cannot plan what that sick stranger, with his changed body, his daily ration of torture, his drug-altered consciousness, will do.

Dr. Reyes *was* thinking of this, once again, toward the end of October.

The breakup of summer on the desert is like the breakup of winter elsewhere. A hardship has been endured, a trying time lived through. A kindlier season is coming. The desert sky, always more steeply arched than elsewhere, bubbles up in a still

246

loftier dome, a height even more crystalline. The stars, always bright, grow larger. The sunset, in summer heat, colors the hills with a wash of water color; when summer ends, the painting is done in oils. Rain is the real seal of summer's ending; and on the desert, a ten-minute splash, from clouds moving fast and with little to give, will mark the transition.

I was sleeping in Blix's room the night of the first rain. A sound too faint to have carried through layers of Seconal, except that it was loud with meanings Seconal could not muffle, awakened me. I sat up in bed quietly, but Blix heard me and turned on her light.

"What is it?" I asked.

"Rain," she said.

"It's too early for rain."

"That's what you think. Open the door. You'll see."

I turned off the air conditioner so that we could hear better, slid open the glass door—and the soft thunder of rain falling onto sand curtained us in. Deaf, we would still have known it was raining: smell would have told us; the smell of dry earth watered, of dehydrated vegetation reconstituted, the smell of resurrection. The first rain in a dry land! It smells better than lilies in July, or the ocean, or the wind in sun-warmed pines, or the irrigated patch of alfalfa you reach after a long haul through dry hills. It is hard to smell that sweetness and believe in death.

I stood in the doorway, letting myself be rained on. Blix's bed, lit by the candle glow of her little bed lamp with its water-lily shade, floated in the darkness of her big dark room. In Blix's place (comparing performances), I would have been out in that rain, I thought, face lifted, remembering the years of rain I'd never feel. But Blix lived her dying. She didn't dramatize it.

I brought her a handful of rain. She put a finger in it. "What're you going to do with it?"

I dumped it in the washbasin and dried my hands. Blix went back to sleep without medication.

It rained through the night—no passing shower, no overexpanded mountain thunderstorm. In the morning the bridge, which usually spanned nothing but sand, spanned a damp streak. The rain had cleaned the air to nothing. It did not exist. The mountains existed. They and their hard colors had moved in so close they were frightening. A horror movie: The Marching Mountains.

Dr. Reyes stopped in, as was his custom, around five. By now, late enough in the season for twilight, a bleached wan-hope twilight that evening, because there was no dust in the air to stain the sunlight.

He rapped on the door and marched into Blix's room, as jubilant about the rain as is any lifelong desert rat.

"Boy, oh boy!" he said. "Wasn't that something? By January this desert's going to look like one king-sized bed of flowers! Sand verbena from Banning to El Centro. Just you wait and see!"

Blix, since Dr. Reyes was going to wake up in the next minute to what he had said, replied matter-of-factly, "I'd like to. Can you arrange it, Doctor?"

Dr. Reyes said, "My God, Blix!" and walked out of the room.

Blix said to me, "You better see if he needs a shot or something."

"Shot of Old Bushmill, probably."

Dr. Reyes was in the kitchen on his usual stool when I came in. Staring at the quail coming out for their usual evening feed. They, too, appeared to have been reconstituted, plumped up by rain, their plumage cleansed of dust, and darker.

"Want a drink?"

"No," he said.

The rain hadn't done anything for Reyes, physically. He wasn't a thin man, but the flesh of his face was taut, and his dark eyes looked hot and dusty.

"Don't worry about Blix," I told him. "She knows there'll be flowers she'll never see."

"Don't give me that old stuff about how she's not going to be sad, because though she dies, she knows that spring goes on forever."

248

"I'm not giving it to you."

"That stuff was written by poets full of beer and with a life expectancy of sixty more years."

" 'Though I am dead, think only this of me,/Some corner of a foreign field is forever England.' " I quoted.

"England! All Blix can do is make some corner of a commercial memorial park Blix for about twenty-five years."

"She won't know. We won't know," I said.

"She knows now. My God, what she's going through is so lonely."

I sat on the drainboard of the sink so that I wouldn't have to look at Dr. Reyes sideways. He faced the windows, and there was no warmth in the sky to soften the hard darkness of his tired face. He had said that he had never had a childhood, and I believed him. There was not a remnant of boyishness in his face. At four or five he had begun accepting responsibilities; at the same time, he had refused to let his face ask for sympathy. It was a cool face now, well disciplined, trained not to "light up," to "glow," become "downcast." It wasn't a face you could read the present in any more than you can read a computer by looking at it. The answers, beneath the skin of enamel, were there, though.

"After a while," he said, "I'll help her. I'll help her all I can. I'll increase the dosage. She's getting more now than she should. She's physically stronger than she was six weeks ago. Heavier, too, I think. But her tumor's growing. And I think her mental state has deteriorated."

I thought he was mistaken, but I kept quiet. I had tried for weeks to get him to talk. I didn't want to stop him now.

"I'll help her. She won't die of cancer, but of lung congestion or heart failure. But she's a strong woman. She has a wonderful constitution. She may live a year. She'll never take those pills. As the opiates increase, the will—the memory becomes fuzzy. You forget what your intentions were. And when you remember them you don't have the will to carry them out. My God, don't you think I've been through this before?"

I thought he had. He'd told me he had. But I kept quiet.

"I'll help her, but look, you get out. You're not doing her any good. She shouldn't get emotionally dependent on someone outside her family."

"Outside? I'm not outside."

"*Her* family, I said. *Her* husband. *Her* daughter. Don't try to replace them."

I didn't think I was, but I didn't argue about it. About Blix's emotional dependence I did. "Emotionally, I'm probably more dependent on Blix than she is on me."

"I'm talking about that, too. This is a rich life for you. Brinksmanship. Combat soldiers sometimes never get over it. Or generals. Life and death in the balance. Each minute. How can you learn to live without that poison?"

"I'm no soldier. My life's not in danger."

"All the worse. All thrill and no chill."

"Thrill? Where's the thrill watching your sister die?"

"Don't ask me. That's down where the mysteries begin. It keeps nurses going."

"And doctors?"

"It wouldn't surprise me."

"But you try to save life."

"Oh, yeh. But down where the mystery is. Face to face with the blackness. How else could we get there? And paid! It's our ticket of admission. You get out. Begin to plant the seeds in Blix's mind that you'll be leaving. You've got a husband and a life of your own. Haven't you? You don't have to be Blix's husband. Or daughter. Or mother. Go home."

"I promised Blix that when I came this time I wouldn't leave while she was alive."

"Break your promise."

"I'm going to stay."

Dr. Reyes got off the stool, got a bottle of beer, opened it, and drank from the bottle.

"I don't know which of you girls is the sickest."

"I'm fine."

"Dr. Orcino, the eminent diagnostician."

He finished the bottle, gave it a nice accurate basketball toss into the metal wastepaper basket.

"Blix heard that," he said. "She can hear the murmur of our voices. She knows we're out here. She has to lie there and ride that." He took a pad out of his inside pocket, looked at it, and put it back.

"You got a plain piece of paper?"

I gave him the kitchen pad. Two-by-four squares, decorated with a forefinger tied round with a bow-knotted string. What he wrote took two seconds.

"Here's what you want to know."

Number of pills, number of hours. The number of pills I already knew. The number of hours I hadn't thought about. It would take as long as it took, that's what I'd thought. It was good to have some specific idea.

"She'll never take them," he said.

"Blix has promised herself," I told him.

Dr. Reyes leaned against the kitchen door, facing me.

"I made a promise too. We call it an Oath. Well, it's broken now."

"No one will know."

"You know. And Vida? The undertaker? Your neighbor? Milt's cronies? You've got that all planned? Drop a stone like this into water and there's no end to the circles. Don't think I don't know what I'm doing. Don't think I believe there are any excuses. And since I'm in this, I'll go whole hog. Tell her to take as little water as possible. Tell me she's sleeping—and I won't come near. But *tell* me. Once in, I'm a doctor again . . . I know that."

He opened the door. "She will never do it. But that piece of paper will relieve *your* mind a little, maybe."

The minute he closed the door I went to Blix's room. She had the TV on, low. But she wasn't watching it. She was watching the door to the hallway. Waiting for me. She wanted too much to know what had gone on to ask.

"It's okay," I said. "We're in. He's with us. We can count on him."

"I knew you could do it, Tassie. I knew right from the start. Okay. The worst is over. We can relax now."

I don't know who else would have thought of it that way. Cancer at hand and self-destruction ahead, but nothing to worry about. But that's the way we were living that fall. Day by day, and that day's accomplishments had been considerable.

"What's that paper?" Blix asked.

I handed her Dr. Reyes's two lines of information.

"I've read about people," she began, but didn't know how to finish. "They're sending out bulletins about some people for weeks, aren't they?" she asked.

"More like days. But they're the people who were found."

"But not me? They won't find me?"

"Not you. That's the promise we got today."

2

Dr. Reyes's co-operation, which we had to have, and had been waiting for, affected Blix for a few days like a setback. She lay against her pillows and rested, neither wholly awake nor truly asleep. I brought in the mail one afternoon; she opened her eyes and saw *Time*, touched it, and said, "This is the first time in my life that that magazine came in the house and I didn't begin to read it."

She gave up for a few days (though she was mostly finished with the work) the packaging and disposal of her belongings. She was determined that when she left her home nothing personal would be left behind. The house would be a shell if she could manage it, washed clean as a seashore conch of any reminders of life.

"I think it was terrible, coming upon purses and scarves of Mama's at home, long after she was gone."

I hadn't felt this. I'd liked coming upon them.

The life we impute to objects, at all times great, grows greater as our own life ebbs. Flesh is wasting, so we hang onto money, cherish old trinkets, begrudge the amount of food it takes to sustain life. Conserve, conserve. Perhaps this is more characteristic of the aged than of the sick. Blix was not without this instinct. Extensions of herself she wanted given away, cleared out, disassociated from the place where she had lived. But the place itself she wanted protected. "Don't put that wet glass on the table." "Don't walk on the rug with those dirty shoes." "Don't leave that chair in the sun." Even to me, who had formed the habit of sitting for an hour in the late afternoon at the top of a ridged sand bank above the pool, she said, "Be careful, when you walk up there, not to break the ridging."

She laughed at herself when she said these things. She excused herself by saying, "I'm trying to keep things nice for Milt's next wife."

There were strange afternoons in that big autumn-lighted, white-carpeted bedroom. Blix was giving away her clothes: her shoes, her scarves, her jewelry. Her furs, coats, negligees, ski pants, imported sweaters. I wasn't a candidate. I was too large; our styles were too different.

Sara was the chief recipient. But before any garment, hat, bracelet was parted with, Blix wanted to see it modeled, to give advice as to suitable combinations, proper hang, possible alterations. She was like an artist at some final showing of his work. Sara walked across the room. The daughters of friends of Blix (Blix had stayed the daughters' size) walked across the room. Heads high, bosoms arched; the pause, with toes properly angled.

Blix sat straight against her pillows, cigarette burning, eyes bright. She was never more alive than when engaged in this appreciating, assessing, rearranging. She was the designer preparing this, her latest (actually her first and last), show. This, not death, was what seemed real. Poor girls, I had thought at first. Asked to try on the castoffs of a soon-to-be-dead woman. It was not so—for them or for Blix. They were all artists. They were all busy creating. No one thought of death.

Blix's closets, when Dr. Reyes handed me that "kitchen memorandum," were already almost empty. After she read Dr. Reyes's figures she lost, for a time, her enthusiasm for emptying them further.

She wasn't in greater pain. She wasn't weaker; but she was, for a while, less responsive.

Blackie drove six hundred miles to see her. She kissed him, then closed her eyes. He sat by her bedside for two hours, and not a word was said.

At three, when Blix had her shot, Blackie took me to town. Except for evening walks and late-afternoon siestas on the hand-built sand dune, I hadn't been out of the house for two months. I was glad to get back again. Everything outside was too loud, too fast, too bright, too unplanned. Too lifelike. I bought the clothes I had gone out for and wouldn't even wait to have a drink downtown with Blackie.

After Blackie left, Blix said, "Show me what you bought."

It was like old times again. Not just pre-Reyes, but premarriage, predivorce, pre-Sara. It was old times in Baranca when Blix and I, trying on possible purchases in the Bon Ton, scanned ourselves in the full-length mirrors, so excited our heartbeats lifted our organdy and voile bodices.

That inspection of my purchases ended Blix's withdrawal. When she had told me what I should keep, what take back, she asked, "Is there any sherry in the house?" There was.

Between sherry and dinnertime, I had half an hour in my deck chair on the sand ridge, up which I climbed as carefully as I could.

We were well into November now, but the air, until sundown, was still warm. From the top of my ridge, I could look over the housetop and across the floor of the valley to the Santa Inez mountains, thirty miles away. Each spur, at that hour a different shade of violet, was distinct. Overhead, the sky was the color of a dried peach. Remembered glories lingered there, the effect sorrowful as well as beautiful.

254

Next to Blix's, on the left, was the neighbor we had to elude. On the right, the desert, unoccupied for as far as the eye could see, stretched, already faintly greening from the October rains, away toward the Colorado. The sun went down. Birds, the shape of children's drawings, the sooty upper half of a crossbow, drifted across the big dried-peach sky. A lizard, beside my chair, shook like an old Ford with the force of its heartbeat. I strained sand through my fingers, a human hourglass. The sand was still warm.

My sister was dying, and I was happy. How could that be? Even she was happy, she said. We were surely both mistaken. I gave up trying to discover explanations. I floated like the crossbow birds in the peach-leather sky. I lay in my body-shaped canvas hammock, bird-brained, air-borne, beatitude where despair should be.

A soft "hoo-hoo" brought me back to earth. Hoo-hoo of Linda and Baranca. "Hoo-hoo," an imitation of Mama's; and Mama's learned back in the Kentucky hills where a knock at the door was too impersonal to announce one's arrival.

Blix's "hoo-hoo." I floundered out of my chair. Blix was out of her bed, out of her room, standing inside the garden, next the wall, looking over the wall and waving to me.

"Hi, up there," she called.

Do all moments last forever? Was this the continuation of some call and waving started long ago? A widening ripple? Or was it the beginning of some act that wouldn't culminate for centuries?

Beginning, ending, or continuing, Blix was waving and calling. She wouldn't do that again, in time. Not outside that particular house. She had taken her walk in the night. She had stepped outside the house at sundown. She was finished with the world, the world outside her room.

"Tassie," she called, "it's getting dark. What're you doing up there?"

"Watching it get dark."

"Come on down. I want to talk to you about something."

"Aren't you afraid I'll mar your artificial sand dune?"

"You've already marred it."

When I was down she said, "Don't climb up and down the same way all the time. You're making a path."

I looked back and saw that she was right. The artificial sand dune had lost the virgin look given it by the bulldozer.

"I'll smooth that out," I promised.

We entered the house like matrons returning from bridge or the supermarket. But Blix's room awaited an invalid, bed turned down and pillows pyramided for a constant occupant. Blix got into her bed. Vida had left the sherry and two glasses on the bedside table. Blix wanted no more, but I poured myself a glass. In the air-conditioned room it was warm and comforting.

"What I want to talk about is my funeral dress. Help me decide."

Blix had recovered from Dr. Reyes's capitulation. She was ready to tackle new problems. She had already decided, as a matter of fact, but she still liked the game of "What shall I wear?" and I liked to play it with her. Who, overhearing us, could have guessed we were speaking of shrouds? Did we understand it ourselves?

I brought out the half-dozen dresses withheld from the modelers' parade. I had a favorite. It fulfilled *my* requirements for shrouds: becoming, of a certain dignity, and associated with happy times.

It was the dress Blix had worn at Sara's wedding, heavy *café au lait* silk, stiff and formal, a costume for an occasion. Blix was not going to be exposed to the view of mourners at her funeral. Still, she would know what she wore, and so would I. A wedding dress for a burial pleased my sense of irony—and neatness. Balance and contradiction achieved at one stroke.

Blix listened to my reasons. But she had no intention of choosing a dress simply to satisfy some ironic sense of balance in my head.

The dress she chose, and had known all along she would wear, was a silk print, foliage of green and silver-green on a cream background: a twining pattern of leaves and grasses. It couldn't

256

have been plainer in cut. If Botticelli's Venus had risen from the sea, clothed, this is the dress she would have worn. This was the dress Blix chose to wear when she departed. When she lay under the burr clover and blue grass, under the sedge and Bermuda, the graft of leaves she wore would take. She would arrive almost indistinguishable from the world she was joining.

When had she bought the dress? Where? For what purpose? A party? A Dunes Club dance? Because it was on sale? Did she remember? Did she think now, "We never know what we're choosing. Never anticipate an ending in a beginning"?

I don't know. I didn't ask. Was mystery what I wanted, not answers? Perhaps Blix couldn't have answered those questions if I had asked them. In any case I didn't ask.

3

After dinner (Vida had put a roast in the oven before she left), when Milt was out at a Boy Scout Eagle Awards dinner, Blix talked some more about the funeral.

"Let's decide on the songs," she said.

Songs! I wouldn't have supposed Blix would care any more about the songs than she would about the color of pallbearers' ties.

"Well, you decide," I told her.

"I have picked out two. There should be three."

"Three? How do you know that?"

"Didn't you ever go to a funeral?"

"Of course. But I didn't count songs."

"Me, either. But sometimes you find out that you've remembered more than you know. Anyway, there's three. I know what I want for the first two. But I can't think of anything to finish with. Maybe I don't *want* to think of anything to finish with. *The* last song."

"Okay. I'll think of that. What're the first two?"

"You'll be shocked."

"I won't be shocked."

"There's no use pretending I've been listening to good music all my life. So I'm going to choose what I like. First of all, I want 'Ah, Sweet Mystery of Life.' I want a man to sing it, someone with a big sweet sexy voice. And I want him just to roll it out. I want the people out on the street to hear it. It may not be very religious. But it's not unreligious, either. There's a lot worse things you could say about life than that."

"Do you really think life's sweet and mysterious?"

"I think it's mysterious. Don't you?"

"It's mysterious, all right."

"And lots of it's been sweet?"

"Some of it, anyway."

"Besides, I love the tune."

"Okay. That takes care of song number one."

I took her answer straight at the time. It never occurred to me that she might be reassuring *me*. Making it possible for me to think "she had a good life."

Had she? Didn't I know anyone, truly? Oh, Mama, Marmion, Everett, Manuel! Oh, Mr. Fetters, the fry cook! The list was endless. Did I never meet any of you? Did I dream you all? Was I captivated by darkness? Devoted to wondering?

I remembered Grove Street, the one-room apartment where I lived while I went to the university. It smelled of gas from the two-burner plate that was my heater as well as my cookstove. With the dark rain of a California winter on my windowpane, I often left the kitchen table, which was also my study table, to stare across the street into the Al Café, where, around the red tablecloths, men and women, laughing and talking, downed bowls of chili and mugs of beer. I stared and wondered. Lonely, I longed. I went back to my table and opened my books. I was a divorced woman of twenty-five. What would my life have been had I been able to go down there, talk, drink beer, eat chili? To stop wondering.

Would I have understood Blix better?

While I was thinking about Grove Street, Blix, concluding that I was really shocked by "Ah, Sweet Mystery of Life," said, "Cheer up. The next one's a real hymn."

"I told you I didn't care."

"I want you to care. It's 'In the Garden.' "

" 'In the Garden'?"

"You know. 'He walks with me and He talks with me and He tells me I am His own.' I never could hear that without crying."

I was a hymn fancier myself. I had favorites that had stayed with me from childhood: Mama's "Bringing in the Sheaves," Papa's "Oh That Will Be Glory for Me." My own "Now the Day is Over." But "He walks with me and He talks with me" I couldn't remember. Searching for it, I began to hum, and, humming, the whole song came back. I liked to sing and I thought I was pleasing Blix. I put my heart into it. I looked at Blix for approval. She was crying.

It was the second time I had seen her cry since I'd been with her. The first was on the afternoon of the pain she had welcomed. Blix's eyes could hold more tears than any other eyes I've ever seen. Deep wells of sadness while her cheeks were dry.

"Oh Blixy," I said, "don't cry. Don't cry. It's not a sad song. I didn't mean to make you cry."

She made fun of herself. "I'm like that Russian dog. Sing that song and I cry."

It was the crying about *that* song that broke my heart. It was Blix the girl who was crying. Or Blix the woman remembering that girl. "Walk with me and talk with me and tell me I am your own." In the cool of the evening where sweet waters flow. What did she remember, hearing those words? Linda? The sea? Mama? Vurl? Milt, in the days of their courting? We'd made a pact before I ever came to Blix about crying. I wasn't to do any. Not before Blix. I had promised, and for the most part I'd been able, at least when with her, to keep my promise. Crying put Blix back into the days when life and death had still been in the balance, the days before acceptance and resignation.

Now, though I wasn't shedding tears, I had a misery in my throat and chest that I couldn't control. I left the room quickly, heading for the outdoors. In the kitchen, Milt sat at the bar with a drink in his hands. He looked up as I came in.

"Don't cry, Tassie," he said.

I wasn't, but my face, I suppose, had the contours of crying. I couldn't answer; my throat was in knots.

"I've cried all my tears," Milt said, as if it had occurred to him that I might find a husband calm-faced and drinking whisky in the house where his wife was dying a revolting sight. "Blix and I have cried them all. We began crying in July, and somewhere in September our tears dried up." He was a little drunk and enunciated his words carefully. "I don't think anything could make me cry now. I would obviously be sorry," he said, "if you walked outside and a rattlesnake bit you. But I wouldn't cry. There is something you maybe don't know, Tassie. You can die alive or you can die dead. Blix and I died in September. Nothing can hurt us now. We're already dead."

I didn't think Blix was already dead. It wasn't a dead woman whose eyes had filled with tears when I hummed that song. Not even a middle-aged woman. I had left a girl back there in her bed. And I had to cry for her; but not before Milt, either.

There was a phone in the cabaña by the pool, and I ran to it. At this time in the early evening Pete often spent a half hour in his office at the club. And even if not there, he could be found by paging. There was direct dialing between Oasis and the club. Pete answered quickly, as though he had been beside me.

"Pete?"

"Tass?"

With his voice the vise about my throat relaxed. I could cry. It was a curious thing to do. As if before I could cry I had to have an audience. I don't know whether what I needed was pity or sympathy. Perhaps it was just Pete. Pete didn't try to hush me up, or make me talk. He did say, "Is everything all right?" Everything was all wrong, and he knew it. "All right, under the circumstances," he meant. Under the circumstances, everything was. He was there and listening, and I had my cry out. Then I explained.

"Blix is choosing the songs for her funeral," I said.

"I'm surprised she cares."

"She doesn't—about funerals. She'd just as lief be put on a platform for birds to eat."

"What?" Pete asked.

"Like the Indians. But it can't be that way. So she's choosing songs. Not hymns. Not real hymns. Songs she liked when she was a girl. A girl is dying, Pete."

I was beginning to cry again.

Pete said, "Tass, listen to me. Blix is damned lucky. Lucky that that girl didn't die when she was twenty-five or thirty. It does with most. You understand me, Tass? It's hard on you to watch, but it's lucky for Blix. She's dying alive."

It was the opposite of what Milt had said, and probably truer.

4

Neither of us slept well that night. I took more sleeping pills than usual and was still wakeful. Blix had larger shots and was still uncomfortable.

When Dr. Reyes had said "I will help her," I took it that he had licensed me as accomplice. Blix kept track of her own schedule. She always knew when, according to the schedule we were presently following, her next shot was due. She wanted to keep on schedule. When the shot was due, she wanted it, whether or not in pain. She didn't want to be a dependent, calling for me or Vida, or made conscious that she was able to keep going only by grace of Numorphan. She knew exactly how much Numorphan she was getting. When I filled the hypodermic she'd say, "Don't shortchange me." She never said, "Don't overpay me." Whether because the idea that we would do so never occurred to her, or because, if we were, she didn't want to hear about it, I don't know.

I was overpaying her. Not much. Not any more than I judged was required to quiet the pain. I tried to find a true balance, the exact amount needed to kill pain and leave her as fully alive as possible. That night, the balance was hard to find. I overpaid and still she was in pain. I overpaid myself and still I could not sleep.

It was our practice not to talk except during "talking periods" —those times when, after I had given her her shot and prepared her food, I sat by her bed.

Once back into bed, even though we couldn't sleep, we didn't talk. Talking then, we believed, would encourage the habit of wakefulness.

But that night, in spite of our combined shrewdness about habits, we permitted ourselves to talk after I got back into bed. I don't know how much we talked or how often. When you are taking sleeping pills, one or two now, one or two later, you slip in and out of sleep. You think you have not been sleeping, but what has been happening could only have happened in a dream. You think you are asleep, but if you were asleep, how could you hear the steady drugged breathing of your sister in the bed next to yours? We would speak, and sleep would interrupt our conversations. We awakened, and repeated what we had said before. Or perhaps we only thought we were repeating ourselves.

It was that night Blix told me what Dr. Reyes had had to say about enemas. Blix had come to them now; they were the necessary, dreadful signposts along the road she was traveling. She hated them, in themselves and as signposts.

"Dr. Reyes," she whispered to me, "says that movie stars have enemas as a regular thing. Every day. A part of their life."

This sounded to me like a dream—or a nightmare. But I was surely awake. I could see through the east windows the dimming stars of an autumn night.

"Big movie stars on location, or making personal-appearance tours, can't be interrupting scenes or running offstage to answer calls of nature. But if they don't answer calls of nature they get constipated. And big movie stars can't be constipated, either.

262

They turn yellow and bilious. So big movie stars have enemas. It's just routine with them, like having their hair washed. They don't waste any emotion on it. They don't say, 'Why can't I have a natural movement like other people?' They aren't like other people, and having enemas is a part of their difference. It's the same with me, Dr. Reyes says."

I thought about this for what seemed quite a long time. Then I said, "Do you think that's true?"

"About the movie stars? Of course I think it's true. Who could make up a story like that?"

Dr. Reyes could, I thought, to make you feel better. But all the same, it might be true; and in any case, I said nothing.

5

Later, I think it was later, Blix said, "You came back for me at Bent."

She must have said something before that, because when I asked "Where?" she answered, "You turned around and came back for me," as if I knew where.

Then I remembered. Blix and I had done what we'd always planned—gone to Europe. Pete was playing golf at St. Andrews; Milt was in Detroit at an automobile dealers' jamboree. We had looked forward forever to the trip. Once on it, we had discovered, not so much that we had become different persons in our years of living apart—we were still the same—but that we had less tolerance for our differences. Or were less able to disguise them as the differences between a mother and a daughter. We had become contemporaries.

The trouble began in Spain, in Segovia. There, an old waiter, peg-legged and peg-toothed, had cared for us like children: walked us the long way down winding halls to the toilet, washed the brandy glasses before he warmed them. I tipped him double the accepted amount, twenty per cent instead of ten: six centavos, perhaps, instead of three, fifteen cents instead of seven and a half.

Blix was disgusted with me. She denounced me as a show-off American tourist, upsetting local economies by throwing my money around. What I had felt (I thought) was real love for the gnarled old fellow, an outflowing of good will in which I never doubted that Blix joined me. My tip was only a kind of blessing (I thought). Blix's words made me see myself as a silly American lady-bountiful, conned by a European versed in conning. The trouble was, I said nothing. I retreated into misunderstood rectitude. I continued to tip generously wherever I went; half my pleasure, now that I wasn't joined in my appreciation of good will, in offending the penny pincher who accompanied me.

It was a dreadful time. When we joined Pete in Scotland and he took over the financial management of our trip, the bitterness died down. Pete wasn't proving anything to anybody by his expenditures. Besides, it was easier for Blix to accept without question what a man did. But I was still wary of opening myself up to Blix. Of expecting her to share feelings I had.

Then one afternoon in Sedbergh, leaving Blix behind, as part of her continuing punishment for daring to criticize me (all this hidden from Pete; I was ashamed for him to know how cruel I could be), Pete and I drove out from our hotel into the surrounding country. It was an afternoon of drizzle and getting on for dusk. Without warning, after driving three or four miles, we came, out of the absolute emptiness of the moors, on the little town of Bent, hidden until you entered it, in a deep fold of the downs. Bent was a single street of stone houses; the town was the color of gorse and twilight, rain-washed. A few lights, watery yellow, had already been lit, or turned on, behind the small many-paned windows. Bent might have been raised by a wand. In California men didn't make—and never had made—towns like this. It *was* a town. Or a hamlet. That was the word for it. It was out-of-doors, life-sized, rained-upon. Yet you entered it like a room. It took you in with a room's comfort. But it also entranced you, like something manufactured by children and left outside overnight. Or something treasured by a grandmother and discovered, after her death, in a box hand-carved by her father.

I couldn't bear for Blix not to see it. Bent was only half my joy, I then clearly understood. The other half was Blix's seeing it with me. If she was to see it before dark, we had to hurry.

Pete drove our Consul dangerously fast on the narrow slippery roads back to Sedbergh. There wasn't time to run up all those flights of stairs to Blix's room, so I stood outside her window and yelled up to her. "Blix, Blix. Hurry, before it gets dark. There's something wonderful to see."

Blix wasn't like me. She didn't hold grudges. If I was through holding mine, fine. She didn't hold my having held it against me. She came down the back way. I could see her, through the window at each landing, coming lickety-split, pulling on the white transparent raincoat she hated as she came.

She banged herself into the car without a word as to the change of heart I had evidently experienced. There had been an interval of separation. Now that was over.

There was still enough light when we reached Bent to see it. The rain had slacked off, and a big clear band of sulphur yellow in the west made the dry dusk lighter than the drizzly afternoon had been.

In Segovia, Blix and I had been separated because I insisted that she feel what I felt. In Bent, because she did feel what I felt we were reunited.

Blix looked and looked for a long time without speaking. Then she said, "Oh, I'm so glad you came back for me."

Now, in November, ten years later, she was saying what she had said then.

"You came back for me."

I hope it wasn't in my dream that I answered, "I should never have left."

XI

Summer on the desert dies like a snake. You think it's done for, dead as a doornail, then there comes another fierce burst of life. And even that violent lashing may not be final.

Summer always dies this way on the desert; and the fact that it does is always forgotten. There are some early sprinkles, or, as that year, a real downpour. Daytime heat gentles; the sky is skimmed over with haze. Nights are cold enough for blankets; the air conditioners, left at 75°, pipe in heat at three o'clock in the morning. Summer is over.

Then the white heat of late November strikes, the last shudder of death from the dying. Thermometers shoot back up into the hundreds. The sky bleaches to paler and paler blues. All the good done by the early rain is lost. The quail nibble on dried grass again. The jack rabbits have greasewood for fodder. The only shadow on the land is that of the mountains, and of the great buzzards drifting down toward the disappearing scent of the fast dehydrating victims. Dust devils dance across the sand ridges. Oily mirages of water shimmer ahead of you on the high-

266

ways. In Palm Springs the exposed haunches of Midwestern matrons show, before the leather is tanned, expanses of baby-bottom heat rash.

Blix may not have noticed the change in the weather. In her room, it didn't change. The air conditioner hummed as usual. Dr. Reyes's ragged roses lasted as well as they ever had. The shots were a little stronger, and though she knew this she didn't remark on it. She did notice my face one morning after a night sleepless for both of us.

"This can't go on," she said.

"Are you feeling worse?"

"Go look at yourself in a mirror. You're the reason."

"I always look this way when I don't sleep. One good night's sleep restores me. Better than Skin Dew. Fresh as a daisy again."

"When do you plan on this good night's sleep?"

By chance I had it that very night. Next morning I went into her room, at ten or eleven, to show her that the restoration had taken place. She and Vida were already watching one of those TV question-and-answer, audience-participation shows.

I sat down and waited until the medicine man delivered his "message." "Buy my snake oil."

While he was speaking, I said to Blix, "Look at me."

Blix said, "I'm looking."

"Well, didn't I tell you one night's sleep would restore me?"

Blix, who was smoking, waved her hand to blow the smoke away. When she had cleared the air she moved her head, propped up against pillow, in negation.

"I'm glad you feel well," she said, emphasizing the feel.

When the commercial was finished, I stayed on to watch. The first thing I did every morning, if I wasn't sleeping in the bed next to Blix's, was to run down to her room to see how she'd made out since I'd last seen her at four or five o'clock. If I heard her TV, I relaxed. She was all right.

The chair I sat in was the only piece of furniture Blix had wanted of Mama's. Blix liked it because of its spare, modern Italianate lines, which did not clash with the simplicity of her modern house. It was a light and easy rocker, perfectly balanced so that slightest movement of the shoulders kept it in motion.

I rocked. The chair whispered. The emcee intoned. Blix smoked. Vida slept. We were happy—I was happy, in the big airy room, while outside November's furnace blazed. Blix had had her long hair cut. She looked younger than she had for years. I saw that what Dr. Reyes had told me might be true, and I no longer resented what he had said as a disparagement of Blix, an underestimation of her resolution and steadfastness.

We certainly planned less than we had. Of course there was less planning to do. All imaginable emergencies had been foreseen. A feasible scheme for getting Vida out of the house on any weekend we wanted her out had been hit upon. Blix, before we had worked on it together, thought she had a solution. She had suggested to Vida that a "personality conflict" might arise between me and Vida. With this idea implanted, she would be able to say to Vida on any Friday afternoon, "Vida, you'll have to go. For some reason you rub Tassie the wrong way."

The first I knew about it, Vida said to me, "What's this personality conflict between you and me?"

I didn't know what it was. I didn't know what she was talking about.

"Is there supposed to be one?" I asked.

"Blix says to expect a blowup at any time."

"Do you feel any clashing?"

"No. I thought we were friends. I never got along better with anyone."

"The same with me," I said. "You know Blix's getting a lot of medication now. There's bound to be distortions in the way she looks at things. If you want to know how I feel, ask me."

"You're taking a lot of sleeping pills yourself."

"I am. But I'm myself by noon every day. Ask me at twelve sharp if we clash."

I asked Blix, after that talk, what this "personality clash" was all about.

After she explained it to me, I said, "We just don't clash."

"Can't you pretend?"

"No, I can't."

"You can pretend to like people. Why can't you pretend to not like them?"

"Lack of practice, I guess. There was never anything to be gained by dislike."

"There's something to be gained now."

"There's an easier way."

"What?"

"Tell Vida she's working too hard. She is. Start giving her weekends off on pay. We'll be rid of her any weekend we want that way, without her being suspicious. And without my having to pretend that I don't like her. That would kill me."

That phrase echoed in my ears, but Blix seemed not to hear. "Tassie," she said, "I think and worry about some problem, then in a second you have a solution."

Actually, the only external problem left to us was that of the pills—hiding them; and losing them. I'm not sure whether Blix really believed that Vida, if she came upon them, would turn them over to Dr. Reyes or not (I think now that she would have), or whether this was a guessing game of her own, a real-life TV quiz program with life and death riding on the right answer. At any rate we played it.

It was the only bit of playing and planning that continued to interest Blix. As the dosage increased she slept more in the daytime; did not truly sleep, she said, was present, aware but uncaring. She was awake, but the life around her was a dream; a dream someone else was dreaming but which she could watch; a TV program with live actors.

Nor was it possible for me, as her days took the shape Dr. Reyes had prophesied, to recall to her her early resolutions. Impossible to say, "Are you sure the time hasn't come?"

The rocker sighed. The air conditioner hummed. Vida, out on a grass widow's date the night before, gave a few relaxed, but ladylike snores. Blix and I looked at each other and smiled. This life, which was not quite a life, which was an interim only, be-

269

tween an experience half-understood and one totally hidden, had somehow become entrancing, I think that's the word. We moved as if in a trance.

It was a blessing for me, I thought, that Blix had given up "the Plan." Endings had always been beyond me.

I had told Blix, "I'm with you in this to the end." I was, I still was. But the nature of the ending was changing, lucky for me. Because if Blix had said, "Tonight's the night," my response would have been what it had been before: "Not yet." "Not yet."

2

Dr. Reyes stopped in that afternoon on his way home from the hospital.

"What's the trouble?" I asked, before I thought.

"What d'you mean, 'trouble'?"

He looked sick. His face was the color of old bones; the heat, if that was it, had drained all the ruddiness from behind the copper. In his yellowed face, his bronze eyes showed up with the blaze of a patch of unhealthy alfalfa in unirrigated land.

"What d'you mean, 'trouble'?" he asked again.

I meant he looked sick. But this is what the doctor tells the patient, not vice versa.

Besides, he didn't act sick. He didn't slump into a chair, as he often did, or rest his head in his hands. He was like a cicada. The hotter it is, the faster they stridulate. He strode around the room burning energy. Examined his own roses. Tested the force of the air flow through the air-conditioner vent. Stopped at Blix's bed and clasped a big toe, which lifted the single sheet that covered her.

" 'Trouble'?" he repeated. " 'Trouble.' Blix, I bet this sister of yours is a born trouble shooter. She's at her best when things have gone wrong and she's hunting solutions. Right? She's down-hearted when the sun shines. Right?"

I changed my diagnosis. Dr. Reyes wasn't sick. He was drunk.

He was neither. He was in good health, cold sober, and covering up. From me as well as from Blix.

"Okay," he admitted. "There *is* something the matter. This heat has got me down. I'm taking two weeks off. I'm taking Lois and the kids to Coronado for two weeks. I want to see fog in the morning. Maybe we'll still be stuck with sand, but it'll be wet sand. I want to hear something besides an air conditioner. Something on the order of wind and waves."

"And see something besides patients?" Blix said.

"Yep. I plan to look at girls in bikinis."

Dr. Reyes hadn't stopped his tour of investigation as he talked. He was examining one of the two cut-glass gold-rimmed toothpick holders, part of Mama's store Blix had on her desk. When Blix said "What's to become of me?" he put it down.

He put the little cup down. "Become of you? I'm not abandoning my patients. For their sake as well as mine I'm taking some time off. Dr. Schroder will take care of my patients while I'm gone."

"Didn't I see him while I was in the hospital?"

"You did. Handsome fellow with a mustache."

"He looked military."

"He acts medical."

"I bet he does."

Dr. Reyes didn't argue this. "When I get back I'm going to send your sister home for two weeks. I gather she thinks I look bedraggled. Well, she ought to have a good look at herself. Don't you think so?"

Blix didn't answer Dr. Reyes. Instead, she turned to me. "Are you going to go, Tassie?"

My answer surprised me. Instead of saying, "This is the first I've heard of going home," or "I gave you my promise," I said, "It might not be a bad idea."

Dr. Reyes had stopped his walking. We both stood at the bottom of Blix's bed, he at one side, I at the other. We formed a triangle, with Blix as our apex. I didn't know then what we were saying, but I suppose Blix did. This is going to be a long siege.

271

Let's face it. Let's get ready for it. Let's stop beating around the bush with any talk about the Plan. The Plan sustained us through a bad time. It was an escape hatch—which we're not going to use.

Blix said, "When are you leaving?"

"Sunday evening." This was Monday. "I want to examine you before I go."

"Why?" asked Blix. "When there isn't anything you can do?"

She was sorry she had said that. She tried to make things easy for Dr. Reyes.

"Your medication hinges on what's going on there. I may want to make changes before I leave."

I didn't make my usual walk through the house to the kitchen door with Dr. Reyes. In the days of getting clearance for the Plan, Blix had wanted me to go and had waited impatiently for my return so that we could talk over what Dr. Reyes had said. Dr. Reyes had had his say to both of us this time. And I had had mine, too. Blix, taking up matters chronologically, didn't mention then what I had said. I was glad she didn't. What did I mean, "Take a vacation"? She wasn't having any vacation, was she? I had said, "I am in this with you till the end." Was I nothing but a summer soldier? My chest was heavy with those words said, and with the words of denial I didn't say. "I agreed with Dr. Reyes to save an argument," I told myself. I hadn't. I had agreed with him for reasons I didn't understand. I wasn't "worn out." Pete and I were in perfect accord about my staying with Blix. My job was well taken care of. "It might not be a bad idea." Where did that come from? Had Dr. Reyes hypnotized me? The words were lead in my heart. But I didn't recant.

Blix said, anxiously, "As if we didn't have enough problems as it is."

"You mean Dr. Schroder's coming?"

"I mean Dr. Reyes's leaving."

"We don't have to have Reyes. Actually, we could get along without any doctor at all for two weeks."

"Of course we could get along without any doctor at all. The point is, we're going to have a doctor. And what a doctor! You don't know Schroder. It wasn't just the patients. All the nurses hated him. He's a machine. He'll be here every evening."

"Well, that won't be too awful. No beer. No roses. But we can ignore him."

"He won't ignore us, though, that's the trouble. One sniff of the Plan and he'd have me back in the hospital in six seconds. He'd have the house searched."

"You know he can't send you back to the hospital without Milt's consent."

"He'd have Milt arrested for interfering with the care of a patient. He'd have Dr. Reyes sued for malpractice. He'd put you in jail."

"Good. I could purify my soul there."

"Good for you, maybe, but hard on me."

"Why did Dr. Reyes choose Schroder, if he's so awful?"

"Maybe he was the only doctor he could get. And he is efficient. No one ever accused him of not being efficient. That's our trouble."

"It's only two weeks."

Blix was silent then, thinking about those two weeks. She leaned away from her stacked pillows, got her cigarettes and lighter from the table drawer. She lit the cigarette with her usual dash.

After the cigarette was lighted, she pulled up her knees and leaned forward, one arm clasped around them. In this position when in pain she would rock back and forth, very slowly, very gently, mothering her pain, hushabying her pain. There would be a sound, hard to name. Not a moan, certainly not a song, but nearer to some sorrowful almost inaudible humming than anything else. Nearer to the pitiful sound a child alone, and without words, makes to comfort his loneliness.

Now she smoked and looked up at me.

She didn't have to tell me what she was thinking. Two weeks

273

with Dr. Reyes gone. Two weeks with Tassie gone. A month when her hands would be tied. Who knew what that month might bring?

I knew what she was thinking and still I didn't say, "Forget what Reyes said. Forget about my going home for two weeks. I'm here for the duration."

I said nothing. Blix said nothing. That was Monday.

3

Bad days followed. Bad nights, too. The Numorphan worked all too well in the daytime. Blix, though not asleep, not in a coma, still lacked the power or the desire to do more than open her eyes when we leaned over her bed. But the dosage that quenched her, as well as her pain, in the daytime, was not effective at night. She was neither truly awake in the day nor truly asleep at night.

On Wednesday night, after Dr. Reyes's announcement on Monday, I, for the first time, slept through the hour when Blix's shot was due. I always set the alarm clock; though on every night before this, I had awakened a half hour before the alarm went off and had then waited, wide awake, for the time to go to Blix.

On Wednesday night I was awakened by a touch. I knew instantly by whom and for what reason. Blix had come down to my room, was sitting on my bed; my light was turned on, the alarm blaring. I quickly reached over and turned off the alarm. Blix was looking down at me as if hunting in my face for some answer. I had the feeling that she had been looking at me for a long time.

"Poor Tassie," she said.

I began to cry.

"Don't cry," Blix said. "I'm all right. I'm not hurting too much. I was asleep. Your alarm clock woke me up. I haven't been waiting for a shot."

I tried to stop my crying. "It's my pride that's hurting," I told her. "I never thought I'd sleep through that alarm. I never thought I'd even need it. I thought something would always tell me when you needed me."

"Maybe that something has worn out," Blix said.

"No, it's not worn out."

I started to get up, but still Blix didn't move.

The air conditioner in my room was turned off. The windows which paralleled my bed, and which Blix faced, were wide open. The hour was five, and the desert air was cold and still. Through my window, on the other side of the valley the long backbone of the mountains was visible, diamond black against the starry glitter of the desert sky. Blix gazed across me out of that window.

"This has been a nice room, hasn't it, Tassie?"

"It has. I like it better than yours."

"What does this remind you of? When did we get up early together?"

"Lots of times, I expect."

"Some one time, I mean."

"The time I remember best is once when I was home from Berkeley and you and I were sleeping together. I had to catch an early bus in Los Angeles. It was November, like this. Thanksgiving vacation, I expect. Papa came in, turned on the lights and woke us up. It was raining. He said, 'It's such a good morning to sleep, I hate to wake you girls.' "

Blix said, "I think that was it. I can remember the sound of the rain and the smell of bacon frying and the bed so snug and warm."

"Le Cid drove us to the bus depot that morning. I remember that. He had that big red Buick roadster, and he didn't turn corners, he skidded round them. We might all of us have died that morning."

"I thought we would. . . . Tassie," Blix said, "Dr. Reyes's going to examine me Friday. I told him he could."

"Do you dread it?"

"Sure."

"Why does he have to do it Friday?"

"He wants to know how I am before he leaves. It's okay with me. I know he has to do it. Will you ask him two questions after it's over?"

"If you want me to."

"First of all, ask him if he thinks I'd be jumping the gun."

"Jumping the gun?"

"If I took the pills now. I told you that as long as I had one decent hour a day left, I wouldn't do it. Ask him if I have."

"He might not know."

"He doesn't have to guarantee anything. The second question is: Will it inconvenience him?"

"You mean, to take them now?"

"Will it spoil his vacation plans? He's leaving Sunday and I wouldn't know until late Friday afternoon."

"He said thirty-six hours would be the greatest of plenty."

"When would that be?"

"Sunday morning—at the latest."

"Maybe Saturday night?"

"Maybe."

"That wouldn't be too bad for him, would it?"

"No."

"So you'll ask him?"

Before I answered, and as if to forestall any objection I might have, she said, "You know Milt can't bring himself to talk to him about this."

"I know."

"Marmion is coming up tomorrow. Sara and Buzz will be here Sunday. So all that works out."

"You promised me 'all that' wasn't going to have anything to do with it."

"It isn't. It just happens to work out that way."

Friday was day after tomorrow. Still, I wasn't worried. Blix had endured many a miserable hour by remembering that she

276

didn't have to go on enduring it. I had advocated postponing and I had come to count on continued postponing. Either I had actually come round to Dr. Reyes's opinion, that no matter how much we planned, Blix would never go through with the Plan, or I chose to believe she never would because that belief protected me.

Blix leaned forward suddenly, cradling her lower abdomen.

"You'd better have your shot before the pain gets a head start on you," I told her.

"It already has a head start," Blix said.

She got up from the bed very slowly and carefully. She bent over, holding herself with her curved arms. Beneath her pajama coat I could see the relaxed bulge of her lower abdomen. She walked ahead of me down the hall to her room. For the first time, I thought, Blix looks sick unto death. Her narrow shoulders drooped away from her neck. Her neck, uncovered by her hair, was thin and corded like an old farmer's, white and damp-looking. She put her feet to the floor before the floor was there so that with each step she was momentarily off balance.

Facing Blix, held up by her pillows, her face made up, the life in her eyes contradicted her sickness. Quenched it. Walking behind her, the sickness in her body was visible. Her body was ruined; its shape had changed, its movement was impeded. She knew this better than I. She felt it. Ruin was what she lived.

She got back into bed gingerly. First, sit on the edge of the bed. Next, get the buttocks as close to the spot they'll occupy when lying down as possible. Finally, gently, carefully lift one leg at a time to the bed. If done expertly, there will be no need for pulling, squirming, adjusting, after the body is in bed. It's that pull of flesh against resistant bedclothes that sets the great pain nerves to vibrating.

There's not much that can be done to help someone with a tumor that alerts nerves which go off like a burglar alarm, shooting warnings of agony over the whole body when touched. I didn't start filling her hypodermic until she was safely settled.

While I was doing that she said, "You will talk to Dr. Reyes Friday, won't you?"

It was easy to say yes, facing her. What this girl, with her smiling ironic eyes, was asking was wholly hypothetical.

4

Next day the great heat storm abated. Oh, it was hot, by any but desert standards—just under a hundred—but the menace was out of it. A few wispy mare's-tails tarnished the blue metal sky. Drops of water deposited by the sprinkler on the leaves of the olive trees and hydrangea bushes hung glistening for a minute, as they did in ordinary regions before they evaporated. The stub-tailed cat walked abroad at midday. Vida came at eight, with a sweater on. "It was cold when I got up at six," she said.

Blix had a rough day Thursday. In spite of the medication, the pain had got ahead of the painkiller and was never really tamed until toward evening.

Marmion arrived at noon, hot, in his hot little compact, full of a lunch of drugstore chili beans and proud of both facts. In a country gone soft, he personally was giving it a little backbone by living close to the bone.

Blix had looked forward to Marmion's coming, and I stayed away from her room while he was there. They had memories to share in which I had no part. But I looked in as I passed the door. There was no talking. Blix was in that world where, neither awake nor asleep, she hid from her pain. Occasionally she opened her eyes to let Marmion know that she knew he was there. The voice of the TV was turned low. Its pictures, stories, and products slipped endlessly past. Sometimes Marmion, caught up in the "will he, won't he" of some dangerous sequence, watched the screen. More often he looked at Blix.

Marmion left at four. Around six o'clock Blix experienced one of her late-day resurrections, when pain and Numorphan, becoming equally matched, left her momentarily free.

When I came in from seeing Marmion off, Blix opened her eyes and said, "I don't think I've had a bite to eat all day. I could eat a real supper tonight."

"If you can eat it, I can cook it."

"Milt won't be here, so I asked Vida to buy us some pork chops."

"Pork chops?"

"Milt hates lamb, and Sara hates pork. I've eaten nothing but club steaks and prime rib roasts all my life. You like pork, don't you?"

"My trouble is that I like food."

"Let's celebrate, then. Cook them the way Mama did, will you?"

"I don't know any other way."

Mama's way was with a skilletful of brown gravy, fairly thick. Since I was cooking an old-time meal, I decided to set an old-time table, too. Blix had a little rectangular table, walnut with casters, which she used as an auxiliary bar when entertaining. I got it out, covered it with a red-checked, hand-fringed table-cloth which had belonged to Grandma. While I boiled sweet potatoes, sliced tomatoes, and tended pork chops with one hand, I set the table with the other. I painted an old-time picture with that table. The picture needed, to be complete, a hanging kerosene lamp above the table and a grate burning beside it. And a "God Bless Our Home" on the wall nearby. I tried to suggest these with what I put on the table: saltcellars, instead of shakers, spoon holder, celery vase, Grandma Mac's "silver," black where the silver plate had worn off. There was no kerosene or wick in the little old "upstairs" lamp of Mama's, but by ramming a candle into the wick holder I made a light for our table. All that was missing was the sweet smell of burning coal oil.

Blix loved the table. "Why didn't we do this every night?"

"You didn't feel like it every night. Me, either. I've pulled stuff out of every cupboard in the kitchen."

"Where's the wine?"

"You don't like it."

"Tonight I do."

The wine bottle took the red tablecloth from a Pilgrim kitchen to an Italian restaurant. Blix sipped wine and ate parts at least of two whole pork chops.

"This is the best food I ever ate," she said.

"Don't kid me."

"I'm not. This has nothing to do with your cooking."

"It has something to do with the wine, I expect."

"It might have."

Blix said nothing about Dr. Reyes's examination next day, or the questions I was to ask him. I thought she had forgotten them. The Plan had taken her safely through another bad period —and would do so again.

"Open the windows," Blix asked, "and turn off the air conditioner, will you? It's cool enough, isn't it?"

It was warm, but the pleasant warm of a summer evening in Baranca. There was a little breeze blowing, and the candle, inside its protecting chimney, wavered like any farmhouse lamp.

Pete called before I rolled the table back to the kitchen. Pete and I had an understanding. I phoned him but when he phoned he always asked first for Blix. He never talked for long. Blix wasn't up to that. But I think she loved his asking for her first. It was as if nothing had changed; Baranca all over again and Blix the belle of the household. For three or four minutes Blix could manage a voice untouched by sickness. The soft inflections of a woman pleased to be talking to a man, she didn't have to manage. They never left her.

Pete was homeward bound from hunting elk in Colorado, calling from some roadside motel and asking Blix to give me news of his whereabouts. It was a thoughtful thing to do. In that way Blix, who was on the receiving end of so much, had a gift of her own to bestow: information. "Pete's in Nevada. He says to call him at the Stockman's Hotel in Elko tomorrow night."

Blix praised me to Pete. "Tassie just cooked me a wonderful dinner."

Then, she was truly herself, Blix pleasing a man.

"But you know something, Pete? The last really good food I ate was that venison you cooked in July. But Tassie tries," she said, and smiled, listening, to Pete's laugh at what he knew was half-truth, half-spoof.

Her face was drawn with the effort to keep all hints of pain and weakness out of her voice. But she asked one more question, the question every huntsman waits to hear.

"Any luck?"

Her sounds of congratulation told me the luck had been good. Pete was homeward bound with elk and deer. Eyes that had seen the great forests and reflected the tarnish of sunsets on mile-high mountain lakes were fixed on emptiness. Pete was homeward bound with a load of death. It was nothing to wince at. Blix didn't. It was an essential strand in the pattern of our living.

The night that followed was easy for both of us. I awakened each time before my alarm went off. At five o'clock I found Blix awake and waiting for me. I had had to rouse her before that for her scheduled shots.

She was leaning back against her pillows smoking.

"Don't worry," she reassured me. "I'm not hurting. Well, that's not exactly true. I'm hurting, but just the usual. You don't have to rush. Or kick yourself because you didn't get here sooner."

After the shot she said, "What kind of a day is it going to be?"

I went to the windows, which had been left open all night. There was still no hint of daylight.

"No telling," I said.

"I wish we would hear a coyote."

"Your wishing it probably spoiled it. Coyotes are contrary. They won't bark, like a dog, just to make a nice sound in the night."

We heard a nice sound though, just then, at the minute Blix wished for it. In the hills back of us, where retired people were building their sun-baked shacks, a rooster crowed. At first, delicately, almost birdlike, as if for practice and still half asleep.

Then twice again, great loud brassy buglings. It wasn't a sound as thrilling as a coyote's lament for a lost wildness. The rooster celebrated what was at hand. And what is at hand is never as thrilling as the lost and remembered.

"If he crows once more," Blix said, "it will be a good sign."

I didn't ask her a sign of what, but whatever sign it was, she got it, the biggest crow yet. A sign to coyotes, maybe, that their rule was over.

That was Friday morning; though for Blix with her shot and me with my sleeping tablets, it was still the time of Thursday's night.

XII

I slept later than usual next morning. It was almost eleven before I went down to Blix's room. The door to her room was open, and as I went down the hall I could see her bed turned back and empty.

"We're in here," Vida called from the bathroom.

Blix, though getting in and out of the tub was difficult, was having, with Vida's help, a bath.

"We're getting ready for Dr. Reyes," Vida said. "Going to give him a real treat."

Blix gave me a look. "A real treat!" Blix exclaimed. "Going to try not to stink."

"How do you feel?" I asked.

She gave Mama's old evasive answer. "With my fingers."

"Not good?"

"Good? What's that?"

Blix didn't like her body, altered by sickness, to be seen. In the daytime she always wore a brassière under her nightgowns. When I gave her shots, she bared an arm, a thigh, a buttock only. Now she kept the mid-section of her body well covered with the tub tray which held her bath needs. I tried not to see her stick-shaped legs and the heavy swell of her lower abdomen. I did see that she would be glad to bathe without an audience.

Blix's lunchtime and mine didn't coincide. Nor did we have the same kind of food. Vida cooked a real lunch, which Blix played with. I ate lunch, usually a slice of brown bread, a cube of cheese, and a bottle of beer, later.

When I next saw Blix, Vida had taken her lunch tray away. She was sitting, propped high against her pyramid of pillows, smoking. She had on one of the prettiest of her many bed costumes: blue silk gown of some chiffon-like material with embroidered bands of what looked like spring wild flowers at the neck and wrists. Over this she wore a matching sleeveless jacket.

She had just had a shot and was in that intermediate stage, perhaps the worst of all, when she still felt considerable pain and was, at the same time, a little dazed by the drug.

I sat on the edge of the chair next to her bed, but not sure whether she wanted me with her.

"Tassie," she said, "you won't forget to ask Dr. Reyes his questions this afternoon?"

"No," I said, "I won't."

"What are they?"

"Are you jumping the gun? Will it upset his plans?"

"You don't have to use those words."

"I'll use the right ones."

Blix's eyes, enlarged by drugs, darkened by pain, were half-covered by her drooping lids.

"Wouldn't you rather have Milt do it?"

"Milt thinks it's easier for Dr. Reyes to talk to you. Someone he won't see again. Besides, I don't know what time Milt'll be back this afternoon."

"I'll do it."

She had closed her eyes, but when I got up, she opened them.

284

"Will you give me a little half-shot before Dr. Reyes comes? It'll be off schedule, but I'd like to have it."

"If you still want it, I'll give it."

2

I put my bread, cheese, beer, and books in a picnic basket of Blix's and climbed up the sandbank—which, just as she had foreseen, was beginning to show the marks of past trips. This was the first day cool enough to be out in the full sun so early. The first day I had ever eaten outside.

It was an afternoon of glancing light: the sky dappled with clouds, the valley floor dappled with their passing shadows. Birds, the size and color of silver thimbles, ate plant lice in the oleander hedge. They made as they ate the snipping sounds of a small pair of pinking shears operated by a fast hand.

The winter tourist season was beginning in the desert. This day of warm sunshine might be overcast in Linda, drizzly in Baranca, cold and windy in Brenner. The highway below me was filled with cars loaded with weekend sun seekers. I raised my eyes from that road to the house a hundred yards below me. All quiet there. Sun or shade, winter or summer not mattering much. Vida asleep in the big chair. Blix in that realm, neither sleeping nor waking, where Percodan and Numorphan reigned.

Neither my food nor my books interested me. My chest was at the same time empty and heavy. A hollow heaviness. Something leaving, something coming. I dreaded the talk with Dr. Reyes. Use whatever words I would, the question was: My sister wants to know if the time for her to die has come? It was an even plainer more bitter question than that. It was: Should my sister now kill herself? Should the Plan, our three months' blessing, a guillotine pleasurable to hone, be lowered?

And beyond those questions, truthfully and brutally or tactfully phrased, the act behind the words, the destruction for which the Plan was only a blueprint. The ordeal of change, oh, the ordeal of change! Has the time come for that ordeal?

The afternoon drifted by: many clouds, many cars, many birds; many passing shadows. Then the birds stopped their eating, and singing began. The morning cock had crowed matins. Now the benediction was sung by lesser birds.

I lifted myself from my chair and went down to the house. It was four-thirty. Vida had gone home. Except for Blix and me the house was empty. Its emptiness rang in my ears with a sea-shell roar as I walked the length of the long hall to Blix's room.

"What is that box you are carrying?" Blix asked.

I held the woven straw picnic basket higher so that she could see it better.

"It looked like a box," she said.

"It's getting dusky in here. Do you still want a shot?"

"I still do. A little one. Enough so I won't feel the examination too much."

"But not so much you won't be able to talk."

"You're going to do the talking."

I was busy fixing the shot and didn't answer.

"Do you mind?" Blix asked.

"In a way. It's not easy for him, either."

"You promised."

"I'm going to do it, all right."

"He's with us, isn't he?"

"Oh, he's with us. I hate to keep reminding him though. And I hate the day we've come to."

"We knew we'd come to it. That's what the Plan was for."

The Plan was heavy as death. The Plan *was* death; expected, but always at some faraway date.

I gave Blix her shot. The rotation system we had worked out called for the top of the right thigh this time. I tried to avoid the sites of recent punctures.

"You don't want me in here during the examination, do you?"

"No."

"I'll go back up my hill and wait until he's through. He should be here in five or ten minutes."

But Blix, who had taken my hand, still held to it, and I sat in my chair of the nighttime rituals. Blix was still keeping up her charade of well-being, but her face no longer played very well the part assigned to it. It was a charade in which I, too, had played the role expected of me, seeing what Blix wanted me to see. In the bleached light of late afternoon I saw what *was*. Perhaps Blix now wanted me to see *that*. There were hollows in her temples no cosmetics could hide. Her tip-tilted nose had grown beaky. Her full lips had thinned, scarcely covering her teeth. Worst of all was the change in her eyes. A stranger looked out of them, a stranger whose experiences were not any that Blix and I had ever shared.

For a long time I had been on the verge of telling Blix a memory of mine. I held back from doing so because I didn't want Blix to think I was trying to "cheer her up," or give her "hope." My reasons were egotistical and self-centered. I simply wondered why the story had stayed in my mind for so long.

When I was in the second or perhaps third grade I had read a story of dragonflies. I could still see the large print, the slick yellowish paper, the hard words at the top of the page divided into syllables for easier pronunciation: drăg'-ŏn—ăs-cend'—rē-main'.

On the page facing the story's beginning was a dragonfly, all eyes and iridescent wings, rising above a muddy swamp into the pure light of a sun-filled sky.

The story was not about that dragonfly but about its brother larvae left behind in the opaque waters of the marsh. These worms discussed among themselves the fate of their recently departed relative. Their lamentations were those of any of the recently bereft. "A friend has died." "Passed into the great beyond." "Lost to life." They moved with sad relish in the slime of their accustomed home. They congratulated themselves on their continuing worminess and the unchanged nature of their sludgy universe.

So they bewailed their lost brother. While, as any second-grader could see, the worms were laboring under a misapprehension, above them, their brother, freed of the horny shell of his chrysalis and the muddy waters of home, had flown into a light they didn't dream of. Perhaps it was the story itself that impressed me. Perhaps it was a seven-year-old's first encounter with dramatic irony. "I know something those worms don't know."

Holding Blix's hand I told her the story and told her how it had stayed with me all these years.

At first, her thought was, I believe, to say nothing. If the story comforted me, let it do so. But dramatic irony, which is only a way of arranging a narrative, was not as satisfying to her as it had been to a seven-year-old. She could not resist biting her teeth down onto the harsher irony of facts.

"Did the story say what happened to the dragonflies?"

"No."

"Didn't you wonder?"

"Not at seven."

"Now?"

I couldn't answer. I knew their wings crumbled, they were broken by beaks, they fell into waters they had intended to skim, they were pulled apart slowly by children. I had seen my cat eat one.

They *were* endings. All of my life I had believed in alternatives, substitutes. Nothing was final, without a solution. There were always ways around every obstacle. Blix had come to a final obstacle. Milt's words about tears came back to me, and I understood them. My tears had dried up. I put Blix's hand to my cheek. She would never have made such a gesture herself, but she didn't pull her hand away.

"Anyway, they flew," she consoled me.

I took her hand down and looked at her. The darkness of pain and drugs had left her eyes; and even the sadness of her young days. They were bright and saucy. Not defeated. Still resolute and relishing, in charge of her own life.

I left her alone for her meeting with the doctor.

3

Before I had seated myself on the sand crest, Milt drove into the carport. Five minutes later Dr. Reyes arrived. I could hear his usual loud knock, followed at once by the opening and firm closing of the door. I was glad Milt was home. Someone, I thought, should be near Blix.

I waited. Across the valley the mountain tops, still sunlit, were darkening: rose to lavender, lavender to dusty blue, dusty blue to slate gray. Darkness was settling. Or rising like a heavy tulle fog from the earth itself. The weekend sun seekers had turned on the lights of their cars. Warmth went with the sun. The air was suddenly cold, the season suddenly winter.

I had intended not to go down to the house until I heard Dr. Reyes close the service-porch door. Then, hurrying through the passageway between carport and walled garden, I would intercept him before he reached his car. The twilight thickened. The door never closed. The examination must surely be over. I was too impatient to wait longer. I went down the sandy slope, hastily, leaving those tracks Blix hated to see.

There were three ways to reach Blix's room: by way of her enclosed garden; through the entire house, after entering by way of the service-porch door which Dr. Reyes always used; or in at the front door and straight down the hall, which ended with the door to her room. The quickest way for me was around the side of the house and in at the front door.

To the right, as I entered, in the direction of Dr. Reyes's usual consultation room, the kitchen, I saw that the lights were on and I heard voices. The door to Blix's room was open, and her water-lily bedside light was on. I went to her at once.

"Go talk to Dr. Reyes." Her voice was tense with anxiety.

"Milt's talking to him."

"He won't ask my questions."

"Dr. Reyes will tell him."

There were sounds of movement in the kitchen.

Blix raised herself on one elbow.

"Go," she said. "You promised you would. He's leaving."

"Did he hurt you?" I asked at the door.

"It doesn't matter. Hurry."

She was right about Dr. Reyes leaving. I passed Milt in the living room going to Blix and overtook Dr. Reyes where I had planned, in the carport.

I don't know that he wanted to talk at all. He wouldn't talk in the carport. He guided me across the road into the open desert land where we had so often watched the quail feeding. When inside the lighted house, I had thought that night had already come. Outside, the white sand still held light and the first stars shed light. I could see Dr. Reyes's face; the outline, not the expression. In outline it was a stone ax, broad at the sharp jaw line, tapering toward the high forehead. His voice, too, was impersonal. He used it as an instrument to report something.

"I've already told Milt," he said.

"Then there's no need . . ." I began, but he cut me off.

"There is need," he said. "You need to know. Your sister wants you to know. She has nothing but agony left. Since last I examined her, her tumor has tripled in size."

"Why has she stayed so well?"

"Stayed so well! She hasn't. She has been sparing you. And Milt. She's not a woman to complain. And she's had an enormous lot of drugs. And she's got a fantastically tough set of organs. Except for the accident of this tumor, she'd live to be a hundred. Heart, liver, kidneys, lungs, they're functioning better in this crisis than many people's function with coddling."

"Well, then," I said, "she might have many more good days . . . into spring, perhaps. . . ."

"She will not have any more good *days*. She hasn't had any good days for a long time. What do you think that tumor is doing? It's at the base of her spine, growing every day, filling her like a stone. Like granite. Pressing on her bladder, on her guts. Reaching up toward liver and stomach. It will choke every

290

organ she has. It will rend and tear. No torture chamber ever had anything like it. She will be smashed and torn. Unable to urinate, defecate, eat, breathe. Finally that tough heart of hers will give up."

I couldn't speak.

"What your sister has endured up to now are pinpricks to what is to come. Pain increasing geometrically as the painkillers fade. Don't look so shocked. What else have I been telling you?"

"Isn't there any chance that the growth . . ."

He anticipated me. "There is a chance that the sun might not come up tomorrow. Would you like to bet on it?"

Blix's first question was answered. She would not be jumping the gun. But I was selfish. I made Dr. Reyes take all the responsibility.

"What would you do?"

"In her place, you mean?"

"Yes."

His answer was short. "Put a gun in my mouth and pull the trigger."

He said this coldly and harshly: an obvious answer to an unnecessary question.

"Blix," I began, for I wanted him to know that the question I was asking was hers, "Blix wants to know if you would be inconvenienced."

"Inconvenienced?" For the first time, his voice was his own. "No, I won't be inconvenienced. Your sister wasn't forgotten in planning this vacation. Or you."

The conversation was over. All questions asked, all answers given. We went back to the carport. Under the carport light, I thought, He shaved before he left the hospital and forgot to rinse off the lather. Then I saw that he'd been crying. His voice had never faltered, but while he talked, tears had run down his cheeks; now his dark face was bright and stiff with the taut glaze of dried tears.

He knew that I saw and he didn't care. He said what he always did when he left. "Call me if you need me." Then he drove away quickly.

In the kitchen Milt was on Reyes's bar stool, bent low over a glass of whisky which he held in both hands. His tanned bald head was the same color as the bourbon in his glass. Vida had put a roast on the rotisserie rod and set the timer. It was turning slowly, with a soft domestic sound: half kitchen rocking chair, half sleepy bird at dusk.

"Did Reyes tell you?" I asked Milt.

"Yes."

"Does Blix know?"

"Yes."

4

There was nothing in Blix's face to show that Dr. Reyes had told her what he had told me. She lay back against her pillows, quiet and reflective. But she knew. She spoke with a glint of cockiness. "I knew all along it would be this weekend."

There was nothing to say. A great dry wind that I could no more feel than see was blowing through the room and hastening all before it.

"What did he tell you?" Blix asked.

I opened my mouth to speak, but had no voice.

Blix said sharply, "Didn't you talk to him? Didn't you ask him my questions?"

"Yes."

"What did he say?"

I told her. In a tape-recorder voice I repeated Dr. Reyes's words. It was her body, her fate, her life. After she knew, I could plead with her, if I wanted to, "Not now. Not this evening." That would be my right. But it was her right to know what I was urging her to continue.

She listened impatiently, as if hearing an old story. When I finished, she said, "See if they're still there."

I sat down on the edge of her bed, something I was careful never to do, because the slightest jar hurt her. I put my arms around her and said, "Poor baby. Poor baby."

"Don't say that or I'll cry."

I took my arms away.

"Hug me, but don't call me 'poor baby.' "

In a minute or so she said, "I'm okay now."

"I'm not," I said, and Blix laughed. Then she said, "Check the pills. We didn't do it this morning."

I stood up, and my mind was blank. This was what I had always feared. We would outsmart ourselves. Hide them so well we'd have to tear the house apart to find them. The wind, as I tried to remember, swept through the room: a bright hot wind, invisible and soundless. But I felt it. I could smell it.

"You put them in the empty Skin Dew jar," Blix said.

She was as sharp with me as if she had a lifetime to make amends. Her manner brought me to. The plastic bottle filled with the cherry-red capsules was where she said it would be.

"No need to hide it any more," Blix said.

I put it in the drawer of her bedside table.

"When?" Blix asked.

"When we've always planned. At bedtime. A lot for you. A few for me. I'll wake up. You won't."

"It would be funny if it turned out the other way around, wouldn't it?" Blix asked.

"I don't know who for," I said.

"It won't, will it?"

"No, it won't."

It was about six then. Time rushed by on that soundless wind. An embarkation, a journey, lay ahead. Blix, eager traveler and careful packer, had last-minute jobs she wanted done. Afternoons of waiting were now finished. Nights of remembering. Mornings of pain. She was leaving.

First of all, call Vida. Get her out of the house over the

weekend. The pattern we had established held. Vida wasn't surprised. Blix took the phone from me.

"Vida? Sara and Buzz are coming up tomorrow and I don't want any nurses around with their enemas and thermometers. Tassie can do it. She's not good, but she's conscientious. Have a good time. Take it easy. See you Monday."

The dusty wind ceaselessly blowing . . . through closed doors . . . through walls . . . from nowhere to nowhere, but passing over us, across us, through us.

For a month Blix had started letters she didn't finish. Something held her back from saying, "Good-by," from sealing, posting. Now she wanted them finished, the final lines added. To Papa: "You should paint your own Christmas cards. Those last pictures you sent me were beautiful. Don't buy cards when those you make yourself are so much better."

To Marmion: "Marmion, the watch you bought me when I was twenty was the nicest present I ever received. I would have given it to you for Louise long ago except that I hated to part with it."

To Milt—she read the half-filled page, then handed it to me. "Is it silly?" she asked.

"No."

"Would he rather not have it?"

"He'd rather have it."

"There's something I'm ashamed of," she said. "Tell Sara for me. When she was here over Labor Day, she and Buzz ran short of cash. They were going to the Sand Trap for dinner. I loaned her fifty dollars. She didn't pay me back, so I asked her for the money. She'd put it in my purse without saying a word. Didn't you do that lots of times with Mama? Put money in her purse and never say a word?"

"I never did. I put it in her hand and said, 'Appreciate me.' "

"Tell Sara I'm sorry."

There were vases and casseroles, which had contained gifts, to be returned.

Then it was finished, packing done, messages concluded.

Blix said, "I smell something cooking."

"Vida put on a roast."

"Do you think it would be a good thing . . . for me to have something . . . in my stomach?"

"I don't know. I suppose so."

5

I gave Blix and Milt their dinner as usual in Blix's room. I didn't, as usual, eat with them.

Instead, I went outside into the cold autumn night; cold and still, nothing moving except the rivers of stars overhead. I made the walk Blix had made two months before. Said another good-by for her, finished and sealed another letter. Good-by, earth. Your present was the best I ever had.

When I got back to the house Blix was alone. "Where's Milt?" I asked.

Blix gave me a merry, scornful look. "He can't take it," she said. Praising us, the two Murphy toughies, whistling in the dark.

I took the plates to the kitchen. Milt was on his stool again, head low over glass again. We didn't speak. I took my own plate back to Blix's room and sat where I usually did, to eat: beside the bed that was "mine" and that I planned to occupy that night. Blix had clicked on her TV, and across the two beds I watched the announcer declaring in his voice of perpetual wonder the perpetual wonder of a circus kaleidoscope.

Tigers, maidens, ponies, clowns. The tight wire, the slack wire, the flying trapeze. Monkeys in panties, men in satin, women in chaps and ten-gallon hats. A world of effort we had never made. Never that renunciation, practice, accomplishment. Never those chances. We had never flown through the air or been in the lion's den. We never would. On and off the cantering white horse, making him her partner, the girl with legs eloquent as wings, performed her flying waltz.

I couldn't eat. The meat was flesh, the wine was blood. I put my plate aside.

Blix, looking at the screen, said, "Tassie, where have we been all of our lives?"

"Clowns and acrobats ask the same question," I told her. Though I wasn't at all sure. She turned away from the screen, held out a pleading hand to me. "Tassie," she said, "do I have to wait?"

I felt, inside myself, a great jar: as if a ball of lead held in my throat had fallen down, down, bruising me as it went. All postponing, all pretense, was past. I got to my feet.

"Of course you don't have to wait."

I had bound her to a sentimentality which made the Plan easy for me. "Falling asleep. Just falling asleep." I was falling asleep. She wasn't. She was departing this life, by her own hand; and she was ready to go. If I would give her my kind permission.

"I am hurting," she said. "Do I have to wait?"

The wind I couldn't see was darker now; it blew off some desert of black sand. I strained to hear it. I wished Blix could hear it—perhaps she did—the Linda sound we both loved.

I stood up. "What I want is a good strong drink."

I believe this was histrionics. I had no desire for a drink. I made it, though, and brought it back to the room. But Blix approved of that act—found it suitable. This was the way we had seen people under stress act in the movies, an act planned by a director to show an audience that his character has strong feelings. The drink was almost pure gin. It was a dream-drink, as the wind was a dream-wind. I could neither taste nor feel it.

Blix had thought of everything. She knew exactly what she wanted done. In those hours when she had lain with eyes closed, this was the hour she had seen.

"Bring me a pair of panties," she said.

There were only two pairs left in the drawer. I held up the best. "Not that." The other was no better. "You've given them all away." She was as sure as bedfast people always are (and usually with reason) that their deputies are careless. "What does it matter anyway?" the deputies say, and spare themselves the effort of search. I held up the second pair, and *she* said, ruefully, "What does it matter anyway?" She was leaving bedfastness behind.

"Don't laugh now," she said. "I want my perfume."

Her perfume at that time was Givenchy's Interdict: a big squat bottle in a box of red moiré silk. The scent was neither girlish and flowery nor heavy and seductive. A fruity, womanly scent: pear orchards, bearing not blooming; a sour hint of marauding wasps and sweaty children, climbing the trees. A big scent, big as an orchard valley and sweet as summer.

Blix used it like toilet water. She rubbed it into her thighs and shoulders; across her stomach.

Do we die as we live? Or some of us better? Depending upon what we have a talent for? Was Blix's talent for dying? For retreating, enduring, acquiring, escaping? For unselfishness? For this perfuming was unselfishness, a gift to me. In the hours that followed, her body's fever, acting on that perfume, filled the room with the scent of orchards and sunshine. She was wordless; but smell, antedating words, spoke for her of some sweet harvest.

When the anointing was over and the miserable everyday panties were on, she said, "Bring me a big bath towel." When I brought it, she said, "Fold it four times and slide it under me."

She arched her hips so I could do so.

Then she said, "You haven't made your bed yet."

"My" bed the past few days had reverted once again to library table. I cleared it of books and papers and took off the spread which hid the mattress.

I had the bottom sheet on. Blix said, "You've put a top sheet on the bottom. That one's not fitted."

I refused to change. "I'll never know tonight," I told her.

Blix knew. She would have liked, particularly in death, to have had things in order: the bed beside her properly made up. I denied her that. Here at the last moment the battle of symbols still rages. I saying, "At this hour what does the position of sheets mean?"

She saying, "At this hour what else matters? How else can I now express my desire for order and seemliness? I, so disordered, and soon to be overpowered by the unseemly."

I didn't think of that then. A properly made bed was the last thing I cared about. Blix had no choice. She, with so few choices left her, had to put up with what I gave her. The bed was made up with two top sheets. As I spread the last sheet, Blix, supporting herself on one elbow, leaned over to my bed and, with a gesture gentle and piteous, helped spread my covers for me.

It is a gesture I do not expect ever to forget. It is in fact the only one out of a lifetime of gestures made lovingly or defiantly in my direction that I remember. I felt mothered and cared for. The mothering had always gone the other way. Now Blix was saying "Baby, baby" to me and I was still as hungry for it as any two-year-old. We can all *be* mothers; even men. But we all *are* babies; tough old shells that house till death the tender infant; and "Baby, baby" is what we long to hear and can never ask for. That invalidates it. It must be a gift.

When the bed was made, I put on my pajamas.

Then I sat in the chair by Blix's bedside and took the plastic bottle from the last hiding place. The red capsules had a holiday sheen. With several folds of Kleenex I made a kind of nest with the palm of my hand. I began to count out the capsules. They reminded me of slippery pomegranate seeds. I counted out loud, and Blix joined me: "Two, four, six, eight, ten." When we reached the final two, I added one more.

"What's that for?" Blix asked.

"Luck," I said.

"Good," Blix said. "I'll make it doubly lucky." She added the second extra.

Then she looked at the glass of water, her usual drinking glass, a perfectly plain tumbler.

"I've got better glasses than that," she said. "And I'd like cold water from the cooler."

I brought the best, a tall leaded glass, monogrammed.

"That's more like it," she said, an old joke between us. So

said a man, his work often interrupted by reports of his wife's illness, on the news that she had died.

She handed the nested capsules back to me and lay against her pillows. I wished she looked, at this minute, more wasted, fragile, suffering. Her gown was a bride's—or so I judged. I had never owned anything like it. Her lips were exactly the right color for a woman in bed.

I spoke without thinking about her reaction, though I was thinking about her, and of the years of our relationship. What it had been. And why. Mother and daughter? Charm admired—but surely not envied—by the charmless? Doer and done-for? Stoic and hedonist? Successful femininity and uncertain femininity? Romantic and realistic? The categorizing uncertain. And in any case, passing. Nothing understood or resolved. In the circle that was closing I wondered about its beginning. Where did it begin?

"When you were born, they put you in my arms," I said.

It was a damnable thing to say. Ask her to travel back those years and miles to an unremembered scene; the baby in my arms never her problem, but mine. And she at this moment working hard to outgrow that comfort-needing infant.

Jaunty about pills and towels and panties and final messages, jaunty about death, those words brought tears to her eyes. The sudden clustering of tears that would never be shed, a glistening bloom.

"I shouldn't have said it. I shouldn't have said it. Drink," I told her. "Take a swallow of water. You can't cry when swallowing."

"Is that true?" she asked.

"It's absolutely true. I've tried it often."

She took three tentative sips. The tears disappeared.

"It is true," she said.

Then, with a motion I never expected to see again, she threw back her sheet, got out of the bed, and standing straight and gaunt went to her desk. There she emptied the writing-table accumulation from the small, two-handled gilt-edged glass toothpick holder which had been Mama's. And before Mama, had been a Hobhouse-Griffith-Pryce keepsake. A reminder of high occasions amid the Murphys of Linda and Baranca.

Back in bed she took my messy little bundle and transferred the shiny capsules to the scalloped-edged jar.

She had no ritual to sustain her. No candles, no incense (except her own perfumed body), no scriptures, no priests, no chanting. No old retainers. No family at her bedside. She was doing the best she could to invest this lonely act with some dignity. And possibly even beauty.

Sparkling glass. Clear water. Perfumed air. The well-accoutered bed. The poison in the best container she could lay her hands on. Ridiculous, but valued; an object with continuity, lovingly preserved, present on high occasions.

She took them two at a time. Her bearing was dashing, her hand steady, her expression proud.

"How can you swallow them two at a time?" I asked.

"Easy," she said. "I want to get it over."

They were down, it seemed, at once. A moment before, and all was to be done. A minute later, and all was over.

She lay back against the pillows and said, somewhat wonderingly, "I can't believe this will do it."

"It will do it," I promised her. "We have Reyes's word. He knows."

We did not anticipate any sudden seizures. Rather, a growing drowsiness. The newspapers had been generous with reports of other deaths of this kind. Persons had been capable of prolonged composition after swallowing their pills. Long notes of farewell.

"Shall I take mine now?" I asked.

"No. Be with me while I go to sleep. And in about ten minutes I want you to help me to the bathroom."

For that trip, she did not usually need help. She was anticipating weakness. And she was trying to make death neat.

"I won't take mine until you're asleep," I promised.

"Fix my blanket, will you?"

Each night I placed a corner of her blanket, folded at the foot of the bed, within reach of her hand, so that she could, if she felt cold, pull it up. She would not feel cold tonight. She would be beyond changing temperatures. Had she forgotten this? I think for the minute she had. She was as precise as ever in her directions, and I as clumsy as usual in following them.

Had I dreamed those glossy capsules and their swallowing? No, the plastic bottle, once brimful, was now half-empty. My own bed, made and turned back, awaited me. But the TV circus still spilled clowns in the sawdust and spun spangled girls by their hair from tent-top machinery. Volunteers from the audience were attempting to leap upon a dappled barrel-shaped rocking horse, who, belying her staid looks, flicked her plump hindquarters and sent them flying. A sober fellow flew one way, his hard hat another.

Blix laughed.

"Blix," I said, "I'm going to get Milt."

Blix had said he "couldn't take it." But this he could surely take. Would want to take. Blix laughing.

She didn't tell me not to.

Milt was where I had left him, same drink, or new drink, in his hands.

"Milt," I said, "the pills are down. All is well. Blix is watching the circus. She is laughing. Don't you want to come?"

I don't know what he wanted, but he came with me. He took the chair next to Blix. I sat on the inside edge of my waiting bed. Blix gave each of us a hand.

Perhaps I should have left. I am sorry for what I heard. And they perhaps were sorry for an audience. What did I expect to hear? This was a real deathbed, not a deathbed scene. A long-married couple, both drugged, worn out, dragged down by grief, they spoke the lines of whisky and Seconal, of Numorphan and fatigue.

Milt said to Blix, "We've had a good time. I love you."

Blix said, "I love you." To me she said, "Milt and I appreciate what you've done."

"Appreciate." I repeated the word, intending to disclaim it.

But the word choked me. I could not get beyond it. "We appreciate your favor of the 16th inst." Could you say, "I appreciate your loving me?" The last three months needed no more appreciation than my breathing. They were the form my living took.

The drug was beginning to affect Blix; she was not drowsy or in any way befuddled, but her knees, which she always drew up when in pain, were trembling. I reached under the covers and straightened them out so that the mattress would support them. When I took her hand again, her thumb, as it had once or twice before when sedation was heavy, jerked spasmodically away from her fingers.

"Milt," she said, "I still hurt. Couldn't I have one more shot?"

"Sure you can," Milt said. Milt always gave Blix her first daytime shot, while I was sleeping and before Vida arrived.

He pushed back the embroidered edge of her sleeve and searched, as we always did, for some puncture-free spot. As the needle went in, Blix began to speak. Not disconnected words or phrases, but a long sentence, its complexities, she hoped, clarified by varying emphases, her voice low, but strong and steady, her tone combining tenderness and scorn.

Not one word she spoke was understandable.

Milt said, afterward, "She was making some crack."

This was perhaps so. In any case, she was smiling. She knew a joke on herself (on all of us, perhaps) and was letting us in on it. She believed we would relish it. She counted on understanding. Her eyes were filled with the satisfaction of truth communicated.

Her language (it sounded like a language, not English slurred) was foreign. It was a soft language, full of vowels and laughter and disillusion. Not Esperanto. Nothing so utopian or utilitarian. Not Spanish or Latin. She believed we understood her. She took pleasure in the points she was making and the phrasing she had achieved. She awaited our reply.

As she waited, Milt took the needle from her arm. As he did so, she sank back against her pillows. Her eyes closed.

6

What took place during the next two or three hours I don't know. How or when Milt left. How or when I took the chair he had vacated. Why I didn't take my pills. Or if I did. Why I didn't go to bed as planned. I don't think I slept. But time went by I can't account for. When I became, once again, aware of myself and of time, I was conscious first of all of a sound. The sound was of my own breathing. Next I was aware that I was breathing in unison with Blix.

She was inhaling with two quick gasping sobs; then, after an interval, she exhaled in a long sigh. I did exactly the same thing. I was breathing as Blix did. Not imitating her so much as trying to be her. Or that was how it seemed to me then. But Blix was dying. If the Plan worked, she was dying. And I could not be Blix by dying. All I would be was dead. Dead me.

I put an end to that kind of breathing—the breathing of a dying woman. I forced myself to inhale slowly, exhale slowly. I was a sister, not a Siamese twin. I was separate. I had to do my own living.

The Late Late Show moved across the screen of the TV, which had never been turned off. Bette Davis, dying histrionically. The remote-control device was on the bed touching Blix's hand. She had used it to turn on a circus. I turned off Bette's suffering.

I took Blix's hand in mine. It was warm, soft, pliable. Not responsive, but Blix. Her mouth was open, but not, she would have been glad to know, in any unseemly fashion. Open with the fatigue of a sleeping traveler or the congestion of a hay-fever sufferer. Her face had all its warm apricot glints. Her mascaraed lashes might lift at any moment—except for that breathing; the intervals between the indrawn breath and the breath expelled were bridges of such duration life might not make the effort to cross them.

At one o'clock I rose from the chair by her side. Without even thinking about it, I left Blix's room and the bed she had helped spread for me and went to my own room and bed. There, without swallowing a single capsule of my own, I stretched myself out. All promises to watch through the night forgotten, no shadow of guilt. Not even, at that moment, remembrance of promises.

Did I sleep? At the time, I thought not. But since I dreamed, I must have slept. What I dreamed, time and again, was that somewhere a phone was ringing. I awakened to answer that phone. But once out of bed, I forgot the phone and ran to Blix's room.

Each time I found her unchanged. I had read that patients in surgery and under deep anesthesia are still able to hear and respond to the conversation of nurses and doctors about them. I talked to Blix. I told her what I thought she would like to hear: that the Plan was working, that she looked fine and smelled sweet. I told her that she was brave and steadfast and that the first night was almost over.

At seven it was over. The wind that had filled the house the day before with its dry harsh voice was silent. Doors were locked. Curtains half-pulled. Milt and I were incapable of making a sound. Our footsteps were noiseless. Doors had velvet edges. Coffee cups were felted. The only sound was Blix's breathing. The motor that powered the world.

Her room was still an orchard, fruity and sweet. Her appearance had not changed. Her body, an organism designed to repel death, didn't distinguish between the poison she had chosen and the cancer which had come without her choosing. It worked as hard against Seconal as against carcinoma. The cancer had said, "Die," and stomach still digested, and heart still beat. The Seconal said, "Die," and lungs still sucked in air and kidneys still expelled the poison. It was a kind of mutiny, crew against captain. Blix had said, "I surrender." But the crew was fighting on.

This was the hard time to be with her. It was hard not to side against Blix and listen instead to the crew's cry for help. The inclination to foster life is very strong—even the fly caught in the web, the rat in the swimming pool. What would black coffee do now? Adrenalin? A changed position? Wouldn't her eyes open and Blix be back with us again? Tell us the meaning of that final sentence? I was pulled toward her bed. I understood what Ulysses felt about the Sirens. My arms, tugged at by my imagination, experienced the weight of her body supported in its struggle for air. I knew what Blix's desire was. But I had never anticipated that those voices, which were also Blix's, would call to me so piteously for help. I could not disassociate Blix from the apparatus by which she lived. And though I knew that if she could speak, she would say, "No, no," I was never positive from minute to minute that I wouldn't go to her, lift her up, and say, "Wake up, Blix. Wake up."

Planning is easy. It has to do with the future. Pill taking is easy. It also has to do with the future. But the body's cry is now. It has not been consulted. It has its own plan, and its plan is life. It goes against the grain of life itself not to be on the side of life. With every suicide, even of those unknown in cities we have never set foot in, we die a little.

At ten-thirty Blix's breathing changed—rhythm and sound. The hard staccato rhythm of two gasping sobs followed first by a long pause, then a long sigh ceased. The indrawn breath was as prolonged as the expelled, and both were heavy, pneumonic. Edema had set in.

I brought Milt to listen.

"Now she is drowning," he said in a broken voice.

The lungs, which still fought for air, fought now behind broken dikes. The water was pouring in.

"We must lower her," Milt said. "We must let her lie flat. It will be easier for her that way."

Easier for her to die, he meant.

I on one side, Milt on the other, lifted her now feverish body off the support of her pillows and placed her, flat and pillowless, lower in the bed. Her breathing became immediately more difficult.

This was the ultimate act—of loyalty or treachery. Loyalty

to what she had planned. Treachery to the life in us which asked for Blix's life.

There must have been some eating and drinking in the house that day. Milt and I must have talked. I cannot remember. All I remember are ceaseless trips down the hall. Sitting by Blix's bedside. Holding her living hand. (She had on silver fingernail polish.) Feeling her pulse. Fast, but steady, I thought. Talking to her: "All goes well. You've nothing to worry about. The pain is past. You have been very brave. We love you."

Twice the doorbell rang. Milt took care of that. And the phone. In mid-afternoon he said, "I think it would be a good thing for me to be seen in town."

We were alone together in the empty house. I made sure that all doors were locked. I listened to the mounting tide in Blix's lungs. I walked the house, rooms I hadn't been in for weeks. Milt's office, with the pile of opened bills on his desk. The guest room, with Chinese screens and a sunken bath in a bamboo-framed alcove. The *lanai*, full of poppies and rattan. The books banking the fireplace in the family room. Many, my gifts; and I remembered the reasons for choosing—sometimes good writing, sometimes great bargains. Room to room, seeing a new landscape because never seen under these circumstances.

I walked the house. I went outside. It was the kind of day that makes you think of the beginning of a new school term. Warm, of course, on the desert, but a beginning—again feel, a touch of haze, some unexplained tenderness. The olive trees made gray rain with the shifting of their double-colored leaves. Ladies still went by in T-Birds bound for cocktail parties. Pick-up trucks with pool-cleaning equipment were homeward bound after a day of fighting algae and sand.

I went up the sand dune back of the house, careless on purpose, not minding my steps, spoiling the contour of carefully shaped dune. Teaching Blix something. And myself. Rubbing salt in my wound. That's the way it's going to be, old kid. The sand disturbed, the blanket any which way, roast beef rare every night. Face it, face it. Our days are as grass and the memory of our names shorter than the duration of the graveyard's granite chiseling. I won't fool you by walking carefully now.

Twilight had come when I returned to the house. A subdued sunset, gentle and pink with a few rosy feathers of cloud overhead.

Blix was still drowning. Her hand in mine was feverish and bony. Dr. Reyes had said thirty-six hours would be enough. It was not yet twenty-four.

I went to her bathroom. I leaned on the window sill. Not a house to be seen. Gray sand, sparse gray-green vegetation, low hills which neither received nor cut off light. I saw what coyotes had seen for thousands of years: a landscape of coyotes and quail and sidewinders.

The evening darkened as I watched, and I was outside in the darkness. Before my mind could tell me, my body knew what had happened, and I, too, stopped breathing. There was complete silence. I ran to Blix. Her hand was still warm and pliable, her face warm and flushed. But she no longer breathed. Her heart no longer beat. The Plan was completed.

7

Milt came in half an hour. He called Dr. Reyes at once. "I'll be with you," I told Milt, "as soon as I change."

"What's wrong with what you've got on?" Milt asked.

"Dr. Reyes will be here," I said, as if that were explanation enough.

Milt shrugged. "You've seen Reyes dozens of times like that."

I had, too. What I had on was a pair of Pete's walking shorts and a *luau* shirt of my own. Clean and decent. Dr. Reyes had scarcely ever seen me in anything else. Milt thought that death was making me ceremonious. He thought death was responsible for the change in me. In a way he was right. Death made it impossible for me, any longer, to point to Blix and say, "There's what I could be if I'd take the trouble. But why do so? *There's* female grace enough for two."

But Blix's beauty was no more. I had lost the person for whom I was a stand-in. I had to play myself.

I met Dr. Reyes at the door of the service porch. This was not a night, I was sure, in which he'd want to announce his arrival with his usual peremptory banging.

I opened the door for him, and he stopped, stock-still, and stared at me.

"My God," he said, "I thought you were Blix."

"It's the dim light."

"No."

"It's a dress and a girdle. And shoes and stockings."

"Maybe," he said.

He put his stethoscope to Blix's chest without once looking at her face. Not once. Blix would have been glad of that.

"She's suffered a pulmonary embolism," he told us.

I tried to say something to him. Something on the order of Blix's "We appreciate what you've done," I expect. But I couldn't even manage Blix's blur of words. Nothing but a strangling sound. Some mechanism at the base of my throat had collapsed.

Dr. Reyes gave me two pills and handed me Blix's half-empty glass. They may not have repaired the mechanism, but they took away the desire to use it.

Before the undertaker took her body from the room, and while he was talking business with Milt, I kissed Blix good-by. I kissed stone. Her forehead was not only cold, it was hard. Though her hair was still Blix's, soft and springy, and her cap of curls still neat. She was well attired for her journey in her silk gown and matching coat. Her scent was still sweet and fruity. And no one who mattered would know that she had on her second-best panties.

I slept that night in the bed she had helped me make. I got into it with as little planning as I had walked away from it the night before. Her arm, curved like a swan's neck, had spread the sheets. It was her gift to me. Here she and I had on many a night gone backward in time. Alone, I went forward. What part the pills Dr. Reyes gave me played in the ordering of my thoughts, I don't know.

Long ago in Baranca Blix had told me that I cared only for what was difficult, reluctant, unoffered. For what was elusive, or past. I could not take what was proffered. I valued the vanished, the stricken. The bird that didn't sing, the kiss withheld, Keats dead; these were my treasures.

All the doors and windows of Blix's room were opened wide that night. In the walled garden her mattress lay across the bridge to nowhere. On top of the mattress the nameless cat sat sphinxlike. Down the street, a car cornered onto the main highway with squealing tires. A tap dripped in the bathroom. A wind, only strong enough to sigh, blew around the jutting corner of her bedroom.

All transitory. What death will take is in an even more precarious position than what death has taken. And death will take all. It is a curious thing to be reconciled to life by death. And at my age. It was as if, though able to discard Santa Claus and the stork, I had never been able to rid myself of the child's belief that the dead are only sleeping. The dead are gone forever. And their going ennobles life. Every living thing, time-stricken and endangered.

At midnight Blix's illuminated clock still ticked on. I awakened, if I had been sleeping. Or stopped thinking, if that was what I had been doing.

Not gone! Forever departed!

My hand, like Blix's, had a life of its own. It moved to touch Blix's bed. My arm took unconsciously the white swan-curve of her arm as she had reached from her deathbed to spread the covers for my sleeping.

Her bed was now empty. Her scent was still in the room. Her cigarette lighter was where she had placed it on her night stand. Roses she had touched still lived.

"Blix," I said.

When I spoke her name I broke the spell that had made speech impossible.

I called Pete in Elko.

Pete answered at once, wide awake, his voice strong and steady.

"Tass? Tassie?"

There was a word I dreaded to say.

"Oh Pete," I began, but couldn't go on. "Pete?"

"I'm here," Pete said. "You've got all the time in the world. I'm not going to hang up."

"Blix," I began again. "Blix."

The minute I said that word there was no need for the other. There had been too much courage. I felt too much pride.

In the middle of the dark night, far across the mountains, Pete listened while I told him about Blix.